Girls' Lips Are Sealed

PHILIPPA KAYE

Editor: @pennycarroll.com.au

Cover design: @kahnsdesign

Paperback ISBN: 978-1-7643332-2-1

eBook ISBN: 978-1-764332-38

To Steve,
and my 'often' lovely adult children
Nique, Wills and Kep,
I love you.

⬯ ⬯ ⬯

I'd like to acknowledge the First Nations People of Australia – the first story tellers of this land. Please be advised that this story is set in the 80s and makes reference to Australian historical events, including those pertaining to Aboriginal and Torres Strait Islander peoples.

Contents

ONE

"Which newly appointed Catholic school principal was caught polishing his desk with a co-teacher's tight backside? Not the 'cleaning equipment' of his ... ahem ... wife. And they say history never repeats."

B IRDIE STIFLED A LAUGH as the words of the latest entry in the *Shame Game, No Names* column tickled the fancy of her sluggish, early morning brain. She knew it wasn't funny. But it was ... just a little bit.

The staffroom of Saint Joan of Arc Ladies' Catholic College was blissfully quiet. She dropped a teabag into a mug, poured in boiling water, added a large dollop of milk and realigned a wayward shoulder pad. She eyed the local paper, nervous energy fizzing in her bones. She shouldn't be curious – she should be outraged – but she couldn't help wondering ... which principal was getting it on with his staff member? And right on his desk. And who, for the love of God, had seen them?

She snavelled a Kingston biscuit – her favourite and unbelievably there was still one in the packet on a Thursday – from the assorted creams and dunked her tea bag. *The*

Gallie Wallen Gazette had welcomed 1985 with its new un-scrupulous column, or should she say – column highlight-ing unscrupulous behaviour. Birdie had been informed, by her Uncle Larry, a friend of the new mayor, that the paper had seen its readership skyrocket. Advertising was through the roof, the money helping to keep it afloat.

Birdie dropped the teabag in the bin, picked up the paper and wandered back to her desk. History never repeats ... what exactly did that mean? Chocolate – and whatever made golden syrup, golden syrup (sugar, she supposed) – swam into her blood as she popped the final morsel into her mouth. The words of the Split Enz song *'History Never Repeats'* trilled through her head and off her lips.

The last three editions of the brazen column had been especially interesting to teachers as the entries had featured careless whispers about them, mostly local school princi-pals, to be precise. In Gallie Wallen, and the neighbouring council of Gibber, there were fourteen Catholic schools – ten primary and four secondary. Birdie could name just about all the principals. And if you took into account those who were of the male variety, surely she could come up with a couple who might fit the backside-desk-polishing bill.

Mist swept forward in a gust, droplets drifting down the outside of the window as she meandered towards her desk. Hundreds of tiny beads clouded the view of the tree that stood just outside. Normally busy with birds, it remained quiet as gentle rain blackened its grey branches. A 'newly appointed' Catholic school principal. Hmm ... that should narrow it down.

The expanse of glass often drew Birdie's attention out-side. It was especially beautiful this time of the year when the autumn hues of changing, falling leaves brought warm, comforting colours. Beyond the trees, bodies hurried along the concrete path. Some teachers held up hands protecting their heads, others – organised humans – huddled under umbrellas and a few simply allowed the water to dust them.

'Oh dear.'

Birdie jumped at the words of her colleague Sabine, a newly recruited French teacher, currently leaning over her shoulder.

Sabine ran a finger over the words in the paper. 'I know this stuff goes on'—she giggled—'but who would be dumb enough to get caught?'

'Do you think it's Dom Walker from next door?' Birdie said. 'He teaches history.'

The principal of Saint Perceval's College for Young Men, the adjoining boys' school, was always very friendly, especially with – as the column suggested – the 'tight' ones. But would he take it further?

'Good guess!' said Sabine. 'He only stepped into the top spot this year.'

Historically, Catholic schools had been run by members of a religious order. Dom was one of the new breed of 'lay' leaders that were popping up.

'And he is a bit of a loveable rascal,' Sabine added as she sashayed towards her desk in the next nook.

Birdie had met Dom's current wife at a work function. She was beautiful in a distant way. His first marriage – to a teacher at one of the primary schools – had been annulled. She was another beauty, European, and similarly detached. Did he choose that kind of woman but entertain fantasies of a different type? A shameless woman happy to be taken sinfully against the principal's desk?

'Meeting in the staffroom, pronto.' The assistant principal marched along the corridor proclaiming her decree. Birdie grabbed the paper and joined the bustle of bodies heading out of the nooks.

The principal of Joan of Arc, or 'Joanie's' for short, was a good friend of Dom Walker. Had Sister Therese Margaret seen the paper? Would she have come to the same conclusion?

Birdie's copy of the *Gallie Wallen Gazette* was plucked out of her hands.

'Hey!' She turned to see Brad Foster's cheeky grin.

Brad, from drama, held it aloft so all the busy eyes surrounding them could sneak a peek. Birdie and Brad had gone to school together. Well, technically, he'd gone to school with Stu – one of her oldest friends. The familiarity of Brad was always a comfort.

'I wonder who the co-teacher is?' said Sabine. 'If Dom is the principal in question, that is?'

Could it be him, though? If he was found out, wouldn't he lose his job? Dom's first marriage had already been annulled. Now the second could be compromised. Not exactly living the Catholic ethos, was it?

'Could it be that new temp? He's very attentive to her. What was her name?' Brad said. 'Something starting with M.'

Birdie had firsthand experience of Dom's interest in women, as – she guessed – would the curvy, pretty, raven haired Sabine. Dom was harmless, though. He was easily placated with a joke and a laugh and a see you later.

'Margie Rogers?' said Sabine.

It would be difficult for Margie to say no if propositioned. She being young and only temporarily employed. Saying no might spell the end of her career.

'I don't think it's Margie,' Sabine said aloud. She leaned closer to Birdie and whispered, 'She's Sister T's niece.'

Sabine's words pulled Birdie from her thoughts. 'I didn't know that.'

'I think Sister T is keeping it quiet.'

'How do you know?'

'On the grapevine.'

'I can't imagine Dom would go there.'

'Definitely not.'

Sister Therese Margaret – Sister T, as she was affectionately known – swept into the staffroom in a cloud of brown linen and incense. 'Just a bit of important news, my lovely people.' All heads turned towards her, and voices ceased. 'Pat Sumner has decided to take term two off on long service leave, so I'm asking for expressions of interest for the first form master's or mistress' role.'

Birdie's ears pricked up. Her heart beat a little faster. She should apply for this. This was her third year at Joanie's. The time to take on a leadership role was now.

'If I could have your expressions of interest by the end of day next Thursday,' Sister T continued, 'that would be excellent.'

Birdie had recently done some professional development in pastoral care and found she had a knack for understanding students' worries, talking things through, offering strategies. Her own unconventional upbringing, being the fatherless daughter of an unwed mother, probably helped. Blood surged hot through her veins; she really wanted this position. She sat straighter.

'Also, a special mass for the outgoing superintendent, Sister Verona, will be held at St Luke's Church with supper afterwards in the parish hall. It's on the last day of term and we'll go straight from school to the church. I know it's encroaching on the anticipated beginning of Easter holidays, but I hope we will have a good representation of staff.'

The end of term was just over two weeks away. Birdie would go to that mass, and she'd submit her expression of interest for the form mistress role, ASAP.

'While I have your attention, I am aware that a spiteful new r-rumour has surfaced this morning.'

A soft murmur spread like an infectious childhood disease throughout the teachers.

'May I ask that we treat this ridiculous tittle-tattle with the contempt it deserves.'

Brad slowly dragged the offending newspaper from the table and onto his lap.

'Our advice is to turn the page before reading.'

He eyed Birdie. His expression said exactly the same as hers: *As if?*

'And give no credence to it whatsoever. The Catholic Schools Board, together with the private and public schools, will meet with the editor of the gazette today in an effort to put an end to this slander. Blessings to you all.' She swept out again, the staffroom instantly filling with chatter.

'Sister T looked harried,' said Brad quietly. He stepped in beside Birdie as they headed off to their desks, dunking his teabag up and down in his cup.

'I suppose it is a little bit wrong of us to engage with such mudslinging,' said Birdie. Guilt that had been sitting under the surface of her skin was on the rise.

'He who is without sin and all that,' said Brad.

'Fools feed on foolishness,' Sabine added. She snatched the gazette and threw it into the nearest bin.

Birdie shuddered. *Fools feed on foolishness.* She remembered those exact words being directed at her in anger years ago.

Brad dropped his teabag on top of the gazette. The liquid turned the white paper splodgy, cacky brown.

No one was without sin. Not even her.

Flirting often suggests that, were it another time, place or arrangement, things could be different. We meet, notice each other, admire and approve, consider what else there might be, notice his lover or mine, smile ruefully and say goodbye — all without words.

'Flirtation:
The art of maybe'
Cleo, March 1985.

TWO

BIRDIE REVERSED THE GYPSY down the driveway of her Vantage Heights home. Driving the little red Holden Gemini wagon sent a buzz through her every time she dropped her bum onto the ribbed seat – even in summer when it melted her skin.

She cruised north along the gentle curves of the bay. The autumn cool would make it too frosty for swimming soon; she'd better have a last swim this weekend. She pulled into the Waverly Park Sports Grounds, already starting to fill up for the 5:20 'Chalkies' Challenge' game, and claimed a parking spot.

Her strong thighs and above-average height were helpful advantages for the school-staff mixed-basketball competition. She was chatting with Brad and several of the crowd from Joanie's, as well as those from other schools, when talk hushed. Dom and the crew from Saint Perceval's – Percy's – wandered in. She was obviously not the only one who suspected the backside-desk-polishing principal might be Dom.

He was making a good show of being bright and breezy – a few elbows from the boys, pats on the back. He threw his hands up in mock surrender. 'I'm innocent!' he said with a big grin. He pointed at a few of the other men sitting in the grandstand who, in turn, also cried innocent. His smile faded quickly as he took a seat away from the ribbing. Flanked on either side by staff, he pulled off his shirt and put on a basketball singlet.

It was such a boy's club sometimes. At least Sister T would throw some oestrogen and progesterone fizzle on this testosterone fire. Where was she? It wasn't like her to be late to a game.

Brad leaned into Birdie. 'Here comes the gorgeous Griff Wheatley,' he said quietly.

A captivatingly hot man's gaze slowly surveyed his surroundings as he sauntered in.

'He's rumoured to be the subject of last week's *Shame Game* entry,' Brad went on. *"Which little teacher-piggy went to market on a graduating fourth form student? And when discovered, by her very angry dad—"*

'*"Went wee, wee, wee, wee all the way home down the Pacific Highway"*?' Birdie finished.

'The very one.'

Griff was outstandingly pleasant to look at: high cheekbones, tanned, flawless complexion, chiselled chin with a dimple adding that little extra something like those on a champion golfer's favourite ball.

'Holy crap, I don't blame the poor girl,' said Brad, salivating. 'Who could resist? He looks like a blond Rob Lowe.'

'Careful, tiger,' Birdie whispered. 'The rumour mill will come for you next.'

Brad's little secret was safe with her. Last year, laws were passed making homosexuality no longer a crime in New South Wales, but who knew what might happen if the gazette's *Shame Game, No Names* started outing gay men, or women. Especially ones who worked in religious schools.

Her eyes drifted back to the young, very good-looking teacher – neither were an excuse to put it about where it didn't belong, she supposed. At the time, Birdie had laughed at that entry. It didn't seem funny now.

'He was teaching at his dad's school. His dad is the principal,' Brad said with a bounce of his brows.

A tiny part of Birdie applauded the editor of the *Gallie Wallen Gazette*. Who did these men think they were?

'But he's back home with Mummy now,' Brad continued. 'She's the secretary at Gallie Wallen Grammar. Apparently he's, you know, the "permanent" casual there.'

Permanent casual? That was an oxymoron. Birdie shook her head at the way the bush telegraph worked in the school systems, not to mention the nepotism. She was surprised he was still able to teach at all, but then, the column was merely hearsay as opposed to hard facts. Innocent until proven guilty and all that.

'Are you right for Sabine's surprise party?' Brad whispered.

'I am,' said Birdie. 'I'm very keen. It's at Fidele's, you know?' Being a patron at Fidele's French le Fair, the restaurant at which Birdie performed for the diners, as opposed to a worker bee, would be fun.

'I do know.' Brad leaned down to pull up his socks just as Griff's eyes swung around to meet Birdie's. 'It says so on the invite.'

Griff stilled, his baby blues laced with interest.

'Strange night for a party,' Brad said from below her.

'Wednesday is Fidele's quietest.' She could almost feel the heat of Griff's attention from across the court. 'It's the best one for him to use for a private function,' Birdie added absently as she maintained eye contact with the gorgeous Griff.

'Right. Well. Will I pick you up?' Brad said, popping up again.

Griff held Birdie's gaze. Both sets of eyes lingered a little longer than was acceptable. Beside her, she felt Brad scan to see what had her mesmerised.

'Oh well, that's me out,' he said behind his hand. 'Our Griff is obviously straight as a die.' He lowered his voice even further. 'And with you, he doesn't even have to worry about Daddy.'

'Low blow.' Birdie elbowed him gently in the ribs. She'd been brushing off jibes about her lack of father all her life, but for some reason, they seemed to land more powerfully of late.

She drew her eyes from Griff and threw her head over, pulled her strawberry blond hair into a ponytail, tied it with a band and flicked it back up.

'Don't look now but our cradle-snatching friend is coming our way,' Brad hissed.

'Birdie Mealing, right?' Griff Wheatley said. 'Music teacher at Joanie's?'

'Yep, that's me.'

'Griff Wheatley. I'm with Gallie Wallen Grammar. It's my first game.'

'Nice to meet you, Griff. This is Brad Foster, drama teacher at Joanie's.'

He shook hands with Brad before turning his attention back to Birdie. 'You're in a band, I hear?'

'I am. Music teacher. Musician. Comes with the territory. I'm a music therapist too, on Fridays at Evesong Retirement Village.'

'Busy girl.' He dragged his bottom lip, roughened by too much time in the sun, through his top teeth. 'Not too busy for fun, I hope?'

'Never too busy for that.'

'Might come see the band. When do you play?'

'Friday nights mostly. This Friday at the Razzle.'

'Cool,' he said, nodding. 'Well, good luck tonight.' He put out his hand.

Joanie's was playing Grammar; the luck needed to be with him. She put her hand in his.

He gave it a shake and then pulled her close. 'I'm a gun at man-on-man defence.' His voice so quiet only she could hear, only she could feel the hum from his touch. 'I'm all over my opponent.' He dropped her hand and went to join his team. When he got there, he glanced over at Birdie again. A grin on his face.

'Geez Louise. Full on flirt,' said Brad. 'Be careful, Birdie.'

'I'm not about to do anything foolish with Griff Wheatley.' Even if he was deliciously dangerous.

'It's all happening tonight,' said Brad. 'Don't look now, but Margie Rogers just crept in.'

Birdie's gaze flicked to the entry once again. The young, 'tight' teacher she had first suspected was the one hinted at in today's rumour – until she found out she was Sister T's niece – made her way towards the players. Margie exchanged a quick look with Dom before squatting to do up a shoelace.

'We better watch each other's backs,' said Brad with a frown. 'And not just on court. I don't particularly want to be the subject of any rumours.' He picked up a ball. His expression turning cheeky. 'Got any skeletons in the closet I should know about?'

Birdie swiped the ball from his hands. 'I think I might shoot some hoops.' She jogged away.

'Avoidance of question noted,' he called after her.

Birdie dribbled, lost in the need to move, to focus on something else. Her hair tickled the back of her neck as she set up for a shot. She bounced the ball, bounced it again and rolled it around in her palm, lifting it to take aim.

Skeletons in the closet. Didn't everyone have them?

'Birdie!' Joanie's assistant principal hurried onto the boards and grabbed Birdie's arm.

'Roseanne.' The ball dropped from Birdie's fingers. The rhythm of its bounce echoed in her ears. 'Is everything okay?'

'Oh Birdie. I'm glad I caught you. I was hoping you could contact your uncle, the solicitor.'

'Uncle Larry? Why?'

'Sister T has been taken into custody.'

'What?' said Brad, coming to join them.

'Into custody?' Birdie said.

'Oh well, I don't know.' Roseanne was clearly flustered. 'She's been taken to the police station.'

'What for?' asked Brad.

'For stabbing the editor of the *Gallie Wallen Gazette*!'

THREE

Uncle Larry smiled over at her as they waited on the uncomfortable seats of the Vantage Bay Police Station foyer. He rested a hand on Birdie's knee, stilling the nervous tapping she'd taken up like a new favourite hobby. 'You okay, darling?'

No! Her treacherous mind kept snagging on memories of Detective Herb Lawson. The cheeky tone of his voice that first time he'd called her 'teach', his sparkling hazel eyes globe round at something 'shocking' she'd done. The warmth of his long fingers on her lower back as he pulled her against him blazed a forgotten thrill across the surface of her skin.

She needed to stop thinking this way. It was doing her no good in trying to move on.

'Just thinking about the last time I was in this station.' Not exactly the truth, but close enough.

She put her hand over her uncle's and squeezed. She'd frequented the station often during Uncle Larry's abduction.

Not that it had helped much. Birdie, with the help of her friends Pia and Stu, had found her 'uncle' – who was not a blood relation but her mother's best friend and Birdie's beloved godfather – without police assistance in the end. It was her determination to find her uncle and her 'sleuthing', as Herb had jokingly called it, that had helped bring an end to the case.

'Let me say thank you once again.' Uncle Larry turned his hand and held hers.

'I'm just glad you're here. I mean here, right now, as well as altogether.' She smiled.

He brought her hand to his lips. 'Me too, my darling child.' He kissed her knuckles and released her hand.

The very last time Birdie had been in this police station was to talk to Constable Celeste Ford. She'd asked Celeste where Herb had disappeared to. The young constable, with sympathy written all over her face, either didn't know or wouldn't tell her.

Celeste had not been the only person she'd asked about Herb. She'd also asked Herb's brother, Cecil. 'Your guess is as good as mine, Birdie,' he'd said. 'Herb's always been about Herb. I'm too busy to concern myself with him, no offence.'

She *had* been slightly offended, but Cecil's busyness in providing advice for Aboriginal people who found themselves in court was never-ending and a good excuse to tolerate his candid response.

She'd also visited the house Herb shared with some mates, had been told they'd let out his room, and then one of the guys reminded her he was free for a date ... now that Herb had moved on. Her so-called sleuthing skills had come to nought.

In the end, Birdie had called Herb's parents. His father had told her he was 'on Country' and couldn't be contacted. Birdie had been too embarrassed to ask for any more information. Too embarrassed to pine for someone who obviously didn't give a shit about her.

'Now, to something much more frivolous but very close to our present situation,' her uncle said, his voice cleared her thoughts. 'Who do you think today's *Shame Game, No Names* post was about?'

Birdie voiced her suspicion about Dom Walker.

'So, that's three weeks in a row the paper has aimed its arrow at teachers,' said Uncle Larry.

'That's true.'

'Must be some good fodder in schools.' *Also, true.*

He checked his watch. It was late. Uncle Larry had been travelling back from an interstate meeting when Birdie rang his office. Birdie had muddled through their basketball game before rushing off to muddle through some light dinner music provided by her voice and guitar at Fidele's. In the time it took them both to finally get to the station, Sister T had been questioned, a liaison officer had escorted her home – where she'd showered, changed and handed over her clothes – and been escorted back.

Uncle Larry closed his eyes and rubbed a finger across each eyelid. *He's tired.* Guilt trickled through her veins. Birdie knew he would do anything for her. He always had. She may not have a dad, but she had the next best thing – an Uncle Larry.

'Well, if it isn't Miss Mealing looking as beautiful as ever.' Sergeant Morton Reynolds wandered into the reception area and beamed across the bulky wooden desk. 'Knew you wouldn't be able to stay away.'

Rolling her eyes on the inside, she smiled on the out. 'It's good to see you, Sergeant.' Best to keep the law on side and, to that end, she jumped in with her request. 'Will we be waiting much longer, do you think?'

He gave her an eyebrow raise. 'You haven't got yourself into more trouble, have you, sweetheart?'

Birdie laughed appropriately. She moved to stand opposite him at the bench. 'You know me too well, Morton.' She morphed her features into an expression of innocence and leaned in. 'A girl can't help it if she was born for mischief.'

He laughed out loud, his big belly pushing even further against the straining buttons of his uniform shirt.

Birdie pulled back. 'You remember my uncle, the solicitor?' She gestured in his direction.

'Of course. Mr Kean, nice to see you again.'

Larry stood, arm outstretched. 'Likewise, Sergeant Reynolds.' The two men shook hands.

Morton gave his attention back to Birdie. 'For you, Miss Mealing, I'd move heaven and earth.'

'I only really need a few doors opened, Morton. Nothing as taxing as heaven and earth.' He laughed again.

She waited until he'd finished. 'We're here to see Sister Therese Margaret.'

The senior policeman winked. 'Let me take you through now, then, and find out what's happening.'

'Birdie, you are a master of manipulation,' Uncle Larry whispered as they walked down the stale corridor.

'Learned from the best,' she whispered back.

Larry touched his chest and feigned surprise.

'Here we go.' Sergeant Reynolds opened the door to the familiar light-green painted room with its familiar chairs.

Her pastoral care course had reported green was a calming colour. Was that the reason they'd decorated this little interview room in a washed-out Granny Smith?

'Take a seat and I'll get the female constable to bring the nun in.' The sergeant left the room.

Birdie threw her eyes to heaven. 'The female constable. Why not just, the constable? She shouldn't be defined by her ... womanliness.'

'Says the girl who just exploited every inch of her womanliness.'

Birdie shrugged a shoulder. 'It got us what we wanted. We're closer to seeing Sister T than we would have been in the waiting room, aren't we?'

He dropped his head back and laughed. She loved the sound. It was one of the things she'd missed while he was lost. Uncle Larry's laugh died away as the door opened and Constable Celeste Ford ushered in a sombre Sister T.

⇔ ⇔ ⇔

The quietly imposing figure Sister T usually embodied was diminished, the fluorescents highlighting the change without mercy.

Birdie rose and hugged her principal, guiding her to one of the empty chairs. 'How are you?'

Sister T shivered, then straightened her shoulders, settling a stoic stance over her torso; a state of being nuns had down pat. 'The Lord is with me. He's keeping me safe.' She fondled her rosary beads.

Uncle Larry conversed quietly with Celeste. The constable handed some papers to him, exchanged a tight-lipped smile with Birdie and left the room.

'Sister, this is my uncle, Larry Kean. He's a solicitor. He's here to help.'

Awe and wonder crept up on Sister T's expression. 'The one who was missing?'

Birdie nodded.

'Lovely to meet you, Sister Therese Margaret.' Larry smiled his most reassuring smile.

'Lovely to meet you too, but I'm not sure I need your help. I didn't stab that poor, unfortunate soul.'

'All the more reason you do, then. Let's remember what the Bible says, Sister: God helps those who help themselves.'

'That's not actually from the Bible, Mr Kean. It's an ancient Greek motto. The gods help those who help themselves.'

'Well.' His eyes darted his goddaughter's way before he cleared his throat. 'That's something I didn't know. Regardless, its sentiment is the same. Now, you've been arrested but not charged as yet. I want to go over your statement with you, before it's signed, and ask you a few questions. Then we can decide whether you need my help.'

Birdie sat and listened while her uncle gently asked his questions.

'I taught him when he was in high school, you know. He was an insecure young man masked by fierce determination, but I wouldn't have said unreasonable.' She rolled a bead from her rosary set in between her fingers. 'Highly intelligent. I thought, if I just visited him personally ...'

She was talking about Warwick Woods, the editor of the *Gallie Wallen Gazette*. He'd met with representatives from the three school systems – state, Catholic and private – earlier that day. A meeting at which Sister T was in attendance due to their history.

'He did not agree with me that the column should be discontinued.' Sister T worried her rosary beads, saying a quick Hail Mary and blessing herself. 'Such behaviour goes against everything we teach. God will judge us on the last day. We don't judge each other.'

'When I went back to Warwick's office later to try to reason with him, the newspaper looked all packed up for the day. It had been about a quarter to five. I knocked. There was no answer, but I went around the back, anyway. That's when I heard the groaning.'

'You could hear it through the door?' asked Larry.

'The back door was open. I rushed in to see what the matter was and ...' Sister T slid her fingers on to the next bead. The words she couldn't say were that she'd found Warwick slumped on the floor in the tiny kitchenette, face down with a knife sticking out of his back.

'I put my hand on the knife to assess how deep it might be, what damage it might have done internally. That's when the lady from the newsagents came in and called, "Do you still need a lift, Warwick?", saw me, and screamed.' Her beads clacked softly against each other. 'Then I started some simple first aid. I trained as a nurse at sixteen, when I first went into the convent.' She grabbed Birdie's hand. 'How is Warwick? They won't tell me if he's okay.'

Birdie checked her uncle, who nodded. 'He's in a coma, Sister,' Birdie said.

Larry had been given this information on route.

Sister T's hand flew to her chest. 'He survived.' She doubled her efforts on her beads, whispering a prayer.

Birdie made out the words 'Holy Spirit'.

Larry reached out a hand and interrupted. 'I would like you to please consider taking me on as your solicitor, Sister. He may be alive but you're looking at a charge of grievous bodily harm, which holds a maximum sentence of twenty-five years imprisonment.'

⊖ ⊖ ⊖

The gentle arms of a couple of the older nuns surrounded Sister T as soon as the convent door opened. They said blessings over Larry and waved him off. His ginger hair caught the glow from the streetlight as he headed back to the car where Birdie had waited. He pulled out of the convent's driveway and into the quiet late-night street.

'So?' Birdie eventually said.

'Well, I don't think she stabbed him, but ...'

'But, what?'

'I can see why the police do. She had his blood all over her; her prints are on the weapon, which she was holding; he's been publishing smut about teachers, of which she is one; and they have a history.'

'Surely, they don't think a little old nun like Sister T could have done this?'

'For a start, she's not little and she's not that old. She's as strong as an ox, I'd wager, and she'd be close to my age.' He speared her with a dare-to-say-I'm-old look.

He was right. She was probably mid-forties. She often had the players on the ropes in the Chalkies' Challenge basketball comp, was fast up and down the court, strong in defence and she could shoot a mean basket. Plus, she swam regular laps and rode a push bike for short trips when the car was unnecessary. She was likely fitter than Birdie.

'I know anyone's capable of anything, but Sister T?'

'She's the only suspect they've got at this stage.'

'Well, if she's the only suspect they've got, we're just going to have to supply them with an alternative.'

'That would be advantageous.' Sister T had been a rock for Birdie when Larry had been missing. 'There's something else I need to tell you.'

'Go on.'

Birdie took a breath. 'Her niece is a temp at Percy's who most people think is the owner of the tight backside Dom, who I told you before could be the principal in question, was swishing over his desk.'

'Oh dear.' Her uncle put his fingers on his cheekbones and massaged. 'This is not helpful. Especially if you add that to the knife and the blood and the fact that Constable Celeste Ford told me, during the meeting earlier in the day witnessed by the representatives from the other school systems, Therese said, "All they that take the sword will perish with the sword."'

'Shit.'

'Bum and damn,' added Larry. 'My thoughts exactly.'

FOUR

Mrs Neslar had styled her beautiful white-grey hair in a French roll today. Her back swanlike, neck held high. She sang softly, her voice a deep alto. Birdie could always pick it among the chorus. She was in the final row of the singers at Evesong Retirement Village. Almost as tall as Birdie, she had always encouraged her surrogate granddaughter not to slouch, to stand tall, to accept she could not avoid looking down on others in stature but could avoid looking down on them with her heart.

She smiled at Birdie as she sang. One of Birdie's favourite times of the week was Friday when she could spend some time with Mrs N. More than their one-time landlady, she was like a mother to Birdie's own mother, Lenore, taking the very young, pregnant and thrown-out-of-home girl under her wing and into her heart. With the Polish woman, who ironically had fled her own home after the war, Lenore and Birdie had made a family of their own.

A bud of warmth bloomed in Birdie's chest.

'I think Sister Therese Margaret did not be stabbing editor of newspaper, Warwick Woods,' Mrs Neslar said when they were alone in her room a little later.

'I don't think so either, Mrs N.'

'Many people here love the sister. She has been teacher of many grandkids.'

'The police will work it out.'

'Like they work out where is Larry. Hmph.'

Mrs N had a point. Birdie still wasn't sure whether the police played a part in making her uncle disappear in the first place or worked to keep him hidden. They certainly didn't find him and bring him home.

The elderly woman placed her fingers ready against the organ keys and started playing the song Birdie had set for practice last week. Birdie had one ear on her charge and one on the thoughts going round her head.

Sister T had taught Warwick Woods. Birdie knew Sister T had previously worked at Percy's next door, obviously when Warwick had attended. The nun had said he was highly intelligent but also insecure. Would being the editor of the local newspaper make you feel secure? Was the *Gallie Wallen Gazette* really the place for a highly intelligent person? He'd expanded the growth of the local paper with *Shame Game, No Names* ... that was clever, but could trying to make his mark with the local paper have compromised Warwick's life?

'Well?' Mrs N focused her eyes on Birdie.

Birdie blinked.

'The playing. Was it good?'

'For a first go, it was. Let's hear it through again, Mrs N.' Birdie hadn't heard a note.

⇔ ⇔ ⇔

Pia King entered the bedroom carrying two plates – a devon sandwich on each – two soft drink cans, and a bottle of tomato sauce as Birdie was getting ready for her gig. To the untrained eye, it looked like a tricky process.

Pia put the sauce bottle on the table. While she placed the plates and drinks down, Birdie attacked the sauce bottle lid.

'It's gotta be one of the other barrr … arseholes at the meeting setting Sister T up.' Pia smiled. The best friends had an unspoken rule: Pia didn't say 'bastard' as an insult, seeing technically Birdie was one due to her lack of father, and Birdie never used the word 'spaz' as it wasn't really funny when you had a congenital hand deformity like Pia did.

Birdie continued to struggle with the lid of the sauce. 'I would have said the same, and actually did to Uncle Larry, but he informed me the other members of the meeting had been interviewed, and all have an alibi for the time the stabbing happened. And I appreciate your use of the word arsehole.' Birdie grinned.

Pia held out her hand. Birdie passed the sauce. Pia took the lid off.

'How did you do that?' Birdie pointed to the now re-lieved-of-its-lid sauce bottle.

'I did read some research that suggested the body compensates for sensory deficits by making other areas stronger. It was referring to the other senses, but the premise is the same. Personally,' Pia said, voice deepened, 'I think it's determination.' She balanced the plates on her knees, kept secured by 'Stumpy', the name she'd given to the hand deemed 'deficit', smothered sauce over the devon, replaced the top pieces of bread and handed one to Birdie.

Birdie took a big bite of the sandwich and shimmied into a short skirt.

'Sister T doesn't have an alibi?' Pia asked.

'She says she was still at school, but no one actually saw her.'

'We could just wait until Warwick Woods wakes up and ask him.'

'He's in an induced coma,' said Birdie.

'Puts a spanner in the works.'

'Enough about that now. How's business?'

'Excellent.' As a food technologist, Pia was a rarity. Not only a woman but also a woman with an impairment. 'We're working on a plastic that can be boiled in water and not deteriorate.'

Birdie sucked in her cheeks and applied blush to her cheekbones. 'Gosh. How does that work?'

'Okay, so, you cook something like, poached pears in syrup, let's say, then you put it in this special type of plastic bag, heat seal it and freeze it. Then, when you want poached pears for dessert, you pop the bag into boiling water, not just the fruit and syrup but the whole plastic bag, until it's heated through. Then you open it and serve with ice cream or custard, or both, and toss away the bag. No cleaning up.'

'You can do that with plastic? Heat it like that?' Birdie applied lipstick.

'This type being developed, you can. It's great for catering, leftovers, camping. They're easy to store, less mess. It's early days, but we'll see.'

'Remember,' Birdie said, facing her friend, 'I'm always here if you need a guinea pig.'

Pia took another bite of her sandwich, a smile on her heart shaped, dimple chinned face. 'Could Warwick have been stabbed by one of the people targeted in the *Shame Game, No Names* column?'

'I thought about that.' Birdie took another big, toothy bite of sandwich – careful not to touch her lips to the bread – chewed quickly and swallowed. 'It could very well be about revenge. Or could it be about stopping the column?'

'Does the attacker think the gossip will stop being printed because Warwick's out of the picture? Whoever's in charge in his absence could just publish it too.'

'I wonder who the person is that's feeding them this sordid information?'

'Good point. It would be much better to target the source if it's about stopping the smut.'

'What if it's got nothing to do with the new column. We are only focusing on the *Shame Game* gossip because that's a good motive to clear Sister T.'

'It's a good motive in general, Birds.' The slices of bread in Pia's sandwich flapped around like a castanet clacker as she used it to emphasise her point. 'And a good place to start.'

'Start?'

'Although, I would love to find out who's supplying the gossip. I wonder whether they should be wary.' Pia flashed a wicked smile at Birdie; her shoulder length, wavy dark hair framed it to perfection. 'Which angle are we investigating?'

Birdie swallowed a mouthful. 'What makes you think we are investigating any angle?'

'That look in your eye. Your determined, can-do attitude. Your pursuit of justice for Sister T.'

'Surely, the best thing to do would be to leave it up to the professionals?' Birdie said, squashing a grin.

'Come now, my friend. You can't kid a kidder.'

⪥ ⪥ ⪥

Common before a gig and not unwelcome, Birdie's stomach windmilled with nerves. They would disappear as soon as she played the first note; she'd churn that whirl into performance energy without even thinking. Let it flow through her like electricity and light up the stage.

'I heard the principal at your school has been accused of stabbing the editor of the gazette?' said Megan, the other female band member of Seasons of Change. Megan, who had completed plugging in and was placing her numerous instruments on their stands, hovered by Birdie's keyboard.

'I don't believe she did it,' said Birdie. *Such a weird topic of conversation.*

'The little pieces about the teachers have been the best ones so far.' Megan extracted a cleaning tool from her bag. 'You know, everyone has gone to school, everyone knows a teacher, loved and hated alike. Everyone has been reprimanded, heard the words – *you're not living up to your potential!* – and spent at least ten years of their lives in an educational institution.' She slipped the tool down the length of her saxophone and worked it back and forth. 'No offence, Birdie, I think teachers are great, but I was having a laugh at the entries about them.'

Megan was right. Almost everyone'd had years of experience in dealing with teachers. Birdie herself thought exposing these men was delicious kismet.

'Perhaps, though, they are not as funny now that a man has been stabbed,' Megan added. She clicked her mouthpiece back into position.

'And a nun has been accused of the attack,' said Birdie.

'Who do you think did do it, if not your nun?' Megan asked.

Any one of those men written about. 'I don't know, but … Uncle Larry's representing Sister T.'

'Oh! Our solicitor-to-the-stars. I love the idea of him representing our very own Gallie Wallen "stars".' Megan smiled. 'It should all work out then, I'm sure.' The talented musician began warming up the mouthpiece.

Rumblings infiltrated their sacred space; the crowd behind the closed curtain was obviously growing. Soon, Drew, the guitarist, technical guru and unofficial manager, would draw back the veil and Seasons of Change would ignite.

Sex-on-legs sauntered onto the stage in the form of their lead singer, Clint. He patted Drew on the back, shook hands with Brett the drummer and stood shoulder to shoulder with Birdie, smiling charmingly at Megan as one hand squeezed the small woman's upper arm in greeting. No one could see the other hand. It secretly drifted, slowly and seductively, over Birdie's backside. She did her best to control the shiver that followed.

'Looks like a big crowd.' Clint slid away from Birdie to fiddle with his mic. He turned and delivered her a subtle glare. 'Might just duck to the gentlemen's.' His shoulder brushed gently against Birdie's as he headed backstage.

'We're right to go when he comes back,' said Drew.

'I might quickly go to the loo myself, then,' said Birdie. She had only taken a few steps down the corridor when she felt arms around her, luring her into the alcove behind the stage area.

'You look extra hot tonight.' Clint's lips met hers and went to work, turning the still-warm shiver into a live wire sizzle.

Her mind flew, as it sometimes did when they played at this venue, to when Herb had caught her in this very place, in a compromising position – much like the one she was currently in – months ago. Clint's kisses consumed her, her thoughts dissolving like fairy floss on a tongue.

Before Herb's kisses, Clint's had been the best. She had never given herself fully to Clint, though, keeping a little piece guarded. Their frontman was only ever a bit of fun. The good thing about Clint was any dalliance would be just that – a dalliance; no strings attached.

She'd never wanted a boyfriend in the first place, but Herb had wormed his way into her heart, her veins, her dreams ... her bed. And had now disappeared. The bastard. The word she never allowed to be used as an adjective seemed appropriate here.

Clint's fingers started to wander, tongue nudged at hers, and Birdie fell deeper into the kiss. No reason not to enjoy it for what it was. As Clint's hands slid up under her skirt, cupped a bum cheek and pulled her against him, she pushed thoughts of Herb aside and allowed herself this stolen morsel of pleasure.

After all, *she* wasn't a nun.

⇔ ⇔ ⇔

Clint's eyes shut tight as he threw his face skyward, dropped his shoulders back and released a soul-battering final note. His shirt was askew, mouth unfastened, pupils alive as he righted himself and swayed towards Drew who was mauling his guitar strings madly. Sweat soaked Brett's shirt. His hair – wet with it – slapped around his cheeks, the drums an extension of his body. Megan's stilettoed feet danced in tune to the sax as she blew the roof off. From her position on the keyboard, stage rear, Birdie was pumped up on the performance.

Clint began gyrating against the microphone stand. 'Goodnight, sexy Randwick. We've had fun!'

The girls in the front row went wild. They reached out for the singer, and he ran his hand along their outstretched fingers.

'Merch and cassettes are available in the foyer after the show,' Drew said. 'Support local Oz music.'

'We're Seasons of Change.' Clint threw his arms in the air. The crowd went wild. 'Thanks for coming!'

Brett played a slow roll on the drums, Birdie jabbed in time at the keys, Megan tooted a few spurts, and Drew slid a heavy finger along the string. Brett gave one final, epic smash with the sticks on skin, and the music stopped.

A hum throbbed through her blood and bloomed in her chest. Birdie stilled under Clint's look of raw desire. His eyes licked her body and lingered on hers, wild and heady, blissed by the beat. She returned the look. Perhaps tonight was the night for having some of her own sexy fun.

'Awesome show, Miss Mealing.' A familiar face entered her peripheral vision, taking her attention.

'Mr Wheatley!'

Griff Wheatly's blond hair shimmered, his eyes – steely blue in the semidarkness – twinkled with promise.

She moved towards the front of stage and squatted. 'Glad you enjoyed it.' She began pulling the gaffer tape off the electrical cord at her feet.

He ran a tongue along his bottom lip. 'Doing anything now?'

Nothing with you. 'Packing up my gear.'

Griff started pulling tape as well. 'And after that?'

Birdie could feel Clint watching the exchange. She glanced over for a second. The spotlights glowed around him, lighting him up like the fallen angel Lucifer.

'Getting a good night's sleep, I hope.'

Griff's focus travelled to Clint and back to her. A sly grin almost took hold of his lips. 'Will I see you Thursday, at Chalkies?'

'You will.'

'Until then.' He handed her some gaffer tape, his hand dawdling in hers as she accepted it. 'Sweet dreams,' he said before letting go. He gave Clint a pointed look and joined the disengaging audience. Not backwards in coming forwards, was our Griff.

As the house lights began to lift and the spotlight faded, Birdie's eye was drawn to another audience member commanding the exit. He was looking down his nose at Griff as he walked around him. The man was slightly taller than those who milled past on their way out. His stance: confident, effortless, elegant. Beautiful cheekbones and a light dusting of hair edged the bow of perfect lips. The man's face, eyes unable to be made out clearly in the dim light, turned towards their lead singer as Clint took that moment to pass by her side, a suggestion whispered in her ear, the back of his hand dusting the curve of her breast. The man in the crowd ran a hand through his hair. Frustration. She'd seen that move on another.

Her heart flew from its chamber and lodged in her throat. *It reminds me of* … 'Herb,' she said in a whisper, the name sucking the air from her lungs.

A coil of cord slapped against Birdie's leg as Drew pulled it tight. He waved a sorry. She rubbed at the sting and stepped to the side to let it glide past. When she looked back for the man, he was gone.

'That guy who was watching you,' said Megan, standing close. 'That wasn't—'

'I'll be back in a minute, hon.'

Birdie ran down the front steps of the stage into the thinning crowd. She searched the heads, the faces, but couldn't see Herb among them. She ran out the front door. The dark car park was scattered with exiting patrons, none of whom were him. Had she dreamt it? She turned in a 360 and stretched onto tiptoes. She couldn't have dreamt it if Megan saw him too. A cool breeze played at her dress sleeves. She wrapped her arms across her chest and clutched her elbows, turned and made her way inside. She glimpsed over her shoulder once more before stepping back through the door.

'It wasn't him?' asked Megan as Birdie began to pack up her gear.

'I'm just seeing things that aren't there.' It wasn't the first time she'd thought she'd recognised Herb in the face, stance, gesture, scent of another. They'd shared the best part of a glorious summer in each other's arms. She knew everything about him. But then he'd taken off, disappeared without a word. *So obviously I hadn't.*

She shouldn't be running like a lost soul to search for him anyway. What had she been thinking? Herb was the one who had decided to go. After she'd put her travel plans on hold for him, he had been the one who had taken himself away. Away from what they'd begun.

Away from me.

Rejection hurt. It was an unforgiving pain Birdie had not reconciled with. Even after all these months her blood boiled at the thought of it, the thought of the ease with which he'd walked away. *Like my father had.* She knew it wasn't entirely the same, but Herb was another man who was happy to turn his back on her.

Which made the lifting of her heart at the mistaken sight of him something she needed to place a brick on. She closed her eyes, took a breath, opened them once more and continued gathering her gear.

Clint would be signing merchandise right now, mixing with the hangers-on, flirting with the playful girls. As if she could seriously consider ever following through with him. She just wanted to go home, shower off the sweat and cigarette smoke and get into bed.

She hurried her packing up, said goodbye to her bandmates – passing up the free drinks – and slipped out the back door.

Her heart was a traitor.

👄 👄 👄

She was aware of him behind her, cradling her back with his warmth. His lean legs sliding along the underside of hers, her feet pushing down as his pushed up, strong tendons gripping bone, caressed by the pads of her big toes.

One hand slipped up her side and cupped a willing breast. She sighed, heat spreading like wildfire. His other hand slinked down the opposite side and around the curve of her bottom. Fingers walking along skin, searching between her legs, his mouth peppering soft kisses on her ear, stubble tickling her shoulder. 'Jesus, I missed you, Bird.' His fingers worked their magic, circling and stroking, gentle but steady.

She was unable to respond, her words dissolving into breathy huffs, her skin on fire, the need for him growing stronger and stronger. She moved in rhythm with his strokes, her body seeking his touch, the intensity of his work rising, building. She was close to the edge, to toppling over.

'I've dreamed about this. Burned for it,' he whispered as he glided a finger inside her.

She gasped, the sound coming from somewhere outside the action. It was a shock to her ears. She chased the solidity of it, the jarring sound, pulled from the hazy chase for ...

'Shit!' Birdie opened her eyes. The Laura Ashley baby blue juniper berries that patterned her walls swam into view. The heat behind her evaporating with every blink. She reached back to touch him, already knowing she'd find an empty space.

Ugh! Just a dream.

Her body tingled all over. Warmth spread from intimate parts to the corners of her entire being. She had been so close. She placed her fingers inside her pyjama bottoms, put pressure on the spot that craved it and brought on her own release. Satisfying ... to a point.

She struggled her arms out of the covers, which had wrapped themselves around her like a lover, and flopped them on top.

'Bloody man.'

It wasn't the first dream she'd had like that about Herb. They always ended the same, with her waking up ... *un*-done.

There are some women for
whom orgasm is part of the
bread and butter of sex;
having sex without orgasm
leaves them frustrated,
angry, perhaps in pain. For
others, it's a bonus.

'Sealed section:
Explore your love/sex feelings'
Cleo, April 1985.

FIVE

T HE BEACH WAS QUIET at this time of day. Seasoned locals bobbed up and down in the April surf. She dropped her gear and slid without preamble into the Ladies Bathing Pool, soaking herself from head to toe. She shot back out again, shivering as she did. She was thoroughly frosty now, outside and in. All thoughts of Herb dunked in cold water as they should be.

She lay back on her towel, listening to the song of other brave-souled swimmers as she dried off. The swishing rhythm of arms slicing through the water, the plonk of a body turning and pushing off again, the lift of a head, an intake of breath, the soft ripple of the liquid as it made room for the oncoming mass. She raised her neck and watched the graceful body. The familiar broad shoulders and long nape, strong taut legs ending in an even four-beat kick. A glance to the side showed the telltale pushbike leaning up against a pole. Sister T was doing her laps. A half hour of time when she'd be able to concentrate on something other than the mess she was in.

The timbre of breaking water deepened as the woman herself glided over to where Birdie was perched on the edge of the pool.

'How are you, Sister?'

'I wish I had that all-consuming belief in the Lord. To put myself in his hands and know that all would be well, Birdie, but I'm finding it hard.'

'Well, lucky you've got me and Uncle Larry then. Your little gifts of the Holy Spirit.'

Sister T managed a smile. Her principal had been there for her when Uncle Larry went missing. Birdie would return the favour, and then some.

'I'm not a perfect person,' Sr T said. 'I can't help thinking this is my penance.'

'None of us are perfect, Therese. And the truth is, you didn't stab Warwick. You need to trust in the truth. That's what I'm going to find.'

To the naked eye, she was doing a valiant job of behaving like nothing was troubling her. But the letters from irate parents, the scrutiny from the Catholic Schools Board, not to mention a visit from the bishop himself, even if – seemingly – in support, must have been weighing on her.

'One thing I've learnt about you, Miss Mealing, is that you're tenacious.' She pushed off from the wall and swam away.

I could say the same thing about you, Sister.

Being a principal meant she wasn't one to shy away from attention, but this was the kind of attention she could not control. She'd refused to stand down from her role, refused to let the whispers, the looks, the comments get to her.

Birdie knew that feeling. She'd dodged throwaway wise-cracks made by shallow, mindless people her whole life. At least in Birdie's case, however unnecessary, they were the truth. But there was no possible way Birdie could reconcile with the idea that Sister T had stabbed Warwick.

'You're right about that, Sis,' Birdie said to herself. She observed for a few more minutes before gathering her towel and bag. 'I always get my man.' She turned and set off for home.

'Apparently, talking to yourself is a healthy sign.' Birdie stumbled at the intrusion. Her oldest friend in the world, Stu Ah Kee, caught her. 'Helps you stay focused, motivated, able to process feelings.'

She threw both arms around him, squeezing tight before releasing. She reached into her bag and flashed her Walkman as she continued to walk. 'I played your mixed tape.'

'Good?' Stu's brown eyes widened with the question.

She bumped his shoulder with hers. 'Amazing! Pia's on her way over. I suppose you've heard about the editor of the *Gallie Wallen Gazette* getting stabbed?' Questions from the week's action looped over in her mind. Who had stabbed Warwick Woods if she was so sure it wasn't Sister T? Who was providing the paper with gossip about the local teachers? And were the two related? 'We're going to try and work out who did it.' They had reached the sand of the beach proper. 'Get wet and then we'll go.'

'I'm concerned about you two getting involved in another crime.'

'We found Uncle Larry.'

'But this kind of finding someone, especially someone who knows how to wield a knife, might not be a sensible idea.' He dropped into the public rock pool and charged back out like a ball from a cannon. 'Shit, that's hypothermic.'

Most people would say 'cold'. *But not my Nurse, Ah Kee.*

'I thought cold water was good for your health,' Birdie said.

'Stick to the point, Birdie. We were discussing the sensibility of your actions. I won't be there to assist this time.'

'So, when you say sensible, you mean, sensible if you're not around?'

He shook his thick black hair; it stuck out at sharp angles. 'Neurological studies show the male brain is better at creating and understanding systems. It's more analytical.'

I bet that will be proven false one day. 'Oh no!' Birdie placed the back of her hand dramatically against her forehead, getting into character. 'Whatever will we do? Without you, we will only have our soft, girly brains to rely on.' She twirled a piece of hair, opened her eyes wide and blinked her eyelashes.

'Very funny. You and Pia are more than capable of doing anything you put your minds to.'

'Gee, thanks.'

'I'm going to be very busy, Birdie.'

Poor Stu. He would be hating missing out on trying to solve this mystery. The nursing degree was moving from a specialised college and hospital setting to courses at university, and Stu, a very dedicated nurse, had been chosen to help design and plan the diploma. It would be interesting to hear his thoughts on the new format for learning when he was able to share them. There was talk the teaching degree would go the same way.

'What if there's danger?' he said, towelling himself off.

Ah, our safety. That's how he was going to spin it. The three had already faced a gunman together – and come out on top. *Thank God!*

'Brad will be there to help.'

'Well, now I feel *so* much better.' Sarcasm dripped off him along with the saltwater. 'Anyway, I better go.'

'But you just got here. Aren't you coming back to the house?'

'Can't. I've got readings to do.'

It was a big thing for him to be asked to help with the set-up of the new style of learning. She sensed the stress swirling through his bones. They walked to the road where Stu would go one way and she the other. She clipped the Walkman onto her hip.

'Please be careful,' he said. 'Homicides have risen to 1.5 per 100,000 of the population. The Emergency department has had to do some training in bloodwork triage.'

'Gee: 1.5 per 100,000. The odds are really against us. Thanks for your concern, *Dad.*' She kissed his cheek, placed her headphones on and pressed play.

Stu grabbed her, stopping her from taking her next step. He lifted one side of the headphones from her ear. 'I mean it, Birdie.'

'I'll be *careful*, Stu.' She removed the earpiece from his fingers and let it snap back into place.

As if she and Pia would be anything but.

One of the twins bounded into her bedroom. Birdie, who had been about to exit her bathroom door, quickly pulled back in. Just out of kindy and now into year one, her little brothers were growing up too fast. Gone was some of the chubbiness of their limbs, the squishiness of their cheeks and their mass of sandy ringlets had been tamed around their ears like newly shorn sheep.

This twin peered around his sister's room, then headed for the hallway that led to the study, bathroom and her entry door.

'Boo!' Birdie called as he poked his little head through. He jumped, a big smile growing across his beautiful face.

'Hey, Big Bird. You scared me half to death.' *Rusty*. Kick would have tackled her or given her a karate chop or something similar. A much more physical specimen was he.

'Gotcha,' said Birdie with a laugh.

'I owe you one now.' And Rusty was the thinker, the softer one, if that was possible for a boy twin at the age of six. He'd be calculating his next move from now until he made it.

'You need something, little man?'

'Dad said to tell you we're on our way to the movies, if you wanted to come?'

'Oo. What are you seeing?'

'*The Care Bears Movie.*'

'Um. Might pass on that one, but thanks for asking. Pia's coming over.'

With the men gone, and her mother's Saturday morning ritual of playing tennis in full swing – pun intended – she had the whole silent house to herself. Not that she didn't always have her privacy. She did live happily in her little suite with her own bedroom, bathroom, study, carport and separate entrance. Courtesy of her mother's husband and the twins' father, who just happened to be a visionary architect, Glen.

'I love Pia,' Rusty said, eyes bright.

'She loves you.'

'I'll see you later, Big Bird.' He flounced out to the main house but turned back. 'You need to be careful, though.

Expect it when you least expect it.' He ran off, leaving her grinning.

Birdie sang along to 'Out of Mind, Out of Sight' by the Models – courtesy of Stu's mixed tape – as she pulled on her jeans and T-shirt. Who else might be a candidate for stabbing Warwick Woods? Warwick was unconscious, so he wasn't talking. Who was the editor-in-charge now? Would they be willing to talk, and would they talk to her?

Maybe she could ask the new mayor to help her gain access to the gazette's staff. After all, if it wasn't for Birdie – and Pia and Stu and Uncle Larry – the mayor might still be under suspicion for misappropriation of council funds.

She called her uncle.

'I don't suppose I can convince you to leave trying to prove it wasn't Sister Therese Margaret to me, can I?' he said.

'I could lie and say yes, but my conscience won't let me. So, no.' He laughed down the line. 'Anyway,' she continued, 'you yourself said it would be advantageous to find out who it was.'

'And how will talking to the staff at the gazette help with that?'

'Pia and I are working on the theory that the stabbing has something to do with *Shame Game, No Names*.'

'Excellent theory.'

'Perhaps the gazette might offer up some clues.'

👄 👄 👄

Pia flopped the *TV Week* magazine down on the coffee table. It was open at a double spread on a new show called *Neighbours.*

'It's like Mrs Mangel,' said Pia, referencing the middle-aged nosey parker, one of the characters featured in the article. She plonked herself onto the lounge in Birdie's room. 'How so?'

'She's a gossip. She's always got her eyes open. Spying on people over the fence, listening in on conversations, watching through windows. She's like the person gathering the dirt to supply to the paper.'

The person supplying the dirt. If Warwick was in fact stabbed as a result of the gossip column, how would *they* be feeling right now?

'Do we know who the subjects of these rumours are?' Pia asked.

'We suspect we do. In two cases, anyway. Firstly, there's hunk of spunk, Griff Wheatley. He's the one that went wee, wee, wee, wee all the way home.'

'Bit dodgy coming onto one of your own students.'

'True. He's now working at his mum's school, Gallie Wallen Grammar.'

Pia scoffed. 'Jobs for the boys.'

'In more ways than one. When in Queensland he worked at his *dad's* school. 'The entry had the phrase: *"I wonder who's the market stallholder?"* added. His dad was the principal.'

'So, what ... he allowed it to happen?'

'Well, the girl was sixteen – age of consent – and just about to graduate.'

'Still.'

'I know.' Birdie sat up on the edge of the mattress and faced her friend. 'You should see him, Pia. He is drop-dead gorgeous. Even I couldn't keep my eyes off him.'

'Put anything else on him?'

'Not yet.'

The girls leaned into a laugh.

'He, on the other hand, was very attentive during the basketball game,' Birdie continued. 'His one-on-one defence was difficult to fault.'

'I'll bet. Any holding fouls?'

'Maybe a couple.' They shared another giggle. Birdie threw herself back down on her pillows. 'Then we think the desk-polishing-with-tight-bum principal was Dom Walker from Percy's. Percy's is a Catholic school, he is very friendly and has only stepped into the role of principal this year.'

'Sounds plausible. Have you worked out who the co-teacher was?'

'Speculation is that it's Margie Rogers, but it wouldn't be her because, and this is not common knowledge, she is Sister T's niece.'

'The plot thickens.'

'The last of the subjects, whose entry was in fact the *first* in the paper—'

'Apart from all the others that didn't concern teachers.'

'Are we worrying about them?' Did the entries that came before the ones aimed at teachers have any bearing on things? 'Should we?'

'Perhaps, but let's concentrate on the present and the fact that Warwick was only just stabbed.'

'Fair point.'

'As I was saying, the other entry was: *Which naughty-notnice principal made sure a fresh teacher didn't get her Christmas wish last year? All because she refused to sit on his lap and make clear it was him she wanted from Santa.'* Birdie gazed at Pia over the paper she was reading from.

Pia lifted her head, closed her eyes slowly and reopened them. 'I'm sorry ... *What?'*

'Don't you read the local?' said Birdie, amused.

'Obviously not close enough.'

'How's that for unwanted sexual advances.'

'So she didn't get a job because she didn't give *him* a job?'

'Pia!' Birdie giggled. 'Gross.'

'He's gross.'

'Naughty-not-nice is the only one we can't place – yet.'

'Poor girl,' said Pia, softly. 'I wonder who she is? In outing the men who had behaved badly, the women involved are inadvertently smeared as well, however innocent. What becomes of the women left in the wake of these appalling men?'

Good question. 'Should we consider the women?'

'We should, but the men are probably easier for now. Do you think one of them might have taken things personally?' Pia asked.

'They might have gone to see Warwick with the intent to harm him, angry that they'd been shamed.' How angry must you need to be to stab someone?

'Okay. Let's focus on the doers of the dirty deeds.' Pia smiled at her alliteration.

Birdie huffed a laugh.

'I wonder who to study first?' Pia tapped an index finger on her cheek in the universal sign for 'wondering'. 'The bumdesk-polisher, Naughty-not-nice or the squealing piggy who just happens to be drop-dead gorgeous.'

Birdie ignored her. 'I think it's about time we wrote this all down,' she said instead.

Pia went into the study and retrieved the little casebook they'd used when trying to find out who had snatched Uncle Larry. Back then, Pia had called their suspects colourful names like: the Scary Gang Lord, the Womanising Letch, the Two-timing Fiancée and the Light-fingered Friend.

'Page one,' Pia began, 'This little piggy Griff, Deskpolishing Dom and Naughty Santa.' She flipped the sheet of paper. 'Page two. Margie Rogers, The Near-Graduate and Santa's little non-helper.'

Birdie laughed at her friend. 'Uncle Larry's set up a meeting with whoever is acting as editor. I suggested he call in a favour from the new mayor.'

'Genius.' Pia steepled her fingers, tapping them together.

'It's for later this morning. Want to come with me?'

Pia's light brown eyes popped. 'Do you even have to ask?' She smiled at Birdie. 'Excellent and very worthwhile deflection but let's get back to Griff as our first to investigate. That little piggy obviously already has thoughts of snuffling around.'

Birdie took a deep breath. 'Well, Griff did also come to the Season's gig last night and asked what I was doing afterwards.'

'That was fast. Even for you.'

Birdie tipped an ear to her shrugged shoulder. 'Cross off the near-graduate. She lives in Queensland. Not only do we not know her, but she probably has no idea herself that she's the subject of a rumour in a different state in the tiny suburb of Gallie Wallen.'

Pia crossed her off.

'And put a question mark next to Margie,' Birdie continued. 'She's not the actual girl Dom was polishing the desk with.'

'However,' said Pia, underlining Margie's name with a harsh strike instead. 'Everyone thinks she is.'

SIX

BIRDIE PICKED UP THE copy of last Thursday's rag as she and Pia waited in the front office of the *Gallie Wallen Gazette*. Drugs were on the rise, heroin apparently. There was talk of a needle exchange program in the face of the AIDS threat, a disease that could be spread through needle sharing. The article made reference to Prime Minister Bob Hawke's daughter, who was an addict. Serious editorial. Interesting how this and *Shame Game, No Names* could compete for space.

'So, how are we playing this?' said Pia.

The second in charge, a lady by the name of Emer Garland, had stepped up into the editor's role. Larry had secured a meeting after the mayor agreed to give the paper a 'day in the life' exclusive.

Birdie rested the newspaper in her lap. 'I thought maybe I'd just be honest. I'm a colleague of Sister T's, and a teacher, and we're all concerned about the rumours and the impact they are having on the teaching community, the community at large.' She flicked through a few pages. 'Uncle Larry told me Dom Walker has been in contact with him too. Apparently, Dom wants to sue the paper.'

'Can he, though, if it doesn't mention him personally?'

Birdie shrugged a shoulder. She continued to flick.

Pia's hand smacked down on a page, stopping Birdie in her tracks. 'I saw that *60 Minutes*,' Pia said. 'Sallie-Anne Huckstepp reckons Roger Rogerson, that detective sergeant in the NSW Police Force, killed her boyfriend in cold blood, not in self-defence. She was very believable. Roger came off looking seriously dodgy.'

Sallie-Anne was a beautiful woman who grew up in Sydney's eastern suburbs, just around the corner from them. She was the girlfriend of murdered mobster Warren Lanfranchi. The article spoke about how she was writing her experiences into a book after a tell-all interview with Ray Martin.

Birdie skimmed the article. 'Far out, Mick Drury was feeding his two-year-old when he was shot through his kitchen window.'

Detective Mick Drury, who, although pressured to, reportedly wouldn't take a bribe to cover up Rogerson's corruption. Roger the Dodger, as Rogerson was known, was rumoured to have been behind the shooting and to have a relationship with organised crime.

Birdie's mind drifted to Vinny Varva – Velvet Vinny, as he was known – an old friend of her uncle and mother. The last time she'd seen him, he was about to be released from jail. He was also a well-known underworld crime boss. Did he know Roger? Did he know how Lanfranchi was really killed?

Vinny knew lots of things, not the least of which was Birdie's original name. The one she was baptised with. The one she'd never been called, except once by Vinny himself. The one her mother changed by deed poll days after her birth.

'Birdie Mealing?' A young woman, not much older than she and Pia, came through a door in front of them. She was above-average height, made taller by the auburn hair she'd twirled into a bun and stabbed through with a pencil that sat atop her head.

Birdie almost laughed. The hairstyle, tortoise-shell rimmed glasses and the mint green cashmere twin set teamed with front pleated tartan pants screamed 'I work with words'. Thoughts of Vinny Varva were pushed aside. She'd think on him later. 'That's me,' said Birdie, standing, resting the newspaper on her empty chair. 'And this is my friend, Pia King.'

'I'm Emer Garland, acting editor. Come this way.'

The inside of the *Gallie Wallen Gazette* opened out to a wide floor of desks, cabinets and shelves. Typewriters, papers, notebooks, telephones, photos and plants all vied for space on top of each desk. Windows poured light over the whole room, including the kitchenette – the kitchenette where Warwick was found stabbed.

Emer's sweet and bookish appearance didn't match her personality, which, after five minutes of semi-polite chatting and the statement – 'Your boss stabbed my boss. I'm not sure how you think I'm going to be much help' – appeared to be hard as nails.

'Are you going to continue with the gossip column, Emer?' Birdie asked.

Her pleasant smile was at odds with her Renée Geyer, contralto voice: gravel, bathed in wood smoke, dripping in Kahlúa. 'Why wouldn't I?'

'Do you think that might have been the reason Warwick was stabbed?'

Emer laughed, deep and leathery like a Chesterfield sofa. Birdie pushed the image of the Chesterfield in Uncle Larry's sitting room out of her mind – along with the memory of what she and Herb had done on it mere months ago.

'You're not suggesting I should be concerned for my life?' Emer said, mid chuckle.

That wasn't the reason Birdie asked the question. She was genuinely asking whether that might have been why Warwick was stabbed. Emer's attention on herself, as opposed to that of her boss, was interesting.

'I suppose that could be a consideration,' Birdie said.

Emer's smile faded. 'The column will continue, whoever is in charge,' she said. 'It's a winner. If it wasn't your nun who stabbed Warwick, and you're suggesting it was a crazed Professor Plum ... with the knife ... in the kitchen'—she scoffed—'they will work out pretty quickly, I can't be stopped.'

Birdie could feel Pia bristle alongside her. She already knew from Sister T that Warwick had refused to shut down the column during the earlier meeting. If it was the attacker's aim to eliminate the problem, after another week and another victim was shamed, they'd realise they hadn't. Emer might be making light with her Professor Plum comment, but unless the column was silenced ...

'Dom Walker, the principal at Saint Perceval's, is ready to sue the paper, you know.'

'Well, good luck with that. We did consult with legal representatives before launch. No one is named directly. Even I don't know the identity of the targets. If this Dom character wants to sue, that only draws attention to the fact that he is possibly the subject of the rumour and therefore guilty of questionable behaviour.'

It seemed there was no chance she was canning *Shame Game, No Names.*

'Did Warwick have any enemies?' Birdie asked.

Emer stood, avoiding eye contact. 'Not that I know of.' She busied herself tidying an already tidy stack of papers on the desk. Birdie and Pia exchanged a glance.

'Why are teachers being targeted?' Birdie asked.

'It's not just teachers who have been the subjects of *Shame Game, No Names.* You may recall the restaurateur, the doctor, the reverend, the politician.'

She did recall those. Fidele had hardly controlled his glee at the entry about a rival restaurant owner who'd boasted truffles but was using porcini mushrooms. The rumoured restaurant had lost its three-hats rating and its customers. Then there was the Church of England minister, the suspected Reverend Arnold, who had been called back to the homeland at the request of the Archbishop of Canterbury to explain why money collected for charity had gone to the purchase of a new bell for the bell tower.

The politician had been of particular interest. An historical case of a man who'd knocked up a staffer and then sacked her. Abandoning his baby. The child would have been in their twenties now, possibly reading the entry along with everyone else. Did this child know about their origins? Did they suspect themselves as the child in question?

That one had hit close to home. Not for the first time did Birdie wonder about her own father.

'There seems to be a string of teachers,' Birdie said, focusing. 'Three in a row.'

'We give the public what they want, and they love the fact that teachers – those who educate the supposed uneducated, who hold themselves to such high standards –

can also act irresponsibly. When this information about teachers came flooding in, it was too good not to print. Our sponsorship is soaring.'

Profiting off others' pain. Where did the guilt lie here? Was it the misbehaver, the paper, the advertisers or the readers?

'Where did this flood of information come from?'

'The source is anonymous.' She sighed. 'But the source is not guilty of stabbing. I mean, why would you supply information and then stab the person who is printing it?'

As Emer continued to find her desk and its surrounds needing attention, Pia sent Birdie a grimace.

'Is this the same way all the rumours came, through the mail?' Birdie asked.

'People love to write into the paper. And I love to follow a story.'

'Could we see the correspondence?'

'I don't think so. You're not the police.'

'You're right. We're not the police. But I must come clean, Emer. As well as working with Sister Therese Margaret, I am also Larry Kean's niece.' *Goddaughter, but close enough.* 'You might have heard of him?'

She smiled. 'Yes. I've heard of the so-called Solicitor to the Stars.'

So-called. It wasn't Larry who named himself that. It was the media – her people. She couldn't have it both ways.

'He is the lawyer representing both Sister Therese Margaret and Dom Walker in this unfortunate chain of events. He will send a legal request for information if he needs to, and he can also secure professional privilege over anything found in a search the police might carry out.'

Emer flinched. The first sign of some sort of acknowledgement of hers and the gazette's role in all of this.

'We both thought a less formal discussion might be better.'

Emer sat back in the chair. Birdie wouldn't describe it as a crumple, more like a stubborn crease.

'It would be very helpful if you could give us the name of the person who is supplying the rumours.' Birdie soldiered on. 'That way we would know for certain who the subjects of the rumours were and therefore provide other possible alternatives to who might have stabbed Warwick.'

Steadying herself once again, Emer answered. 'As I've already said, the source is anonymous. There is no signature attached and no sender's address.'

Birdie exhaled and side-eyed Pia. Out of sight, Pia made her hand into a fist and knuckled it into Stumpy – the signal for 'sock it to her'.

'It's also possible that this person is in danger themselves,' said Birdie. 'What if the assailant comes after them? You'll have two attacks on your conscience.'

Emer's face faltered briefly before reverting to its steely façade. 'We don't know the attack on Warwick has anything to do with the *Shame Game, No Names* column.'

The TV news had run with the column leading to the stabbing. It was a solid hypothesis, and Emer would have definitely come to the same conclusion despite the brush-off. The timing was pretty clear. Birdie caught Pia's eye. Emer's comment inadvertantly suggested there might be another reason Warwick Woods was the victim of a stabbing...

'And if I don't even know who the author of the rumours is,' Emer went on, 'how will anyone else?'

'It's not like showing us this correspondence is giving me any information I don't already know, Emer.' Still no response. The room remained silent for a few ticks of the very loud clock. 'In fact, you're not giving me any information that your highly successful column hasn't given to almost everyone in Gallie Wallen.'

Eventually, Emer leaned forward and opened her top drawer. She passed some letters to Birdie. The words were typed on thin blue paper.

Birdie looked them over. 'Could I get a photocopy of these?' She passed them to Pia, who did the same.

'I'm not sure I can do that,' Emer responded.

Birdie took a deep, frustrated breath.

'This is a lovely office, Emer,' said Pia, who had remained silent until now. Pia stood and wandered for a moment.

Birdie watched her friend in action. She knew Pia only too well. There would be a point to her little trip around the office. Pia fingered several framed newspaper cut-outs propped up against the neatly stocked books in the bookshelf. Birdie kept a close eye on everything she touched. An article published in Gaelic, one in English, one in French.

Interesting. Who was writing in three different languages?

Pia moved on to an article about Pope John Paul II from the *Polish Catholic Guardian* newspaper that was also on display. A fourth language? Pia shot a look at Birdie.

Yes, Pia. I can see them.

'You've written lots of articles,' Pia said.

These were Emer's articles!

'I did a lot of freelance, dabbled in overseas markets.' And now, as acting editor, she'd decorated her 'new' office with them. 'It's all good practice.'

Birdie scanned the room. There didn't seem to be any evidence of such experience from Warwick.

Pia moved on and picked up a photo frame. 'This is Warwick Woods, I take it?' The frame held a picture of a man and his dog.

Emer gestured with an arm to the room. 'This is the editor's office.'

Into which Emer had moved her little trophies. To sit alongside Warwick's 'Walkley' winning picture of him and his dog.

Pia threw another glance at Birdie above the frame, an eyebrow slightly raised. She turned back to the shelves. 'Well then, where are his articles?' Pia must have been thinking along the same lines as Birdie. Why would Warwick be in the position of editor when Emer seemed to have more experience?

'You'd have to ask him.' Did that response mean Emer also wondered about their roles? Could they read anything into her tone?

'Are you enjoying your new role as editor, Emer?' Pia continued.

'I'm feeling my way.'

'Have you been to visit the boss in hospital?'

'The secretary has sent some flowers.'

Pia turned to Emer and tilted her head.

'Warwick not being here means we are very busy. Someone needs to keep the paper running.'

Pia walked back to the chair next to Birdie and sat down. She placed her elbows on the desk, clasped her hands and rested her chin on top. 'Warwick Woods was the type of jerk who was happy to verbally shoot down a little old nun,' Pia said. 'That puts him in the nasty-basket for mine. He is photographed with his dog. So, I'm guessing, no girlfriend. Plus, he was getting a lift home from the owner of the newsagents, not someone in his own office. That tells me he might not have any friends here.' Pia leaned back in the chair and crossed her arms. 'Maybe he was a bit of an arsehole as a boss.'

Finally, a shadow of emotion registered on Emer's face. Pia was onto something.

'I bet you've got some great ideas for improvements that might not have been taken seriously under Warwick?' Pia said.

Birdie could have kissed her deviously minded friend.

'Perhaps you're not overly interested in finding out who stabbed Mr Woods,' Pia added. 'It could be said you appear quite happy here without him.'

Emer sat back and crossed her arms as well. She eyeballed Pia. 'I hope you're not suggesting I had anything to do with—'

'We're suggesting you make me a copy of the letters,' Birdie jumped in. 'My uncle will request a copy anyway. It might be best for all concerned if you are seen as helpful.'

'Fine,' Emer spat, mouth pursed. 'If there's nothing else?' She stood. 'I think I've given you enough of my Saturday morning. I'll copy them for you'—she began walking to the door—'on the way out.'

⇔ ⇔ ⇔

The ocean glistened in the background as Birdie crested the hill at Vantage Tops. Not a real suburb, but the name given to the streets that were so high up they overlooked the town and beach below.

They had gone straight to Uncle Larry's from the gazette. The feeling of home that filled her whenever she visited her uncle's place settled in her chest. The thought that she'd almost lost him followed close behind.

But they hadn't. He was safe and alive and doing what he loved. Navigating the law. His eyes widened with excitement as they retold their visit with the evasive Emer Garland.

'So you moved the conversation to the source of the rumours. It's probably a good angle to follow,' her uncle agreed. 'Plus, the source could tell us who the other target was as well as confirm Dom and this Griff Wheatley person as the two we think we know.'

Birdie smiled. 'Giving us an alternative to Sister T as the attacker.'

It was a short-lived feeling of victory, though, as there was nothing in the copies that could help them identify who the source might be. Not the postmark, not the stamps. 'The use of blue paper doesn't really help,' said Uncle Larry. 'Even though these are airmail grade and this one isn't. Even though the odd one out has a watermark.' It was the piece that had the desk-wiper story on it. The same watermark that was on every ream of paper. Paper that would be sold in every local newsagency. 'A virtually impossible lead,' her uncle said as he brought two tubs of YoGo to the table and placed them in front of the girls.

'We can't identify handwriting, but it's someone with a typewriter,' said Birdie.

'Narrows it down.' Pia peeled the top off the strawber-ry-flavoured custardy treat and licked it with her sarcastic tongue.

'You did learn one thing.' Larry took a seat at the table. 'Thanks to Pia.'

Pia sat up straight. 'Of course we did.' She scooped out a giant spoonful. 'Which particular piece of information are you referring to?'

Larry chuffed in amusement. 'That Warwick Woods might not have been well-liked by his assistant editor, or possibly anyone at the paper.'

'Need to add Emer slash gazette staff to our casebook,' Pia said through a swallow.

'Maybe someone he works with is responsible for stabbing him and it has nothing to do with *Shame Game, No Names*.' Birdie began eating from the banana tub.

'Who do you think is creatively rewriting: "There. Is. A. Principal",' Pia started reading in a robotic voice, "Blah, blah, blah", into the juicy offerings we read?' said Pia.

'Who's got the by-line?' said Birdie.

'One guess.' Pia flicked through last Thursday's copy of the *Gallie Wallen Gazette*. 'None other than our friend with the husky – frog in your throat on the first day of the flu – Kathleen Turner, *Romancing the Stone* voice ... Emer Garland.'

'She's obviously talented and ambitious. Plus, she's re-searched extra information like the identity of the market's "stallholder" in Griff's entry, which is not mentioned in the original letter from the source.' Larry held up the note in question. 'And the whole desk visual that's not included in the one you've got, Pia.'

'What if Warwick *did* decide to discontinue the column after all, after he took some time to think about Sister T's request?' said Birdie.

'Our ambitious friend Emer might not have been happy about that,' said Pia, popping another spoonful of YoGo into her mouth.

'Hmm.' Larry tapped his chin. 'I might suggest to the police that they ask some questions about staff relationships at the gazette.'

SEVEN

RAIN SPLATTERED THE WINDSCREEN as Birdie drove the cloudy streets. It matched her mood. She'd been without Herb for twelve weeks now. When would she feel better? She wiped her eyes with a tissue and blew her dripping nose. Hopefully, no oncoming drivers would be able to see her tears inside while the cloud's tears streamed Gypsy's windows on the outside.

She carefully navigated the long driveway; the tiny native violets struggled to perform their normal cheery welcome under the rain's patters. The downpour increased, pounding on the roof of her car and blocking her of all visibility, all sound from the world around her. She parked on the concrete slab and turned the car off. Taking a breath, she closed her eyes, leaned her head against the headrest and put her mind on something other than her broken heart.

The meeting with Emer was still spinning in her head. But it was Monday she was thinking forward to, and ballroom dancing classes. The girls would make their debut at the Roundhouse at the University of New South Wales, a big deal and an event which was creating excitement as well as angst, especially with the dances. While the boys and girls bumbled through the Pride of Erin, in the hall that Joanie's and Percy's shared, she would have an excuse ... to wander.

Surely, this sorry business must be impacting Dom's job; his new position as principal would be under scrutiny. *Would that make you angry enough to stab someone?* She could seek Dom out. Find out where he had been on Thursday afternoon before basketball.

She checked herself in the rear-view mirror. Her eyes were a little puffy, but the redness had eased. The rain softened some more, so Birdie took her chance. She opened the car door and ran.

The noise of her little brothers welcomed her as she peeled off her soggy clothes, dropped them on her bathroom floor, shook out the wetness of her hair and threw on her dressing gown.

'Hey, Mum,' she said, heading into the main house.

Cotton cord being formed into a macrame hanging plant holder slid through her mother's fingers as she sat at the dining table. Shoulders loose. Posture calm. A day out with girlfriends, exercising and being free of children, as well as a craft project, would do that.

'Hi, love.' She scanned her daughter. 'Bit wet out?'

Birdie kissed the top of the other woman's head. Lenore Mealing was petite in stature as opposed to her daughter. Soft where Birdie was angled, dark where Birdie was fair. Her mother was a walking, talking reminder of the fact that Birdie must look like her father. *Whoever and wherever he was.* Lenore Mealing was a natural beauty who, in her early forties, still drew the eye.

'Just a bit.' Birdie smiled. She pointed at the macrame. 'This looks good.'

'Ta.' Lenore folded up the strings and packed them into a material pouch. 'Am just about to start dinner.'

'I can help.'

Lenore passed over a chopping board and some potatoes.

'I just came from Uncle Larry's.' Birdie washed and peeled the potatoes. The shavings dropping onto an old page of the *Gallie Wallen Gazette*. 'The Sister Therese Margaret thing?' Birdie nodded.

'Any headway?'

'Not yet.'

'I don't know how I'd feel if my secrets were exposed.'

Like the secret about who my father is? Lately, Birdie could feel herself considering her father's identity much more than she ever had before. Had the column ignited her curiosity or coincided with it? After meeting Vinny Varva months ago and watching him interact with her mother, she'd thought about the possibility it might be him, often. She'd tried to engage Lenore in conversation about it, with little success. Should she try again?

'How'd you go at tennis?'

'Great. I won.' Lenore put a hand under her chin and curtsied.

Birdie laughed. 'Well done, you!'

She cut the potatoes into chip sizes and lined them up on the baking tray. She sprayed them with Pure & Simple and put them in the oven. Then wandered into the living room.

The boys had set up their toys in front of the TV. Birdie plopped onto the lounge behind them. Kick's warm, little fingers tickled her skin as he manoeuvred his Matchbox car between her feet and behind her heels, all the while humming a *vroom-vroom*. He began to take his car up one leg to her knee and then down the other to her toes.

'A man rang for you today. Glen wrote a message. It's on the pad next to the phone in the hall,' her mother called from the kitchen.

'Thanks, Mum.'

'Jonathon someone. I think Glen said he wants you to call him back. Naylor. Jonathon Naylor.' Birdie's stomach dropped. 'Sounds familiar,' her mother went on. Birdie hadn't spoken to Jonathon Naylor in about five years. Lenore faced her, knife poised. 'Who is he again?'

Birdie swallowed. 'He was the teacher who supervised me on my first prac.'

'That's right.' Her mother went back to chopping. 'Wonder what he wants?'

Kick pushed her knees together, pulled both feet out forward at an angle and lifted her toes to the sky. *A jump.* He slid the car from her knees down the join. When it reached her feet, he flew it through the air. It crashed to the floor – like a mirror to her stomach.

'I'll call him back later.' She wouldn't call him back later. She never wanted to speak to Jonathon Naylor ever again.

👄 👄 👄

Birdie made straight for the bar. A drink or maybe a few was what she needed. She felt Pia next to her.

'What's going on underneath all that strawberry hair?' Pia said. 'Something's bothering you.'

'Jonathon called me.'

'Jonathon?' Pia said, looking over at her and then around them to see who was in earshot. 'Jonathon? As in, married-should-have-known-better Jonathon?'

'Yep. Him.'

A connection to the man had been immediate. So polite and helpful, so knowledgeable about teaching, so serious about the craft and her emerging part in it. But also ... so handsome. She'd felt the spark between them. It had been intense, visceral, weaving around everything they did. But she'd thought she was safely off limits; he was married, had a family, was older.

He was the acting assistant principal. As an eighteenyear-old, first-year student, on her very first prac, she'd lucked out. She had an excellent supervising teacher; everyone said so. Everyone told her he was one of the best.

'Shit! Why?' Pia asked.

The concern in her voice pulled at Birdie's chest. 'I don't know. Glen took a message. I've been commanded to call him back on Monday morning.'

Pia rolled her eyes. 'Wanker. Are you going to call him?'

'I don't want to. I don't want to talk to him ever again but wondering about what he wants is sure to slowly kill me.'

'Me too.' Pia placed a hand on Birdie's arm. She suddenly slammed the other hand down on the top of the bar and speared Birdie straight in the eye. 'You have to call him.'

'What can I get ya, pet?' Birdie focused on the smiling barmaid.

'One chicken schnitzel burger'—she eyed Pia who nodded—'and one Aussie burger, please.'

'Chips?'

'Yes, please.' She'd need the stodge to soak up the alcohol; she was not driving and was in no mood to count drinks tonight.

'I'll have a cheeseburger and chips, please,' said a familiar voice behind her right ear. Melon and musk filled her nostrils.

'Stu!' Birdie turned and hugged her friend. 'I wasn't sure we'd be seeing you?'

'I was hoping we wouldn't,' mumbled Pia.

'Get stuffed,' Stu said. He turned back to Birdie. 'I'm giving myself the night off. I needed to get out. See normal people. Not that you two are anything close to normal.'

Pia hugged Stu. 'That's the nicest thing you've said to me.'

Birdie laughed. Stu rolled his eyes and pushed Pia away. Her two best friends had always been like this. Tit for tat. Trying to get the better of each other. The pastel lemon shirt Stu was wearing highlighted a sallowness to his brown skin. His shiny, dark hair also at odds with his washed out features. He appeared tired.

'Actually, make that two cheeseburgers,' Stu said. His appetite obviously hadn't been affected, though.

'We're having Fluffy Ducks,' Birdie said as the barmaid placed the buttery yellow vessels of deliciousness on a tray in front of them. 'Want one?'

Stu raised an eyebrow at the drinks. 'Ummm, might just get a beer.'

'Spoil sport,' said Pia.

The club was starting to fill up nicely. Stu held court as he ate, telling detailed stories of his planning while old friends packed in around them. Birdie waved at Brad and Sabine, who had arrived mid-bite.

Brad removed her burger and inhaled about a quarter before putting it back in her hands and leaning in close to her ear. 'Griff Wheatley might be coming. He asked about places to hang out, and I mentioned the Sailo on a Saturday night. Just thought I'd give you the heads up in case he arrives.'

Birdie swallowed her last mouthful and started wiping her hands on a serviette. 'Don't look now, Brad, but he's here.'

Griff's easy swagger and Patrick Swayze smile were heading their way. 'Miss Mealing,' he said, dropping his gorgeous limbs next to hers.

'Mr Wheatley.' She moved slightly to make room.

After several rounds of Fluffy Ducks, and the same in interrogation of Griff, they found out he was originally from the Sutherland Shire. His mum had moved in with her own mother at Vantage Beach after her father had died. A simple solution now that her sons were grown, and her marriage had ended.

Griff had done an 'out-of-area' prac in Queensland where his dad, a principal, now lived with his new family. He'd liked it so much he'd spent the first couple of years of his teaching career doing casual work up there. No strings, no programming, no responsibilities. Just swan in, teach, and swan back out again: his words.

'I could get a surf in before work and then one again after it,' he said. 'And the Gold Coast is always ready to party.' He winked at Birdie. 'You would have loved it.'

With all the booze on board, Birdie found it hard to keep the grin from her face.

'So, I've heard whispers, Griff.' Pia leaned her merry self forward. 'Are you the little pig who slept with the student'— she made clumsy air quotation marks on the word student—'and then came wee, wee, wee, wee all the way home?' Her golden eyes sparkled at her forwardness. Her cheeks were flushed, her smile bright against her olive skin.

Griff opened his piercing blue eyes wide. 'I'm not telling you that.'

'That's not a "no".' Pia laughed, rolling into Stu, who in turn rolled into Sabine as they both laughed along.

'It's definitely you,' said Sabine.

'The girl in question was well and truly sixteen and mere days off finishing school,' Griff said to Pia.

'I know the sordid facts, mate. I need a confession.'

'Facts,' Griff muttered under his breath with a half grin. 'That's an interesting concept.'

Brad squeezed Birdie's leg. He was trying, and failing in his sozzled state, to contain his excitement. Not that she could blame him. The mood was definitely cheeky. Everyone pushing just a little close to the edge.

Birdie stood now with her elbows on the bar, waiting for another round and trying to wrangle the thoughts swirling through her buzzed mind. It didn't appear that Griff cared too much about his reputation. He was happy to do the job, get the money and enjoy the free time casual teaching gave him.

Besides, as a casual, you didn't sign a contract that said you would behave in a certain way. Did this man have the type of personality that stabbed someone who had wronged him?

Really, Griff could do whatever he liked – within reason – and he'd still get work. All schools were in need of competent casuals. Part of her was envious.

Birdie narrowed her eyes and tapped her bottom lip in contemplation. So, if Griff didn't care about his reputation, could they come to the conclusion that it probably wasn't he who'd attacked Warwick? That might narrow down the suspects. They could focus on Dom or Naughty Santa.

Facts – that's an interesting concept.

Wasn't that what Griff had said? What was factual about anonymous slander written in a gossip column in the local paper? Perhaps Griff was totally innocent.

Laughter grabbed her attention, and she glanced at her rowdy little group. Griff's baby blues caught her eye. He'd made it clear he was interested in her again tonight. Subtle touches, suggestive comments. Currently, his gaze licked over her like Baileys poured on ice.

This footloose boy's motto in life was what hers *used* to be ... before Herb.

Perhaps she needed to be more like Griff. Embrace her motto again.

No promises, no demands.

EIGHT

O N Monday morning, Birdie studied the clock that hung on the wall in the staffroom. It confirmed for the tenth time that it was just past eight twenty-five.

She moved towards the little glass-windowed booth tucked away in the corner that housed the phone. She sat on the cushioned seat and smoothed over the crumpled piece of paper that she'd previously scrunched up and thrown at her bin. Glen's architect's capitals informed her that Jonathon wanted her to call him back on Monday at the number given between eight o'clock and eight thirty. She'd waited until the last minute – *Bossy son of a bitch*, telling her what time to call and on what number. Who did these men think they were?

Her heart hammered a military tattoo in her chest. She breathed deeply, and deeply again, picked up the receiver and pressed for an outside line. The rattle of the dial tone assaulted her ear; the tattoo revved up a notch. She pressed in the number and listened as it connected and trilled.

'Mr Naylor's office. Mrs Larobe speaking.'

Jonathon had an office? And someone to answer his phone? 'Good morning, Mrs Larobe. Could I speak to Mr Naylor, please?'

'Mr Naylor is in conference with the leadership team at the moment.'

Leadership team? In conference? Jonathon had always been looking to move up the food chain. He obviously had.

'Who may I say is calling?' the secretary asked.

'My name is Birdie Mealing. He asked me to call him this morning between eight and eight thirty.'

'Yes, Miss Mealing. Thanks so much for calling. Mr Naylor has requested a meeting with you. He is free this afternoon at three thirty.'

'*Is* he?'

'Can he expect you then?'

No, he bloody could not. The military tattoo had turned into The Angels' 'Am I Ever Gonna See Your Face Again?' with an emphasis on its accompanying crowd-sung response. The hide of the man to boss her around like a subordinate.

'I'm not sure I'll be available then, Mrs Larobe. Do you know what the meeting might be about?'

'Oh. Well. I only know that it's terribly important that you meet with him as soon as possible.' The woman was getting flustered. 'I was told not to take no for an answer.'

Oh, for God's sake. What a prick. It would be just like Jonathon to put pressure on his secretary.

'I'm afraid we have a staff meeting at Joanie's on a Monday afternoon. I won't be finished until at least 4:30, probably five.'

'Oh dear. He won't be happy.'

'It's not your fault, Mrs Larobe.' Through the glass, she saw Brad wander into the staffroom and start making himself a cuppa. He signalled to her with a held-up mug. She nodded. 'Really, Mr Naylor should have already guessed that might be the case. Please give him my apologies.' Birdie hung up the phone.

'Morning, Miss Mealing.'

'Mr Foster,' Birdie said exiting the booth. 'Did you pull up alright after Saturday night?'

'Bit dusty but otherwise okay. You?'

'A minor headache. What did you think of our Mr Wheatley?'

'He's utterly shameless. I'm quite jealous, if I'm being honest. Although I hope it doesn't bite him in the arse like it has Dom Walker. His wife's left him, did you hear?'

'Shit.' *No, I hadn't heard.* 'I've got ballroom dancing supervision first period. Wonder what the mood is like over there? It's bad enough here with the whole Sister T business.'

'Rumour is they are looking to give Sister T some well earned "leave".'

'Gee. That move won't make everyone think she's guilty.' She couldn't keep the sarcasm from coating her words.

'I know, poor chimp. She's holding firm, so I'm told.'

'So she should. She hasn't been charged with anything.' *Yet.*

Uncle Larry had told Birdie he couldn't find anyone on staff who had seen Sister T at school at the time Warwick was stabbed. No one at present could corroborate her alibi. Her job being in jeopardy and her lack of alibi confirmation were another two very solid reasons Birdie needed to expose some other likely suspects.

'Just as well you and I are beyond reproach!' Brad laughed. He handed her a fresh brew. 'Although ... you have yet to confirm the lack of skeletons in your closet.'

Birdie considered Brad's remark as she herded the fourth form girls out of the school gates and into the adjoining hall moments later. She couldn't shift the churning in her stomach that she'd nursed all morning since dismissing Jonathon's attempt to meet with her. *Beyond reproach.*

She could hear the deep voices of the boys as they neared the hall. She hoped the teacher supervising the boys wouldn't mind her ducking off to have a word with Dom. She encouraged the girls to form a circle around the hall, and right on cue, the boys entered in single file. They ambled self-consciously around the outside of it to secure their first dance partner. Their teacher bringing up the rear.

Jesus, Mary and Joseph. It was Margie Rogers, of all people. Margie placed herself just inside the door. Head down and with her back leaning against the cold bricks. *Keeping herself to herself.* Margie had made herself into a tiny mouse.

What was Birdie's role here? This woman was the victim of whispers and scorn, probably more so now that Dom's wife had left him. There was a bit of a walking-on-eggshells feeling around Joanie's. Surely it would be similar at Percy's. And unfortunately, it would be Margie who bore the brunt of any anger, even though Dom himself, being the one who was actually married and the person in power, was the one who should have behaved better. Not to mention, she probably definitely was not the girl in question. Who were they to judge? Who actually *was* without reproach?

The PE teacher was showing the students the positions of their bodies and feet and going through the steps. Birdie walked around the circle, making a compliment here, a suggestion there, until she was closer to the withdrawn woman. Eventually, the PE teacher played the tape, and the students started to move. If Miss Rogers was in low spirits, Birdie would not make her day any gloomier.

'It's Margie, isn't it?' she said as the music played on.

The girl goggled at Birdie – a deer-in-the-headlights.

Birdie smiled. 'Hi, I'm Birdie Mealing.'

Recognition flashed behind the enormous pupils. 'Larry Kean's niece.'

'Yes.'

'Your uncle is representing Aun ...' She swallowed. 'Sister Therese Margaret.'

'Yes, that's right.' They were both silent. *Now what?* Birdie smiled again. Should she tell Margie she knew Sister T was her aunty? If the women in question were keeping it quiet, she probably should too.

The PE teacher's voice carried instructions over the music. Margie squeezed her left hand in her right.

'Uncle Larry knows what he's doing, Margie.'

The young woman nodded and gave a semblance of a smile in return.

'Are you okay, though?' Birdie asked.

She considered Birdie, a frown allowing her wide eyes to relax. Had anybody asked her that question? Surely she'd have at least one friend on staff who cared. Birdie smiled again.

Eventually, the other woman's eyes softened. 'I've been better, Birdie. Thanks for asking.'

'Do you want to talk about it?'

'Not really.'

'It will all blow over soon. In a couple of days, you'll be yesterday's news.'

'So, I should be happy that a new rumour will surface, and some other poor soul might feel like I do.'

Good point. Who would be the next target? 'I know Dom is speaking to my uncle about a possible case of slander.'

'Honestly, the man's old enough to be my father. What are people thinking?' She fiddled with a loose thread at her elbow. 'He pushed for me to get the job. Probably because ...' she trailed off.

Because you are Sister T's niece?

'Anyway,' Margie continued, 'people feel like I was given privilege ahead of others who deserved it more.' A blessing and a curse, and it would only add fuel to the suspicions that she and Dom were sleeping together. 'He's a lovely bloke but ...'

'I know. It's ridiculous.' Birdie didn't really have an issue with age gaps between partners, but she knew it was probably unlikely that Margie and Dom were together.

'I'm glad your uncle is helping out,' Margie said.

And here is my 'in'. 'Actually, Margie, do you mind if I go and have a chat with Dom? I told my uncle I'd touch base and see how he's faring.' *Tiny, white lie.*

'That might be nice. Thanks, Birdie.'

Birdie had a quick look over at the girls. Some were giggling, others watched their feet, and a couple stared starry-eyed at their partners.

'Go,' Margie said. 'I'll hold the fort here.' She managed a tight smile.

The secretary was sitting at her desk when Birdie neared. She inspected the intruder over the top of silver rimmed glasses and frowned, somewhat bemused – probably because Birdie had entered the office from the staff entrance while not actually being a member of staff.

'Hi there, Sue.' God bless her, she was wearing a name badge. 'My name's Birdie Mealing. I'm a teacher at Joanie's. I'm supervising the girls doing ballroom dancing.'

'Oh, right. Hello, Birdie. How can I help?'

'I was wondering if Dom was available to talk to?'

'Sorry, he's on class.'

'Never mind. I hope he's doing okay. All these silly rumours and accusations flying.'

'Yes, and an assailant on the loose because I don't believe for a second Sister Therese Margaret harmed the editor of the paper.'

'Us either. We're all very worried about her over at ours as you can imagine.'

'We're in a bit of a tither over here as well.'

'I play basketball in the Chalkies' Challenge, and I saw Dom on Thursday evening. He often arrives with Sister T. He gives her a lift, I think. Which is quite sweet.' Another tiny lie. 'It's just that Dom arrived solo last week, and I was wondering whether you would know if he tried to bring Sister T, like he sometimes does, or just headed off on his own?'

'Well, I'm not sure I would know. He didn't say anything to me. The last time I saw him was in my rear-view mirror, at his car, collecting his gym bag.'

Collecting his gym bag or getting in his car to drive off?

'About what time do you think? If he did collect Sister T, it might help to establish whether it was possible for her to have even been at the newspaper offices at the actual time the editor was stabbed.' *Or whether your principal could have been.*

'Oh dear, let me think. I said goodbye at about a quarter to four. He was in his office. I got some petty cash from the girls at the main office to buy milk. Then I left.'

'So the last time you saw him, was at his car, at four.'

'Just before.'

'Thanks for your help. Better get back to the girls.' Birdie turned to go.

'It's terrible business,' Sue said. 'That *Shame Game, No Names* column has a lot to answer for.'

Hmm. There was nothing Birdie liked better than a chatty secretary. She turned back around. 'I think perhaps the paper thought it was just a bit of fun.'

'Fun until someone almost gets killed.'

Yes indeed, Sue. 'So you're convinced Warwick's stabbing has to do with *Shame Game, No Names*?'

'Well, of course, isn't everyone? I mean, Warwick Woods probably shouldn't be printing such nonsense, but in saying that, did he deserve to get stabbed because of it?'

'Sister T taught Warwick back in the day. Did you know him?'

'No. He left well before I started.'

'What about any old teachers? What do they think about him being stabbed?'

'We've been told by the bishop not to engage in gossip.' She pursed her lips together and mimed turning a key. When she opened them, she whispered, 'Our lips are sealed.'

Not surprising. The Bish had told Joanie's staff the same thing. 'Thanks for the chat, Sue. I'd better get back to the girls.'

'Would you like me to tell Mr Walker you dropped by?' Sue called as Birdie dashed away.

'No need. I'll see him on Thursday. I'll tell him then.'

What did Dom do after four? What time had he arrived at the stadium? Birdie tried to work it out as she passed the school's little chapel. She'd always loved the stained-glass windows created by an ex-student that showed the story of Mary MacKillop. She doubled back.

Dom could easily have got into said car and visited the gazette office, stabbed Warwick, got changed and then still made it to basketball on time. He and his mates pretty much arrived at the same time Birdie had. In time to put their singlets on and warm up. Had Dom stabbed Warwick?

Birdie ran a finger along the stained glass in the door panel. She'd been baptised in a chapel. The chapel at the hospital where she was born. Just her, her mum and Uncle Larry as her godfather. She'd always been drawn to them. A quiet space. A peaceful place to be. A place that was bittersweet, reminding her of how much she was loved while also reminding her there was one person missing from her life. One person who wasn't at her baptism. One person's love she'd never known.

She ducked inside, lit a candle and said a quick prayer for him, wherever he was, and for Sister T.

'It wasn't me who stabbed him.' An urgent voice startled her from prayer. 'And I know it wasn't you.' She recognised that voice. It was Dom Walker.

'You and I are both fully aware of who that womanising Santa is.' The second voice, Sister Therese Margaret's, was louder. Closer.

'Do you think he took offence and acted out?' Dom again.

The pair were in the corridor she'd just been in, outside the chapel. Birdie lifted her ear. It sounded like they were discussing the identity of Naughty Santa, and they thought whoever it was had stabbed Warwick?

Sister T made a shushing sound. 'Let's go into the chapel,' she whispered. 'Before we say anything else.'

Shit!

Birdie darted her eyeballs around. Pews, altar – she could crouch behind the altar – kneeler, confessional box.

The confessional box!

With her eyes glued to the chapel entry, Birdie backed towards the confessional box – a tiny cupboard probably only a metre by a metre. She twisted her hand behind her and opened the door just as the chapel door began to push inwards. She shuffled backwards quickly into the booth – she could watch the action through the mesh that separated the priest from the sinner – and closed the door silently.

A rough hand grabbed her around the waist from behind. It pulled her back against the body it was attached to. Birdie opened her mouth to scream. Another hand flew to cover it, stopping the sound. Birdie's heartbeat fought against the confines of her chest. She struggled against the firm hold.

Muscled arms slammed her body against its own, tightening its grip. A puff of hot air accompanied the words, 'Be. Still.'

NINE

B IRDIE FROZE. HER HEART pounded in her ears.

'It wouldn't be the first time he retaliated against something Warwick did.' Sister T's voice was competing with the whooshing.

Birdie's legs were like jelly.

'I doubt that pretty boy Wheatley was responsible,' said Dom.

Sweat flushed across Birdie's skin.

'If anything, the rumour has made him more bloody appealing.' Jealousy clipped Dom's tone. 'The women on staff are all talking about him, thinly disguising their interest with disgust. They think he's their very own Robert Redford.'

Curls tickled the side of Birdie's face. She flinched, trying desperately to slow her breathing. Soft breath stroked her ears. 'Didn't mean to scare you, teach.'

It couldn't be.

'You okay?' he breathed.

Herb.

She nodded. He dropped his hand from her mouth but still held her around the waist. Lucky, because her legs were having trouble holding her up. She sank into his arms. He moulded around her like a favourite song. She closed her eyes, lost in the feeling. His long, strong fingers an overture against her skin through the fabric of her dress.

'For God's sake, Dom.' Sister T's words from outside the confessional swam clearly in through the grill. 'Enough with your midlife crisis. Our focus should be on serving the Lord not carnal needs.'

'Forgive me.' There was a shuffling of feet. 'My wife's left me.'

'I heard. I am sorry.'

'I'm not.'

'Don't talk like that. It's not her fault.'

'It wasn't a surprise, though, Terri. You must know that.'

A long sigh. 'Are you okay?'

'I'm in trouble with Brother Zachariah. And the bishop.'

Sister T chuckled sadly. 'Join the club.'

'How are *you*?'

'A bit shaken, but good.'

Honeyed spices filled Birdie's nostrils. She ran her hands along Herb's fingers, pressed the side of her cheek against his neck. She couldn't resist the feel of him. Herb dropped his mouth and kissed her forehead, her temple, dropped it further to kiss her collarbone. His left hand slid forwards across her lower belly, pulling her back into him; his right skimmed the underside of her breast. Birdie shivered.

'We both know the Saint is capable of losing his temper, and there's bad blood between them,' said Dom.

Focusing on the conversation between Dom and Sister T took Birdie some effort.

'That was years ago,' Sister T countered. 'They were just kids. They are both adults now. I can't believe he'd do this.'

'I admire your loyalty.'

'My loyalty lies with both boys.'

'If he's stabbed Warwick, he needs to come forward,' Dom said softly. 'He could have killed him.'

'Well, the knife obviously hit something vital. A nerve, perhaps. The liver.'

'Did the doctors tell you that?'

'I could tell by the amount of blood. Although that could have been from the length of time he sat there until I found him. With the position of the blade, the spleen could have been damaged.'

'Jeez. You sound so clinical.'

'I'm a biology teacher, was a trainee nurse – once upon a time.'

'The police already think you did it. I wouldn't go explaining the happy circumstance that you noticed vital organs were affected.'

Dom was probably correct. Knowing how to plunge a knife into flesh in order to pierce vital organs only made her look more guilty.

'I got someone to call an ambulance, applied pressure, made sure the knife wasn't removed.'

'Terri, not everybody knows that those things might save someone.'

'It's not my fault that I do. Besides, why would I have acted in such a *clinical* way if it was me who'd stabbed him? Wouldn't I want him dead?'

'Just be careful what you say.'

'The Lord will watch over me.'

Sister T had walked as she talked, standing right outside the confessional, using its immediate presence to ram home her point about God's watch. Inside the box, Birdie and Herb stiffened. Only a mesh grill separated them from the nun. Herb pulled Birdie slowly backwards and leaned against the rear of the tiny structure.

'Although, I *could* have stabbed him myself,' Sister T said, 'with the way he's sullied Margie's name.'

'Don't even joke about stabbing someone, Terri.'

'I never dreamed my … niece might be implicated in all this. Poor girl. It wasn't *Margie* you were swishing across the desk.'

'Not this time or the last,' Dom said softly.

Birdie's skin tingled with awareness. The whole back side of her body was flat out against the front of Herb's. There was silence for a few moments. Birdie imagined Dom must have moved closer to Sister T.

He spoke to her now in a softer tone. 'If it was the Saint, he may have done you a favour. With Little Buddy indisposed, you have less chance of exposure. *Your* secret stays safe.'

The Saint and Little Buddy. They were using some sort of nicknames. Code names?

Birdie heard the fabric of Sister T's dress rustle as she turned away from his advocacy.

'You want me to be happy Warwick was attacked?' Sister T said.

Was Little Buddy code for Warwick? He was the one who was 'indisposed'. She knew Gilligan from *Gilligan's Island* was referred to as 'Little Buddy' by Skipper.

'No, of course not.' More shuffling of feet. 'I'm worried about you.'

'Don't be. No one *really* suspects a nun.' The voices moved from the confessional back to the pews. 'We'd better get back before we're missed.' The scraping sound of the retrieval of a candle could be heard. 'You go first,' Sister T added.

The door of the chapel opened and closed. A female voice murmured a prayer and then the door opened and closed again.

She and Herb were alone.

Her body was humming with adrenaline, relief, desire. Herb twisted her expertly in his arms. They were face to face, his perfect lips centimetres from hers. She ran a finger along the smattering of a moustache that outlined their brilliance. She lifted her eyes, her world shrinking to just him. His dark brown hair had grown. She lengthened a soft curl, one of the many that were falling around his face, and let it spring back. She ran a finger along the side of his stubbly cheek, across the bounce of his bottom lip.

'Birdie.' His voice was a hoarse whisper.

You are really here.

His fingers pulled her closer, igniting the skin at her hips.

She had to get back to the dancing, to the girls.

She had to get back to Margie. She could not deal with Herb. Could not deal with the ache that had started in her stomach muscles but was rising, the roar in her ears, the fear.

She knew she was being a coward. She knew Herb couldn't follow; he wouldn't even be able to call out.

Birdie backed away, opened the door to the confessional box and ran.

TEN

Rainbow lorikeets hopped in the branches outside the window, as Birdie sat at her desk, chattering and vying for territory. A family of ducks waddled along the edge of the shared oval, plopping into the creek adjoining it. Everyone else had gone directly home from the staff meeting. But Birdie had taken the chance to tidy up her workspace and grab her things. The staff nooks were quiet and still. She doodled in her daybook, watched the birds ... and thought of Herb.

What had he been doing in the confessional box? What was he doing back in Vantage? Where the hell had he been? She shook her body loose, scribbled a few evaluations from the day's lessons, wrote up her daybook for tomorrow, packed her bag and pushed Herb from her mind.

Sister T and Dom had some serious concerns about whether Naughty Santa had been the one to stab Warwick Woods. How could she find out who he was? Who was Naughty Santa, referred to by them – ironically – as the Saint? There was a TV show called *The Saint* about a spy, if Birdie remembered correctly. Glen watched it.

She picked up her bag and stood too quickly, slightly overbalancing. She could still feel Herb's strong hands on her, keeping her steady. Feel them burning against the skin at the back of her ribs. Who was she kidding thinking she'd be able to get over him? His soft, puffy lips swam into view. She'd wanted them so badly to brush hers.

Her face flushed. She held a cool hand to her warm cheek. *Far out.* She exhaled a long, slow breath and walked away from her desk and towards the doorway.

'Hello, Birdie.'

Straight into the path of a very attractive man.

'Jonathon?' Birdie's heart was tapping its tiny fists against her breastbone. 'What are you doing here?'

'You refused to heed my call.'

The tiny fists clenched and assumed a boxing stance. 'I'm not a bloody dog.'

'We need to talk.'

'I'm on my way home.'

'This can't wait.' He walked past her, back into the nook.

Typical Jonathon. She should have known she couldn't avoid him. She turned slowly back around.

He speared her with a look. 'With whom have you discussed ... us?'

'P-pardon?'

'Who have you told about us?' He said the words more slowly and with more emphasis on each.

Birdie sucked a few breaths in and out. She watched Jonathon walk back and forth, head down. His thick fair hair was greying at the temples. His endless ocean eyes glittered their magic. The carpet – which was getting the full treatment – was not responding.

'This is what you wanted to t-talk to me about?'

'Someone is blackmailing me.' His eyes flicked up to hers. 'If I don't pay up, they will reveal a little secret about my past,' he said, spitting the words. 'I know you're prone to engaging in gossip.' He flashed with anger.

Fools feed on foolishness. He'd always had an issue with idle gossip. Any time she indulged in any – listening to or passing on of juicy news – he'd been verbal in attack.

'I'd be surprised if I'm the only secret in your past, Jonathon.' Her words an angry snark.

Her mind raced. *Shame Game, No Names.* Was Jonathon Naylor the next victim? And if so, did the other subjects also get threats before disclosure?

He studied her. 'Have you got something to do with this indecent threat?'

'Why do you think I would have something to do with it?'

He slumped onto the edge of the desk that ran along the side of the nook and buried his face in his hands. 'The infidelity with you was my only slip-up.' He ran his fingers through his neatly done hair.

Nausea swam around Birdie's stomach.

He shook his head. 'As you probably know, if this gets out, my new position will be seriously in jeopardy.'

'This may surprise you, Jonathon, but I haven't actually been following your career.'

He contemplated her with a half grin. 'Is your staff being encouraged to go to Sister Verona's farewell?'

Why was he asking about poor old Sister Verona's mass? What did the retiring Catholic Schools' superintendent have to do with the price of fish?

Birdie's eyes flew open wide. 'Holy shit. You're not ...'

'I've just been appointed the new superintendent for the Catholic schools in our diocese.'

'God almighty!'

'Not exactly, but close.'

She speared him with a look.

'Sorry, this is not really a good time to make jokes, is it?' He buried his head again. 'I can see your use of colourful language hasn't improved.'

She let that comment go through to the keeper. Jonathon had never been keen on her swearing. *My swearing, my gossiping, my talking about money, my drinking, my short skirts.* Birdie put a hand on his shoulder. She knew he'd been ambitious, but she had no idea he'd moved through the ranks like this.

'I've got my own career, you know,' she said, the first form mistress' role coming to mind. 'It's not like I'd want this getting out.'

Blue-sky eyes drifted up. Scared. Clouds brewing.

She felt a pang of pity. 'What do they actually know, Jonathon?'

'My dirty little secret, apparently. I've just been asked to put a sum of money into an envelope and deposit it in an account, or it will be revealed.'

'Have you paid it?'

'Not yet. But I will.'

'How much is it?'

'It's impolite to discuss money matters, Birdie.' He paced and then sat against the edge of the desk again.

She waited.

'It's substantial.'

Birdie drew a long breath in and out. For all his rules and regulations about life, he was certainly okay with putting it about when he was married. Bringing that to his attention, though, would not be helpful.

Birdie took another deep breath in. 'How do you know the secret is *our* relationship?' she said on exhale and began to pace.

'I don't. I was just hoping ...' He grabbed her hand. 'I don't know what I was hoping.'

Perched where he was, they were eye to eye. The seductive pools that she had dived deeply into were doing their best to draw her back down. She'd been so blissfully lost in them once.

Jonathon ran a finger down her face. 'You are still as beautiful as ever, Bell.'

Birdie's mouth felt dry. She needed to get away from here. *Bell*. Short for bellbird. A play on her name, her voice, her bronze-gold hair.

'How's Linda?' she asked.

Jonathon flinched.

Once Birdie had conceded she'd crossed a line, she had a compulsion to know everything. Forced herself to put a name, an identity, a soul to what she'd compromised. Linda was the name of Jonathon's wife.

Birdie broke out in a sweat. 'It's time for you to go,' she said, pulling him up. 'This behaviour was what got you into the mess you're in.' She lifted her hair off the back of her neck and let it fall again, then pushed Jonathon towards the doorway. 'I haven't said anything to anyone. No one knows about us but us. Whatever the secret is, it's not us. You're going to have to pay the money and hope for the best.'

Would his wife, Linda, notice the withdrawal from their bank account?

'But Bell—'

'Remember what's at stake,' Birdie said. 'Your job, your marriage, your child.'

'My child.' Jonathon dropped his head, gave it a small shake.

Birdie frowned. 'Is everything okay with ...' She couldn't remember the boy's name. He was about ten back then. He'd be an adolescent now.

'Johnny,' Jonathon provided.

Of course. *Named after his father.*

'Things are less than perfect with Johnny. His school seems to think he has a behaviour problem. They've suggested we see a psychologist.'

Oh. 'Based on what?'

'They've accused him of dropping some lab mice out the window of a second-floor science classroom, apart from other things.'

'Was he trying to free them?'

'Either that or watch them fall to their deaths.'

Eeek!

He turned and stepped in close. 'Linda's not taking the suggestion well. She's ready to murder someone. The principal at present.' He grabbed her arm. 'I miss you. I miss this. You were always so easy to talk to.'

As opposed to his wife, who wasn't. She remembered him saying those words to her years ago. Words she fell for, words that made her feel important.

'Is there anyone else you've said those words to?' She removed his hand. *Someone else who could be the dirty little secret?* Some other delusional young woman. She didn't wait for an answer. She felt bad for Jonathon and his family, but she was not going to fall back into this. She turned him towards the door once more. 'Go, Jonathon. And make sure no one sees you.'

She listened to the swish of his clothes get softer and softer until she heard the door to the outside world open and close.

She sank into her seat. Her head was pounding.

Would the secret be about them? Other rumours had involved women. Although not naming her, Margie had been implicated. And what about the poor girl from Naughty Santa's entry?

Who knew about her and Jonathon?

Pia. Jonathon. Birdie herself. Who else? Did his wife know?

In three days, the *Gallie Wallen Gazette* would be flung onto the front lawns of every resident in the council area. They would open up to everyone's favourite column: *Shame Game, No Names*.

Birdie needed to make sure she was not the person they read about.

➤ ➤ ➤

'We don't know that Jonathon's secret will be in this Thursday's *Shame Game*, you know.'

Birdie had just filled Pia in on Jonathon's visit and the possibility that he could be the next victim. She'd rushed straight to the staffroom phone as soon as Jonathon left. She twirled the phone cord around and around her finger, nerves making her skin itch.

It had been a long day. The sun was setting. Purple and gold splashes of sky painted the high windows of the staffroom. Normally, a view Birdie would marvel at, but right now, registering its beauty went quickly into her brain and out again.

'I know,' she said into the mouthpiece, 'and paying up might stop it altogether.'

Although, they might take the money and still send the information. How much longer will teachers be in the spotlight? What had Emer said? *It was too good not to print?*

'There's a real chance this is going to happen, Pia. With Jonathon about to take on an integral role in the diocese, this would be gold.'

'Who else is clued-in about you two?'

'Only you.' Birdie twirled; the cord stretched. She exhaled forcefully. 'And I suppose anyone who was watching super closely while I was on prac.' She'd only been on prac for four weeks. She walked to the door of the cubicle and closed it. She lowered her voice. 'We only slept together that one time.' A shiver ran across Birdie's shoulders. Once had been enough to spook her, appal her, make her feel sick to the stomach.

Regret. That was the main emotion she felt when she thought of Jonathon. Shame. That was another one. She'd considered the old adage: *Je ne regrette rien.* No regrets. Your mistakes, your triumphs, they make you who you are. And it was true. She had definitely learned about herself. It had made her look at the person she did – and didn't – want to be.

But the selfishness of the phrase 'no regrets' made her blood boil. She'd always regret what she'd done. She'd always regret the hurt she may have caused someone else.

'You might not be the dirty little secret? Have you thought of that?'

'Jonathon said I was the only infidelity in his marriage.'

'I don't believe that for a second. I'd put money on he's done something else worthy of blackmail.'

'An upstanding, righteous model of society like Jonathon?' Birdie pressed her forehead against the glass window.

'How the mighty have fallen. That's from the Bible, you know.'

'I hope there *is* something else he's done, as horrible as that sounds.' Birdie dropped the coil of line and began to twirl again.

Leaders of all systems: Catholic, state and private had been targeted. Who worked across all systems? Who would meet with, see the actions of, and listen to discussions about these people? Cleaners, security, maintenance, delivery men, presenters of professional development? A casual teacher?

She also filled Pia in on the incident in the confessional box – well, overhearing Sister T and Dom, anyway. She kept the Herb bit to herself. *For now.*

'The way they were talking made it sound like Warwick and Santa knew each other.' Birdie said.

There's bad blood between them.

What might that be? Could Warwick have targeted Naughty Santa because of this bad blood? But how could that be if he was only printing the gossip and not mailing it in? Could Naughty Santa have stabbed Warwick because of this bad blood, taken exception to the gossip and confronted his old mate, who wasn't really a 'mate' at all?

'Who's Naughty Santa, also known as the Saint, how do we find out, and will that help us work out who stabbed Warwick Woods?' Pia mused.

'Three very good questions.'

'Do they still have yearbooks in the library? Remember we used to have them?'

Birdie visualised the library shelves. 'They probably do. Are you thinking we might be able to work out who Naughty Santa is by looking through them?'

'Both Sister T and Dom know Santa and Warwick. We know Sister T taught Warwick.'

'Yes, when she was at Percy's with Dom before they both climbed their respective ladders.'

'Stands to reason they taught Santa as well,' Pia said.

'Warwick Woods and Santa are older than us. I think Larry said Warwick was thirty-seven. So they'd appear in the yearbooks around 1964, 65? It's worth a look at least.'

She'd head to the library in the morning. The sky continued to darken outside, purples turning to dark blue. Too late for the librarians to be around. She should probably get home herself. A cleaner wandered into the staffroom, set the vacuum down and started to wipe the lunch tables. Birdie wondered briefly if this was the only school she cleaned. 'Something else happened in the confessional box,' she said into the mouthpiece.

'Ooh. Something of a divine nature?'

'You could say that.' Heat spread across her skin. *But not the type of divine you mean, Pia.* 'I saw Herb.'

'Like ... as an apparition?'

'No, you boofhead, as a real live person. In real life. He was there.'

'Dead set?' Birdie heard the rustle of movement as Pia was obviously sitting up straight. 'Shit. Herb's back? What did you say to him? What was he doing in there? Did he explain why he left?'

'I didn't really give him the chance. I ran out as soon as I could.'

'Out of the confessional box?'

'Yes, after Sister T and Dom had gone.'

'So ... your two, long-limbed, angular-boned bodies were squashed in that tiny confessional box. Together?'

Birdie felt his lips on her forehead, her neck, his front against her back.

'Cosy,' Pia said.

'Part of me wanted to slap him and the other part wanted to run my fingers through his hair and kiss his perfect lips.'

'Just like old times then.'

Whereas men tend to be aggressive in their climb up the ladder, women compete more against themselves and the job. There's almost an element of 'hey, I can do it and I really like proving it.'

'The Cleo three S report:
Status'
Cleo, March 1985.

ELEVEN

BY THE TIME BIRDIE had made it home to her door, it was dark out. A figure, illuminated under the glow provided by the Gypsy's parking lights, lounged in the shadows.

Recognition replaced panic in a split second.

She manoeuvred up the rest of the driveway carefully, hands sweating against the steering wheel. If she got out, she would have to talk to him; the presence she'd longed for, had begun to accept she'd live without. She would have to see his eyes, feel the warmth that always radiated from him, stand too close to the fire.

'What are you doing here?' She tried to keep the swift rush of anger under control as she stepped from her car.

He stood up straight. The new sensor light Glen had just installed threw them both into an unnatural gold spotlight.

'I could have been anyone, Birdie, and you just walked straight up to me.'

She exhaled heavily. 'You are not anyone, Herb. And you don't get to tell me to be careful anymore. You gave that up when you gave me up.'

He ran a hand over his barely there moustache and beard, squeezing his chin between index finger and thumb. Her heart clenched. It was a movement so familiar. The time between this action right now and the last time she'd seen him do it faded into nothing. He nibbled his perfect bottom lip. Her lips tingled in response, remembering the way his felt against them, against other parts of her body. Against her neck in the confessional box.

'What the hell were you doing in the confessional box, Herb?'

'Could ask you the same thing.'

'Well, too bad. I asked first.' She waited. He held her gaze, mouth unmoving. She kept pushing. 'I mean, I can understand you might have had sins to confess.'

'Was that why you were there?'

She should have known he was just as good at this game as she was. *Fine.* She'd just have to play harder. 'Forgive me, Lord, for I have sinned. I've felt pride, greed, anger, been filled with hot, raging lus—'

'You might want to speak to your uncle,' he spat.

What the hell does my uncle have to do with this? 'Why?'

'He's representing both Sister T and Dom Walker, isn't he?'

'Yes. And that's your business because …?'

Herb had taken 'leave' from the NSW Police Force. The official reason was so he could recover after being shot. The real reason, Birdie guessed, was much more complicated.

'Are you working for my uncle?' she said.

Herb had once told her, Inspector Draper had him over a barrel. She suspected Herb's boss was somewhat of a bully.

He dropped his head. 'As I said, Birdie. You might want to have this conversation with your uncle.'

I'll be having a conversation with my uncle, alright.

'I've answered your question,' Herb continued. 'Now—'

'With a nonanswer.'

Herb took a breath. Ignored her retort. 'Now,' he tried again, 'what were you doing in the chapel?'

She dragged her gaze away. 'That's easy.' She pushed down the anger. She'd put some distance between them. 'I work at the school. I went in to say a prayer.' She put her key in the door and started to turn it.

'Good gig, Friday night?' Herb said evenly.

It had been him I'd seen. 'You were there.' She stilled. 'What did you think?'

'Prefer not to comment on what I saw.'

'What? You've got nothing to say about the mighty performance by Seasons of Change?' She pushed open the solid, pale blue door and hurried into the tiny entryway, turning quickly to close it behind her. A large-booted foot stopped her progress. Her glare lifted from the boot to the face that owned it.

'You know what I'm talking about.' His voice was low and not at all happy.

'Get your foot out of my doorway.' She matched his menace. He had no right to make a comment about the look between her and Clint or the interest from Griff. He shouldn't even have been watching. How bloody dare he.

'And Saturday night at the Sailo?' he said.

Bloody voyeur.

'Oh, come on, Herb. Do you really think I'm sitting at home, pining away for you? Keeping myself tidy?'

'Not if last weekend or this afternoon are anything to go by. Had your choice of three.'

Shit! He'd seen Jonathon?

'Jealousy's a curse.' She slammed the door, but it hit solid leather and bounced back. She caught it mid-swing. 'Get your bloody foot out of my doorway.' She peered at him, exasperated.

He grinned.

Arsehole.

Her hands clenched the door and frame, anger flowing from her fingertips into the wood. He was so close she could smell him, clean and fresh. He'd only recently showered. The thought of water cascading down his naked body made her involuntarily gasp.

He was so close she could have slapped him, which she'd done, once before and vowed she never would again ... *but I'd make an exception tonight.*

He was so close she could have run her fingers through the soft, loose ringlets around his head, grown out from his neat, close-cropped former style. The mischievous curl that used to escape when he was hot and bothered – or just after he'd exerted himself in pleasure above her, or in pleasuring her below him – was joined by many now, all in wild abandon. He looked amazing, more gorgeous than before, if that was possible. She shivered. A dangerously traitorous thrill danced a twirl through her blood.

'Cold, teach?' A tiny lift at the corner of his mouth.

'Go away, Detective.' She shouldn't be engaging. This was not a game. 'Stop following me.'

'You once pleaded with me to stay.' His voice was thick and throaty. 'Right here, in this very bedroom.' He indicated her bed, its foot just visible from the doorway. 'Right next to that bed.'

'And if I remember correctly, you left me then too.'

'Birdie.' He grabbed her hand; she pulled it back. He held tight until she was looking at him. His eyes searched hers. He would not find what he was looking for. 'I'm sorry.'

She pulled her hand away again. This time, he let her. 'Keep your apology.'

'I can see you're upset.'

'You see that now, do you? Almost three months after the event?'

'Birdie, you don't understand.'

'I am not unintelligent, Herb. If there was something I needed to understand, you should have explained it.'

'You also once said you'd walk with me on the fight.'

Birdie felt the statement like a punch in the gut – She never got the chance.

It was understanding more about his Aboriginal culture, more about himself, more about the 'fight' that she had thought led him away. He had always planned to visit his country. They'd spoken about it. She was excited for him. It's just that he'd left months earlier than he told her he would and with no goodbye. And in fact, she wasn't even sure that's where he'd gone – home to Country. She just presumed it was.

'That was below the belt, officer, using your culture to make me feel guilty for being upset you'd disappeared.'

'Careful, Bird.'

She ignored the edge in his voice. 'I'm past being careful here, Herb.' She grabbed a handful of his shirt and pulled him close. His eyes widened. She could see the blue flecks of heat flickering among the hazel. 'I would have walked with you on the fight, but I wasn't invited. Don't use reverse psychology on me.'

'You've got your job, Birdie, your family. I couldn't ask you to leave them.' His voice soft and pleading.

'That's a decision for me to make, you misogynistic prick.' She let go of his shirt and pushed him away. He stammered backwards. 'Do what you do best, Herb: disappear.'

'Birdie.' He came towards her.

She shut the door quickly, before he could get his foot back in, and pressed her head and hands against the wood.

'Birdie, please.' A muffled yell came through the door.

Tears sprouted. She turned her back, slid down the hard wood until her bum hit the soft plush runner and cried.

TWELVE

Birdie worked on her expression of interest for the first form mistress' position during her free period on Tuesday morning. Brad and Sabine had been keeping an ear open for who else might be applying. The job was only for the second term, thirteen weeks in total, so she was hoping not many.

'The woman who applies for everything and gets nothing, Kelly Lane from home economics, is throwing her hat in again.' Brad rolled his eyes.

'Kelly Lane really should take a hint.' Sabine juggled a bundle of notes. 'This role requires you to be at least civil, if not pleasant, to the students,' she added, breezing through the nook. 'She is neither. There's no way Sister T will give it to her.' Sabine reached the exit and kept going. '*Au revoir.* I'm off to class.' She stopped, turned back and addressed Brad. 'Tell her what I found out about Robin.' Then, she was gone.

'Robin Michael's from maths is the other possibility. She's done a few fill-ins before, although we've heard on the grapevine, she might be pregnant.'

'That doesn't mean she won't be able to do the job for the term, Brad.'

'I *know* that.'

Birdie was reminded of an article Emer Garland had written in the gazette, which she'd read when she got around to actually looking at the rest of the paper. It was about 'The Glass Ceiling', a recent discussion on the fact that women could see leadership roles but couldn't reach them. Motherhood being one of the reasons they couldn't break through. Ironic – or coincidental? – that when Emer was such a clever and talented writer, it was a gossip column that brought in the big bucks.

'But I've also heard on the grapevine that Pat Sumner may be taking more than one term's leave,' Brad continued. 'He's planning on using up all his long service leave before he *retires*, is what I've heard.'

'Shit!'

'I know. They won't want to have to fill the position again if Robin goes on maternity leave.' Brad leaned over her shoulder as she organised her application. 'Which means they might be looking for someone long term.'

Is that what Birdie wanted? Was she ready?

'Are you going to the mass for Sister Verona?' Brad said. 'It's a Friday, so not a Joanie's day for you, but it might be good to come. Show your dedication.'

'She's a sweet old thing,' Birdie said. 'I'm definitely going.'

'I wonder who's going to replace her?'

'I actually know who's replacing her, but if I tell you, you'll have to take it to the grave.'

Brad drew an X on his chest. 'Cross my heart and hope to die, stick a needle in my eye. Who?'

'Jonathon Naylor.'

'Oh, that man is a spunk!' Brad almost purred the words. 'He can superintend me anytime. He could superintend the bejesus out of me.'

Birdie swallowed. In the role of superintendent, Jonathon would come in contact with lots of people. Would that give him more of a chance to philander?

'Interesting that they've gone with a layperson,' Brad went on. 'Leadership roles normally go to those in the religious orders. Case in point, Sister Verona. But then I suppose that's the way of things now. Look at Dom.'

Birdie had heard those in religious orders were channelling their work into places other than schools and hospitals. More into areas such as missionaries and social work.

'You know Jonathon Naylor's son goes to the school at which a friend of mine is the principal,' Brad continued. 'The kid's a bit of a brat, by all accounts.'

So I've heard.

'How do you know that it's Jonathon Naylor who's taking over?' Brad asked.

'I bumped into him the other day.' Bumped into was a stretch but not exactly a lie. 'He was my supervisor for my first prac, an old acquaintance, so we had a chat and he mentioned it.'

'Lucky you.'

Lucky was not the word she would have used.

👄 👄 👄

Birdie watched Uncle Larry's face lift into a smile. All innocent and chatty as she and Pia sat at his table and he stood in the kitchen putting teacups on the bench.

'Any luck with Sister T and the identity of Naughty Santa?' Birdie asked.

'She insists she has no idea who the target of the first rumour was, has no idea who might have wanted to harm Warwick and will not provide any alternatives as to who might have stabbed him.' Larry put teabags in cups. 'Which means she is not going to give up the name of Naughty Santa aka the Saint.'

'Did you ask Dom?' said Birdie.

'Same vague response,' her uncle said.

'Did you know that "Santa" actually means "saint" in Italian?' said Pia. 'How's that for a coincidence?'

'Freaky,' said Birdie.

'She also insists she was at school on the afternoon in question, even though I can't find anyone who saw her,' Uncle Larry continued.

Why was Sister T being so stubborn, so secretive? Was she covering for someone? Perhaps the yearbooks might shed some light. She'd visited the library to find them after school, only to be informed that they were probably in the archives and the librarian would have to search them out.

She knew someone else who was keeping secrets, and he was currently making tea in his kitchen.

'Are you free tonight, Birdie?' her secretive uncle said. 'We could use some of your magic at the ALS.'

'Of course.'

'Never know who you might see at the ALS,' Pia whispered. 'Which on-leave policeman you might be able to throw a few ideas around with.'

'I'd rather ask Sergeant Morton Reynolds,' Birdie mumbled under her breath.

'Gutless wonder,' Pia mumbled back.

Birdie pulled a face and bit into her Tim Tam. 'Speaking of on-leave policemen,' she said under her breath to Pia. She switched her gaze to her uncle. 'Uncle Larry?'

'Yes, darling.'

'What would you think about someone who betrayed one of the people they supposedly loved?'

'Well, it depends on the circumstances.' He unplugged the now-boiled kettle and made his way with it towards the bench.

'Let's say the "supposedly loved" person, in this scenario, was a young lady in her mid-twenties. Successful, vibrant, had her heart recently broken by her boyfriend who disappeared without a word.'

Boiling water spilled over the side of the cup Larry was filling. He pulled up the tip of the kettle and jumped back in alarm.

'Oh dear,' Birdie mocked. 'You've spilled some water, Unky. You really should watch what you're doing.'

He put the kettle down. 'Birdie. I need to tell you something.' He pulled a tea towel from the oven door and scrunched the material over and over.

'But Uncle Larry, I haven't finished *my* story.' She tapped her chin. 'Now, where was I?' She consulted the ceiling. 'Oh, I remember. Let's say, the person who was doing the betraying, in this hypothetical situation, was the young woman's uncle.'

'B-Birdie, it's not what you think.' Larry put the tea towel over the spill.

Pia stopped crunching. Her eyes flicked from Birdie to Larry.

'Her godfather and honorary uncle. Her only uncle. The man she grew up admiring, worshipping and loving unconditionally, who she saved from near death only months ago.'

'Birdie.' Water dripped from the towel Larry had used to mop up with. He gave up and plonked the tea towel back into the pooled liquid. He held up a finger. 'Just hold on a minute.'

'You want me to stop and listen to you explain away the fact that you knew'—she slammed her hand against the table—'that Herb was back in town.' She stood up and put her hands on her hips. 'And you'd hired him to find out who stabbed Warwick Woods?'

'Can I be frank, darling?'

'I wish you would be before my head explodes *right* off my shoulders!' She held her head and threw her arms in the air to add to the effect.

Pia was watching the exchange with a devil in her eye and a great, open-mouthed grin. *Sadist.*

Uncle Larry pointed over to the biscuits. 'I suggest you eat more of those. Sugar energy.'

Birdie plonked back into her seat, pushed the plate away and crossed her arms against her chest, waiting.

Larry held the end of the bench for strength. 'Herb is doing some work at the ALS.'

Pia grabbed a biscuit from the tray that was now in front of her. Her almond eyes moved from one combatant to the other like she was watching a game of tennis.

'This we know,' Birdie said.

Larry took a deep breath. 'And he's also doing some work for me, personally.'

Birdie's eyes grew wide. 'Uncle Larry!'

'Before you get all huffy, darling, let me explain.'

She had every right to be huffy, and her uncle would just have to deal with it. She sat up and put her hands on her hips again.

'We were all working together at the ALS before he ... left. Well, he has returned, and Cecil has got him helping again. He's also doing some groundwork for me. He's branching out into private investigation while he's on leave from the police.'

'Why didn't you tell me?'

'I just did.'

'*Magnum PI.*' Pia was wide-eyed.

That explained your presence in the confessional box, Herb Lawson.

'Something like that,' said Larry to Pia.

Tom Selleck's dimpled cheeks and big blue eyes swam into Birdie's mind. That moustache and wavy dark hair reminded her briefly of the look Herb was currently rocking. *Very sexy.* She smiled to herself. A warm, fuzzy, hot chocolate fudge on a sundae feeling dripped into her chest. She turned away as her lower eyelids suddenly filled with tears. There's a fine line between pleasure and pain. *Just ask Chrissy Amphlett.*

She blinked them back.

'He wants to talk to you, Birdie.'

She rounded on her uncle. Mouth open, ready to pounce. 'And you told him I'd listen?'

He put his hands up, fingertips to the sky and palms out. 'I told him you might not be agreeable to that.' He came out from behind the kitchen bench and hugged her shoulder. 'I'm on your side, darling. I know he's hurt you, and I will never forgive him for that.' Her uncle squeezed again and let go. 'But he is doing some fine work for ALS, which is really needed. I think, deep down, he's a good guy.'

Uncle Larry finished making the tea. 'You might be seeing more of him if you are invested in Sister Therese Margaret's case.' He picked up the cups and carried them to the table. 'And even more of him again'—he returned to the safety of the kitchen—'as ... it's possible'—he took a sip from his mug—'he might have moved in with me.'

'What?' Birdie was on her feet again.

Pia laughed out loud. 'This is gold.' She picked up another biscuit, eyes never leaving the spectacle.

'Remain calm, Birdie,' her uncle said, moving further back into the kitchen and extending a hand.

'You're ...' Birdie swung her arm towards the front rooms of her uncle's house and whispered, 'You're housing him?'

'Don't worry. He's not here now.'

Birdie breathed deeply. Pia continued to grin.

'What else could I do?' Larry said, voice pleading. He came towards the table tentatively. 'He had to give up the room at his old place. He's been bunking down with a friend, but it's not really conducive to good sleep habits, and he needs to be firing on all cylinders.'

'I thought *I* was helping with the investigation,' she said.

'You are, my sweetheart.'

Pia laughed into her teacup.

Larry silenced Pia with a glare. 'And I'm very appreciative. But I also have a responsibility to my clients. The more informed I am, the better the outcome for Dom and Sister Therese Margaret.' He sipped his tea. 'Could you at least *try* being friends with him?' He held his hand out for a biscuit. Birdie slammed one into his palm. He took a bite and swallowed. 'I need you both.'

Not long after, Birdie walked Pia to her car, lost in her own little world.

'You want to talk about it?' Pia asked as they reached her car door.

'You were no help. Laughing and eating all the bikkies.'

'Couldn't help myself. You two are very entertaining sometimes. I'm listening now, though.'

'I don't know, Pia. Herb was lurking around my door when I got home from work last night.'

'Shit, Birds.'

'I know.'

'What happened?'

She pictured his boot jammed in her door, his shirt fisted in her fingers. She retold the few heated lines of their exchange. 'You should see him. He's stopped gelling his curls down, and they've grown out a bit. They're all messy and free. It makes him look wild, more ...'

'Of a spunk?'

'If that's possible.'

'You still love him, Birdie,' she said, matter-of-fact.

'Do I?'

'Don't you?'

'I can't trust him. I should never have trusted him in the first place.' He'd buzzed her on his bike, spied on her, tried to keep her from finding the truth. Sure, he had a good excuse for his former erratic behaviour – his superior having him 'over a barrel' – but could he be trusted?

'I love you, Birdie Mealing, but have you ever considered that he may not be able to trust *you*?'

'What does that mean?'

'You are a free spirit. There's really nothing in your manner that contradicts that. Perhaps he thought he had Buckley's of holding you. Of nailing you down.'

Birdie was taken aback. Griff with his lingering looks, Clint running a finger down her side, and Jonathon saying 'I miss you' played out behind her eyes.

'That's not to say you don't love with all your heart,' Pia continued. 'Are not loyal to a T.' She squeezed Birdie's hand. 'You love *me* with all your heart. Stu, the twins, Larry, Lenore, Mrs N, and Glen.' Pia got into her car, shut her door and leaned out the window. 'We know you'd do anything for us. But how many of your boyfriends would be able to say the same?'

Birdie contemplated her statement. 'Enough with the character analysis. Get your smug, Sophia Loren face out of here, moll.' Birdie smiled. Pia laughed.

Her wise friend started the car and pulled away. Birdie watched her disappear around the corner before stepping back from the kerb, tears spilling over the bottom of her lashes.

She had loved Herb, and he *had* known it, hadn't he? She blinked her eyes tightly, pushing away the glassy balls of salty water threatening to obstruct her vision. She'd not followed through on her plans to travel overseas for him. Admittedly, she hadn't made any firm travel plans and was currently vying for a leadership role at St Joanie's, but the intention was there.

She hadn't loved anyone else. She'd had feelings for many men, but Pia was right about one thing: she hadn't loved them. Not really. Even if she might have had a chance, she made sure she didn't. She'd left before the opportunity arose, before the feelings spilled over, and even once – immaturely and regretfully – she'd chosen a man whom she knew she could never have.

She had let Herb right in, all the way, and had allowed herself to love him. She'd told him she loved him, hadn't she?

Regardless, he had felt that love.

Hadn't you, Herb?

THIRTEEN

THE POSSIBILITY OF BUMPING into Herb tonight sent equal parts thrill and dread careening along Birdie's veins. It irked her that her blood ran its own race with no consideration whatsoever for the intentions of her mind.

'It's only boring paperwork, darling.' Uncle Larry drove out of Vantage towards the ALS offices in Redfern.

'If it helps the legals be more hands-on, then I'm happy to do it.' Plus, it would keep her busy, her mind full. She had Jonathon, Herb and Sister T, all swimming around in there. Pia kept reassuring her she'd be fine. There is no way Jonathon would not pay whatever it took to keep his reputation squeaky clean.

'You're a treasure.' He looked across at her sheepishly. 'I don't deserve you.'

She'd forgiven her uncle. It was hard to stay angry with a man who was driving them both to the ALS – the Aboriginal Legal Service – where he'd put in a few volunteer hours to help those in need.

As they rode through the streets getting closer to Redfern, she was reminded of the time that Herb had brought her to see the mural. When she'd got up to road level from the train station platform, it had been right in front of her in all its beauty. The enormous rainbow snake that ran its length, the footprints, the pictures telling the story of the Aboriginal people's journey. He had trusted her with his insecurities back then. Had talked through his muddled thoughts about what he should be doing with his life, where he wanted to be, who he really was.

Now look at them. Perhaps Pia was right. Why hadn't he trusted her with the truth about whatever he was so desperate to do? Was it because she gave the impression she was flighty, not solid? She inhaled – long and deep – and exhaled a ragged breath. She focused on the window of her uncle's Alfa Romeo Spider, fighting back the tears.

'You okay, darling?'

She nodded, not trusting her voice.

'Thinking about Herbert?' he asked.

As if he ever leaves my mind. While he was gone, she could hate him, but he'd returned. He was here. In all his beautiful glory. Did she really never want to see him again, to write the relationship off?

'Birdie, you need to talk to him. Listen to what he has to say.'

She swallowed. 'Do you think he can explain away the fact that he just up and left and broke my heart in the p-process?' Her voice choked on the last word. Tears, warm against her cheeks.

'Oh, darling.' Her uncle's hand groped for hers. 'Are you okay to come tonight?'

She hadn't told her uncle about Jonathon and the blackmail. She hoped no one would ever know. Whether she was okay or not, she needed to be busy.

'I'm fine.' Consideration for others before her own.

'Birdie, my darling. Do you honestly think I would allow some inconsiderate arsehole, who stomped on my god-daughter's heart, to reside under my roof if I wasn't satisfied that he had a good reason for leaving? Not only would it break my own heart, your mother would have my guts for garters.'

She frowned at her uncle. 'You know why he left?'

'You need to talk to him, Birdie. Find out for yourself.'

She turned back to the dark glass as he pulled into the kerb out the front of the ALS building.

'Will you be okay if he's here?' Uncle Larry's quiet question met her ears.

Birdie gazed out the window. Maybe her uncle was right. He was always on her side, and he would never let her be hurt if he could prevent it.

'Yes.' She *would* be okay. She always was.

⇔ ⇔ ⇔

Birdie sat at what was used as the reception desk inside the ALS offices. She shifted papers into files and placed files into the filing cabinet. She typed up handwritten notes and placed them into those files. She transferred the scribbled messages on random bits of paper neatly onto the calendar and tidied everyone's desks.

Her uncle's voice – a soft hum of reassuring presence as she worked – conversed with a client in an adjoining room. The reception desk bin was overflowing – as usual. She picked it up, and a few others that littered the various rooms with their contents also spilling over the sides – the ALS was a very busy place, so emptying bins was not a priority – and took them towards the back door to be emptied into the bigger receptacles outside.

Birdie opened the door with her elbow and placed a footstep onto the landing at the top of the emergency exit stairs. Scritching against the tin roof above her head had her heart skipping. The heavy door clicked shut behind her, bumping into her bum and pushing her further out onto the tiny concrete slab. The scurrying came closer; she sucked in a breath. A possum with a joey on its back scrambled from the gutter to the powerline.

Her breath released in a whoosh. Just a possum. *Not a knife-wielding assassin.*

'Sorry, little mumma,' she said exhaling slowly. 'Didn't mean to disturb you.' Her heart settled back to its normal rhythm.

The night was inky, but the moon and a few streetlights threw a pale filter on the world below. She descended the concrete stairs on tiptoes, so as not to scare the possum any further, and emptied the under-desk bins into the larger silver cylindrical ones, securing their metal lids tightly. The possum watched her every move. She tiptoed back up the staircase and placed her elbow on the handle of the heavy door.

A rumble of wheels and the carefree voices of a group of young adolescent boys made her turn her head. The noise came closer. Birdie strained to see the group as they rode their skateboards and bikes down the street, laughing and calling to each other. A boy hitching a piggyback from another lifted a hand and waved. From up high, Birdie followed his line of sight. The wave was returned by one of two men, lurking in the dark, as he leaned against a car at the kerb. He turned his face momentarily towards the moonlight. Strong cheekbones, soft-lipped smile, face framed in wild, dark brown curls.

Birdie's heart stilled.

Herb.

The feeling of – devastation ... amazement ... giddiness? – that took her every time she saw him unsuspectingly – and sometimes when she knew he'd be soon in view – hit her again.

The boys rumbled along down the street. Cheeky words were exchanged before Herb turned back to the man he was standing with. The other man struck a match to light the cigarette that hung from his lip, his face briefly flooded with a golden glow.

Birdie's heart stilled again, but for a very different reason.

The man who had been concealed under a tree, talking to Herb, out on the dusky footpath, under the light of a filtered moon, was ... Vincent Varva.

And therein lies the rub, because most of us, however cynical, like to believe that one day we will meet our knight in shining armour, fall in love and live happily ever after. In the early, heady days of passion, it doesn't occur to us that something as destructive as mistrust may creep in.

'You may love him … but do you trust him?'
Cleo, December 1983.

FOURTEEN

B IRDIE DREW IN A sharp breath. What the hell was Herb doing hiding in the dark in private conversation with a mob boss?

Her mind raced like 'Flight of the Bumblebee' back to a conversation she'd had with Herb just before Christmas. At the time, he was still working as a detective, had been ordered to carry out certain tasks. Tasks he didn't ask questions about. Tasks he knew were questionable. Wasn't that part of the reason he was reevaluating his career?

Cavorting with Vinny Varva was surely stepping from the frying pan into the fire!

A shiver burst along Birdie's spine, making her shake violently – and involuntarily. The grip she'd had on the bins loosened, and one fell to her feet. It bounced off the concrete, sending an echo out over the night. Two heads lifted in her direction. She ducked down quickly, picked up the fallen bin, put her back towards the pair, turned the handle – sweaty now under her palm – and rushed back through the fire exit door. Inside, the steady voices of client and worker welcomed her return.

Why did she care that Herb was meeting with a man who had spent the best part of the last ten years in jail for murdering four people? Sure, said crime lord was also a teenage friend of her uncle's and her mother's *and* had been recently acquitted, which she'd – through uncovering the real murderer – had a hand in helping to achieve, but he was still dangerous and deceitful and getting involved with him could be deadly. You didn't become a crime overlord by being sweet.

She put the bins silently back under busy desks and set about tidying up the tiny alcove that served as a kitchen. Her mind eased with the violent scouring of teacups and teaspoons. She huffed a laugh. The disregard for clean-yourown-cup-after-use was universal, it seemed. Soggy teabags and well-past-it sponges that peppered the drip tray and sink were chucked in the kitchen tidy, which she noticed, also needed to be emptied.

With the sink, benchtops, cupboard doors, and a little of the floor nicely Gumption'd, Birdie wriggled and jiggled the full-to-the-brim-but-we'll-still-shove-more-into-it kitchen bin liner and secured it with a twist tie. The kitchen tidy itself would also probably need a clean. She tugged at the stuffed rubbish bag to loosen it.

Lengthy fingers reached over her shoulder and lifted the full bag into the air. 'I've got it.'

Birdie turned to see Herb behind her, a half grin and a twinkle in his eye.

'It's dark out.' He searched her face. 'Plus, pretty sure you've already been to the bins once tonight.'

'I'm quite capable, thank you.'

He leaned in; she could smell cigarette smoke amongst his usual honey, spice and sweat. 'Well aware of your capabilities, teach.' He headed off in the direction of the fire exit.

Birdie's ears, neck and chest flushed with heat. She closed her eyes and let it pass. Nostrils flaring, she set about cleaning the kitchen tidy, wiping it out vigorously and refitting a plastic bag liner. She tossed the dirty hand and tea towels on the floor in a pile, ready to take home to launder, washed and dried her hands and grabbed some new linen.

Herb returned, washed his own hands and stood facing her. 'Say it,' he said with a lift of his chin. He held out wet hands for a handtowel.

Birdie slammed a clean one against his palm. 'Say what?' *That you're an idiot for thinking anything good will come of an association with Vinny Varva. What the bloody hell are you playing at?!*

He dried his hands. 'Whatever's running through that dangerous mind.' He grinned.

'I don't know what you're talking about.' *Dangerous mind! Who's the one dicing with danger here?*

He leaned his backside against the – now spotlessly clean – sink and crossed one foot over the other. His long legs had always impressed the taller-than-average Birdie. He crossed his arms, rested them against his broad chest and considered her. Birdie could almost see the cogs turning. That was the problem with Herb; he read her just as well as she read him. He was watching her cogs turn just as intently.

He handed her back the towel. 'Have it your way.' He turned and pulled down two mugs.

'If I had it my way, I wouldn't be standing in the kitchen with you,' she said under her breath as she placed clean linen on the little hooks. His cheeks lifted with his smile as he continued making the tea. Even as the words came out, she knew they needed to talk, however sick to the stomach it made her feel.

He passed her a mug but held on as she went to retrieve it. 'Wanna tell me about the yearbooks?'

She had wondered how soon he'd come to the same conclusions she and Pia had. 'They're a record of the school year in photos and—'

'Cut the bullshit, Birdie.' His voice rose, anger bouncing off the close walls.

Cec Lawson appeared in the doorway of the room opposite. 'Watch your mouth, brother.'

They waited for him to go back to his client.

Herb's attention retrained on her. 'The yearbooks, Birdie.'

'Why don't you just talk to the staff at St Percy's?'

'They've closed ranks.'

She smiled again. 'Their lips are sealed.'

'I need those books.'

'I got them first.' Birdie sipped her tea.

'You trying to play girl detective again?'

'Succeeding, I'd call it.' He moved in closer. She kept eye contact. 'We seem to be having some sort of communication breakdown, Herb.'

'Whose fault is that?'

'Are you suggesting it's mine?' Birdie's voice rose on the last word, her volume increasing as the anger surged through her veins. 'I wasn't the one who racked off for three months.' She slammed her teacup onto the sink.

Her uncle's head poked out from another doorway. 'Everything alright, darling?'

Birdie opened her mouth to answer.

'We're fine,' said Herb, intercepting. He grabbed Birdie's wrist and pulled her back out the fire exit.

It wasn't the ideal place to be having this discussion, or any discussion. They were up high; a small railing behind

Herb the only thing that might keep him from toppling to his death on the ground below.

'You've put a hold on them,' he said.

'I can't help it if I worked it out first.'

'I'm on the investigation now. You can step back.'

'Up yours.'

'Christ, Birdie. This is my job, my livelihood. This is not a game for me.'

'What game are you playing with Vinny?'

A grin spread slowly over Herb's lips. 'Knew it,' he said. 'You're dying to have a go at me about that.'

'There are so many things I want to have a go at you about, Detective. Vinny is way down the list.'

'Start at the top, teach.'

'I don't think so.'

'Get it off your chest.' He eyed the area in question.

She crossed her arms across her breasts—'Get stuffed, Herb'—and turned back for the handle.

Herb grabbed her, spun her around and held her still. 'Let me have it.' His voice soft, eyes reflecting the lights above as they captured hers.

Birdie controlled her breaths.

Herb joggled her gently. 'Give it to me, Birdie.'

'Where the hell were you? Why did you disappear from my life for almost three months?'

he straightened. 'Needed to take some time out. Was on Country. We'd talked about it. I told you.'

'You didn't say goodbye, you didn't tell me where you were going, how long you'd be. You never rang me to tell me you were okay. I had to call your home and talk to your dad.' She jabbed his chest. 'You know how embarrassing that was?'

'Birdie, I *told* you.'

Air pushed in and out of heavy lungs as they squared up.

Birdie flicked her head. 'After about eight weeks, I started to feel okay, you know. A bit lighter, a little less sad.'

Herb exhaled angrily. 'Don't do this.'

'What? You just asked me to talk to you. I'm doing what you asked.'

'Would be a first,' he mumbled.

She breathed in and out, her teeth grinding. 'After about ten weeks I was almost feeling good. I was going out, having fun.' She loosened her jaw. 'Flirting a little even.'

Herb opened his mouth.

'Shut up,' Birdie said. 'You're not in a position to say anything.'

He sensibly closed it again.

'If you were on Country, I'm glad about that. But that's not all of it. What else were you doing?'

A tiny backward step. 'I was on Country.'

She considered him – olive skin toasted with stubble, hair woolly and wild, eyes comfortable in the shadows. 'The man I fell in love with would never have left without saying goodbye.'

He shook his head. 'You don't understand, Birdie.'

'Then explain it.'

They faced off for a few seconds. Herb dropped his gaze.

'That's the second time I've asked you to.'

'Birdie.'

'You haven't told me the whole truth,' she continued. 'For some reason, you won't. You're right, I don't understand, but after seeing you with Vinny tonight, things are becoming clearer.'

Herb's wide eyes clouded with worry. The boy never could pull a poker face. What was going on with Vinny and Herb?

'You've got it wrong, Bird.'

'You haven't shared what the right way is. And you're not going to. We need to end this now.'

'End it?' he whispered. 'This argument?'

'Us.'

'Are you serious?'

'I've already spent three months alone, Herb. I'm already halfway over you.'

He flinched. 'Birdie.' Herb searched her face.

Her words might have been tough, but the pain in her chest was crushing her. 'I'm so angry Herb Lawson, it's hard to look at you.' Tears filled Birdie's eyes. 'I'm only talking to you right now so we can get this over with.' She took a breath and swallowed the lump in her throat. 'And move on.'

'I don't want to move on.' He grabbed her hand.

'Too bad.' She pulled it away. 'It's not your choice.' She breathed in and out. 'You do have a choice about something, though.'

'Birdie, could we just—'

'You can choose to tell me the truth.' She eyeballed him and waited. Almost certain he would not.

He grabbed her arms. 'Don't do this, Birdie. Please.'

'This is how it's going to go, Herb.' The tears rolled over her bottom lashes. 'We are friends.' She pushed the words through the burn in her throat. 'But that's all. Just friends.'

'No.' His hold on her arms tightened.

'I will not jeopardise your work with my uncle. No more games.'

'Come on, Bird. You don't mean this.'

'If you want to see the yearbooks, we can work on them together, for Uncle Larry's sake, as co-workers.'

'No, Birdie.'

She wiped away his hands like they were sand stuck on zinc cream. 'You had your chance,' she said quietly. Now she had to take hers.

Birdie opened the door, went back inside and headed straight for the bathroom. She sat on the closed toilet seat and hugged her legs – allowed herself a few minutes of crying.

She was not lying when she said she'd been healing for months, but she hadn't counted on the pain she was feeling now. The heaviness of her heart.

⬮ ⬮ ⬮

They avoided each other for the rest of the night.

Head down as he read the address Cec placed in his hand, Herb had stalked out the door later on. He hadn't said goodbye. Hadn't looked back.

Birdie had never been especially good at accepting defeat. In letting things go. Especially when she had the chance to regain a morsel of control. Herb should have known better than to keep something from her.

She'd met with Vinny Varva while he was in jail, when she was trying to find Uncle Larry. He had been cautious, compelling, cryptic in his responses. He'd answered her questions mostly because her mother had accompanied her; he'd felt an historical obligation. Would Vinny Varva meet with her now that he was not compelled to? When he wasn't chained and bound?

Would he have the answers?

'What's going on with Herb and Vinny Varva?' Birdie asked when she and her uncle were on their way home. The moon was full and followed them like a winged pixie as they twisted and turned through the quiet streets.

Her uncle laughed. 'Nothing, that I'm aware of.'

'So *something*, but you don't know what it is.'

'Is that what I said?'

She ignored his intended vagueness. 'I saw Vinny and Herb talking tonight.'

'Tonight? At the ALS?'

'Out on the footpath, under some trees.'

'That's ... interesting.'

What was interesting was her uncle's very low-grade re-action to Herb and Vinny being in conversation. *Listen to what Herb has to say.* Wasn't that what Uncle Larry had advised? Well, Herb was saying very little, and her uncle was proving just as tight-lipped.

'I need to speak with Vinny.'

'For what purpose?'

'Uncle Larry. I know you know how to contact him. Can you give me his number or organise a meeting, please?'

'It's too dangerous, Birdie, plus your mother would kill me.'

'Why does she need to know? I need to speak to him and quickly – like yesterday.'

'No.'

'How about tomorrow?'

'No!'

'You can come too. Then it wouldn't be dangerous. Please, Uncle Larry. You're the one who told me to listen to Herb. He won't tell me what's going on. I'm scared for him.' *Scared and majorly pissed off he hasn't levelled with me.* 'It would help me understand everything. Help me know if I've made the right decision ending things with him.' Would it? She'd already decided, hadn't she? Damn Herb and his secret. What was stopping him from telling her?!

She peeked across at her uncle. A frown worried his brow. *Yes!* Frowning meant he was thinking. She was getting to him. It was not often she didn't win an argument with her uncle. 'I would hate to pull the "you owe me one" card.'

'Birdie Laura Mealing, are you calling *quid pro quo*?'

'Will you honour it?'

He laughed. 'No.'

'Uncle Larry!'

'No.'

FIFTEEN

'**U**NFINISHED BUSINESS,' SAID PIA very simply.

Birdie had headed straight to Pia's after school. After she'd bundled the discarded musical scripts and made them into a neat pile. The *Little Shop of Horrors* – a musical that centred around an alien plant that fed voraciously on human blood. The irony was not lost on her.

She'd come to the sanctuary of Pia's room to hear her friend tell her once more it would not be her and Jonathon's blood the rumour mill would be feeding on tomorrow but was getting an earful of Pia's opinion about her relationship with Herb instead.

'I've already told him we're done.' Birdie scowled as Pia rolled her eyes. 'It's him working with Vinny I can't let go of. It's not safe.'

Pia had upturned her dirty clothes basket all over her room and was picking up articles of clothing, considering them and dropping them again. 'Leaving without saying goodbye pissed you off and'—Birdie opened her mouth to protest. Pia raised her voice to stop the interruption—'him not telling you why he left has also pissed you off. *That's* why you can't let go.'

Pia could have a point. Birdie's first move had been to want to contact Vinny Varva to get information. Her heart seemed to be caught in an epic rock ballad. Every time she thought of Herb, it squeezed an octave higher. She rubbed the spot.

'What are we doing with your clothes?' Birdie said, after Pia picked up the third article of black clothing.

'Door knocker earrings. Pocket of black stirrup pants. Belonging to Giulia. She wants them back.'

Birdie picked up said stirrup pants, retrieved the earrings and handed them over.

'I don't blame you for wanting to know what happened, and, my friend, I'm here to assist,' said Pia.

'Assist me with finding out who really stabbed Warwick Woods. That's probably more important,' Birdie called as Pia left her room, went into her sister's and dropped off the earrings.

'What's the latest?' Pia said on return.

'We still don't know who Santa the Saint is, but the yearbooks are being retrieved from the archives as we speak. Herb has discussed our suspicion of tension at the *Gallie Wallen Gazette* with Constable Celeste, suggesting background checks might be a good idea, and we still don't know Sister T's secret and if knowing it might help or hinder her case.'

'Is the secret juicy enough for Sister T to stab Warwick to keep it quiet?'

'That's the thing; her alibi is sketchy.' Birdie found a clothing-free spot on Pia's bed and sat. 'And obviously, with the whole *Shame Game* business, she could be worried that whatever this secret is might come to light.'

'It's a good motive.'

It might've been, if Birdie didn't firmly believe that Sister T was not capable of such an act. 'But it's not Warwick who's supplying the gossip. It's from an unknown source. So why stab him?'

Pia paced her room. 'What if Warwick – who might *already* be in possession of gossip that is similar to the gossip that he's already publishing in the paper he's in charge of – used the platform *already* available to him to slip in some of his own?' Pia stopped and shrugged a shoulder at Birdie. 'I would.'

'That's a thought.'

'Here's another possibility.' Pia began pacing again. 'Could Warwick have mentioned he has some gossip similar to the stuff they'd been printing? *He says* he can't print it due to his past affiliation with the subject. Emer gets the shits with him – not for the first time. *She says* they should print it. He refuses. They argue – there's no love lost there.' Pia thrust an imaginary knife forward. 'She stabs him.'

'Did we put Emer in our little casebook?'

'Sure did. We have four things to focus on.'

'And they are?'

Pia straightened a finger for each of her points. 'One: as before, we need to find out Sister T's secret. Two: work out if Emer is capable of stabbing her boss. She's tall, she's fierce; my money's on yes. And three: decipher who Saint Santa is.' Pia picked up the T-shirt under her foot, sniffed it and threw it in the dirty clothes basket.

Birdie picked up one from the bed and did the same. 'What's the fourth?' she said.

Pia steepled her fingers and tapped the tips rhythmically together. 'What's hunky Herb been up to?'

⬤ ⬤ ⬤

Birdie completed her routine of shower, pyjamas and dressing gown. It seemed that after a full day of living, she had to remove all items from her body, including perspiration. She went out into the main living area. The boys had also had their baths. They were currently rolling a ball down the hallway to each other, Rusty with his back leaning against the front door and Kick, legs straddled wide, blocking off the hall to the kitchen.

What if it was someone at the paper who was the blackmailer? Once they had the juicy gossip, they either used it or not, depending on who paid up. Could it be Emer? Was it the secretary or the person who opened the mail? Whoever stabbed Warwick might have thought Warwick himself was the one doing the blackmail. Rather than pay up, they could just remove the need to.

The twins laughed and niggled each other as they played their game. Lost in their fun. Tomorrow's edition was only hours away. What would have happened if she and Herb were still together, and he'd found out about her affair? She didn't particularly want *anyone* to find out, but especially not Herb. Was it right for her to expect the truth from him when she herself was lying by omission? Perhaps it was for the best that they weren't together anymore.

The ball bounced over Rusty's leg and sailed into the kitchen. Birdie snatched it out of the air by reflex. The twins, in shock for a split second, roared with approval, their happiness instantly lifting her mood. Birdie stood halfway between her brothers in the middle of the hallway and put her feet shoulder-width apart, filling the space from skirting board to skirting board.

'An obstacle,' she said, passing the ball back to her brother.

Grins spread across their cute faces. They rolled the ball through her legs a few times, very pleased with themselves.

She brought her feet closer together. 'It's getting harder.'

They rolled again.

She put her feet closer together. 'Harder still.'

The ball occasionally skimmed the inside of her ankle or leg, but made it through.

Eventually, she put them closer again. 'Super hard now.'

They hooted their delight, eyes and mouths wide with anticipation and excitement. Rusty began the quest to make it through the ten or so centimetres she'd left them, deep in concentration, his twin supplying hints. His roll was careful and slow, making it through with much relief. Kick lined up his attempt in a split second and threw. The ball shot through Birdie's legs and slammed against the front door. Rusty shimmied from his place just in time to avoid the attack *and* just as a knock sounded from the door at his back.

In one fluid movement, he jumped up, clutched the wayward ball from its rebound, opened the front door and threw himself into the arms of the visitor. 'Herb!'

Herb's eyes met Birdie's as he shuffled inside, dropped briefly to her chest area, her gown having opened in the effort of the game, and then lower to the little man attached to his left leg. He put a hand on her brother's back in greeting. She pulled her dressing gown across her body.

'No need on my account,' Herb said with a wink, holding tight to the human koala.

She tilted her head and raised an eyebrow. 'Too bad I'm off limits now, Detective.' She tied the belt with exaggerated force. 'I'm glad you came, though, I've got questions.'

'And I have the answers?'

'If you know what's good for you.' She started down the hall to the kitchen.

'Know what's good for me? Just can't get it,' she heard him mumble.

She spun and met his eyes. 'You can get it. You choose not to.'

He continued to struggle up the hall, a koala on his left *and* right legs now as Kick joined his brother. Long thigh muscles strained against the fabric of his jeans as he carried a laughing boy with each step. Would she never stop noticing how beautifully put together this man was?

'Mrs Mealing,' Herb said with a nod, as he reached the kitchen.

Her mother, making lunches for the next day, turned to greet him. Her face moved from surprise to a frown. She placed a hand on her hip. 'You're a brave man, Herb Lawson.' She made eye contact with Birdie.

'I'm sure you've used lesser words to describe me.'

'You'd be right.' Lenore turned back to her work.

Herb's eyes lowered, mouth made a thin line. He took a long breath, physically stung. He rubbed Kick's head absently. The comfort of little people; she knew the feeling. 'I'm sorry, Mrs Mealing. It was not my intention to upset your daughter.'

'I'm sure it wasn't, but you did.'

Sadness swam through the muddy gold pools. 'Something I'm learning to accept the consequences of,' he said quietly.

Birdie's heart ached in a way that had her struggling to cool the heat that was suddenly in her throat. She coughed. 'Okay, boys. Leave Herb alone now.'

'Actually, you should be heading off to bed,' said their mother. She shooed them away, ignoring their protests.

'Read us a book, Herb?' Rusty said.

Herb checked Lenore for approval.

'Just one and then Herb and Birdie have work to do for Uncle Larry.'

Birdie entered the kitchen and pulled two mugs out of the cupboard. She waited until she could hear the mumbling voice of Herb before turning to her mother.

'Sugar, Birdie,' whispered Lenore. 'He's got some guts. If Glen was here, he'd get a grilling. Lucky he's on that conference.'

'I know. I thought he'd just come round to *my* door.' Birdie set about making cups of tea. 'Not come to the front.'

'I hate to be on his side, love, but facing the parents is an admirable trait.'

'We were friends once.' Again, heat burnt her throat. *I'd rather him in my life than not.* 'Perhaps we can be friends again.'

'He's a sweet kid, love. You know what you're doing.'

Birdie hugged her mother. 'Thanks for sticking up for me.'

They chuckled conspiratorially. 'As if I wouldn't.'

Herb appeared from the boys' rooms.

Lenore stepped out of Birdie's embrace. 'Thanks for doing that, Herb,' she said. 'The boys do adore you.'

Herb said nothing, just nodded. Birdie passed him a cup and ushered him down the small hallway and into her suite.

'They might adore me, but your mum hates me.' Herb dropped onto the lounge in her bedroom.

'She doesn't. And if she did, it's all your own doing.' He raised a brow at her response. She shrugged a shoulder and sat on the edge of her bed, opposite. 'What have you got for me?'

'On the afternoon in question, your mate Griff Wheatley went straight from work to have a surf, on his own. His alibi is flimsy. Only one beach bum recognised *this little pig* from his photo.'

'He's not my mate.'

'Evidence would suggest otherwise.'

She opened her mouth to argue but shut it again. Let him stew over Griff. What did she care? She'd neither confirm nor deny. She steeled herself; she was not going to play. 'What about Dom?' she said, all business.

'Dom was at work until he left for basketball.'

'Is that what he told you?'

'That's what he told his solicitor.'

Birdie sipped her tea and stood. What if Dom had got into his car when Sue, the secretary, said she saw him? What if he'd driven over to the *Gallie Wallen Gazette*, stabbed Warwick and then driven onto the game? She put down her tea and reached towards the little bedside table for last night's water glass.

Warm fingers nabbed her wrist mid-flight. 'What do you know, Birdie?'

She side-eyed their owner. 'About?' She slid her hand out, grabbed the water and went over to her plant.

'Dom's alibi.'

She watered the soil but didn't turn around. 'I think I've mentioned everything I know.' *Tiny lie.*

'Think again.' She heard the frustration in his voice, the sound of his fingers dragging through his hair, him lifting from the lounge. 'Mention it again,' he said, his voice behind her ear, demanding. *So* Herb. She turned to face him. *Big mistake.* He was too close. Fervour shimmered from him.

She swallowed. 'His secretary said—'

'You spoke to his secretary?'

'I might have bumped into her.'

'When you were at Percy's three days ago.'

'That might have been when.'

'There's no might about it, Birdie.' His voice was deep and boiling.

He'd never really let her get away with much, and he was obviously not going to start now. *Bold move in your fragile position, Detective.*

'What did she say?' he pushed.

She considered him for a moment. 'She saw Dom at his car when she left at about four.'

'Getting in?'

'She presumed he was retrieving his gym bag to get ready for basketball. The game was at 5:20.'

'But he could have got in and driven away?'

That's what I thought, but she said nothing.

'I needed this information, Birdie. You said you wouldn't get between me and my work for your uncle.'

'I can't help it if I ask the right questions of the right people'—she raised her chin—'*Detective.*'

His eyes searched hers. Black, ginger-tipped lashes framed gold circles of flame. Her mind flew to another time when they'd been in this room, discussing a case. When Herb hadn't been able to keep his hands off her as they threw ideas around.

You're hot when you're worked up, teach.

She'd brought those hands – as they'd circled her waist, dragged her to him, her dressing gown opening ... and those lips, as they'd kissed her soundly and then dropped to brush the skin of her breast – to mind many a time when she'd been in her bed, on her own, in the dark. Heat surged through her. She could feel it rising up her neck.

Herb leaned in. 'Anything else you want to share?' His whisper caressed the burn of her skin, a half grin changing the temper of his face. Did he read the memory in her eyes? *Recognise my flush?*

'I think that's all.' She wrapped her dressing gown tighter and stepped back, breaking the tiny fever bubble they'd been in. 'I'm committed to working together on this ... for Uncle Larry.'

'Are you?'

'That's all we have now, Herb.'

He reached up and dragged a hand down one silk sleeve. 'Yet you tempt me in your PJs and dressing gown. Like old times.'

You have been remembering too. Heat shot from her neck down through her torso and then on to places below. She could kiss him. His beautiful mouth was so close. She could *feel* those lips on her instead of having to reminisce, imagine.

She reached her hand up and ran a finger gently across the softness of his bottom lip, heard the intake of his breath. 'Where were you, Herb?'

'Birdie please,' he all but whispered. 'Can't we just—

'Do you know how many times I've had to imagine these lips on mine? Months of imagining. And here they are. Round and soft and so very close.' She traced the top lip back the other way.

'Jesus.'

'I've imagined them here.' She ran a finger along her lips. His eyes followed.

'Here.' She ran a hand down her chest, cupped a breast. He let out a short breath.

Her hand continued down her body. 'And here,' she whispered.

'Christ's sake, Birdie.' He reached for her, but she stopped his hand.

'Where were you?'

'Please, teach. It's best you don't know.'

She stepped back. 'So you *weren't* on Country.'

His eyes grew wide. Guilt was written all over them. Herb was never good at disguising emotion.

Hers narrowed. 'Where were you?'

A knock on the door stopped any further interrogation on her part. Birdie's head swung towards the knock. Herb left her side and was through the bathroom door in two large steps.

Lenore stuck her head around the doorframe. 'I'm off to bed.'

'Night, Mum.'

'Herb?' She assessed the arch through which three doors – one that led to the study, one to an ensuite and one that led outside – were located.

'In the bathroom,' Birdie answered.

'Say goodnight for me.'

'Will do.'

Birdie *knew* there was more to it than being on Country. He had planned to go to Country, that was true. They'd discussed it. But he'd left too soon. They'd discussed her settling back into school before he left, but she'd started the term alone. If he had decided to go earlier, why hadn't he at least said goodbye? This was something else. Something before Country. Something sudden. What could have happened?

Herb ambled from the bathroom and picked up his tea.

'We have to work out who else might have stabbed Warwick, Herb. Let's focus on that.' She'd focus on where he'd *actually* gone in her own time and perhaps with Vinny's help.

'And we need to know if Dom went somewhere in his car,' Herb said.

Griff, Santa, Dom and even Sister T all had an obvious motive and, technically, opportunity. *What was the other one?* Means!

'What about the knife?' Birdie said.

'Came from the kitchen of the gazette.' And so, they all had means.

'This is getting us nowhere. Money, power, revenge, love.' She smiled at Herb.

He returned the smile. It was a familiar list of motives. During Uncle Larry's disappearance, Stu had prescribed these four things were the reasons people committed a crime.

Revenge seemed obvious. One stabbing for one dirty secret published.

Power. By circumstance in Emer's case, over an old friend, if it was Santa.

Money? Did anyone stand to benefit financially? Only the blackmailer, but they could benefit whether Warwick was editor or not.

'Love,' they both said at the same time.

Herb held Birdie's gaze. He may profess love, but if that were true, why did he leave, and why was he keeping secrets?

She broke the contact. 'Dom and Sister T are very close. He knows her secret and is very protective. We know that from listening in on their chat in the ...' Birdie's mind raced back to the confessional box. Herb's hand on her skin, his lips on her neck. His front pressed against her back.

Herb shifted in his seat. Readjusting himself after having the same thoughts, she guessed. Could she have a physical relationship with Herb and be done with the consequences?

'Did you see anyone else while you were ... gone, Herb?'

'See anyone?'

'Romantically?'

'Birdie.' Herb stood, anger on his face.

'It's a legitimate question.'

'Did you?'

'I asked you first.'

He exhaled. 'You know I didn't.'

She studied him. She did know. She could feel it. Whatever Herb had been doing, it wasn't sleeping around. She wasn't going to let him get off that easily, though. 'I only have your word for it, Herb. The word of a man who keeps secrets.'

He shook his head and flopped back onto the lounge, lifting his eyes to the ceiling. She should change the subject. She herself had not been exactly honest when it came to lovers. Herb had seen her with Jonathon. Had he heard what they'd discussed?

Love. Was this what it was like? This push and pull?

Sister T was a nun. She had no man to love, no children to love.

Birdie considered Herb. 'Would you kill for love?'

Herb met her eyes and held them for a moment. He stood again. 'Probably should go.' He rubbed his fingers back and forth across his forehead.

'Herb?'

'Need to speak to Larry about Dom's lack of alibi.'

She'd upset him. Why couldn't she upset him and be happy about it? 'Are you okay?'

'Yeah. Just getting late.' He squeezed her arm.

And he was gone.

SIXTEEN

BIRDIE'S EYES JERKED OPEN.

It was Thursday morning.

She sat up straight in bed.

The paper had already been delivered to hundreds of homes.

She threw back the covers and ran for the bathroom. Their delivery boy didn't come until the afternoon, but she'd be able to get a copy from the gazette's offices. A freshly printed pile was always available outside its doors.

Birdie evaluated herself in the mirror. She had tossed and turned, not thinking she'd ever be able to get to sleep the night before, but she must have eventually dropped off. Her hair was a bird's nest of knots, her eyes puffy and resting in shadow. Why hadn't she made stopping the *Gallie Wallen Gazette*'s next edition a priority?

She showered, dressed, applied a little concealer, and picked up her hairbrush. Her fingers were shaking.

Calm down, Birdie. Jonathon has paid the money. The entry would not be about him, about you.

She dealt with the knots, made a piece of toast, packed her things, jumped in the car, pulled out the choke, waited for the Gypsy to warm up and headed for the Little Shops.

The town tempted her into a false security with its silence. The milkman with his giant Clydesdale the only sign a new day was beginning. She watched the placid strides of the enormous horse before manoeuvring safely around him. A wave to the runner as the horse led itself, riderless, along the familiar path and stopped outside the next house.

Did the mayor have the power to shut a paper down? Could the law? Probably not, seeing there was such a thing as freedom of the press. Although a man *had* been stabbed. Could that be seen as a danger to the public? Why hadn't she at least enquired about a possible shutdown? Or a wrapping up of the *Shame Game, No Names* feature? She had connections to the mayor.

She pulled up in front of the office of the Gallie Wallan Gazette, her heart beating wildly. It was in the same row of shops as Fidele's. There was also a bottle shop, a general store, a milk bar, a hairdresser's and the post office slash dry cleaners. Plus, the library across the road. She opened her door, darted out and grabbed a copy of the latest edition.

Inside the Gypsy, she rifled through the pages until she got to *Shame Game, No Names*.

She ran her finger along the words: *'Which MIA state school TOOL of a principal "accidentally" overordered on building supplies ...'*

She expelled an enormous breath.

It wasn't about Jonathon.

It wasn't about her.

Relief soared through her bones like a love song.

When she'd stopped shaking, she focused on the entry again and read it all the way through.

Which MIA state school TOOL of a principal "accidentally" overordered on school building supplies? What could the tool possibly do with all the excess? ... Add a room (and value) to his own house, perhaps? Is that a "For Sale" sign I see?

Oh dear! This opportunistic principal had used funds – provided by the government and meant to improve his school – to fix up his own home. To make a greater profit when he sold it.

The relief that it hadn't been about her only made her realise that if she was feeling this ragged wondering her fate, what about Sister T – if she was feeling any of the anxiety that Birdie had this morning, it was a wonder she was still standing. Luckily, no women were mentioned in today's entry. Although 'family home' suggested a family. A wife.

Birdie was momentarily lost in the world of Uncle Doug, the irreverent DJ who ruled morning radio. As the song finished, his voice broke through.

'Scorpio'—Doug began in a loose Hungarian accent. He was performing as one of his alter-egos, star-woman Venus Imayour—'you remember that the words "follow the money" are figurative and not literal a little too late today, when you dive off a cliff after a twenty-dollar note that was blown away on the wind.'

Birdie giggled – feeling able to, now that her fate had not ended in dire straits.

Follow the money.

Why hadn't she thought of that? If they'd followed the money, they could have found out who the blackmailer and possible supplier of gossip was. She hated to admit that Stu probably would have thought it.

Although, if she followed the money ... would she have to explain how she knew to follow the money? That being: blackmail. Uncle Larry would certainly want to know why looking into bank accounts had any bearing on the situation. Admitting an affair was not a conversation she wanted to have with her uncle. How could she pass on the information without revealing her connection to it?

Would Herb find out?

Could she pass on this information without anyone she loved finding out about what she'd done?

Birdie pulled into the staff car park at Saint Joan of Arc and stepped out of her car. Another car door shut as she closed her own. Jonathon started walking towards her, having stepped out of the only other vehicle – thank God – in the car park. The morning sun caught the gold in his hair, sparkled off the blue of his eyes and reflected the white of his smile.

'We're safe,' he said.

'Alive to fight another day.' She offered a close-lipped smile.

He hugged her, moved a lock of hair from her face with way too much familiarity. 'That was close. Perhaps we could get a drink later to celebrate?'

She stayed still. She could not entertain any thoughts he may have. 'Good luck with the new job, Jonathon.' She removed his hand from her face. 'I hope it goes well.' He contemplated her for a moment before nodding.

She watched his car leave, grabbed her things from the Gypsy and closed the door. When she turned, she was face to face with Herb.

'Who's the guy?' A heatwave of hostility.

Shit! Birdie's heartbeat sped up. 'Get back, Jojo,' she said (the Beatles had a lyric for every possible occasion) and started walking towards the school.

Herb moved into her path. His interest locked on her. 'I'm exactly ... where I belong.'

Shithead. Damn him. *And the Beatles.*

She tried to step around him, but he moved with her.

Arsehole.

His temper sparked. 'Answer the question.'

She would not answer his bloody question. Anger pushed up through the fear. Her teeth clenched. She moved air back and forth through her nose. She needed to keep her cool. She fought to shove the fire down. 'He's just an old teaching friend.'

'*Name*, Birdie.'

Bloody hell. 'Jonathon.' She fixed her attention on the school building.

He cupped her chin and dragged her face to his. Commanded her devotion and waited. She pushed her lips together. She was saying no more.

'I'm dogged, Birdie,' he said slowly. 'You of all people should know that.'

She stared at him.

'Isn't he the same guy you were speaking to last week?'

She shifted her focus.

'If he's a teacher, he shouldn't be too hard to find.'

She flicked her eyes back to his. Would Herb be able to find out about her and Jonathon through his contacts on the force, or elsewhere? 'Naylor,' she answered through her teeth. Perhaps if she didn't resist, he wouldn't bother.

He dropped his hand. 'What does he want?'

Birdie started to sweat. She'd tried so hard to keep Jonathon a secret. Was their liaison about to be revealed? 'He was worried he'd be the next victim of *Shame Game, No Names.*' Not a lie.

'Done something wrong, has he?'

She began to walk again. 'He slept with someone he shouldn't have.' God, she was skirting close to the truth.

'Why is he meeting with you?'

'Why the twenty questions?'

He stopped her again. 'Answer them.' His growly tone did nothing to calm her.

'He knows Uncle Larry's representing Sister T and Dom.' *It's possible he did. People would know.* 'He thought I might be able to help.'

'Why did you hug him?'

'Did it look like I had a choice?' She grabbed Herb's chin, mirroring his action from before, and moved his face to hers. 'Sometimes men think they can touch you however they want.' She could see his cogs turning, anger flashing. She let go of his chin. 'It's easier to go with it.' And it was definitely easier to just go with it this morning with Jonathon.

'So you didn't want to?'

'Did I look like I did? Did I lean into it, Detective?' She leaned into him for effect, then pulled away. She started for the school again. 'What do you think?' she continued as he kept pace. 'You've been watching me closely. I thought your job was to discover anything that might help Sister T and Dom. Does Uncle Larry know you're scrutinising my every move?'

Herb's face registered the guilt she'd been vying for. *Alleluia.* She slid past him quickly and pushed open the door.

'Birdie, I am not finished with this.'

She turned. 'I think I've made it pretty clear that I am.' She went straight to the toilet and let out a breath that fogged the glass. *That was close.*

It was quiet in the nooks. Cradling a cup of tea, with shaking hands, she scanned beyond the window and wondered what Herb would do now, if he was still out there watching.

'I need to talk to you.'

Birdie jumped. She turned to see Brad's face alive with concern.

'Did you see the newest *Shame Game, No Names*?' he hissed.

She nodded. *Gratefully, not about me.*

'That's what I want to talk to you about.'

Birdie thought back to the entry. Surely Brad had nothing to do with the latest entry. He wasn't a state school principal syphoning building supplies.

'My friend is in a bit of a predicament,' he whispered, looking around the nook, even though, clearly, at this time of the morning, they were the only two people around.

She shuffled him to her desk. 'Your friend who's building a new room onto his house using school materials?'

'No, I'm not friends with him. I don't even know who he is. This is someone different.'

'Ohhkay?'

'I can't tell you who it is and actually, it's probably best you don't know for now anyway.' Slightly dramatic, but then again, it was Brad.

'What's your friend's predicament then?' She tapped the side of her nose – the sign for *I know your friend is really you, but I'll keep your secret* – and winked at him.

He lifted his eyes to the ceiling. 'It's not me. This friend is a principal. I told you about him the other day, Jonathon Naylor's son's principal.'

'But not the tool?'

'No! Will you forget about the tool?' Brad pushed his clasped hands together. He wiped a hand over his mouth. 'My friend, who is also a principal, *not the tool*, has been getting threatening mail regarding something he did years ago that is probably not in the principal's code of conduct. A dirty little secret.'

Dirty little secret.

Birdie's mind raced to her conversation with Jonathon. *Threatening mail.* She inhaled. Not the subject of today's entry but possibly the next. 'Are they asking for money?'

'Yes, someone's blackmailing my friend.'

'Holy shit, Brad.'

'How did you know?'

'What did he do?'

'He's the principal of a religious school. Their views on homosexuality are much more, shall we say, conservative than most. They don't even tolerate staff being gay, so if the principal was found out, he'd be crucified. And probably, literally.'

'There are heaps of gay people in schools. So long as they are sensible about their lifestyle, it shouldn't be a problem. I know it's ridiculous, but if he's quiet, he'll be right. How will they be able to prove it?'

'They have video evidence.'

Shit! 'Of what ... exactly?'

'I'm concerned your virgin ears may be a bit shocked when I describe it.'

She slapped his arm. 'Just tell me!'

'When he was younger, he was at a disco and was approached by the producers of a reputable gay porno production company. My friend was very good-looking and had a very spunky body when he was a tadpole – I think he still does, personally. At the time, he had just turned sixteen.'

'Sixteen! Far out that's young.'

'I know. At sixteen, I was definitely not going to discos.'

'Except school discos.'

'Yes, Birdie. I went to those. I was talking about gay discos. Come to think of it, I was even still trying out girls at sixteen, though I was fairly sure they didn't fit!'

Birdie remembered Brad from school. Tall, dark and handsome. Their very own Clark Kent. He'd had lots of girlfriends. She'd fancied him herself for a bit. Had passed notes back and forth through Stu for a couple of weeks.

'Anyway, as you can imagine, they dangled more cash than he could count in front of him and said porno was made. I've seen it. It's very tame. That porno and several more kept him afloat while at teachers' college.'

'But who would have seen it? If the school is that against homosexuality, no offence, then who would have *actually* seen it?'

'That's a good point. Although, the lady doth protest too much, methinks, so ... probably the whole school board.'

Birdie laughed. 'If he was sixteen, would anybody even recognise him now?'

'All I know is, he's devastated, and packing shit and I have to *help* him.'

'He doesn't need to worry. Just pay the blackmail money and all will be well.'

'I think he is going to, but he's concerned that even if he pays it, there's no guarantee the scandal won't be brought to light anyway.'

This might very well be the time to explain how she knew that paying the blackmail money would keep them safe. 'I have to tell you something, but you can't tell anyone.'

'Cross my heart and hope to die, stick a needle in my eye.' Birdie explained how she knew this to be the case – in a roundabout way, using no names and not implicating herself.

'I wondered how you knew about the money. That does make me feel better. I will pass it on.'

If the gossip about Jonathon *wasn't* published, then Griff, Dom, Naughty Santa, and the subject of today's entry, 'the tool', mustn't've paid up.

Why wouldn't they?

Granted, they might not have taken the threat seriously, but everyone had seen the first entry. It stands to reason that after the second, then the third, there was clearly intent behind the threat. Why wouldn't you pay? Birdie remembered Jonathon had said the amount was substantial. Had it been too much for the others?

The sounds of other teachers entering the staff area signalled the end of their discussion.

'Might make a cuppa and a phone call,' Brad said, heading for the archway.

'Just how friendly is this friend, Brad?'

He glimpsed back over his shoulder and flashed a smile. 'The friendliest kind.'

Certain types of men out
there aren't going to make
you very happy, and some may
make you downright
miserable. Since women still
tend to connect sex and
romance, many casual
encounters fuelled by lust
turn into more durable
relationships, often ending
badly.

'Looking for Mr Right?
Twelve types of men to avoid'
Cleo, December 1983.

SEVENTEEN

B IRDIE WANDERED FROM ROOM to room in the music block, supervising rehearsals. Some girls were preparing for performances that needed grading and some for the end-ofterm liturgy. She rehearsed a song of her own in her head, going through the chords and lyrics for a new addition to her playlist at Fidele's

She checked out the clock. Five minutes to recess. Her eye was taken by Charmaine's dancer's frame as it moved irregularly in the contemporary style of ballet that was all the rage. With Carly's haunting acapella vocals of 'Somebody' by Depeche Mode, she was mesmerised for a moment. It was almost a shame to pack them up.

The staffroom was abuzz with bodies as she took a seat at the table next to Brad. Speculation about who might be 'the tool' was the topic of conversation.

'It's got to be Todd Jones from Kingsdown West. They've had work being done all term,' said Brad.

'It would be easy to check too,' someone said. 'All you'd have to do is see if Todd's house is up for sale.'

The gossip column was situated about halfway through the rag. Birdie read the entry again and absentmindedly turned the pages backwards to view the serious news. Reading the paper in full had become of secondary importance since *Shame Game*.

'She's right,' said Brad. 'Does anyone know where he lives?'

A headline caught Birdie's eye. She froze, sucked in a breath. Her eyes darted to the people around her, oblivious to her state of panic.

Why hadn't she noticed this article before? Why hadn't anyone pointed it out to her? Was everyone, including herself, so caught up in *Shame Game, No Names* that they'd missed it? She pulled the paper onto her lap under the table and read the headline again.

> **What do we really know about Larry Kean, Solicitor to the Stars? By Emer Garland.**

'Apparently, Todd's taken leave and is holidaying with his family at their property in Huskisson,' said Sabine. 'Makes him look a bit guilty, doesn't it?'

Birdie let the conversation carry on around her as she focused on the paper and skimmed the story.

> It's been almost four months since solicitor-to-the-stars, Larry Kean, was reportedly bundled into a black car and driven away from his workplace, leaving family and friends terrified for his safety. But police have never revealed who seized him. Do they know who it was? Are they keeping this information quiet? Was he actually abducted at all?

What! What the hell was Emer playing at?

'I heard Todd's got a job down south and has no intention of returning,' a teacher said.

'What better reason to sell your home,' someone else agreed.

Birdie read on.

> Laurence Bertram Kean grew up in the suburb of West Innisfail to working-class parents. He was an intelligent student and won a scholarship to the prestigious Queen Elizabeth College in Sydney. There, he met another intelligent scholarship recipient, and son of Czech immigrants, Vincent Vel Varva. They were drawn together by circumstance and became firm friends. Years later, Kean – originally trained as an accountant – decided to become a lawyer, turning his back on the increasingly worrisome actions of his buddy Vinny in favour of the law. This is when their friendship dissolved ... But did it?

There was a picture of Vinny and Uncle Larry in high school, arms around each other and smiles on their faces. Another person was in the photo. A girl. Her arm was around Vinny's on the opposite side to Uncle Larry, and her face was turned, speaking to someone over her shoulder. It looked like ... Birdie pulled the paper closer to her face ... *Lenore*. They would have been about fourteen. She knew they'd gone to high school together but seeing proof was ... unsettling.

As reported by ABC's investigative affairs program *Uncovered,* while working as an accountant, Kean's main client was the now-infamous crime figure Velvet Vinny Varva. Velvet Vinny has recently been released from jail after serving almost ten years for murder. A crime of which he has since been acquitted. Kean was instrumental in securing Varva's release after uncovering "new" information. But where was this information during the first investigation and the subsequent investigation for Vincent Varva's first appeal? Are we to believe that Larry Kean is that good that he was the only person to stumble upon this new evidence? Evidence that freed Vinny.

Yes, you bloody-well are. And yes, he bloody-well is! Not only that, but Birdie helped find some of this evidence, with help from Stu and Pia.

Kean's ties with Velvet Vinny run deep. Did Vinny have anything to do with Kean's disappearance or his reappearance? Was it just a coincidence that Kean's abduction coincided with Vinny's acquittal?

Admittedly, this was a question Birdie had asked herself and one she'd asked Vinny. Emer Garland was speculating about nothing that she hadn't already asked herself. She just wished it wasn't being done in such a public forum.

We've already had a visit from an associate of Kean's seeking our cooperation.

What!

The cocktail sipping – think Tequila Sunrises, Fluffy Ducks – goddaughter/honorary niece/band member/music therapist/teacher (how she has time to teach, one wonders)/self-determined investigative assistant, Birdie Mealing, who was also instrumental in the activities surrounding Vinny's case.

What the hell was Emer playing at? Was she suggesting Birdie was some sort of undefinable, directionless ... drunk?

But if Larry Kean is still thick with Velvet Vinny Varva, should we here at the gazette be concerned about our interactions with him or his associates? Should the people of Gallie Wallen Shire be concerned? Do we have mob bosses and ambitious attorneys and amateur sleuths – who are obviously upset about our spotlight on unscrupulous teachers – running our town, deciding who's guilty and when? And if so, will the truth of who tried to kill our editor see the light of day? The clues point to Sister Scarlett ... with the knife ... in the kitchen.

Birdie gasped. She'd used the joke she'd invented when they'd met and tweaked it to suit Sister T!

>But will the events of this case be manipulated to suit the players who seem to have all the power? Are they planning on taking over the paper? Making our community gazette a vessel for propaganda the way Hitler did?

Hitler! Now, that was a bit of a stretch.

>You might scoff: all the above is pure speculation.

Ya think?!

>And to be honest, this editor's normal practice of digging deep is coming up with very few definitive answers.

Ha! Sucked in.

>Which only makes my speculation more interesting, wouldn't you say?

She tapped Brad on the knee. 'Did you see this article?' She pointed at the paper.

He pulled the page closer. 'No! I only looked at *Shame Game.*'

'Emer is trying to make it look like Larry is dodgy. And that he's in cahoots with Vinny.' *And I'm a ditsy sidekick.*

No one had mentioned the article that morning. It made sense, she supposed. At present, teachers were only interested in finding out if they were the subject of *Shame Game, No Names*, or – once clarifying they weren't the subject – if they could work out who it was?

'You're famous – again!' whispered Brad.

'For all the wrong reasons.' Birdie grabbed the offending page, smashed it into a ball and lobbed it into the bin.

Brad's expression displayed instant glee, but he wisely kept his lips tightly pulled together.

'Nice shot, Miss Mealing!' Sister T said as she marched into the staffroom.

Brad folded the rest of the paper in half and slid it under his leg.

'I hope, like Birdie, everyone's ready for Chalkies' Challenge this afternoon.' There was a general murmur of agreement. 'Excellent. We're playing Percy's tonight and I want to wipe the floor with them,' she said in a growl, a hand sweeping across the tabletop. She resumed her pleasant persona. 'See you there.'

Birdie grinned. If Sister T *was* the person who had stabbed Warwick, then she was obviously a sociopath if that last exchange was any indicator.

Had it only been a week since Warwick had been stabbed? It felt like much longer.

At least they could rule out 'the tool', if the tool was Todd Jones. Surely it would be a difficult task to stab someone when you're currently living four hours south.

❦ ❦ ❦

Fidele's smelled like heaven as Birdie made her way inside from the back entrance and past the kitchen. Aromas wrapped around her and floated her in. Whatever the special was, she was looking forward to it. She was *hungry*!

The game against Percy's had been hard won, much to Sister T's delight. It was good to see her worry-free for a few minutes.

Fidele beamed when he saw her. *'Bonjour, alouette.'*

'Bonjour, monsieur,' Birdie replied.

Fidele had started calling her alouette – 'lark' in English – from the time she'd sung *'La Vie en Rose'* and stopped his heart. Falling in love sounded so much better in French.

'Ah. You will love the special tonight. *Il est Langoustine.'*

'Langoustine?'

'Urm. Lobster.'

'Oh wow! Okay.'

Fidele was right. She did love the special. The lobster was served in a melted butter sauce and had a side of greens. It was amazing, had made her stomach sing. Fitting really. She was about to make her voice do the same.

Birdie watched the action from her little stage in the corner, patrons enjoying their meals, waitstaff smiling and nodding, Fidele flitting around like a dragonfly – swoop, hover, dart off again.

A familiar face stood just inside the door. The woman waved a hand at those already seated at a table, spoke briefly to Fidele and then moved over to join them.

Emer Garland, acting editor.

Singing at a restaurant was an interesting gig. Birdie people-watched the lovers, friends, business associates, loners. Some would clap after each song, others were so caught up in the moment they didn't even realise she was there. Someone on Emer's table applauded as Birdie finished her latest song, 'Jesse', obviously a fan of Carly Simon's. Emer absentmindedly joined in, lifting her head for the first time to look at the musician who was supplying the tunes. Birdie met her surprised eye and smiled. Emer's face fell flat and turned back to the table.

'Hi, Emer,' Birdie said as she wandered over on her break.

'Hello, Miss Mealing.'

'I caught the latest edition this morning.'

'Did you?'

'You have such an incredible way with words.' *The article about my uncle, for example.*

A small grin crept into the left side of Emer's lips.

Birdie was ready to wipe that smile away. 'Did you know that whoever is supplying your paper with the gossip for *Shame Game, No Names* is also blackmailing their victims?'

Emer's face told Birdie that she did *not* know that. It also told her the acting editor was probably not the blackmailer, as Birdie had considered.

Emer recovered quickly. 'I don't think that's true.'

'Well, think again. How does it feel to take advantage of people who can't afford to keep their secrets quiet?'

'How much money someone makes is really none of my business. Besides, unless you are behaving badly, you have nothing to worry about.'

One of the men at the table leaned into Emer. 'We should review this place in the gazette, boss. This lobster is amazing.'

'Boss?' It seemed Emer continued to own her new role. 'A work function? How lovely.' Emer didn't respond. Birdie smiled. 'Enjoy your night.' Obviously, their real boss being in the hospital hadn't dampened their spirits. Before she walked away, Birdie leaned down and whispered in Emer's ear, 'Off the record, I was the one who worked out the real killer of Robert Crown. I wonder whether I'll be the one who works out that Warwick Woods was assaulted because of your nasty column?' Birdie didn't look back as she walked away.

The *Gallie Wallen Gazette* staff were fixing up the bill and gathering their belongings as Birdie started her last song. She was finishing with the one she'd been practising all day, 'I Should Have Known Better' by English artist Jim Diamond.

Just as Emer was making her way out the doors, Herb made his way in. His eyes met Birdie's as she crooned about lies, regret and losing love.

⇔ ⇔ ⇔

Birdie sat on the stool next to Herb at the bar. 'Good timing,' she said.

'Not my first rodeo.'

She laughed despite herself.

He gave her a half grin. 'Was that song for my benefit?'

'You're a bit up yourself. Although, I'll take victories where I can get them. Especially when it comes to you.'

He turned to face her, expression sincere. 'Sorry I went off my nut this morning.'

'Did you? I hadn't noticed.' Birdie did *not* want to revisit Jonathon's appearance this morning or Herb's push for answers. Luckily, the bartender took that moment to pass over her post-performance champagne.

'This is where we first met, Bird.' He smoothed his hands along the bar. 'Just like this.'

She lifted her glass and watched the tiny bubbles pop. 'Why did you take me home with you that first night?'

He side-eyed her as if it was pretty obvious.

'Apart from the sex,' she said.

Herb fiddled with the basket of *pomme frites* in front of him.

Birdie lifted a chip and blew on it. 'I've known you for a while now'—she popped it in her mouth and swallowed—'and it doesn't strike me as something you'd do, picking up strange girls at a bar.'

'You were the one and only, Bird. You weren't strange. And this is not a bar.' He ate another *frite*. 'I'd watched you for weeks. Was devvo when you slunk away in the morning.'

Birdie remembered trying to leave Herb's house as quietly as possible the morning after. She'd got halfway across his front lawn, the sun only just beginning to rise before she'd heard his voice calling her name.

'Would have liked you to have hung around.' Herb went back to fiddling with the chips.

Girls just wanna have fun had been Birdie's motto back then. She hadn't wanted to be tied down.

He lifted his head to the side. 'Do you think we could start over?'

Birdie sipped her champagne. 'I don't think so, Herb. We haven't really finished the first time. Don't we need to end one thing before beginning another?'

Herb drank his beer. The grin on his face widening into a full smile.

'What are you smiling at?'

'You just said we haven't finished yet.'

'Herb.'

'No take-backs.'

She huffed a laugh. Why couldn't she just ignore everything that had gone before and pick up where they'd left off? Why could her uncle welcome him into his home, but she couldn't welcome him into her heart, her bed?

She pondered the arm that rested against the bar – lean forearm muscles toned and dusted with fine hair, those amazing hands attached. Not only did they look beautiful, but they did beautiful things. She could reach out, run her fingers along them, pull them around her waist. Have them do those beautiful things tonight. Why had she made that bold statement that they were over? Now she couldn't go back on her word. Tears threatened the bottom of her lids.

'I'm tired,' she said, getting up to go. 'It's been a big week.'

'Birdie.' Herb grabbed her forearm; his hand slid down her wrist and stopped in hers.

The intimacy sent electricity through her. She met his eyes – dragonfly wings trapped in amber – her resolve slipping. She felt the hook. Felt her body being reeled in. 'Emer Garland from the gazette was in the restaurant tonight,' she said. 'A staff night out.'

'Interesting, teach,' he said in a whisper. 'But not really what I was hoping to hear.'

She regarded him for a moment, willing herself to say the words he wanted to hear. 'I know that feeling,' she said instead and pulled her hand away.

⧓ ⧓ ⧓

'You look tired, love.'

Lenore was still awake when Birdie had showered, put on her pyjamas and wandered into the main house to get a drink. Her mother looked tired too. Glen would be home tomorrow morning to share the load.

'It's been a big week, Mum. Did you see the paper?'

'The article about you and Larry?'

Birdie nodded.

'He's already had a few clients on the phone seeking reassurance,' said Lenore.

The faster Birdie worked out who stabbed Warwick Woods, the better. 'Is he okay?'

'Larry's tough.' She smiled at Birdie. 'Like you. And he *was* friends with Vincent once.' The next words she mumbled. *'Still is'* was what Birdie was sure she'd said. Lenore ran her hand down her ponytail. 'His connection to Vinny can never be erased.'

And your connection to Vinny, Mum?

Lenore cleared her throat. 'You okay?'

Birdie thought about her exchange with Emer at Fidele's. 'Yep.'

'The librarian called. The yearbooks are ready for collection.'

'Excellent. Might pop in and pick them up tomorrow.' She sat next to her mum on the lounge. 'Speaking of Vinny, Mum. How would you feel about me meeting with him?'

'Why? About what? Do you think that's wise after that article?'

'I saw Vinny and Herb having a discussion under the cover of darkness the other night. I think Vinny might have something to do with where Herb disappeared to.'

Her mother sat up straight. 'Sugar, Birdie. I'm not sure I like the sound of this.'

'I really need to know, Mum. Uncle Larry won't set it up without your okay.'

Her mother frowned.

'He said you'd kill him if he did.'

'Smart man, your uncle.'

'I've met with him before.'

'That was when he was behind bars, in handcuffs, a security guard watching, and me beside you.'

'Uncle Larry will come.'

'And throw further speculation his way? I don't know, Birdie.'

It wasn't Larry's connection to Vinny that was the issue. It was Emer's attempt to discredit him. More popularity for the paper. More 'hard-hitting' reporting in Emer's name.

'I need to understand why Herb left and why he won't tell me. It's stopping me from going forward with him or cutting him off completely.' Is that what she wanted? To cut him off completely. The dull ache in her heart sent out a sharp tendril. She started to cry.

'Have you considered that Herb is doing what's best for you by not telling you?'

'He said something similar.' She blew her nose on the tissue Lenore offered. 'Are you on his side?'

'No. I'm not. All I'm saying is, if he's doing something for Vinny, it could be dangerous. Perhaps Herb wants to keep you from it.'

'Then, I need to know that too.'

Lenore smoothed a lock of hair. 'I suppose you do.' She pushed the lock behind her ear and worried her bottom lip, thinking. She untucked the hair she'd just put behind her ear.

Not for the first time did Birdie wonder about her mother's relationship with Vinny.

'I'll speak to Larry.'

EIGHTEEN

THE NERVOUSNESS OF MEETING Vinny bubbled back to the surface – her mother had spoken to Larry, and a meeting was set – as her day at Evesong was coming to an end. The familiar chords of 'The Happy Wanderer' had brought a smile to the faces of the choir. They loved it, its yodelling chorus always a favourite.

Luckily she had Mrs N's chatter to fill her thoughts as they walked to Uncle Larry's car.

'How you going with who stab Warwick?' Mrs N said.

'We have a list of suspects.' Birdie sighed. 'Just working through them. What's the word on the Retirement Village street?'

'Everyone has opinion. But, I find funny, no one is big sorry Warwick is stabbed.'

'They don't like him?'

'Many think gazette should be about them, their worries. Warwick'—she lifted her shoulders and dropped them—'not so much, thought this.'

Birdie hid a grin. Oldies were a great group for sending in complaints and opinions to the local rag. Potholes and traffic, buildings going up, dogs barking, rubbish, late buses and trains, crime. Not to mention character and morals.

'Anything in particular that might warrant substantial rage?' Not that she could ever imagine one of the Evesong community attacking.

'My friends can't even sing with note, as if one could stab.'

Birdie laughed out loud.

'Scared are some. Dangerous man is on loose.'

'Let's hope it is a dangerous man, so Sister T is cleared.'

'Yes, great! Dangerous man is running free, such is a good thought.'

Birdie laughed again. 'Sarcasm is the lowest form of wit, Mrs N.'

'But highest form of intelligence, is rest of quote. Oscar Wilde.'

Mrs N waved at Larry who had just pulled up. 'You will work it out,' she said. Not a question. She was always so confident in Birdie's abilities.

'I hope so.'

Mrs N bent down to say hello to Larry through the car window. When she straightened, she hugged Birdie good-bye. ' Herb is good boy. I'm sure this is something important that kept him away. You will see.' Mrs N said quietly.

⬭ ⬭ ⬭

A large window spanned most of the little coffee shop, in Alexandria's, frontage. A signwriter's graphics mirrored an arched window and a ledge briming with flowers. Gold leaf swirls bringing to life the steam rising from a cup of coffee perched in the centre. The solitary figure seated inside, encased in all the charm, could only have been Velvet Vinny Varva.

'Do you want me to come in?' her uncle asked, turning off the car at the kerb.

'I'll be right.'

She studied Vinny, drinking from a small, handleless ceramic cup, as she walked towards his table. He stood as she approached, taller than she remembered.

'What are you doing with Herb?' Birdie was supposed to start with 'hello', but the rage had rushed along her arms into her chest and through her mouth like a broken dam – like the escape of water from Mickey's pails in *Fantasia*.

'Didn't your mother ever teach you to greet someone politely when you meet them?'

'Interesting you should jump straight to my mother. I'd be eager to hear what the story is with you and Lennie?'

By using the nickname Vinny himself had used for her mother, Lennie, she hoped to rattle him a little. Rattling a mobster may not be a sensible idea, but she'd chance it.

He resumed his seat. The aroma of coffee wafted from his cup as he brought it to his lips and back again. 'Sit.' He indicated with a brief nod. Birdie didn't move. He sighed. 'Please sit down, Miss Mealing.'

She dropped into the chair.

He leaned back and rested an ankle on the knee of his other leg. He lit a cigarette. 'Herb Lawson interviewed me when he was working Illario's, your Uncle Larry's, case. I met with him because I wanted to say thank you.'

'Bullshit.'

He coughed out a laugh. 'I would offer you coffee.' He held up the small cup. 'But this is too sweet a drop for that mouth.'

She ignored his jibe and continued. 'The trial was months ago. Why did you meet on the street, in the dark, just this week?' She leaned forward. 'Were you waiting for a gibbous moon?'

Another laugh. 'So like your mother.'

'Oh. So, *now* you want to talk about Mum?' He'd ignored her last reference to her mother. Would he bite at this one? 'How long have you known her?'

'You know the answer to that.'

'Since high school.'

He stared at her.

'I wonder what severed ties?'

Nothing. Just a drag on his cigarette.

'Was *only* you going bad?' she tapped her chin.

They continued to maintain eye contact. Since her uncle's case, Birdie had wondered whether Vinny Varva might be her biological father. His barely contained visceral connection to her mother, the fact that he knew her baptismal name, the way he spoke to Birdie like he owned her, like she was a child – *his child?* – had made her curious.

He blew out the smoke. 'You finished, *holčička*?'

Case in point. 'For now.'

'Herb has been away. This was simply the first chance I got.'

'More bullshit.'

He sat forward. 'I humoured you when I was in jail.' His voice unnervingly low, she could smell the coffee and cigarettes on his breath. 'I am a free man now.'

Birdie swallowed. She turned towards the window, the outline of Uncle Larry in his car just outside. She took a deep breath and refocused on Vinny, matching his menace, and leaned in. 'You might remember that a certain someone had a hand in finding their uncle, which in turn helped secure *your* freedom.'

He sat back. 'And for that, I will always be indebted to you.' He bowed his head. '*Dekuju*, Birdie.' He held up his cup and drank.

She sat back too. 'Why did Herb disappear?'

'I wasn't aware that he did.'

'You just said he did.'

'I said, he'd been away.'

'Where did he go?'

'On Country, as far as I know.'

'What's your connection to my mother?'

'We are old friends.'

'What do you have Herb working on?'

'Herb doesn't work for me.'

She searched his face. Could feel him searching hers. He looked better than the last time she'd seen him – less drawn, more radiant, younger. She wouldn't have said so before, but he was actually quite an attractive man. Lush dark brown hair with streaks of auburn, strong forehead and deep-set blue-green eyes that were speckled with gold. *Hair that threw red, eyes that swam with green.*

His dusty pink lips sucked on his cigarette and puffed into a pout as he blew out another drag. 'Ask him,' Vinny said.

She could see the attraction her mother might have harboured. If she indeed harboured one.

'I have asked him. He's telling me nothing.'

She caught a small raise of Vinny's left eyebrow, a slight lift at the corner of his mouth.

She leaned forward. 'Whatever secret Herb's keeping for you is keeping us apart. Think on that, Vinny.'

He placed his cigarette in the ashtray and held his forehead in his hand, his elbow resting on his knee. Cigarette smoke floated slowly from his lips along with a muttered: '*Snesl bych ti modré z nebe.*' She had no idea what that meant. He picked up the ciggy again, waving it around as he spoke. 'He would do anything for you.' He sipped his coffee. 'You should be true to him.'

She stood up and put her hands on her hips. 'Who I'm true to is *no* concern of yours.'

Vinny lurched up too, big hands banging on the table. His coffee cup wobbled. His nostrils flared.

She burnt his gaze with her own. 'Herb just got up and walked off. Didn't look back. And you're okay with a man who does that. You think I should be true to a man who just up and leaves?' *Is that what you did to my mother?* 'Interesting.'

His hands gripped the edge of the table. The cup fell. Out of the corner of her eye, Birdie saw a thin but determined line of brown liquid spill onto the tabletop and run towards the edge. Lenore never lost her temper. Not like Birdie and the man in front of her did.

She leaned forward. 'I'll find out what's going on,' she said, anxious energy powering her words, '*Starý muz.*'

Her legs shook with anger and a little terror at the fact that she was facing off with a crime lord. Vinny's face went from fury to surprise at her use of the Czech phrase for 'old man', which sounded like *starry moosh*. He opened his mouth, threw his head back and belted out a belly laugh.

Birdie turned on her heel and marched to the door, Vinny's laughter vibrating in her ears. 'And the fact that you ignored my question about Mother, did not go unnoticed.'

Birdie just got into her uncle's car before her legs collapsed like a disturbed soufflé.

'That was quick,' Larry said.

She took a few deep breaths. 'I think I made him angry.'

'Oh, yes?'

'He slammed the table, and his nostrils were flaring.'

'Sounds like Vinny.'

'Plus, I called him an "old man" in Czechoslovakian.'

'Birdie! That's ... disrespectful,' he said, chuckling. 'How do you know how to speak Czechoslovakian?'

'He calls me *holčička*, which means "young girl" (as well as kiddo, baby girl), so I asked one of the teachers who migrated from Czechoslovakia how to say "old man". Not sure I said it correctly, though. He thought it was hilarious.'

More chuckling from her uncle. 'Did you get the answers you were looking for, darling?'

Did she? She took one last look at the shop window before Uncle Larry pulled into the traffic.

Herb doesn't work for me. Something was going on between Herb and Vinny, and it had been for some time. Birdie thought back to a discussion she'd had with Herb just after Uncle Larry had been found. Herb had suspected Vinny, and those like him, had had something to do with the activities he'd been involved in. She knew street lords had tentacles in the NSW Police Force.

I wanted to say thank you. In what way might Vinny say thanks?

If Herb was caught up in something for which his boss 'had him over a barrel', might getting out of the force be hard to do?

So many questions.

Not to mention the one she'd been thinking a lot about lately: Was Velvet Vinny Varva her father?

⇔ ⇔ ⇔

Birdie ran into the school's library and back out again with the yearbooks.

'A little bit of light reading?' said her uncle, as she jumped back into the car.

'These are the yearbooks from the archives I requested. Herb and I are supposed to be going through them ... together.' Although at present she'd rather slap him than sit down with him.

'Thanks for working with him, Birdie.'

'We're hoping to identify Saint Santa and therefore provide yet another possibility for who might have stabbed Warwick.' She needed to focus on proving Sister T was innocent.

'I appreciate how uncomfortable this may be for you. Herb seems to brighten when you're around.'

'Has he been down?'

'Perhaps there is something brewing underneath the surface.'

'Well, he's not telling me anything.'

Uncle Larry's mouth became a straight line. He breathed out a sigh but said nothing.

'How much do you know about the corruption in the NSW Police Force?' Birdie asked.

'Not a lot. Why?'

'When you were missing, the inspector told Herb to keep an eye on me. That was his job.'

'Hmm ... keep talking.' Uncle Larry pulled the handbrake on.

Birdie turned to face him. 'That Herb was trying to find out where you were seemed of ... secondary importance. As you suspected, it wasn't the main priority for the force. Pia, Stu and I thought that some of their actions were carried out so that they looked like they were following procedure but might have just been for show. Is it possible that they knew where you were because *they* put you there?'

'Are you ruminating on today's story by our intrepid reporter, Emer?'

'It's been playing on my mind.' And tensing up all her limbs and making her want to go and tell Emer to retract every word.

'I *was* given food and drink and bedding, access to a toilet.' Larry tapped his chin.

'Did anything you were working on have to do with organised crime?'

'Let me see ... misappropriation of council funds, the murder of a prominent Sydney entrepreneur, making millions from dodgy land sales ... Do you want me to go on?'

'Okay, stupid question, but could Vinny have been involved somehow?'

'Vinny does have grandiose ideas that he's in charge of everything. And actually, he has many fingers in many pies. I stopped asking about his business years ago. I was only concerned with finding out who really planted the bomb. It wouldn't surprise me what Vinny's caught up in.'

'I think Vinny is in cahoots with the police. That he's a player in organised crime and perhaps he's using his position to help Herb.'

'Interesting.'

But not really for Uncle Larry because he probably knew some of this. Was her beloved uncle letting her run her mind, her mouth, to see how close she'd get?

'Herb told me once that Inspector Draper had him over a barrel.'

'Well, that is one man I don't trust. This could be dangerous, Birdie.' Her uncle put his hands together and chewed on a nail. 'I wonder whether that explains why Herb left without a goodbye?' He raised a brow.

Smartarse. 'Because he was in immediate danger?' Birdie asked.

'Yes, definitely that, but you're missing something vital, darling.'

'Being?'

'By default, you might have been in danger too.' Both brows were arched now.

Birdie shivered. Herb had always been protective of her, regardless of his heavy-handedness at times when doing so and of her insistence it was unwarranted. 'If that's true, he'll *never* tell me.' As much as Herb understood her desire for liberation and admired Birdie's and Pia's spunk, he also held onto the chivalrous need to protect.

'But you'll still push?' said Larry.

'Are you telling me not to?'

'I would never suggest such a thing.'

She wondered for a moment whether her penchant for sarcasm came straight from her uncle.

They drove on in silence. Narrow tree-lined streets and perfect gardens announced their closeness to her uncle's place. As they crested the hill a spectacular view over the, currently dark blue and choppy, ocean of the Pacific took her focus.

Larry dropped her on the verge. 'I'm going into the office. Let me know how you go with those,' he said, indicating the yearbooks.

Birdie had let herself into her uncle's house before, any number of times, but felt a little like an intruder today. It wasn't just *his* house anymore. When normally she'd walk right in, grab a snack and put the kettle on, she stood inside the door and called out, 'Herb.'

'Out in a minute.'

The sound of Herb's voice came from down the hall, from the rooms at the front of the house. She made her way into the kitchen and put on the kettle.

'Hey, Bird.'

She turned to say hello, but the word caught in her throat as her heart sizzled like it had swallowed some Wizz Fizz. Herb was shirtless, exposed skin slightly ruddy from the shower, hair was wet and flopping around his head in ringlets. She steadied her breath. Her fingers actually twitched with wanting to reach for him. The flow of his arms, the curve of his waist, the tiny spots of water on the fabric of his T-shirt that he was only just pulling over wet skin. She dropped her eyes and lifted them to focus on the kitchen cupboards. 'Cuppa?' she said.

'Ta. Those the books.' Herb picked up the yearbooks and flicked through them as he moved into the lounge room.

She felt a small urge to grab them back. She'd organised them, not him. She smiled into her tea. Always a competition with Herb. She reminded herself they were in it together. One of the few things they could do together – *your rules, Birdie.*

She stepped into the living room and was taken by the stirring in her chest. The completely satisfying feeling the man sitting on the lounge gave her. A birthday present she'd tucked away unopened, forgotten about and recently found.

His eyes caught hers. The stirring in her chest had dropped much lower. She wanted to peel away the wrapping. She could feel the slight lift of her mouth as she thought about what she'd find inside.

'What?' he said.

She'd never been great at following rules.

NINETEEN

THE PICTURES WERE GRAINY. Many tiny faces jammed into class and grade groups. Birdie had no idea how she might find these boys when they all looked so young. Newlysprouting-hair-dappled chins, pimples and braces and standard-issue, black-framed glasses. Masses of messy hair or, in contrast, neatly cropped.

She searched the names and could not find a Warwick Woods amongst them. If she couldn't find him, she'd have no chance of guessing at his probable enemy. She scanned the almost two hundred names per grade, none of which sounded familiar; the two hundred faces, none of which looked familiar.

'Anything?' said Herb.

'This is useless. It was twenty years ago that these boys were at school. We don't know the name of the other guy, and I can't find Warwick's at all.'

Sister T's reluctance to talk was making life difficult. She could have told them everything they needed to know about the Saint. Or Dom could have. Then again, the pair had used code names in the chapel. They were probably never going to spill the beans, no matter how hard Larry had tried.

'Got the right book?'

'I don't know. What about you?'

'You've got a better chance at this one, teach.'

Why his words hit her with such a force, she couldn't tell, but her stomach did a little flip at the confidence he had in her. Birdie analysed the staff photo. She knew the boys were there when Sister T and Dom were teaching. She found the adults easily in each book.

'Sister T and Dom.' She showed Herb.

'On the right track then.' She was caught in his smiling multicoloured eyes for a moment.

Herb searched for the staff photo in the other years' books. Sister T and Dom were recognisable in all of them, except the last one where Sister T was absent.

She opened the pages of the 1964 book and began again. She scanned the faces of the young men who were lined up in neat rows, smiling obediently – for the most part – into the camera lens.

After all the class photos, there were the extracurricular groups. The sports teams, the academic clubs, the award recipients and then lots of candid ones from each year group. She focused on the fourth form cohort. There were photos from the swimming carnival, liturgies, discos, leadership camp. Happy young faces smiled out from among the prefects' group that had spent three days on retreat at Huntington House at Terrigal. She turned back to the group photos, back to the photo of the boys chosen as prefects. She flicked back to the sports teams and found the rugby league team photo. The captain of the school had also been the captain of the league team. He'd also been a member of the rugby union team, hockey team, cricket team and athletics team. He was very good-looking and well-built.

He would have been a heartbreaker. For a moment, she forgot that he'd be in his mid-thirties now.

'The captain of the school in 1964 as Simon Templeton-Cox.'

Herb's eyes grew wide. 'Would have been the hero of the school with a surname like Cox,' he said with a wink.

Birdie shook her head at Herb and peered more closely at the picture. The vice-captain was called Budhwar Critterwood. Another interesting name. Budhwar was present in the debating team, the chess club, Maths Olympiad and the school band. The captain was a jock and the vice a straight-one-eighty. Total opposites.

'Do you remember when we were in the confessional box—'

'I do.' He grinned and bounced his eyebrows.

She sighed and shook her head again. 'Sister T and Dom were talking about whether this person we're looking for was capable of injuring Warwick.'

'Yep.'

'Dom referred to Naughty Santa as—'

'The Saint,' said Herb.

'Correct, and Warwick as—'

'Little Buddy.'

'Right again. Look at this.' Birdie covered the 'Budh' in Budhwar with the fingernail of her left pointer and the 'Critter' in Critterwood with her right.

'War wood,' said Herb. A question in his expression.

'Add "wick" onto the end of "war".'

'War. Wick.'

'And an "s" on the end of Wood.'

'War. Wick. Woods.' Herb's face still held a frown.

'Faster.'

'Warwickwoods.' Pushing the words together as one. 'Warwick Woods.' Herb's face lit up. 'Shit, Birdie.'

'I think Budhwar is now known as Warwick Woods. His nickname back then could have been Bud or Buddy if you consider his original first name of Budhwar.'

'Little Buddy,' said Herb in awe. Herb pored over the pictures of the boys in their various groups.

Birdie put her finger under another boy's face. 'You know how Gilligan from *Gilligan's Island* is called Little Buddy by Skipper?'

'Yes?'

'I remembered there was also another TV show called *The Saint.*'

'Great show,' said Herb. 'Saw it in re-runs and the sequel.'

Birdie pointed to the captain's name: Simon Templeton-Cox.

'Shit!' said Herb. 'The Saint's real name is Simon Templar.'

'Close enough to Simon Templeton-Cox, do you think?'

'Christ, teach. You're a genius.'

'But wait, there's more. The principal of South Vantage Public is called Sy Templeton. I've only ever been introduced to him as Sy, but I'm guessing that's short for Simon. And maybe he dropped the "Cox" as an adult? I know you said he'd be a hero in the playground, but maybe he got sick of being the subject of dick jokes or there was a parents' divorce?'

Herb curbed his grin. 'Think it's him?'

Birdie scrutinised the school photo. 'He looks like the Sy I remember.' Same dark hair. Same broad shoulders. Same cocky smile. Was he the naughty-not-nice principal who didn't give a job to the fresh young teacher who rejected his advances? The one entry whose identity they had yet to uncover?

From captain of the school to bad Santa?

'I remember going to an in-service on improving literacy. Sy Templeton was there, as was Dom and a few of their less egotistical hangers-on. They were very … friendly.'

Birdie had been able to hold her own – just. She could feel their eyes on her. Their pack mentality sizzling. She was young and new – fresh meat. Their mouths grinning and firing off questions, personal as well as professional, and their suggestion that she should join them for drinks afterwards. The pheromones had been thick in the air. She had smiled and laughed and flirted safely away.

'He's quite charming. Charismatic and likeable. Good-looking. Very sure of himself. And definitely a man's man. I wonder what he would be like at a Christmas event when he was a little merry, uninhibited, letting his libido run wild. I wouldn't want to be alone with him in a situation like that.'

Herb was looking at her intently. A tiny frown above his eyebrows. Before she knew what she was doing, she'd reached out and smoothed it. 'It's okay, Herb.'

He caught her hand in his, eyes searching. 'Birdie, that's …' He shook his head, searching for words.

She dropped her gaze. 'It's like that sometimes. I'm sure they didn't mean any harm. Girls are quite equipped at handling themselves.' She pulled her hand away.

The girl at the Christmas party had resisted. Where was she now, though? Firstly, with no job and secondly, with a mention in the local gossip pages. Angry enough to retaliate?

'Might look into this, Templeton-Cox,' said Herb flatly, slamming his book shut.

'The person we're looking for had a history with Warwick, and Sy fits that, especially if they were captain and vice.' Birdie threw the yearbook onto the coffee table. 'My eyes are hurting.' She stood up from the table and gave them a rub. 'This could all just be a coincidence, though.' These boys might not even be the men we're looking for.

The sun was streaming through the sheer curtains that covered Uncle Larry's lounge room window. She turned, followed the stream, closed her eyes and soaked it up.

'Got a gig tonight?' Herb's voice wafted in.

Small talk.

Sadness moved along Birdie's skin like fingers on a harp, settling on her heart. Should she tell him she'd met with Vinny earlier this morning? Would Vinny tell him? Would Uncle Larry? She could imagine his reaction. It wouldn't be pretty. At least it wouldn't be small talk.

She flopped back into her uncle's comfy lounge and rested her long legs on the coffee table. Herb's even longer legs followed suit. She focused on their feet, sitting together in a row. His foot tapped against hers. She smiled to herself. Wasn't this what she'd said she wanted – just to be friends?

'Yep.' She closed her eyes again. Heaviness settled against her eyelids. If she wasn't careful, she'd fall asleep right here. She'd tell Herb about Vinny, just not today. She sat up abruptly. 'I might head home. Try and get some zeds in before tonight.'

'There's a bed right down this hall.'

Her stomach flipped again. He grinned, face instantly beautiful. Flirting with Herb was much better than small talk.

She laughed at his cheeky arched eyebrow. 'You wish.' She stood, collected her things and slapped him on the shoulder. 'Get up and see me to my car, officer.'

⬯ ⬯ ⬯

Birdie was disinterested in Clint's advances. Something to do with Herb being back in town, she guessed. After she indulged in one kiss, she pulled back.

'Have I lost you to him, kitten?'

'Don't you start too, Clint, for shit's sake.'

He laughed and rested his forehead against hers. 'When will it be our time?'

'You and I both know, it never will.'

He took her hand and placed it against his chest. '*Mon cœur est brisé.*'

She doubted that very much.

He kissed her forehead, grabbed her hand, pulled her down the corridor and onto the stage. She watched him flick the microphone from its stand, twirl it in the air and catch it. He turned back and winked at her, then set the room alight. Clint's heart was not broken; it would be fine.

When the show was over, Griff Wheatley was hanging around.

'Did this one not get the hint, bunny?' Clint said, jerking a finger in Griff's direction.

'Ah, now this one's a need, not a want. He has useful information for me,' she whispered.

Clint grinned. He grabbed her ponytail and pulled it gently. 'Naughty girl,' he whispered in her ear.

A hint of what might have been wafted around them in a smoky fog. She fought her way clear. 'Mr Wheatley,' she said. 'Two weeks in a row.'

'What can I say, I can't resist a musician.' He should have stopped at *I can't resist* which would have been more like it.

'Well then, I can introduce you to Megan if you like?'

Griff laughed. 'A musician *and* a comedian. How lucky can one guy get?'

'Lucky enough for me to buy you a drink if you help me with my stuff.'

Griff helped Birdie sort her gear into the boot of the Gypsy. Then they joined the other band members at the bar.

'Have the police spoken to you?' Birdie asked.

'We've had a conversation.'

'They wanted an alibi, I'm guessing?'

'You're taking this Sister Therese Margaret accusation very personally.'

'My uncle is representing her. He's a solicitor. I'm invested in this for many reasons.' The obvious ones, being Uncle Larry and the fate of Sister T, and the ones Griff wouldn't even have considered – as Pia put it: *the women left in their wake.*

'I didn't stab Warwick Woods, Birdie.'

'And I'm supposed to believe that because of your exemplary character.'

He laughed again. 'You're a tough nut to crack.'

'I hope you've worked out that this nut won't be cracked by you, Griff.'

'Might need some extra tuition to help me understand.'

Birdie shook her head. 'So, what is your alibi?'

'I went for a surf straight from school and then from the surf straight to the game.'

'And the only witness was some beach bum.'

'I'm very lucky the hodad saw me at all. I'm new in town. You and Brad and a few people from Grammar are my only'—he raised an eyebrow—'friends?' He said the word 'friends' as if he wasn't sure that they were.

She nodded at him and smiled. 'We're friends, Griff.'

He smiled in return. 'If I hadn't stopped and chatted to old mate, I'd have *no* alibi.'

Birdie hadn't known he'd chatted to anyone. Her information from Herb, through Constable Celeste, was that the beach bum recognised a *picture* of Griff. Did the circumstances of the recognition mean anything? Was this something she should tell Herb?

Megan leaned over on her stool. 'I know you're trying to prove it wasn't your nun, Birdie, but the longer it takes to arrest someone for Warwick Woods' attack, the more nervous I get.'

'I don't think you're in danger, honey. Uncle Larry's working on the assumption Warwick was specifically targeted because of *Shame Game*.'

Megan shivered. 'I wish that made me feel better.'

Griff did give his attention to Megan then. His naturally charming manner was treated with interest, if not a little caution, by her clued-in band mate.

She watched them interact. Where were his old friends? He'd told them he'd grown up in the Sutherland Shire. Why was he happy to stay in Queensland after his prac and work up there? Why was he happy to relocate with his mum to live with his grandma in the sleepy municipality of Gallie Wallen?

Drinks were winding up. Griff had moved on to engage with Brett and Drew. Birdie was happy to call it a night, go home and shower, toddle off to bed.

She gave Griff a lift home. Technically, his grandma's home, where he was living with both his grandma and his mum. Not really conducive to his pulling-the-ladies lifestyle.

'Did you really sleep with that girl in Queensland, Griff?'

'Don't tell me you're softening, Birdie.'

She laughed at his craftiness. 'No.'

'What makes you think I didn't?'

'I don't think you didn't. I was just wondering whether you'd answer a direct question.'

He smiled. 'Perhaps when you get to know me better, you'll be able to work out the answer for yourself.'

'Have you kept in touch with her?'

'Well, that would depend on whether I slept with her.'

'So, that's a no then.'

'You don't think I slept with her?'

'I don't think you can answer a direct question.'

'How upset would you be if the answer was yes?' He reached out and held her hand. 'Would you like me to level with you, Birdie?' He lifted her hand and kissed her palm.

Did she? His invitation to level with her held more than just having a chat. What was stopping her from accepting his real offer? What was stopping her from hearing him tell her of his intentions?

'Not tonight, Griff.'

She knew what was stopping her. *Herb*.

Griff got out of the car and stuck his head through the open window. 'Don't see this arse walking away as defeat,

Birdie Mealing.' He tapped the open window ledge and, with a final grin, turned on his heel.

'Who says I'm going to watch it?' she called after him.

'You will.'

He lifted his shirt so his jean-covered, impressive backside was in full view, and sauntered inside.

Birdie laughed and shook her head. He was right. *I was always going to look.*

She started the car and pulled away from the kerb.

Would knowing him better solidify his reputation or clear it?

As Birdie climbed into bed that night, she realised she'd forgotten to ask him about why he didn't pay the blackmail demand.

Traditionally, society
labelled women in terms of
who they belong to ... wife,
mother, mistress, Mrs,
daughter ... But if the
possessive packaging
persists, women's attitudes
towards their own identity
have changed dramatically in
the past 20 years ... the
majority of Australian women
now regard their 'sense of
self' as one of the most
important, if not the single
most important, thing in
their lives.

'The Cleo three S report:
Self'
Cleo, March 1985.

TWENTY

THE LOCAL PAPER LAY open on the benchtop. Birdie poured cereal into a bowl and covered it with milk. She'd still not read it thoroughly after the nervousness of making sure she wasn't in its gossip pages and finding the editorial by Emer. As she crunched a scoop of Frosties, her attention was drawn to a follow-up article on Sallie-Anne Huckstepp. Birdie wondered how she continued to carry on after losing her boyfriend, doing that exposé on *60 Minutes* and now writing her tell-all book. Birdie would be living in fear if it were her.

Her mother wandered into the kitchen in her Saturday morning tennis whites. 'You're up early,' she whispered.

'My tummy was rumbling. I'll take this back to my room. I don't want to wake the men,' Birdie whispered back. Not on a morning they could all sleep in.

'How did you go with Vincent?'

'I'm still trying to decide whether I'm reading too much into the discussion. You know what Vinny's like. Not sure I can trust anything he says.' Although, in hindsight, he had been very honest in the past, if not a little cryptic.

'How is he?' Lenore busied herself checking that her bag had all the needed equipment. She repacked her perfectly packed tennis racquet and a tube of balls.

'He seems good. He looks good too. Really good. He's a handsome man, Mum.' Birdie dropped her eyes back to her brekky. Now might be a good time to ask the question she'd been wanting to ask for a while.

She and her mother had danced around this topic. This topic of Vinny and Lennie.

She twirled a yellow flake of sugar, disguised as cereal, around in her bowl. 'Did you and he ever ... you know?'

When Birdie looked up, her mother was already scooting out the back door towards the garage. She whispered, 'I'd better go, love. We'll talk later,' as she went.

'Sure,' Birdie mumbled to herself. She took the paper and the cereal back to her room.

⇔ ⇔ ⇔

'Herb and I checked over the yearbooks yesterday,' Birdie said as she and Pia neared the Sailo that night. Birdie pulled the Gypsy into the rocky driveway of the car park. 'The vice-captain of the school in 1964 was a guy called Budhwar Critterwood.'

'Budhwar,' said Pia, 'as in, "Budh" plus "war" and so therefore, let's keep the war and add wick?'

'Well done.'

'And Critterwood, as in, let's get rid of the critter, add an "s" and anglicise it to just Woods?'

Birdie pulled into a spot and put the handbrake on. She turned and contemplated Pia. 'You're amazing.' She really shouldn't be surprised her clever friend had hypothesised the reasoning exactly as she had.

'Did you know Mum's real surname was Campabello?' Pia said. 'After arriving in Australia to start a new life, they went through customs where it was suggested to her father that he just make it Campbell?'

'Is that so?'

'*Si*. And as a child, she was called Lucy, not Lucia-Rosa.'

'Ah, Lucy Campbell.'

'*Comprehende?*'

'Comprehende.'

Birdie explained seeing Simon Templeton-Cox, better known as Sy Templeton, in the yearbooks as they got out of the car and closed their doors. Why did no one mention Warwick was really Budhwar Critterwood? The paper hadn't even mentioned it.

'And you think this Sy might be the subject of the first entry – our Naughty Santa?' asked Pia.

'Sister T and Dom called Naughty Santa "the Saint".'

'Because Sy Templeton's initials are "ST", short for "saint". Makes sense.' Pia locked up the car and flicked her doorhandle to check. 'Dad loved that show.'

'Glen too.' Birdie flicked her handle as well. 'Why would they change their names so late in the game?'

'Hmm.' Pia put on the TV voice of a news anchor. 'Here's our report from Budhwar Critterwood?' Pia grimaced.

'Mouthful.'

Birdie adopted the same TV voice. 'And now let's cross to Warwick Woods.'

Pia smiled. 'I think we might've just answered our question.'

'Warwick knows Sister T's secret. Did he also know that one about Sy?'

'But the rumours came from an outside source,' said Pia. 'So he couldn't have.'

'That's true.'

'And if the rumours are still coming, it can't be Warwick that's supplying them, unless he can send rumours while in a coma,' said Pia.

They manoeuvred through the car park to the club's entrance.

'Sister T and Dom were concerned that Sy Templeton, our Saint, was the one who stabbed Warwick,' Birdie said.

'Out of anger?' mused Pia.

'Holding a grudge from school?' added Birdie.

'Hang on,' said Pia. 'What if Warwick, seeing the information coming in on blue paper, decided to copy that?'

'He typed his secrets on blue paper and posted them in?' said Birdie.

Pia pushed the door open. 'It's possible. There were three entries before he was taken out of the picture,' she said with a 'this is getting interesting' look.

They spotted the table of their friends straight away, having gravitated to the same area each week. After waving their hellos, they headed to the bar where Pia ordered some West Coast Coolers. 'There's a hole in our theory.'

'What's that?'

'How would Warwick know about Sy's behaviour at that Christmas party?'

'Good point,' Birdie said.

'Have you heard from Stu? Should we be buying him a drink?' Pia asked.

'I left a message with Mrs Ah Kee. She wasn't sure what he was doing. He wasn't home yet.'

Pia paid the barman. A loud proclamation of woe at a table in the sports bar part of the club had them both straining their necks to see across the island counter.

Dom Walker was holding court. His familiar tone now registering in Birdie's auditory memory. He must have been there for a while. He and his mates were on their way to being merry. She pointed him out to Pia.

'Maybe you should go speak to him. Beers are a good lip loosener. He knows Sister T's secret,' Pia said.

Before she got a chance to move, Brad was whispering in her face. 'My friend is beside himself with worry.'

Birdie reared back, but then her brain switched into gear, recalling the conversation on Thursday morning she'd had with Brad regarding his 'friend'. She said hello to Sabine who had walked in with him, waited for Sabine and Pia to start chatting, and turned back to Brad. 'Has he paid the blackmail?' she whispered.

'Yes. Although, I did have to lend him some money to cover it. He has a wife, three kids and a mortgage. He doesn't have cash lying around. The bank account is a joint one. Any withdrawal would be noticed. It's been very stressful.'

'It will be fine now that he's paid it. Tell him to relax. And you can relax too. What's going on with you two anyway?'

'I'm sure you're clever enough to work it out. If a queer man wants to be taken seriously by this society, he has to behave accordingly. That doesn't mean his other needs can necessarily be ignored.'

'It's shit, Brad.'

His eyebrows moved into a frown above his wide eyes.

'I don't mean you are shit, just the whole situation.' *An affair with a married man; who'd have thought it?*

His face softened. 'It might be, Birdie, but it's just the way it is. It works out perfectly for both of us. I'm happy.'

Birdie hugged her friend fiercely. 'So long as you're both okay.'

Dom Walker caught Birdie's eye as she hung over Brad's shoulder. He was at the bar ordering another.

'My shout,' she said to no one in particular and gave Pia a knowing look before making her way towards Dom.

'Hello, there.'

'Birdie Mealing. Legs that go all the way up to her bum.'

'I should hope so, Mr Walker. Can I buy you a beer?'

'Of course.'

Birdie ordered the drinks. 'You get the beer in exchange for the answer to my question?'

'Some might think you're a bit too young for me, Birdie, but my answer would always be yes.'

'I am too young for you. You're almost old enough to be my father.' A throwaway line with a sting in its tail that registered as the words themselves left her lips. Birdie held the beer in front of Dom. 'What's Sister T's secret?'

The machinations of a slightly inebriated brain were slowly moving. He grinned. 'What secret?' He reached for the beer.

She held onto it tightly. 'I know she has one, and she won't tell my uncle what it is. Plus, I know you know it.'

He pulled the beer towards him. 'I don't know what you're talking about.'

'It could get her off a charge of manslaughter if Warwick dies.' A big statement used to shock. 'The police are putting a case together as we speak.' Speculation, but based on fact.

'It could also make her look even more guilty,' said Dom.

'Let me be the judge of that. What's the secret?'

'I would do anything for that woman. She's one of the best. But I'm not going to do anything that makes her look worse, no matter how many drinks I've had.'

'You've been friends for a long time.' A statement, not a question.

'Since she started teaching. She was a nurse first.'

'She's a talented woman.'

'She certainly is.'

'So, what's her secret?'

'Is this beer worth all these questions, I wonder?' Dom smiled.

'She doesn't have an alibi.'

'She was at school.'

'Was she? Were you at school?'

'Miss Mealing, are you suggesting Therese is lying? Nuns are very respectable people. A woman makes certain vows when she becomes a nun, you know.' His gaze sparked with a hint of something. 'Breaking these is not done lightly.'

Breaking her vows. *Poverty, chastity and obedience.* Were Dom's words laced with meaning or beer? Birdie let go of the glass holding said amber fluid.

'So, the editorial in the paper has a ring of truth, then? Asking questions is the action of an investigator.'

'I have an inquiring mind, Mr Walker. And as such, I have another question. Were Sy Templeton – previously known as Simon Templeton-Cox, and Warwick Woods – previously known as Budhwar Critterwood, friends at school?'

Dom's glass slipped through his fingers. He clutched at it to save it from falling. Beer splashed over the rim, down his hand and onto his shoes. He shook his foot free of the foamy liquid.

Hmm ... Jumpy or drunk? Birdie grabbed some serviettes from the bar and handed them across. As her eyes met Dom's, she could see the surprise behind them.

'You're not wrong about your mind.' His tone was suddenly serious. 'They were captain and vice-captain. They should have been friends, but they weren't.'

'Why not?'

'Budhwar, as he was known then, was an insecure character, worked hard for what he won. Simon had talent, looks, personality, popularity; things came easily to him. Buddy was embarrassed by his background, by his multitude of siblings, his presumed lower status, his name. Buddy hated looking like a fool, Sy revelled in playing one.' Dom's expression danced with scorn. 'But Buddy has definitely turned that around. He's changed his name, his status and got himself into a position where he could make fools of all of us.' He took a big sip of his beer. 'Luckily this'—he held up his almost empty glass. Birdie could see the hurt, the pain. When he spoke again, anger laced his words—'will help me forget just how much of a fool he's made out of me. Thanks for the beer.' He turned to go.

'One last question.'

His cheeky grin was back. Birdie was reminded of images of Jekyll and Hyde. 'Does your investigation hinge on my responses?' he said.

She laughed. 'Perhaps,' she said with a smile. 'Why didn't you pay the blackmail money?'

'What blackmail money?'

'The blackmail money that would have prevented the lines about you and your desk-polishing being published by our vengeful friend.'

'I'm not following.' He shook his head, trying to clear the fog. 'Who asked for money?'

'The person who called you.'

Dom's face was blank.

Birdie pushed on. 'Didn't you get a call asking for money?'

'No.'

'So no one called you at work and asked you to deposit money into an account?'

Shouts from Dom's mates had him lifting his head in their direction. 'No, Birdie Mealing, Girl Detective.' He began walking over to rejoin them.

'Did you get a call at the house?' Birdie tried again.

He didn't even bother to turn around. 'Good night, Miss Mealing,' he called, waving a hand in the air. 'Thanks for the beer.'

Birdie watched Dom sway slightly as he walked away. Why did the whistleblower only blackmail some of their victims? It didn't make sense.

Dom stopped in his tracks. He put a wobbly hand to his forehead. 'Holy crap,' she heard him say. He turned back to Birdie, arm up, hand out, palm open. 'Hang on.' He drank a big gulp of beer, focus wandering over the carpet. 'My wife did take a weird call. She wouldn't tell me who it was. She didn't call them by name.' Bloodshot eyes trained on Birdie. 'She just stared at me as she said "Please don't call here again" into the mouthpiece, and then hung up. Guilt stopped me from asking any questions. The look on her face was enough, you know?'

'I think I'm following,' said Birdie.

'When she got off the phone, she said I was a son of a bitch, I deserved everything that was coming to me, and she hoped I'd rot in hell.'

Damn.

'How do you know it was someone extorting money?' he asked.

'I don't know for sure, but I have heard of a couple of teachers who have been contacted and asked to put a substantial amount of money into a bank account or their dirty little secrets would become public. At least one, I do know for certain, followed through on that demand, paid the blackmail money and his secret has remained just that.'

And luckily for her, it did.

'Jeez.' He massaged his forehead.

Dom's entry was the third about teachers. His wife would have known it would make the paper if the demand wasn't paid. Perhaps she figured any money they had was better off coming to her in a divorce settlement than ending up in the pocket of the whistleblower.

'Sorry, Dom.' Birdie *was* sorry, but also a little bit in admiration of Dom's discarded wife.

She took her drinks back to the table.

'Well?' Pia said.

'Brad, do you know Sy Templeton, the principal at South Vantage?' Birdie said as she sat down.

'Sy?' Brad drank his beer. 'Yeah, vaguely.'

'He's not the principal there at the moment. He's on leave,' said Sabine. 'Why are you asking about him?'

'I think he might be Naughty Santa.'

'Ew,' said Brad. 'Gross.'

'No wonder he's taken leave,' said Sabine. 'What a coward. He has leave for all of term two as well. He's got a job as the Randwick Bluebottles reserves coach.'

'How do you know that?'

'Three older brothers. Plus, I'm in first place on the staff tipping ladder. You have to keep up to date with these things.'

Captain of the football team at school, now a football coach. A footy-head. In Birdie's experience, they had little respect for women. He took leave before the paper printed the column *allegedly* about him, which points to his guilt and to him knowing it was coming. Why didn't he pay the blackmail money?

'Do you think Sy Templeton refused to pay the extortion money?' said Brad.

'What money?' said Sabine.

Perhaps he didn't believe it would be printed. Although his was the first in the string of entries about teachers, the column had already impacted the lives of four non-teachers. He knew there was a real possibility it would be. Did he think he was untouchable? Was it arrogance? It fit the bill. Or maybe he didn't care that the rumour would be published because he'd organised another job anyway.

'Maybe he didn't have the money to pay the blackmail.' Brad gave Birdie a knowing look.

'Are you saying someone was blackmailing these guys?' asked Sabine with a frown. 'Someone at the paper?' she said softly.

'Or the person supplying the rumours,' said Birdie.

Sabine's leg connected with the table. Everyone grabbed for their unsteady drinks. Fizzy alcoholic liquid spilled out of Sabine's bottle as it toppled over and splashed onto her jean leg. 'Bugger.' She reached for a coaster to blot the liquid.

Brad grabbed a serviette and started to dab at the spot. 'Perhaps some water from the bathrooms,' he said, leading her away.

The fact that Sy had not hung around to face the music also pointed very securely at his guilt.

She waited until Brad and Sabine were out of earshot before whispering to Pia. 'Dom mentioned the vows a woman makes when becoming a nun.'

'Poverty, chastity and obedience,' the honey-eyed beauty said. 'Are we thinking Sister T's secret has something to do with her being irreverent, living lavishly or having sex?'

'If she's living lavishly and having sex, then she *is* being irreverent,' Birdie said with a grin. 'The breaking of which of these vows do you think is the most scandalous?' she continued, with an of-course-it's-she's-having-sex look on her face.

'Get out!' said Pia.

'Who's she having sex with?' Birdie said, coughing a laugh. Pia giggled into her drink.

Two Fluffy Duck cocktails materialised from behind their shoulders to levitate before them. Not actually levitating, but held out by the familiar hands of ...

'Stu!' They each retrieved their prize and dragged him into their threesome.

'Who's who having sex with?' he said.

TWENTY-ONE

THE HEAVINESS OF STU'S brow lifted as Pia's and Birdie's summary of the last few days tumbled out. Birdie smiled to herself as the line of Stu's mouth softened and his eyes began to sparkle.

'You've concluded with intelligence that the blackmail angle is worth pursuing,' Stu said.

'Thanks for your insight, Obi-Wan,' Pia said with a bow.

Stu ignored her sarcasm. 'Have you spoken to the non-teachers who have been blackmailed?'

Why hadn't she thought of that? She'd been so caught up in the plight of teachers she'd all but forgotten those who came before.

'Dr Lee plays poker with Dad,' Stu said. 'It's the only gambling he's allowed to partake in; they play for matchsticks.'

Dr Lee was the doctor who featured in his own *Shame Game, No Names* entry. He had dipped into the till to pay his gambling debts and had been given a suspension from duty while an inquiry was being held.

'The next game is set to take place in our garage,' continued Stu. 'I can offer to be barman for the night. Medically speaking, alcohol lowers inhibitions.'

Moments later, Birdie stood at the bar for her shout and watched Stu hold court. The nursing course 'think tank' had wrapped up, and he was back to shifts at the hospital on Monday. Birdie sensed he was happy to be returning to the wards once again and to Sister T's case. She smiled to herself. It was good to have him back.

'Plotting something dangerous, teach?'

Warmth tickled Birdie's neck. She shivered and raised her eyes to the beautiful face of Herb Lawson. Her heart stopped. She straightened, willed it to beat, and hoped he hadn't noticed her body's reaction. She raised an eyebrow. 'Perhaps I am.' She leaned in close. 'Are you feeling nervous, Detective?'

He took a step towards her. 'Ever since I met you.'

The soft hairs that poked from the top of his shirt caught her eye; the tiny auburn curls. He smelled of clean and promise. She imagined droplets of water peppering his chest, rivulets running down his body, pooling at his crotch. She leaned in further. The impulse to undo his buttons and touch skin she knew would be just-washed-soft was overwhelming.

He dropped his head to her ear. 'See something you like?' he said, soft and deep.

She snapped back like a broken guitar string. He chuckled to himself and lifted his hand to order a beer.

Birdie cleared her throat. 'I think Sister T's secret has something to do with breaking her vows as a nun.'

'Poverty, obedience and chastity.'

'Those are the ones.'

He swallowed his beer. 'You think she's sleeping with someone?'

'Interesting that was your first thought, Herb.' She flicked his arm, his muscly arm, his freshly washed, soft muscly arm. 'Mind out of the gutter.'

'Tell me that wasn't your first thought.'

She grinned again. *My first thought?* Her thoughts right now on the topic of sleeping with someone were an echo of his words: *See something you like.*

She moved onto safer ground. 'Sy Templeton has left education to pursue a career as a football coach.'

'Wealth of information tonight, teach.'

'He's the coach of the Bluebottles reserve team.'

'Easy to find then.'

'Also, I was just thinking, there was a new entry in this week's paper, which might prove Warwick can't be the supplier of gossip.'

'Did we think he was?'

'Pia and I thought he might be, that he may have been pretending someone was sending rumours in but was really supplying them himself.'

'Interesting theory.'

'We thought he might have published the gossip about his old mate Sy just to piss him off.'

'And Sy snapped and stabbed him?'

'That's what we were considering.'

'And because he's out of action, you decided against it?' *That and the blackmail.*

Blackmail that was still happening in Warwick's absence. Blackmail she knew was happening but hadn't told Herb about. Blackmail that suggested gossip would be leaked if the payment didn't come. She knew he'd ask questions and, for some reason, she still cared about Herb knowing the answers.

'Why did Sy, if it was Sy, wait so long to strike?' she said instead. 'He didn't attack until three weeks later.'

'Snapped. Fed up. If Dom's keeping Sy's identity disguised, they must be mates. Maybe he didn't like seeing his mate upset, knowing Dom was feeling the same way he did.'

Would it make a difference to the case if the information about blackmail was revealed? Birdie knew the answer, but she pushed its importance deep down. Easier to do when a barmaid places a new round of cocktails on the bar. She reached for the tray.

'How did you get here?' Herb's face held that look it often did. The one that said 'Are you making good decisions, Birdie?'

'I drove. How did *you* get here?'

'How much have you had to drink?'

'None of your bloody business.' His scrutiny was unwavering. She exhaled. 'I've only had a West Coast and a cocktail.' *Or two. This might in fact be my third.*

'Police are trialling what's called random breath testing. They park in the streets that flow from clubs and pubs, and as people drive home, they test the level of alcohol in their system.'

'You'd be a riot at a party.'

'They're trialling it in this area.'

'Meaning?'

'You've had too much to drink to drive.'

When she and Pia had been in their second year of high school, they'd been coming home on a Friday afternoon when, in front of them, two young guys ran their car straight into the back of a parked Mack Truck.

She leaned forward and tapped his chest. 'Thanks for the tip, officer.'

'Being under the influence makes you an unsafe driver.' Herb put down his beer. 'Might take you home.'

'No, you won't.'

Pia and her dad had been the first people to stop to assist at the accident. By coincidence, Birdie and Lenore had been the second.

'I'm here with Pia and Stu and Brad and Sabine.' She pointed at her friends back at the table. She could still see the twisted metal, the car's insides spilling onto the grey road. 'We'll work something out.'

'Birdie.' His voice was fierce; he stood up tall, eyes flashing with purpose.

Lenore and Mr King had tried in vain to keep the damaged pair alive. Trying to shield Pia and Birdie from the horrific scene. The young men had been 500 metres up the road from the local pub. Lenore had rung the hospital later to inquire about them. Both young men had died. The trauma of that accident, the sadness of the loss of two young men – who would probably have been younger than the age she and Pia were now – had stayed with them.

'We've been through this, Herb. You have no claim on me,' she said, matching his intensity. She lifted the tray. 'And by the way, I met with Vinny.' She turned on her heel, her stomach swimming with butterflies and maybe a few wasps, and walked back to the table.

'Hunky Herb's not happy,' said Pia, looking over Birdie's shoulder as she sat down.

'No, but that's his problem.' She sucked on her drink. 'He's worried about me driving home under the influence of alcohol.' The girls exchanged a knowing look: *as if*.

She flicked a look back at the bar. Herb caught her eye as she sucked on the straw. He held her gaze. Would it always be this way with them? Like Pia said: love and hate. She glued her eyes onto his as she sucked up more cocktail than she'd planned to, felt the anger meet the alcohol that was spreading along her limbs. She didn't need him to tell her she'd had enough to drink or how to get home after being at the club. She already knew she was incapable of driving. She turned her back and refocused her attention on her friends. When she looked back a little later, he was having a conversation with some guy. When she looked back later still, he had gone.

Birdie had finished up drinking after the Fluffy Duck she'd guzzled down – quickly for Herb's benefit – sat, along with her memories, unsteadily in her stomach, but Stu, Brad and Sabine had continued and then moved onto Sambuca shots. So, it was hours later that the little group stumbled out the door of the club and zigzagged through the car park. They were loud, speech slurring as they meandered towards Birdie's car. She wasn't going to drive. She just wanted to make sure the Gypsy was locked.

Birdie noticed a couple of men loitering nearby, watching them. As Birdie checked the car, Brad stumbled. He grabbed for Stu, who also stumbled. Both tumbled to the ground. The boys roared with laughter as they tried to right themselves.

Brad eyeballed the loitering men. 'What are you looking at?' He snorted as he picked himself up. The men turned and leisurely ambled away.

Was one of them the guy who was with Herb at the bar? She kept an eye on the men, and Gypsy, as she and her friends moved on, back towards the club's entrance and to the taxi rank. A taxi driver slowed down and leaned over the passenger seat to speak to them through the window.

'Can you take all five of us?' asked Birdie. Hopefully, the driver would allow four across the back seat or two in the front.

'Sorry, love, I've already got a warnin' about overcrowding. Can only take enough for the seat belts. They are mandatory now. I'll lose my licence.'

Perhaps she'd been too hasty in telling Herb to shove his lift. She surveyed the car park. His motorbike was amongst the others parked, which meant he was still here somewhere. She could get him to drop her home, and then the others could get the taxi. Only problem was, she still had a little issue with motorbikes and, after their last conversation, a little issue with Herb.

Birdie pointed out the motorbike to Pia. 'Herb's still here.' She shrugged a shoulder. 'I can get a lift with him.'

Pia frowned and leaned into the car's window. 'Can you call another taxi to come?'

'There's one guy who just left. He said he was knockin' off after taking a couple into the city. I can see if he'll come back out. Could be a while, though.' The taxi driver started talking on his CB radio. Stu, Brad and Sabine swayed and laughed into each other.

'I can wait with you, and we can go in the next one.'

Birdie was being silly. It was just a bike. And Herb was a *very* safe driver. Perhaps he could drive the Gypsy home and come back for his bike in the morning. That might be a better idea.

He'd do anything for you.

Vinny's words came back to her on the still night air. Herb might do anything for her, but he also might kill her when he gets his hands on her. She'd told him she'd met with Vinny. *Shit!* If she went home with Herb, he'd want to know all about the meeting. She crossed her fingers that another taxi was coming.

'He's finished up, love. Not comin' back out, and I've just got another call. What are you lot gonna do, cause if it's not gettin' in, I'll have to go.'

Brad and Stu had already opened the cab's door and, with Sabine, were piling in the back.

'Could Herb take us both?' said Pia.

Not on the bike and not in the Gypsy either. It only had the two front seats. She couldn't imagine cranky Herb would let her or Pia roll around in the boot without a seatbelt, or squash into the Gypsy's cab.

Birdie hugged her friend. 'I'll be fine. There's gotta be some advantage to having Herb trying to win me over, or in this case, being cranky with me. Besides, he'll love the win.'

'You two.' Pia rolled her eyes. 'I don't really want to leave you, Birds.'

'You aren't gonna chuck in my cab, are you?' the cabby said to the delinquents across the back seat. He glared up at the girls.

'Someone needs to see them home, Pia. It's either you or me.'

'They are not going to spew,' Pia said to the driver. She slid into the front seat and turned to the drunkards in the back. 'Wind down the windows.' Then back to the driver. 'We're not going until I see her safely back inside the club doors.'

Birdie shut Pia's door and hugged her through the window. She hurried back towards the Sailo's entrance, opened the door, turned and waved, watched the cab pull away from the kerb and wandered back inside to find Herb.

Bloody hell, he would just love the fact that she was going to ask for a lift.

She'd got a few steps inside before Herb was at her shoulder. He put a hand around her waist and whispered in her ear. 'We have to go.'

'Well, lucky I was just coming in to see if you'd drop me home, then.'

He pushed her towards the corridor that led to the bathrooms.

Birdie hesitated. 'Where are we going?'

He said nothing, moving her firmly along, bypassing the toilet doors and continuing to the door at the end.

'Are we leaving via the emergency exit?'

'Stay close, Birdie,' he whispered in her ear. The hand around her waist tightening.

The protectiveness of Herb's actions, the tone of his voice, the seriousness of his demeanour set her heart hammering in her chest.

They got out into the laneway beside the club where the sounds of the kitchen could be heard. Food had stopped being served a while ago, and the clean-up must have been in progress. Birdie could hear the voices of the workers singing along to the radio over the sound of gushing tap water.

'What's happening, Herb?'

He scanned the car park. 'Don't leave my side.'

TWENTY-TWO

S ENSES WERE ON HIGH alert – fermenting vegetable scraps, a chilly breeze coming off the bay, its tickle of the on-end hairs of her arm, the clacking of her heels forcing her onto tiptoe.

She was shuffled along in a dream. Their bodies hugged the building. She pushed her breath out and pulled it in, lungs forgetting how it was done.

'Bike,' he whispered. They weaved between the rows of parked cars until they reached it.

Herb handed her the helmet. He grabbed the bike's handles and threw his long leg over its body, kicked back the stand, flicked out the starter pedal and slammed his foot down. The rumbling of the throttle surged up into her torso, fuelling her fear.

Herb eyed her and frowned. 'Put that on.'

Birdie held the helmet in her shaking hands. She could see a faint glow streaming from the back of the club.

Herb's head darted at the flash of light and then back to Birdie. 'Birdie!'

She couldn't move. A roar reverberated in her ears, spun round her head; the smell of petrol filled her nostrils. She could see Herb's mouth moving, his face the picture of panic, but the engine's grumble held her in a mystic trance, the vibration inside her hijacking her heartbeat. Herb circled her on the bike, putting himself between her and what approached.

'Put it on, Birdie!' His voice crashed through the balloon of silent fear. Urgent over the soft idle of the engine, the shuffle of leather soles on the asphalt. 'They're coming.'

She was rooted to the spot.

'Christ.' He pulled her towards him, slammed the helmet onto her head.

'Herb.' She dug in her heels. The helmet added a fresh feeling of claustrophobia to the fear. She jiggled her head. 'I can't—'

'For the love of God, Birdie,' he said in a low growl. 'Could you, just for once'—he flicked the visor up and urged her towards the bike—'do what I bloody-well ask?'

She could see the men now, shouting to each other. Chins raised as eyes darted over the tops of cars. The same guy she'd seen before at the bar with Herb, in the car park near her car.

'It's your bloody fault, Herb.' She was marching on the spot. 'It's *your* fault I can't get on this bike,' she hissed in a whisper, pushing the words through the helmet's restrictive covering, tears dampening her skin.

'I'm sorry.' He placed his thumbs into the space left open by the visor, wiped the wetness from her cheeks, drawing her focus. 'I'm sorry, Bird. You know, if I could take that back, I would.'

A loud *click* filled the night air, followed by a giant mozzie whistling past. It smacked into the fence behind them. Herb's eyes went from fierce concern to wide with panic.

That wasn't a mozzie. 'Was that a bul—?'

'They're shooting at us, Birdie.'

'But it sounded like a moz—'

'They've got a silencer.'

'A silencer?' *To muffle the sound!*

Bodies came towards them from a few fronts.

Herb put his hands back on the handles, revved the engine. 'Get the hell on the bike! NOW!'

She lifted a leg and slid onto the seat behind him, her body throbbing with the engine's roar. She wrapped her arms around him.

He slipped one long forearm over hers. 'Head down. Hold tight.'

The tiny rear-view mirror exploded like a silver firework with the mark of another shot. Birdie screamed, burying her head further.

'Fuck,' she heard Herb say as the bike convulsed into motion.

🗣 🗣 🗣

They were flying down the road, looping and zipping through the streets. The muscles of Herb's back twisted against her chest, his torso slipping within her hold as he checked over his shoulder every few minutes. Her heart was just returning to some semblance of a normal rhythm when she felt the bike start to slow.

She chanced opening her eyes.

The row of dahlias that Uncle Larry so loved to grow in autumn swam into focus just before Herb cut the lights and puttered into her uncle's driveway. He glided the bike around the edge of the house, parking it alongside the underneath part of the concrete pool.

He lifted Birdie off and removed the helmet. 'You okay?'

She nodded, couldn't speak.

He hugged her to him, held her tight against his chest and stroked her hair. 'You did well, teach.'

Herb took her hand and led her towards the door that connected the downstairs rooms of the house – her uncle's bedroom and ensuite – with the backyard. Uncle Larry appeared at his bedroom door, hair sticking up in spikes and dressing gown hanging open. She heard a female voice make a query from within – Shelly, her uncle's fiancée, she guessed.

Her uncle glared at Herb and sized up Birdie. He pulled Birdie into his arms and spoke to Herb above her head. 'Something to share?'

Herb started to recall events in a hushed tone. Larry moved his goddaughter back into Herb's arms. He responded to Shelly with a 'not to worry, be back in a sec' and closed the bedroom door.

Birdie zoned out as Herb tucked her under his wing and pulled her along to the living areas. The men's muffled conversation continued around her. Uncle Larry engaged in a three-second phone call while he put the kettle on. She heard the hushed words '*malý drobeček*'. Herb sat her on a chair at the kitchen table, checked the doors and windows, pulled down the blinds and turned off all the lights. The only glow came from the oven light and the fridge as he got out the milk.

'What the hell just happened?' Birdie asked in a whisper, her tongue furry.

Her uncle put a heaped teaspoon of sugar in a cup of milky tea. The tinkle of the spoon against the side of the cup nursed the rhythm of exhaustion that was settling in her bones. Uncle Larry placed the tea in front of her. 'Drink this, darling.'

The first sip shocked. She normally had no sugar in her tea. In a second, she was twelve again. She drank another sip and then another. Sweetness cradling her fear and rocking it calm.

Even in her sloppy mind, the idea of being shot at and chased on a motorbike felt a little like overkill, but from past experience she knew that if she got too close to the truth, someone might try and stop her. Her sloppy mind chugged into action. What was the latest clue they'd uncovered? Who might she have rattled?

'Do you think that shooting had anything to do with us looking into Warwick's stabbing?' Her gaze clashed with Herb's. She read his features perfectly. *Perhaps my mind is not so sloppy after all.* No. Herb did not think the incident had anything to do with Warwick's stabbing which meant ... 'Herb, who were those men?'

She watched as he calculated just how much he could get away with, without actually telling her anything. *Think again, Detective.* She stood, the sugar now fuelled her fire, and flew at him. 'Don't you dare, Herb Lawson,' she said in a hissed whisper, long legs making light work of the distance between the table and the kitchen. 'I just got shot at.'

Her uncle and Herb exchanged a look.

She pushed both hands into Herb's chest. He stumbled back. She pushed again, and again, kept going across the kitchen floor until his back slammed into a cupboard. He gawked at her. 'Take it easy, teach.'

Take it easy! Before she could stop herself, she pulled back her elbow and punched him in the stomach.

He doubled over, hands supported on his knees, and gaped up at her. 'For Christ's sake, Birdie.'

She grabbed his chin with her forefinger and thumb and brought his eyes to hers. 'Don't. You. DARE try and cover this up.'

'Alright, alright.' He shrugged out of her hold and rubbed his stomach. 'If you stop attacking me. I'll tell you.'

'The truth.'

'Yes, the truth. It began on the afternoon of the twenty-seventh of June 1981.'

Birdie was shocked into silence. When he said he'd tell the truth, he really meant it.

'Was helping a mate paint the outside of his house. We were up a ladder on the first-floor balcony when we heard a conversation between two men down on the street below. One pulled out a gun and shot the other.'

'Shit,' whispered Birdie.

'Oh dear,' said Larry.

'Yeah. Well, before I could do anything, a car full of plain-clothed policemen were on the scene. Looked intense. Left them to it. Later, my mate and I went to the station and gave an account of what happened. Turned out, the victim was Warren Lanfranchi, a drug dealer, and the shooter was Detective Sergeant Roger Rogerson.'

'Roger Rogerson?' said Birdie. She knew that name. 'Wasn't he just recently done for shooting Mick Drury?'

'Six months ago, in November, actually,' Uncle Larry corrected as he continued making tea. 'And he wasn't convicted of murder; he was tried for offering a bribe to Mick Drury and for engineering his attempted murder. He was suspended for offering the bribe but found *not guilty* of shooting Mick Drury.'

Rogerson obviously had friends not only in low but in high places.

'His trial was part of the reason I had to leave quickly,' said Herb. 'I was contacted by internal affairs. They were collecting information on Roger Rogerson, hoping to open a new investigation.'

Larry passed Herb a cup of tea. 'I'm guessing they weren't the only party interested in what you knew?'

Herb put his hands around the cup, like it was his favourite childhood teddy. 'No.' He dropped his head. 'My mate took off. Though there was no evidence to suggest foul play, I've never heard from him again.'

Larry sat at the table. 'This doesn't sound good.'

Birdie collapsed onto the chair next to him.

'I'd already been approached by a senior cop,' Herb continued, 'and offered twenty thousand dollars to change my statement. They wanted me to say Lanfranchi had pulled a gun on Senior Officer Rogerson, and the detective had been left with no choice but to shoot Lanfranchi in self-defence.'

Detective Mick Drury was shot after refusing to take a bribe – he alleged – to change his statement. He'd been feeding dinner to his two-year-old daughter when he was shot through his kitchen window.

'Did you change it?' Birdie asked.

He sighed. 'Went and spoke to Draper.'

Birdie and Larry exchanged a glance; nothing good would have come of Herb talking to his boss.

'He impressed upon me the severity of the situation. If I stuck to my original story, I'd be dead. Was well known around the boys that several witnesses, drug dealers and cops had met a sticky end at the hands of Roger Rogerson's "associates".'

And possibly Herb's never-heard-from-again mate.

Birdie's skin prickled.

'I didn't take the bribe, but I did quietly alter my original statement, with Inspector Draper's support.'

Birdie was sure Inspector Draper had been 'supportive'.

'Changed it to say I couldn't be completely positive about what I'd seen that afternoon. My mate's statement had conveniently disappeared.'

'Is this what Draper has over you?' said Birdie.

He dropped his head. His teacup his best friend again. 'That was the original thing.'

'Herbert.' Herb's focus shifted to Larry. Her uncle's tone took Birdie's attention as well. 'You had no choice. And all the choices you've made since then have been about survival. Don't forget that.'

Herb nodded. His eyes flicked briefly to Birdie's and then away. Did he need her to say she agreed? Because she did.

He swallowed. 'Changing my statement didn't stop me from being on their radar, though, or as I said, at Draper's beck and call or at the end of threats about what might happen if I didn't do his bidding from then on.'

Herb finally sipped some tea. He stared into the cup. Tea wasn't really that interesting. Either Herb was lost in memories, or there was more he needed to tell. Larry must have sensed the same. Both Birdie and her uncle waited.

'I was also contacted by one of Rogerson's associates.' Herb shuffled the cup around in his hands. His voice was quiet when he said, 'He threatened Mum, Dad ... the girls.'

'Oh no,' Birdie breathed the words out. No wonder he'd disappeared. His family was in danger. She would have done exactly the same thing.

'But that wasn't all.' Herb's gaze focused on Birdie. 'They also threatened my "leggy girlfriend".'

Women have as much right as
men do to declare their
intentions, to reach for what
appeals to us, to court, woo
or conquer as we please. Why
should we wait to be asked,
allowing men the power of
asking?

'Man-chasing:
Win and keep his attention'
Cleo, April 1985.

TWENTY-THREE

B IRDIE LAY IN HER bed at her uncle's house. The
room she'd spent many nights in at Uncle Larry's for
a sleepover. Where she'd laid a million times, looking
up at the tiny patch of midnight that streamed through the
gap where the curtains didn't quite meet.

They had moved about the house in silence and darkness
until her uncle received a phone call and spoke in whispered
code again with Herb.

'Maybe, darling, don't mention this to your mother,'
Larry had said when he'd finally kissed her goodnight.

They were all safer now, apparently. Protection surrounded her uncle's home. She could imagine who was
providing it. She understood enough about the linguistic
and phonetic features of the Czech language to recognise it
when it was spoken, even in a whisper.

The dark sky was freckled with tiny lights far, far away.
They were already into the early hours of a new day, though
sleep seemed as far away as the stars. She focused on the
biggest star. It was Venus, actually. Not a star but a planet.

Goddess of love.

Sneezel beach demodray neebay.

That's what Vinny had said when she'd met with him.
That's what it sounded like – phonetically anyway. Birdie

had tried to remember the words. Had said them to herself over and over so she could repeat them to her Czechoslovakian workmate.

'*Snesl bych ti modré z nebe,*' her friend had corrected. 'I will bring you blue from the sky.'

Bloody Vinny.

Birdie had wondered whether Herb was working for Vinny, then wondered whether Vinny was working for Herb. Whatever it was, their connection was evident. It was Vinny's men who guarded this very house. Vinny obviously knew what was going on with Herb; in his clumsy way, he'd been trying to tell Birdie that Herb would do anything for her. *He would bring her the blue from the sky.*

She put her hand against the wall that separated them. Herb was right there behind thin layers of plasterboard. She wanted to go to him. Was he thinking about her? Her body burned, a wave of heat that would surely blaze right through the panels. She closed her eyes and metered her short breaths.

Herb couldn't have stayed. He had to disappear. There was too much danger, too close. He'd put the word out that he'd broken up with Birdie, was estranged from his family – 'Even fed into the Aboriginal stereotype of going "walkabout",' he'd said with a grin – and disappeared.

The stars flickered. She watched them meditatively, listened to the beat of her heart. Moments later, she rolled over and sat on the edge of the bed, her feet flat on the floor, pulse echoing in her ears. Would he be happy to see her? He would probably already be asleep. It had been a big day for him – for them both – but especially him. He'd taken the lead. Got them out of danger.

On unsteady legs, she tiptoed across the carpeted floor and opened her door.

She'd ignored his pleas to trust him. Instead, she'd put an ultimatum on their love. But when it came to the crunch, she *had* trusted him. She'd allowed him to lead her from the club without question. She'd got on the bike behind him, held onto his body like a buoy, knew in her heart that there must be a logical explanation for his absence.

She made her way silently down the hall and stopped in front of his door.

After the battering it had taken today, how could her heart be capable of galloping so wildly again? The wave of the pulse in her ears was overwhelming. She forced her breath to steady.

Then lifted her hand and knocked.

Birdie waited. And waited a little more.

Herb must be asleep, as she had guessed. She couldn't blame him. He'd be exhausted.

Disappointment sat in her stomach like cooling soup. She stepped away. She should go back to bed. Instead put her ear to the door. Could she let herself in? Could she wake him up? Would he be happy if she did?

'No need to knock, teach.'

She whirled around to find him standing at the entry of the hallway. A glass of water in his hand and moonlight throwing shadows across his face.

'Door's always open to you,' he said softly. He walked towards her, so close she could smell the fading mint from his brushed teeth, soap and sweat on his skin. 'Need something in particular?'

She could pretend.

Then again, she was standing in the hallway, in the middle of the night, in nothing but her undies and an old T-shirt she'd fished out of her teenage drawer, knocking on the door of the only man she'd ever loved – who by the way was *only* wearing pyjama pants. It was fairly obvious what she needed.

She ran a hand across his bare chest. He sucked in a breath. She kissed his collarbone. He rested his cheek on her hair. The fact that they could have died tonight was not lost on her as she peeled off her T-shirt and pushed her breasts against his skin. The comfort of his warmth surged through her. Her heart calmed and slowed.

She dragged her gaze up. 'Something very in particular.' And then his perfect mouth was on hers.

❦ ❦ ❦

They pulled apart once they made it to the bed. Herb taking her in with sleepy eyes. He ran his fingers lazily across her stomach, down her side, up along the swell of her breast as she leaned on her side facing him. She tilted forward, kissed his chest, his neck, ran a hand down his torso and found his shaft, already hard and hot. The softest skin imaginable against her steady grip.

'Christ,' was all he could manage before his mouth met hers again. He kissed her until she was lost, until she was gasping for air.

She pulled away and breathed in. 'Herb,' she breathed out. 'Why did you come back?'

'*Right now*, Bird?' He kissed her again.

She ceased her hand movement.

'Don't stop,' he pleaded into her neck, putting his hand over hers.

She started again, long and slow, capturing him momentarily in her spell. His breath ragged as he accepted her touch. He ran his tongue along her bottom lip, nipped the skin and then moulded his soft lips with hers. She was lost for a few heady seconds of her own, breathless again, maintaining the rhythm of her hand before she ceased it once more.

'*Birdie*,' he rumbled.

He was still in danger. Those men were still out there.

She gripped him tight. 'Answer me.'

She heard the grin in his voice. 'You holding my manhood hostage?'

She squeezed tighter. 'Why did you come back?'

'Jesus Christ, Birdie.' He rolled her onto her back and straddled her. He loomed above her, strong arms taking his weight, muscles tense and straining.

She slid her hands up and down his biceps, across the tendons in his chest. He was so beautiful.

He lowered himself down and caught her nipple in his mouth; he sucked, rolled it around with his tongue. 'Later.' Warm breath tickled her wet skin; he sucked again.

A deep groan escaped her throat.

He shuffled back towards her feet. Kissed her ankle, her calves, the outside of her knees, dragged his tongue along the inside of her thighs, her breaths coming fast. His tongue flicked against her spot. She held her breath in anticipation. He licked her again, long and slow. He pushed his soft lips against hers; kissing her down there as he had her mouth, sucking as he had her nipple, her exhales frayed and careless. 'Not happy I came back, teach?' he whispered into her.

She grabbed his hair as he went to work. Her body moving to his beat, hips arching towards his mouth. She could feel the tension rising, feel herself losing the edge.

She'd gone months without his hands on her. Months without his mouth – his kisses and warm whispers and the flickers of joy it gave her. Feeling grateful that she'd had a shower before bed, floated into her thoughts, and out again, as she lost the ability to care where she was or what she was doing.

Herb gripped her thighs, held her to him as she bucked and cried out. She finally slipped over and welcomed the explosion.

Moments later, she dreamily watched him sip some water and rummage around on the bed. He put on a condom and was above her again. He kissed her lips, the head of him poking below at her entrance. She guided him in. Once more, her hips rose to meet him as he moved inside her, against her, making her orgasm again.

He stopped still. Stopped moving. She opened her eyes to see his searching hers. 'If anything had happened to you.' His perusal dark and glassy. 'You scared the shit out of me when you wouldn't get on the bike.'

'I did get on the bike,' she whispered and kissed him softly.

He lowered his eyes. 'I shouldn't have come back.'

She grabbed his arse and pulled him in, re-establishing his rhythm, raising herself to meet each thrust. She held him firm as his thrusts became erratic, as his throat ground out incomprehensible sounds, until he too let himself go, collapsing against her chest. She ran her fingers through his messy hair, kissed the top of his head. 'I'm glad you did.'

TWENTY-FOUR

Birdie woke on Sunday morning to the soft puff of Herb's tiny snore-breathing, the sound he made when he slept on his back. She'd forgotten about it until now, listening to its beat, proof of the life beside her. She wanted to relearn all the other things she'd forgotten.

She rolled towards him and slid a hand across his stomach.

He lifted his own groggily to cover it. 'Morning,' he murmured through the sleep.

She ran her hand lower, meeting more of him, much more. 'It is for some.'

'Natural hormone shifts, Bird. Don't flatter yourself,' he said, eyes still closed.

'Oh, how rude,' she said, slapping his arm.

She began to roll away but was pinned in place as Herb lifted from the bed like a wave and crashed onto her. 'Shame not to make good use of it, though,' he whispered, nibbling her ear.

'Get off me, you dag.' She laughed, pushing him aside. 'I'm having a shower.'

'Sounds good,' he said, rising.

'On my own.' She pushed him back down. Pain had her sucking in a breath. She flicked and then cradled her wrist as Herb rolled dramatically across the covers.

He lent up on his elbows and considered her. 'You alright?'

'My wrist is sore.'

He came towards her, lifted it in his fingers and kissed it gently. 'That will teach you for punching your boyfriend in his rock-hard stomach,' he said over her skin.

'Won't make that mistake twice, *boyfriend*.' She kissed his lips and slipped away from his grip.

'Appreciate that, teach. Nice to know you won't be punching me again.' He leaned back on the mattress, his head resting on the hand he placed behind his head.

'I didn't say *that*. I just mean I'll aim for a softer spot next time.'

'She-devil.' He leaped across the bed and threw an arm out to grab her, but she scurried out of reach with a squeal, made it into the bathroom and closed the door just in time.

Sounds and smells of cooking wafted in from the kitchen as she stepped out of the shower. Bacon and eggs, if she wasn't mistaken. She dressed in a clean bra and undies, an old pair of shorts and a T-shirt, and wandered into the kitchen.

'Breakfast, madam.' Herb swept a hand towards a plate of food and kissed the top of her head as she sat down. 'I'm going to shower too.'

Her uncle wandered out also, tying his dressing gown, slippers scuffing on the tiles. Shelly was beside him, already dressed for the day.

'Morning, Shelly,' said Birdie.

'Morning, Birdie,' she replied with a smile.

'Hope we didn't upset your sleep too much last night.'

'I'm just glad you two are safe.' Shelly kissed her fiancé. 'I'll see you at the office tomorrow.' She turned to Birdie. 'I'm off to Mum's. Enjoy your day.'

Her uncle helped himself to breakfast and sat with her at the table. She eyeballed him. He glanced up briefly. She crossed her arms and raised an eyebrow. He shovelled food into his mouth. She tapped her foot against the lino.

'It's not me you're cranky with, goddaughter dear,' he said between bites.

'Yes, it is actually. You knew what he'd been through. You kept information from me.'

'I didn't know the extent of it, Birdie, honestly, darling.'

'You knew it was bad.'

'Bad enough to disappear, perhaps?' He held his knife and fork still. '*You* knew that too.'

She should have known he wouldn't have left her, and a little part of her was never fully content, could never quite believe that he had.

Her uncle poked at some scrambled egg. 'I do remember telling you to be patient.'

'Be patient! He only told me because I was almost shot.' He flinched.

A shudder ran through her. 'And because I insisted he did. What if I hadn't found all this out? I could have gone on hating him.'

'I distinctly recall saying to you that I would not have had him under my roof if I wasn't satisfied that he had a good reason for his previous actions. You should have trusted your old uncle.'

'Fat chance now, Uncle dear.' She stood and removed her plate. She put it in the sink and pulled down two cups.

'Tea?'

'Please.'

'Hmm. Now, where did I put that arsenic?' she mumbled as she pulled out drawers and opened cupboards.

'Birdie!'

She laughed. She couldn't blame her uncle, really. 'He hasn't told me all of it.' Her uncle opened his mouth to speak, but she quickly cut him off. 'And don't start defending his lack of disclosure.'

'You mean with a statement like, perhaps he thinks it's safer if you don't know?' He ate another mouthful.

'Too bad,' she said.

They engaged in another staring match. He put his knife and fork down and sighed.

'I don't care if it's safer,' she continued. 'He should know better. And so should you.'

'Some are slower to learn than others.' He smiled and picked up his utensils again. 'Will he have a chance to learn?'

'We've made up. But if he doesn't come clean with the rest of it. He'll be in some deep shit.'

'Language, darling. You'll curdle my eggs.'

Birdie continued making tea and a plate for Herb who'd wandered in. Why had he come back if the danger was still imminent? He had left, without saying goodbye, because he was worried about safety. Why now was it okay to return when safety was obviously still a real issue? She placed the plate of food and the tea in front of him. He smiled at her, hazel eyes shining with streaks of gold. He wouldn't tell her. She knew him too well. He'd told her all he dared to. He'd keep her away from any perceived menace. She wasn't sure if it was chivalrous or irritating. Maybe a bit of both.

'You haven't answered my question yet,' Birdie said after breakfast as she and Herb tidied up the bedrooms.

'Your question being?'

'Why did you come back when there is still trouble brewing?'

'Thought I'd dealt with it.'

'How did you deal with it?'

'Birdie.'

"'If I could take anything back, it would be that.'" Birdie adopted a manly voice in an effort to replicate Herb's.

Herb's mouth twitched up at the side as he put toothpaste on his brush.

'You owe me one,' she said.

'Emotionally blackmailing me now?' He started brushing his teeth.

'I like to call it evening the score.' She folded articles of clothing and made the bed.

He spat into the sink and rinsed his mouth. 'I wanted you to get on the bike.' He leaned over and kissed her cheek. Minty freshness filled her nostrils. He lifted his mouth to her ear and said in a low voice, 'Would have admitted any wrong to get your arse behind mine on that seat, teach.' He slapped the body part in question.

She pushed him away and plumped the pillows, smoothed the bedspread. She turned and ambled into her room. He followed her, his hands sliding around her tummy from behind.

'You're avoiding the question.' She began tidying up her bed.

'Trying to.'

'Herb.'

He moved her hair aside, kissed the back of her neck. 'Not answering it.' A shiver ran through her. He felt it, took advantage and slid his hand down her thigh.

She spun in his arms and held his hands at bay. 'I can make life difficult for you.'

'More than you already do?'

Birdie widened her eyes and let out a frustrated puff of air. 'Know this, Herb Lawson...' She poked his chest.

He put his hands in his pockets and peered down at her, a cheeky grin spread across his beautiful face.

'I will find out,' Birdie said.

A tiny flash of fear crossed his face. *Good, you should be scared.*

'Need to do something about that competitive streak, Bird.'

She pushed him onto the bed and climbed on top of him. 'I know what to do about it.' She kissed him deeply.

'What's that?' he asked, coming up for air.

'Win.'

⇔ ⇔ ⇔

Birdie sat across from her friends, the casebook she'd just retrieved from her study in her hands. Pia and Stu chatted as they always did. They had a connection that often fizzled with electricity – sometimes creating a spark, sometimes a nasty burn.

Her mind wandered to Herb and what he might be doing now. Spending the night with him seemed somehow unreal. The gooey feeling filling her bones was a lovely little reminder that he was hers once again.

'I need to tell you something.'

Pia tilted her head. 'Herb didn't act like an arsehole last night, did he?'

'The opposite. But what I have to tell you does concern him.'

She gave them an abridged version of the reason he needed to disappear. Both sat with mouths open listening to the story. Roger Rogerson, Mick Drury, Warren Lanfranchi, Sally-Anne Huckstepp were all names they'd heard before.

'Holy shit,' Pia said. 'Talk about a good excuse.'

'Are you alright, Birdie?' Stu asked.

She didn't know what the answer to that question was. She hadn't told them about being shot at. Her uncle's request that she keep it secret from her mother was still fresh in her mind. She knew if she told them, they'd take it to the grave; she trusted them both implicitly. But voicing what had happened, reliving it, made it vivid and real. She was happy to just be blissed out on Herb. Fear pushed aside for now.

She was grateful when Pia held out her hand for the casebook and they could focus on something else. 'My money's still on Emer,' said Pia as Birdie passed it over. 'Where was she when it happened?'

'Up the coast doing some research for a story. Constable Celeste confirmed she was seen by the owner of the sandwich shop, the guy who put petrol in her car at the servo, the stewards at the hotel she stayed in and the publican where she had a drink.'

'Solid alibi,' said Stu.

'I stand corrected,' Pia said.

Birdie hid a grin. 'Perhaps put a line through Griff and Emer. apart from her alibi, I'm not convinced snagging the editor's gig at the local rag is reason enough for attempted murder.'

Pia did just that. 'The girl in Sy's entry,' she continued. 'She lost a permanent job prospect and her reputation.'

'Application paperwork would indicate which young woman went for a job at his school and missed out, although that would be confidential and locked up in the office,' said Stu.

'Yeah, but no one in education suspects it's Sy except us,' said Birdie. 'The woman in Sy's wake has no need to retaliate because there's no threat to her.'

'Her reputation is ... intact, *in fact*.' Pia grinned.

Birdie wobbled her head. Nothing like alliteration to brighten the mood.

'And, if she was going to stab someone, surely it would be Sy,' Pia continued. 'That's who I'd stab, not Warwick.'

'Logical point,' said Stu.

'What about Margie Rogers?' said Pia. '*We* know it wasn't her who was with Dom, but because he made sure she got the job as a favour to Sister T, she's been implicated. Do you think the fallout would be enough for her to stab someone?'

'It's not a bad theory. And it could be the reason Sister T refuses to prove her innocence beyond a doubt. She might think, or know, Margie did it and is protecting her niece,' said Stu.

'Did you get to talk to Dr Lee?' Birdie asked Stu.

'Poker games are on Tuesday nights. I swapped a shift at the hospital, so I'm home for it. Dr Lee loves a brandy.

Hopefully, I'll have some info for you on Wednesday morning.'

'Okay, in order of who we need to look into,' said Birdie.

'Sy: He's left his job. His name has been dragged through the mud. If we can work out it's him, others – in time – will too. His historical enemy, and subordinate vice-captain, has embarrassed him,' said Stu.

'Margie: Her reputation has been damaged. Sister T – with the flimsy alibi – could be taking the fall for her,' said Pia.

'Sister T: Warwick knows her secret – possibly who she's sleeping with – she was actually at the scene, holding the knife and covered in blood,' added Stu.

'Right. Herb still needs to approach Sy. He also has to try and get the staff at Percy's to open up, see if anyone saw Dom at school *after* he went out to his car. Sister T's not talking, which only leaves Margie,' said Birdie.

'How are we going to infiltrate there?' said Pia.

'I'm supervising ballroom dancing practice again tomorrow. I can chat to her then. In the meantime, I have a favour.' They focused on her and waited. 'I have an interview for the form mistress position on Tuesday afternoon. Brad snavelled a list of possible questions from an informed acquaintance. I need you to ask me some.'

She took the list from her desk and handed it to her friends. Pia and Stu looked over it and then at each other.

Pia pointed at one and began. 'Miss Mealing, as you know, the sanctity of marriage is the only place where a man and woman can engage in an activity in order to procreate. Could you please tell us if you're a virgin?'

Birdie dragged in a breath. 'It doesn't say that?' She grabbed the paper.

Pia and Stu laughed. 'Gotcha!' Stu said.

'Wankers.' She passed back the questions. 'Be serious.'

There was already too much focus on sexual activities of late. She was screwed, pun intended, if one of the questions did touch on relationships outside marriage. Luckily, thanks to Jonathon paying the blackmail money – and her ability to keep secrets – no one would ever know about hers.

TWENTY-FIVE

'MONEY FOR THE POOR.'

The singsong voices of Charmaine and Carly did nothing to break Birdie's anxiety on Monday morning. She watched in a daze as a couple of classmates delved into their pockets and put a one or two cent piece in the pair's outstretched palms.

Someone had threatened her life. She couldn't seem to get over the loop that kept playing in her mind.

'Money for the poor.'

She'd been shot at. Someone had threatened Herb's family. The threat so real that Herb had disappeared to keep them all safe. *Keep me safe.*

'Money for the poor.'

Her eyes ran along the rabble of girls. Were they in danger? Would being in her care put these girls in danger? She'd read a book a few years ago, *Fortress* it was called, about a teacher in a small country town who, together with her little class, had been kidnapped by scary masked men and held ransom for a million dollars.

'We've got enough for a Peppermint Freddo,' said Carly.

'Or a Caramello Koala,' said Charmaine.

She smiled at their eager faces. 'Good job, girls.' She remembered when she and Pia used to do the same. Sometimes it took them almost a whole lunchtime to gather the coins they needed to buy whatever it was they wanted. 'Now, ya big scabs, get back in the line.'

'Harsh, Miss.'

School students – even her very young adults – were great levellers. Her focus had already shifted to the here and now, which was a good thing. She would focus on her job, on the girls. She'd leave Herb to focus on the other.

'Straighten up the line, girls,' she called as they neared the hall.

The girls got themselves into a single file, forwarded into the hall and created a circle. Bit lopsided, but close enough. The boys came in moments later and took up their positions. Birdie craned her neck to see Margie accompanying them and smiled at the other teacher as she met her eye. As with the previous practice, the PE teacher gave some directions and the music started.

'How are you this week?' Birdie asked.

'Better. Things have died down. You were right, I think people are starting to realise it's not actually me Dom is slee … having a relationship with, which is such a relief.'

'Do you know who it is?'

Margie laughed. 'You would think I'd be staying right away from idle gossip, but I have a feeling …' She pulled in her lips. 'I really don't think it's someone on staff.'

'But *Shame Game* said a "co-teacher".'

'I know. Maybe their information was wrong? I don't know.'

Birdie made a mental note to have a closer look at what the informer had originally written in their letter and how that was interpreted and reworked by Emer.

'How is Dom? I saw him at the Sailo on Saturday night. He'd been drinking a bit.'

'You know Dom. He just bounces back.'

'Sister T is pretty much life-as-usual too.'

'Those two are a rock for each other. Excuse me.' She moved off quickly and reprimanded one of the boys.

Should Birdie mention she knew Sister T was her aunty?

'The evening Warwick was stabbed,' Birdie said when Margie returned 'a few of the guys from Percy's arrived at the basketball game together. Did they go in the same car?'

Margie frowned at Birdie. 'I'm not sure. I was working in my classroom. I went to the game on my own from there.'

Interesting.

'Where were you teaching before Percy's?'

'I was doing a bit of casual. Percy's is my first full-time job. I was lucky to get it too. The position only became available on the last day of school, last year. Dom put my name forward.'

'So you knew Dom from before?'

'He is an old mate of my mum's.'

I bet he was.

Margie read Birdie's look. 'Not like that. Not in the way you're thinking. They were in teachers' college together. I'm not sure I'm Dom's greatest defender at the moment, but Mum won't have a bad word said about him.'

'Your mum's a teacher too?'

'She mostly works with Dad now. He's a dentist. She's his dental nurse.'

Cute.

So Margie got the job at the last minute, a job that wasn't advertised. Birdie had heard there were different rules for the filling of last-minute positions. Two of the girls she went to college with were offered their jobs while in their final prac during the dying weeks of school. In his position, Dom would have known the job was going to become available. No wonder people on staff were dirty with Margie getting the position over some others.

Unless someone saw Margie still at school, she had no alibi. She could have left, stabbed Warwick and then gone to basketball. She was the girl thought to be the subject of the *Shame Game* entry at the time of the stabbing. Only *now* – a week and a new *Shame Game* later – had people quietened down about her. Could she have lashed out in anger and embarrassment?

'Margie, do you know anything that might help Sister T's case?'

Margie pondered for a moment. She opened her mouth – Birdie thought she was about to speak – but then her top lip closed over her bottom one.

'My uncle is trying hard to make sure she's not convicted of Warwick's stabbing, but he feels like she's keeping something from him. It might be important.'

They held each other's gaze for another moment. It wasn't such an odd request. Not when you took into account that Sister T was Margie's aunty.

'Perhaps you should talk to my mum.' She leaned in close and whispered. 'You probably know Therese and my mum, Rebecca, are sisters.'

Birdie had known. She smiled at Margie. 'I'll pass that on to my uncle.'

'They're on the phone more often than usual. Mum didn't say anything specific, but she has been ... extra attentive.'

Was that because of *Shame Game*'s implication, or was something else at play?

'Can I have her number for Larry?'

'Thanks for helping her, Birdie. I know Aunty Terri didn't stab that man. She's a giver of life, not a taker. She worked as a nurse in the country, you know, before they placed her in schools. She even helped bring me into the world. Mum had a complicated pregnancy. She went into premature labour at home. I'm named after my lovely aunty. I owe my life to her.'

It sounded like she owed Therese Margaret a debt of gratitude. Did Margie know her aunty had a secret? Would Margie silence a man in an effort to keep her aunty's – to whom she owed her life – secret safe?

Did Sister T's sister know the secret?

She'd go straight to the phone and call her uncle with this little tidbit. She considered the young teacher as the information was passed over.

Did Margie seem like someone who could stab a man and leave him to die?

⇔ ⇔ ⇔

Birdie missed the question. Herb had been asking her many in preparation for her interview on Tuesday. Surely this was the last one. It felt like they'd been practising for ages.

'Miss Mealing,' Herb said a little louder. 'Would you like me to repeat the question?' He sat on the lounge in her bedroom. The list of questions held delicately in his far-reaching fingers, forearms leaning casually on his knees, hair tousled and eyes like changing autumn leaves.

'No.' She didn't want him to repeat the question. She wanted to run her fingers through that messy hair, get lost in those autumn jewels. Feel those fingers touch her delicately, and then afterwards ... maybe not so delicately.

'Name two strengths,' he said, ignoring her no, 'one as a classroom teacher and one as a member of staff that you can bring to the role?'

She moved towards him – she'd already had this one a few times and had committed a response to memory – and stopped in front of him. She kneeled on the lounge – her left knee on the outside of Herb's right, her other leg slipped over his lap, straddling him.

He gazed up at her. 'Is there anything else...'

She kissed his neck, removing the paper from his hands.

'That you want us to know, Miss Mealing...'

She kissed his collarbone. He groaned, hands slipping along her thighs and settling on her hips. 'Before we finish up?'

'I think we're finished,' she said softly into his mouth as she leaned in to kiss him. She'd kissed Herb's lips too many times to count but was delighted by the softness of them, every time. 'And besides, that question's not on the list.'

'What about ... Have you had any dealings with notorious crime lord, Vinny Varva?'

'Also'—she kissed him again—'not on the list.' She moved on to the other side of his neck.

'Haven't properly discussed your secret meeting with him yet, Bird.'

She pushed his shirt open, feathered kisses along his shoulder. 'You're misguided if you think I'm going to share every move I make with you, Detective.'

His hand found her left breast and thumbed the nipple. Her breath left her. She bit into his skin. When she found her voice, she said, 'Besides, there are things you aren't telling me.'

He thumbed the nipple again. A line of heat ran straight from it to between her legs. He pulled her top down. Her breast bounced over the collar and popped up into his face.

He set his lips to it, suckling and licking. He kept his eyes pinned on hers as his tongue darted over her. 'Some things you don't need to know,' he breathed across her wet skin.

Her breath rushed out, her back arching towards him. 'And some things *you* don't need to know,' she answered, her voice strained.

Herb popped out her other breast and pushed them to-gether. Birdie grabbed Herb's hair as he placed both nipples in his mouth. She wouldn't be able to put up with much more of this. Her body already floating and aching for fric-tion.

Apart from her connection to Vinny, she could think of a few other things she didn't want her employers to know. Like what she was doing right now. Like what she wanted to do. She leaned down and whispered a few suggestions in Herb's ear.

'Jesus, Birdie.' He sucked in a breath and captured her mouth in his. His kisses hot and searching. 'That wicked mouth on you.' He readjusted her on his lap so that his growing hardness sat nicely between her legs.

She slid her tongue up his neck and across to his ear-lobe, nuzzled his ear. A shiver ricocheted across his body;

he pulled her further onto him. *Friction.* This is what she needed.

'What would you like me to do with my wicked mouth?' She rocked against him.

The sound of Glen's low voice drifted an undercurrent through the rooms outside her door. The boys' brash, clanging arrival followed closely.

She popped her breasts back into place. 'Raincheck, Detective?' And slid off his lap.

'I won, Big Bird.' Rusty came running into her room and stood holding high a painting he'd done. It had a big blue ribbon stuck on it.

She appraised the picture and then its artist – face beaming, arm muscles taut, sandy curls slick with sweat from footy practice. 'That's excellent, little man. What a colourful painting.'

'We had to do a portrait of Father Wim. He's going to Italy, you know, to the Baticave. We're making a book for him to take with him.'

Birdie observed the painting more closely, that of a blond-haired man wearing square, black-rimmed glasses. A red jumper with two blue stripes covered a very broad chest.

'Mine gets to go on the cover. Father Wim said it looks like how fat he'll be when he's eated all that pasta.'

'Because he's going to the *Vatican* in Italy, where pasta is *eaten*.'

'Yeah.'

She held up the painting and admired it. 'Well done. It looks tops.'

'Hey, Herb,' he said quickly before he grabbed the painting and ran back out into the main house.

Birdie shook her head.

Herb grabbed her hand and pressed a kiss to her wrist.

Fire danced along her limbs again.

'Did you get in touch with Rebecca Rogers?' she said.

Herb narrowed his eyes at her as she extracted her wrist but picked up the chain of conversation. 'Made an appointment as soon as I got off the phone with Larry. Saw her at about lunchtime.'

Birdie bit her fingernail. 'Your efficiency is a bit of a turn-on, Herb.'

He reached for her, but she danced away. 'Not fair, teach.'

She stayed at a safe distance and flicked her hand at him. 'Continue your story.'

He exhaled but went on. 'Rebecca confirmed Sister T had stayed with her before Margie was born. But there's something Rebecca's not saying. Husband popped into the little kitchen we were talking in and sat down to join us. Became more reserved with what she shared after that.'

'Oh. I wonder why?'

'Is it usual for a religious nun to step back from her duties to care for a family member?'

'I know the church can be controlling, but they're not unfeeling. How could they stop her? Besides, Sister T worked as a nurse before she trained as a teacher. Surely, they could see that she'd be a comfort to her pregnant sister in such a situation.'

'Was one interesting thing Larry's friend in hospital records found.'

'Larry looked into hospital records?'

'Something you said triggered it. He thinks the sun shines out of you, Bird.'

'It does.' She glimpsed over her shoulder as she lifted and dropped it.

'I do too.'

'Well, of course you do, Detective.' She rewarded him with a kiss, which – she was sure – was what he was vying for. 'It's only natural.' But she was ready, when he inevitably reached for her again, to dart away.

'Anyway,' Herb continued through a grin. 'A Rebecca Rogers had a hospital stay while she was pregnant.'

'That makes sense. Margie said her mum experienced a troubling pregnancy.'

'Records show that Mrs Rogers had a miscarriage not long before Margie was born.'

'A miscarriage? That can't be right. Is it the same Rebecca Rogers?' Birdie's face lifted to the door where Kick entered, dragging his feet. 'How was your day, little man?'

'I didn't win.' He flopped into Birdie's arms as she held them out. His bony back was damp with perspiration.

'We can't all be good at painting.' She kissed the top of his sweaty head. 'How was training? I bet you did well at that?'

'Yeah, I got three goals for my team when we had the game at the end.'

'There you go.'

He went and sat next to Herb on the lounge, snuggling in.

'Hey, mate,' Herb said, putting an arm around him. Birdie sat on the other side.

'I told Rusty his painting was good,' Kick said grumpily.

'That's excellent sportsmanship, Kick. Very mature,' she said.

He snuggled Herb for a moment longer and then stood up again.

Birdie watched his downhearted flounce back towards the door. 'Hey, Kick?'

He turned, bottom lip extended.

She dug around in her work bag for a lollipop. She gave them out to the students every so often. 'Here, for being a good sport. Don't tell Rusty.'

He smiled, took the offering, pocketed it, and happily headed out again.

Birdie watched him go for a moment before turning back to Herb. 'Perhaps Rebecca was carrying twins?'

Herb rubbed his chin. 'Lost one but the other survived?'

'It happens.' Her mother's second pregnancy was monitored more vigilantly because she was carrying two foetuses.

'No record of any other birth in the hospital's data, though.'

'That could be because Margie was a home birth.'

Herb threw her a look. 'How do you know that?' he said accusingly.

'Don't get the shits, Herb.' She ran a finger along his cheek. 'I only just remembered I knew it. Margie said her aunty helped bring her into the world. Do you think Rebecca held the pregnancy of the second baby and delivered Margie at home with Therese's help?'

'Only logical explanation there is.'

Having one baby after a difficult pregnancy was probably better than having none. But only having one of the twins? She loved both boys in equal amounts. A rush of heartache at their possible non-existence crashed against her chest.

'Are we being watched, Herb?' she asked without making eye contact.

'Whadoya mean?'

'Is someone making sure we're safe? What if those men come back?'

'Birdie.' He lifted off the lounge and came towards her. 'I don't want you to worry about that.'

'Is Vinny also protecting *us*?'

'Birdie,' he warned.

She turned to face him. 'I was shot at. Don't tell me not to be concerned. I have to consider the boys, Herb; they're only little.' She pointed at the door. 'Lenore. Glen. My students.'

Birdie had tried to play down the events of last Saturday night – she didn't want to make a big deal about it, didn't want Herb to feel the need to disappear again. A tear sprang up on her. *But the boys.* She searched Herb's face through the swell.

'*You* don't need to worry,' he said brushing it away.

Fear spread through her veins, anger hot on its heels. She grabbed his shirt. 'I *do* need to worry. Tell me.'

His eyes grew wide. 'Birdie, come on. I can't—'

'Can't discuss my safety with me, or that of my family. Can't share your dark secrets? Stop bloody keeping things from me.' She twisted tighter, her voice gaining power. 'Are. We. SAFE?' The tears dropped over onto her cheeks.

Herb's hands closed over hers. 'Vinny's watching, Bird.'

'The boys?'

'Making it a priority.'

She released her grip and dropped her head to his chest. Herb's arms came around her. Her hands still shook where they rested on Herb's pecs. She wondered, once again, about Vinny's involvement in their lives.

In Herb's life.

In Lenore's life.

In my life.

Vinny was the wrong colouring. She was more like Uncle Larry in that respect. The other man she often daydreamed might be her father, him being the ginger one. But Vinny was the right height, and on the few occasions she'd had dealings with him, she recognised – for the first time in her life – someone who shared her temper. She couldn't be the daughter of a street lord, could she?

She'd always wondered where it came from, the rage. Lenore was pretty much a passive person, very calm, slow to anger. The way Birdie's blood filled with heat, limbs burst with violent energy, she'd presumed was an hereditary gene passed down from her grandparents. They had angrily disowned their daughter after all. But did that suggest a quick temper or a much deeper condition such as narrow-mindedness or embarrassment ... stupidity?

'I'm here too, Bird.'

But you might go, Herb. Disappear again.

He held her face in his hands. 'I'm not going anywhere,' he said reading her mind like he often did. She took in the fiery intensity of his golden gaze, blue flames contrasted against the soft red veins. 'Not going anywhere, teach.'

'You can't promise that, Herb.'

He put his forehead against hers. 'I do promise.' But was it a promise he could keep?

Flirting is not like
football. There are no tackles
or passes or goals to score.
It's more like shuttlecock,
the deft pat of something
going back and forth, back
and forth. A good flirt is
like a good tickle.

'Flirtation:
The art of maybe'
Cleo, March 1985.

TWENTY-SIX

Birdie drove towards the Little Shops. It was the May birthdays' morning tea at recess today, and seeing that Sabine was one of the staff who celebrated her birthday in May, Birdie had asked Fidele to organise some petit fours. She drove the Gypsy into the very small parking area behind the shops and stepped out of the car.

Two heated, female voices invaded the still morning air, followed immediately by wild colour and movement. The birthday girl in question, Sabine, was flinging words at ... *Emer*.

Both women were unaware of Birdie's presence at this early Tuesday morning hour.

Sabine's arms were flailing. Her face was alive with anger. Instinctively, Birdie crouched behind her car. The acting editor looked taken aback at Sabine's words; it was the most emotion she'd ever seen from her. Emer grabbed Sabine's outstretched arm and ushered her inside. Birdie hadn't caught the words that were said, but the feeling of fury behind them was deafening. She slid along the side of Gypsy and edged closer to the back entrance of the gazette office.

A shiver ran up her spine.

This was where the person who had stabbed Warwick exited.

She moved closer. Just behind this door was where the newsagent's owner found Sister T, knife in hand and covered in blood.

She could hear the voices of Sabine and Emer inside, but as she neared, she realised their heated conversation was being held ... in French.

She heard the phrase '*es-tu*', then some words she didn't understand and then '*personnes*?' before the door to the *Gallie Wallen Gazette* was soundly shut. 'Are you' and 'people'. Sabine was asking Emer a question. Are you ... *something, something, something* ... people?

She moved closer to the door and listened for a few minutes. Not only could she no longer hear the conversation very well, but she couldn't understand enough French to decipher what was being spoken about.

The door suddenly flew open. Birdie dropped behind the incinerator. Sabine marched away. Emer stood in the open doorway watching her departure. Suddenly Sabine turned back and pointed a finger at the editor. '*Na touche pas à mon Birdie Mealing.*'

Birdie sucked in a breath, heart beating madly. She stayed still for the count of sixty, then walked back across the car park and through the back door of Fidele's.

Don't touch Birdie Mealing.

Birdie understood those words loud and clear.

☘☘☘

Welcome sun streamed through the front window and across Birdie's chest as she pulled out of the car park at Fidele's.

Why were Emer and Sabine arguing? Surely the whole argument couldn't have been about Birdie, even with Sabine's final comment demanding Emer stay away? If only she'd taken more notice of Fidele's attempt to educate her in French. The rising unrest in her stomach was not helped by the sweet-smelling pastries on the seat beside her or the fact that she'd been met with an armoured back door when she'd gone to collect them.

Fidele's voice had risen, and he'd waved his hands around in demonstration when she'd asked why, all of a sudden, it was locked. *'C'est impératif* my personnel, my patrons are safe.'

She hadn't thought about the impact Warwick's stabbing might be having on the Little Shops; that Fidele and the patrons of the French le Faire might feel unsafe. It felt like life at the moment was one gut-wrenching event after another.

At the pedestrian crossing, she stopped to let a board rider stroll across. The rider turned and gifted her a very attractive grin.

'You'll be late for work if you don't get a wriggle on,' she called through the window, dragging her attention from her worries to Griff Wheatley.

Griff's smile broadened. He put a hand through his blond hair – shaking off excess water – wandered over to her car and leaned in the window. A couple of drips dropped into the casing in which the glass of the window recessed.

'Are you offering me a lift?'

'Very funny. I'm going in the opposite direction.'

'If only you could be persuaded to go my way, Birdie.'

Birdie shook her head.

'Whatcha got there?' He tipped his head at the pink-lidded dessert box on the passenger seat.

'Petit fours. May birthdays' morning tea. Sabine is one of them.'

'Pretty girl, Sabine. Wonder whether *she'd* be happy to give me a lift.'

'Play nice, Griff.' Birdie grinned.

He laughed.

'Actually,' she said, 'I've been meaning to ask you a question.'

'Oh, yeah?'

'Why didn't you pay the blackmail money?'

'What are you talking about?'

'The blackmail money that would have stopped the story about your relationship with the schoolgirl from Queensland being published in the paper?'

Griff frowned. 'No one asked me for any money.'

Perhaps he couldn't be contacted. 'Where were you staying in Queensland? Did you have a phone?'

'I stayed with my dad. He has a phone. People called me on it.' He flicked his head to the right and shook a droplet from his ear. The frown deepened on his bronzed forehead as he straightened his head. 'Are you saying that other people were contacted before their story was printed and asked for money to prevent it from happening?'

Could he have missed the call? 'Yes, that's exactly what I'm saying.'

'How do you know?'

'I have a couple of teaching friends who were contacted recently. If they didn't pay up, then their "dirty little secret" would get out. They did pay up, and it wasn't printed.'

'Shit!' Griff rubbed a hand through his hair, sending droplets flying. It stuck back for a moment before flopping down again. 'But then, what about the entries that made it into the paper? Didn't those guys get contacted either?'

'The desk-polisher-with-co-worker's-arse did, but his wife answered the phone and didn't tell him the nature of the call. Her only response when she hung up the phone was to smile and say he deserved what was coming.'

'Whoa. Gnarly.'

'Yep, that. He had no idea who had been on the phone. I haven't asked the other two.'

'Maybe Dad took the message, or his girlfriend did. Why wouldn't they have told me, though?'

Good question.

'Hey, I've just had a thought! Maybe the informer wanted certain stories to be told regardless.' She huffed a laugh. 'If everybody paid up, there'd be no gossip to share, would there?'

He slapped his hand against the window ledge. 'This is my life you're tossing around.' He pointing out to sea. 'Like a boat in the storm.' His tone shocked her. It seemed the normally Zen man had a limit. 'She was a school leaver, by the way, not a schoolgirl,' Griff ground out.

'Sorry, Griff. I didn't mean to—'

'No'—he took a deep breath—'I'm sorry, Birdie. Didn't mean to snap.' He resumed his nonchalant nature and flashed a smile. 'Catch you later.' She watched as he ran up the road barefoot and into the driveway of his gran's house.

She wondered whether Sy or Todd *had* been contacted or whether it was always the intention for Sy's, Todd's and Griff's stories to be told.

Maybe not everyone got the opportunity to have their dirty little secret kept secret.

⸜ ⸜ ⸜

Was it possible for a heartbeat to be heard outside someone's chest?

Birdie went over questions and answers in her head as she passed the moments before the form mistress interview. The little waiting area was silent, except for her noisy heart. The wooden chair hard against the back of her thighs, the smell of Mr Sheen, the worn carpet that led to Sister T's office door, all wandered in and out of her consciousness as she waited. She had kept herself busy over the last couple of days; dark thoughts crept in when she wasn't busy. Was Herb safe? Were she and her family? Would Vinny's protection be enough?

She'd seen Herb around Joanie's. Since her worried outburst the other night, he'd made an appearance dressed as a maintenance staff member. Glasses and a hat on at all times. He'd also been 'maintaining' things at her brothers' primary school, so Rusty said. Lenore had eyeballed her at that news. Birdie mentioned Uncle Larry had Herb working on a case. Her mother seemed to have bought it. As Uncle Larry had requested, Birdie had kept her mouth shut about the shots fired on Saturday night as well as the subsequent protection detail.

Knowing Herb was hovering around had calmed her. She looked over her shoulder every now and then to see if she could spot Vinny's people – a familiar car, a recognisable face, some sort of presence – but didn't see anyone. Except Herb. Would Vinny's people get to her first if the bad guys did approach? Would they get to Herb?

Birdie's mouth was suddenly dry. Her nerves increasing as the thoughts flooded in. She needed to focus on the interview. She could use a sugar hit from today's petit fours right about now. She rummaged in her bag, her fingers resting on a lollipop – momentarily reminding her of Kick's sad face at not winning the portrait prize – before finding a packet of Tic Tacs. She popped one into her mouth and calmed her mind.

The door in front of her opened. Birdie jumped. She recovered quickly and formed her face into a smile.

Sister T beamed back. 'Come in, Birdie.'

She heard the click of the other door, from which the previous interviewee had exited, as she entered. She smiled at the assistant principal and pastoral care coordinator, who were already seated, and took the chair her principal offered.

She answered the questions as best she could, aware of the heat that filled her cheeks, the flush and the tickle of perspiration behind her knees. Most questions were similar to the ones she'd practised; a few she had to formulate answers to on the spot. The question of who might do the Friday was discussed. To Birdie's relief, it didn't seem a problem that someone would act in the role for one day a week. The panel saw it as an opportunity for someone else. *Maybe Brad?* There was lots of smiling and nodding and an assurance she would know the outcome before the end of the week.

'That was an excellent interview,' Sister T whispered as Birdie was seen out via the other door. Now all she could do was wait.

The corridors were empty so late in the afternoon; the cleaner the only person she saw as she made her way to her car. The staff car park held a few cars, probably those of the panel. This back end of school was surrounded by bush on three of its sides. She was suddenly aware of her vulnerability in the dying light. She opened her car, got in, locked it again – something she rarely did – and started the engine.

How must Herb be faring if she was so skittish? Was he always looking over his shoulder? He said he'd thought he had eliminated the problem. What had made him think he had, made him happy enough to return to Vantage and her?

And what about the gazette staff? Granted, no attack had been made on Emer after Thursday's edition, but it still could be. Someone had the balls to stab Warwick. Someone in Gallie Wallen. An attempted murderer was at large.

She was almost home before noticing an envelope that had been stuck under the windscreen wiper on the passenger side.

TWENTY-SEVEN

THE CONSTANT GRUNTS AND groans of young men struck Birdie, much as the blows that conjured them, as she sat in the stands of the local footy ground. The Randwick Bluebottles were training tonight, and Herb had picked her up on the way.

'What's my role?' she'd asked.

'Watch and listen.'

She'd given him a rundown of how she thought she went and of Sister T's words, still slightly buzzing from her interview. His mouth created a satisfied grin – Such confidence in her ability.

She'd positively identified Sy – which wasn't difficult seeing the older man in the middle of the young players was obviously the coach – and was now keeping out of Herb's way but *also* watching and listening, as ordered.

She could hardly do anything *but* listen. Sy bellowed cranky orders and sporadic praise as he lumbered up and down the field, verbally – and at times physically – squeezing the most from his players. The only couple of times she'd seen him was in a suit. Tonight, he was fleshy and free. His muscles cut loose in the tiny shorts and team T-shirt.

And she definitely could watch. She couldn't take her eyes off the twenty-odd fit, young men decked out in shorts and singlets, flexing their sweat-slicked muscles under ambient lighting. *Watching was not a problem.*

Sy was up in the face of one of the players, a smaller guy, berating him. Would Sy have been a challenge to work for in the school environment? Had he got into Warwick's face like this when they were kids? Was this his normal behaviour, or was it unique to the field? The player ran back to the others, head down.

Herb walked towards her. 'Apparently, they'll finish up in a few minutes.'

'That's a shame,' Birdie mumbled, keeping her eyes on the show.

'Birdie.'

'You're the one who told me to watch.'

Herb stood in front of her, blocking the scene.

Her focus lifted. 'Just doing as I was asked, Detective.'

'Be a first.' He rubbed a hand above his top lip, then down around and under his chin, pinching the skin in his fingertips. A sure sign he was thinking. 'Actually, I can't believe I'm asking you to do this, but perhaps you could pick one of the players and ask some questions?'

'Are you suggesting I use my wily, feminine charms to obtain information?' Birdie fluttered her eyelashes.

'Jesus Christ.'

'How close should I get?'

'On second thoughts.'

'Flirting, teasing, touching.' She ran a finger up his thigh. He snapped his hand to catch it before it found its intended mark.

'So help me, Birdie, if you put your hands anywhere near another guy's—'

'Herb,' she whispered, pointing. 'They're coming off the field.'

She hadn't really dressed for seduction, still in the dusty pink linen, knee-length pencil skirt and matching jacket she'd worn to work, picked out especially for her afternoon interview. She rolled up the waistband of her skirt till it was a mini, removed the jacket – she had a silk camisole on underneath – and hung it over her shoulder, then pulled her hair out of its low pony. She waited until a stream of squeaky clean, aftershave-smelling men emerged from the changerooms and stepped nonchalantly into the light.

An immediate wolf whistle greeted her. She laughed and continued to walk. Shouts from the group and then the sound of one man walking in step.

'Hey, there.'

'Hi.' She kept walking.

'I'm Jed.'

'Hi, Jed.'

'And your name is?'

'A secret.'

He huffed a laugh. 'Where are you headed?'

Good question. Where am I headed? There was nowhere to go. What was she gonna do – a lap around the oval? She stopped. 'Just stretching my legs and waiting for my ... brother.'

They turned back to the field.

'They *are* incredible legs.'

'Thanks.' Birdie viewed him properly. He was smaller than the regular footballer. Much smaller than her. A winger, perhaps. Five-eighth? She didn't know a lot about football, but these players were lighter, made for speed rather than strength, she was led to believe.

'Who's your brother?'

She stepped in close. 'I'd never get a chance to talk to anyone if I announced that.'

He laughed. 'Bit protective, is he?'

'The new coach looks like a bit of a ... bully?'

'Yeah, he had a bee in his bonnet tonight. He does that sometimes. Just blows his stack. Picks on you.'

'He seems very ... physically intimidating.'

'Yeah, he can be.'

Sy and Herb were walking towards the boundary in a heated discussion. Herb had height on his side; Sy had width.

'He has a weird gait. Is he limping?'

'Yeah, he did something to his ankle coupla weeks back. Hasn't stopped him, though.'

'Did he do it at training?'

'Nah. At home.'

'Well, here comes my brother.'

Jed followed Birdie's eye as Herb and Sy had reached the fence. 'He's not on the team.'

'I didn't say he was.' Birdie offered a guilty smile as she walked off. 'Nice to meet you, Jed.'

Jed scurried away – 'I don't need to tell you anything, mate' – as Sy's angry voice echoed loudly out over the night.

'You went to school with the victim. Weren't the best of friends, I hear.' Herb was still pushing.

'No. He's a righteous git. Always on top of organising things, always making sure everyone knew I wasn't. He was jealous. Resented me for finding life ... fun.'

Fun? Is that what he called misogyny?

'Can't say I'm surprised someone stabbed him,' Sy continued, 'but it wasn't me.'

'So where were you when it happened?'

'As I said, mate, none of your business.'

Birdie stepped forward. 'What happened to your leg?'

Sy looked her up and down, his focus finally landing on her face.

Herb did the same – more alarming, less leering.

'Miss Mealing,' Sy cooed, 'from the literacy in-service.'

'Yes, that's right. Hello, Sy.'

Herb bristled beside him.

Sy smiled. 'A box fell on it.'

Birdie smiled back. 'Of Christmas party decorations?'

Sy's face morphed from smiley to fuck-you. 'I beg your pardon?'

But Herb had already placed a firm hand under her elbow and was leading her away. 'He did not like the suggestion he might be Naughty Santa at all, Bird,' he whispered against her ear. Herb didn't turn around and say goodbye and didn't stop moving until they reached the car. Once in the sanctuary of the car, he looked Birdie up and down again. 'I didn't say strip for the man.' He drove off.

'I just ... loosened up my outfit a touch.'

Herb shook his head. 'What did the little guy have to say?'

'His name is Jed, Herb.'

She saw the side of his mouth tug into a smile.

'He was the one who was pulled up by Sy during that last five minutes of training. I implied Sy might be physically intimidating and a bit of a bully. He didn't disagree. He said Coach got a bee in his bonnet sometimes and tended to pick on individuals.'

Herb tapped his hand on the steering wheel as they were stopped at the lights. 'Fits with the aggression he aimed at me. He was not impressed at my claim he'd taken leave in a hurry, and that it made him look questionable.'

'Surely Warwick would have fought for his life. Perhaps there was a struggle and Sy was hurt, and that's why he's limping.'

'So not a dropped box of Christmas party decorations then?'

Birdie rolled her lips over covering a smile. 'Sorry. Couldn't help myself.'

Once more, Herb shook his head. 'Not sure a bung leg fits with the stab in the back, teach. He wouldn't answer my questions about where he was.' He rubbed his forehead. 'Perhaps Celeste might be able to get it out of him. Though could be too late.'

'Why?'

'He'll be wise to it.'

'So he might organise an alibi if he hasn't got one?'

'Exactly.'

⇔ ⇔ ⇔

Herb drove her uncle's car towards Redfern. With him at the wheel, she could play voyeur. He really was quite breathtaking. Light travelled through the iris of his eye. Banana topping, champagne, even searing flames in certain radiance and the flecks of blue that added a simple reminder that nothing was perfect. That chaos could still reign in beauty.

'Are you going to stare at me all night?' His gaze slid to her, a grin tugging his lips.

The full effect of those eyes on her – alone with him in the darkness, like it was only the two of them in the whole world – sent a zing along her skin. Did he know he did that to her? Should she tell him? 'Dream on.'

The ALS was filled with bodies when they stepped inside.

Herb lifted an eyebrow at Birdie. 'Koori party,' he said, putting an arm around her waist and leading her into the mix.

'Bring ya gubba over here?' called an elderly man sprawled on the lounge.

'Hands off, Norm. She's mine.'

'Would you like a cup of tea, Norm?' asked Birdie over her shoulder as Herb continued to steer her towards the kitchenette at the back.

'Old fella wouldn't say no.'

Herb grinned, pinched Birdie's backside and headed for the phone.

Birdie's eyes picked their way through the crowd until she spotted her uncle. He acknowledged her with a wave, pausing his conversation with the client in front of him. 'Cecil is still at the courts. Might need Herb to run some liaison with the police,' he called over the din.

'He's making a call to Constable Celeste, but he'll be back in a tic.'

Her uncle nodded.

Birdie heard snippets of conversation as she passed out cups of tea and bikkies. It seemed that Radio Redfern was getting some legal advice.

'Radio Redfern?' said Birdie to Herb as he hurried by.

'Concern about occupying a building currently owned by the government.' Herb jerked his eyebrows. 'Back soon.'

Radio Redfern was more than just a radio station; it was a meeting place, a place to chill, have a cuppa, catch up. Much like the ALS tonight. Uncle Larry had already assisted with applications for funding, for equipment. A voice for the people, it was currently pumping out of the radio on the windowsill. It lifted her spirits as she tidied the office bins and cleaned up in the kitchen, lost in the rhythm of making order out of mayhem.

'Was everything okay at the pub?' Birdie asked Herb at the conclusion of their evening; time at the ALS always seemed to fly.

'Just the usual. Took some notes. Be a witness if needed.'

He didn't say anymore. Birdie knew the usual. The trifecta, it was called. At closing time, the police would wait outside the pub. Once the Aboriginal patrons stepped outside, the police would swoop to arrest them for being drunk in a public place. That was number one in the trifecta. Unseemly language and resisting police were two and three.

'What was Constable Celeste's reaction to our ideas about Sy?'

'Looking into it.' Herb yawned and dragged a hand over his eyes. She directed him to the passenger seat and took her uncle's keys. Shelly would pick up Larry on her way home from dinner with friends.

The pub hadn't been Herb's only stop that night. Intent on arresting her grandson, the police had entered the home of an elderly Aboriginal woman.

'The boy hadn't been there.' She'd heard Herb tell her uncle. 'Probably got wind they were coming and buggered off. Didn't stop them from making their presence known, though. Aunty put up a fight.' Having been a policeman himself for the last ten years, the heavy-handed treatment of certain police teams towards the Aboriginal community meant Herb was tired and a little cranky.

Birdie rubbed his leg and offered a close-lipped smile as they drove towards Vantage. He rested his head back and closed his eyes.

She drove in silence until she pulled up in front of her door. 'Does a witness chatting to a suspect make an alibi more viable than the witness just seeing the suspect from afar?'

Herb sat up and pushed the hair back from his forehead. Washed-out. He released a deep sigh. 'Out with it.'

'Out with what?'

'Whatever's behind your loaded question.'

'I don't know what you mean.' It's not that she intentionally kept things from Herb. *Apart from the fact that I know the subjects had been blackmailed and still have not found a way – that doesn't incriminate me – to tell you.*

'Yes you do.'

Perhaps now was not a good time to chat.

'Waiting, Birdie.'

She swallowed. 'Griff told me he *spoke* to the old beach bum. You told me the old beach bum recognised his photo as being one of the surfers in the water.'

Herb ran his forefinger under his bottom lip and, with it and his thumb, gripped his chin. 'Two different versions.'

'Surely speaking to someone confirms his presence?'

'Why wouldn't he tell the cops something that would make his alibi more solid?' Herb searched Birdie's face as he obviously tossed hypotheses back and forth like *Pong*.

'Either it's true and he forgot to mention it or it's a lie he wants *you* to believe.'

'Perhaps he thinks, because he's innocent, the details don't matter.'

'More like he'd perjure himself if he lied to the cops in his initial statement and then changed it later on.' Herb gave her a searching look. 'What does he want from you, Birdie?'

'Nothing.'

He narrowed his eyes. 'Why have you sat on this? When did you speak to him? Saturday night? It's Tuesday today.'

It was Friday night, actually. Not to mention our conversation this morning.

'Herb, a lot has happened since Saturday night.' *Like being shot at, sleeping together.* She smiled over at him.

'Fair enough.' A slip of a grin. 'Could be telling you what he wants only you to hear with a motive behind it.'

Possibly. But what if it was the truth?

'So, you need to answer my question. What does he want from you?'

Griff had made that pretty clear, but Birdie wasn't sure Herb would be happy with that truth. And being innocent of attempted murder *would* make him more attractive. 'The closer I get, Herb, the more I find out.'

'You're leading him on?'

Better than being *led* on. His frown made her heart twist.

'Excuse me. Who was the one who asked me, just this evening, to cosy up to one of the football players?'

'I was right there, Birdie. There was no danger.'

'Griff's not dangerous.' *Was he?* He *had* got a little cranky when she spoke to him this morning; a side she'd never seen before.

Herb glared at her. 'Unless it was Griff who stabbed Warwick.'

'Isn't that why *speaking* to someone would be a better alibi than seeing someone?'

'How close are you?'

'Are you asking for the sake of the case or other reasons?'

'Is the reason I'm asking more or less important than the fact that you won't answer?'

The push-pull. The signature of their relationship. It made her angry that she'd need to answer. Made her defiant in not wanting to. She breathed in and out. 'We're friends.'

'Have you asked your friend why he would sleep with a girl in the fourth form? What made him move to Queensland? Why he doesn't hold a permanent job?' *She knew all those answers, didn't she?* 'For someone with a calculating mind like yours, Bird, you've left this man's motives pretty much alone.'

'I'm questioning them now, Detective.'

'Have you let him think he's in with a chance?'

'Herb, a little harmless flir—'

'Birdie,' he warned.

She sat up straight. 'Don't you trust me?' she said, a smile in her voice.

'*Can* I trust you?'

Her smile dropped. *I love you, Birdie Mealing, but have you ever considered that he may not be able to trust you.* Pia's words from a week ago rang in her ears.

She was flirty, not disloyal. Perhaps she was hard to pin down, but once committed, she was unwavering. Had Herb's disappearance – subsequent keeping of his cards close to his chest, secretive relationship with Vinny – meant she'd allowed herself a bit of breathing room? Her little backstage trysts with Clint had picked up where they'd left off. She'd even been thinking of taking things further.

She once slept with a married man. *Could* she be trusted?

'Your silence speaks volumes, teach.' He got out of the car and slammed the door.

'Oh, come on, Herb.' She got out of the car and followed him. 'I could ask you the same thing about trust. You haven't exactly been totally honest with me.' *Good. Turn it around on him.*

He spun around to face her. 'Are you into this guy?'

Once upon a time, she would have been. She would have definitely been into a little Griff fun, but not now.

'Again with the silence! For fuck's sake, Birdie.' Herb growled.

'You were gone for months, Herb.'

He stormed towards her and took her face in his hands, a palm on either cheek. 'Was I so easy to forget, teach?' His eyes blazed with anger, insecurity.

'Herb,' she said softly. If only he knew the truth. That she'd thought about him every day. Had begun to coach herself not to. 'I'm a hopeless flirt, but not so hopeless that I'd step over the line.' *Except with Jonathon.*

His eyes searched hers.

'Think about it,' she said.

She thought about it too. She'd kissed Clint, but that was because Herb had abandoned her. Anger made her decide all bets were off. She hadn't slept with him. And since Herb had been back, she'd retreated from Clint. The only reason she put up with Griff's advances was because it suited her, *wasn't it*? She was getting info for the case. Griff was a teddy bear, plus, he needed a friend.

She tilted her head. 'We might have a slight issue with trust, Detective.'

'Birdie, how many times can I explain myself?'

'I don't know. Probably about the same number of times I put myself in a man's path to gain information.'

A heavy breath wafted towards her from his lips. 'I don't want to argue.'

Could they get past this? Did all couples keep secrets from each other?

He still held her face. More gently now, rubbing his thumbs across her skin.

She reached up and held his cheeks, too. 'Then kiss me, Herb.'

TWENTY-EIGHT

BIRDIE READ THE WORDS, barely believing their existence, glad that she hadn't opened the envelope while Herb was there.

She'd forgotten all about it when she'd pulled into the driveway after her interview. Herb had been waiting for her, wanting her to go to footy practice with him. Then from footy, they'd gone to the ALS. She'd got out of one car and straight into another. Then when they'd got home, in the dark and kissed, kissed after they'd just had an argument about trust – the irony – she'd been caught up again. She'd only remembered the envelope after Herb had left. She'd tiptoed out in her nightie and bare feet in what felt like the middle of the night to retrieve it.

The paper shook in her hand as she read it again.

> I know all about your dirty little secret. I also know you're up for a promotion. If you want your secret to remain so, you'll need to deposit $5,000 cash into the attached account.

> P.S. I'm not sure a good Catholic school
> teacher, who sleeps with a married man, has a
> gay best friend and seduces policemen is really
> leadership material. Do you?

Who the hell was this person? How did they know so much about her life?

Birdie's breath was coming hard and fast. She concentrated on regulating it, stopping her head from spinning.

Why hadn't she asked Uncle Larry to: *Follow. The. Money?*

She knew why. This very note was the reason why. She hadn't wanted anyone to find out about her and Jonathon.

Well, that seemed a little inconsequential now, didn't it!

She paced her bedroom floor.

She could ask her uncle to locate the account owner tomorrow ... no, tonight. Uncle Larry could do it. Birdie could use Brad as the catalyst. She could ask her uncle to follow the money because Brad's mate had been threatened. No one needed to know it was actually *her* who had been threatened. It wasn't a lie that Brad's friend had been blackmailed.

Where was she going to get $5000? Perhaps that could also come from her uncle. But, how would she explain it? Maybe a new car, but then what would happen when she didn't buy a new car? Maybe some musical equipment, but what piece of equipment would cost that much?

Uncle Larry would mention the money to her mother. Unless she asked him not to. He'd asked her to keep the shooting a secret. But then he'd want to know why it was to be kept a secret. Five thousand dollars was such a lot of money. It was like a fifth of her whole year's wage. Wouldn't

Uncle Larry want to know where his hard-earned money was going? Of course he would.

Birdie's mind was going at a hundred miles an hour as she massaged the soft skin that covered the bone beneath her eyebrows. Behind there, thoughts tumbled over each other; she didn't even attempt to rein them in.

Perhaps she could say it was for Brad. But then, he might want to talk to Brad. Discuss his predicament. That wouldn't do. She hadn't levelled with Brad about her real relationship with Jonathon. The only person who knew about her dirty little secret was Pia.

Pia! Would Pia have that much money? Or could she say it was for Pia? But why? Why would Pia need five thousand dollars, and why couldn't her parents supply it?

Far out! Birdie took a deep breath in and out.

Vinny!

I could ask Vinny.

Herb would be ropeable if he knew she'd made contact again. God, she was keeping so much from him. No wonder they had an issue with trust.

Could she *decipher* who this blackmailer was?

They would have to know that she was up for a promotion, that she'd slept with Jonathon all those years ago, that Brad was gay. Who would know so many secrets about the teachers of Gallie Wallan Shire? Who would know those things about *her*? Could she work out who before Thursday?

Two days away!

She would talk to Uncle Larry about the money trail.

No ... She would ask Vinny for a loan.

No ... She would ask her uncle for a loan.

No!

Her head was throbbing.

Jonathon.

Of course.

She could ask Jonathon for the money. If she was going to be the subject of the next *Shame Game* rumour, then Jonathon would be implicated too. He'd already paid to keep the story from being written once. He could do it again.

She pushed her fingers into her skull. Her head tight and hot. That's if he had the money. He'd already said the blackmail was a substantial amount. What if he had no money left?

She ran into her study and picked up the phone. She needed to talk to someone.

'It doesn't make sense, Birds,' Pia said sleepily into her ear.

Birdie knew it was past the respectable hour to be calling, but she hadn't been able to stop herself. Luckily, Giulia, who had just hung up from her fiancé, had answered on the first ring and had passed the phone, without judgement, over to Pia.

'All the other victims have been men in leadership roles,' Pia said. 'Why target you?'

That was a good question. Number one, she was a woman, and number two, she wasn't a principal. She didn't really fit the mould.

'What about Griff? He's not leadership.'

'Yeah, but his dad is. He was the "market stallholder". That was clearly part of the entry. Remember?'

'Did I tell you that Griff reckons no one called him asking for money?'

'That's bizarre.' Pia yawned. 'His entry was one of the first ones about teachers, wasn't it?'

'Yes. Sy, then Griff, then Dom.'

'Then Warwick was stabbed.'

'Yes. And since then, we've had Todd the Tool.'

'You might be right, Birds. Perhaps the blackmailer always intended to print some information but use other information as extortion. This person is taking down men. Men who think they can get away with whatever they want. I reckon they are just trying to get money out of you because they know who you are after discovering *Jonathon's* dirty deed. They're just trying to make a buck out of you.'

'I hope you're right. I wonder whether the woman Dom had on the desk or Sy tried to get onto his lap or Griff slept with in Queensland were approached?'

'Good girl. We need to find that out. Could Griff be trusted to get that information?'

'Griff got a bit angry the last time I spoke to him about it all.'

'Griff? Angry?'

'I know.'

'It might help us determine whether this person will publish your secret or whether this information is just for bribery.' She yawned again. 'Is there a connection we're missing?'

'I might have a D-and-M with Brad about his principal.'

'Good idea. Right. Don't panic. Don't ring Vinny or Larry or Jonathon yet. I really don't think anything about you, a woman and one with no power – no offence—'

'None taken.' She'd never been happier being a woman, and one with no power, before in her life.

'—is going to end up written about in *Shame Game, No Names.*'

The modern woman knows what
she wants from life and sets
out to achieve it. She enjoys
competition in her work, all
the better if her rivals are
men. Her view of life is
pragmatic and positive.

Who are you?'
Cleo, April 1985.

TWENTY-NINE

T HE THOUGHT OF SABINE'S surprise party wasn't thrilling Birdie as it should have been. She'd made it all the way through Wednesday, somehow, with a crowd of thoughts swimming around her already overcrowded mind.

There was her little argument with Herb – although they'd made up, she couldn't plug the tiny hole that was leaking when it came to her and him. Then, the blackmail threat – even with all of Pia's reassurances, ones she'd given before and had proved correct, she was still nervous about what might happen there. And finally, there was the first form mistress position. Sister T had told her she had been successful in being appointed as the acting first form mistress, but to keep the news quiet. An official announcement would be made at tomorrow morning's meeting. This had made her excited for a few minutes before the dread set in again.

She stared vacantly into her wardrobe. She'd originally cleaned and ironed a short, tiered, ruffle skirt and top combination in baby pink with tiny flowers, but at present just felt like pulling on a pair of pyjamas instead.

'You, okay?' Brad said, reading her face as she slid into the passenger seat of his maroon Ford Escort. 'Where'd you get to this afternoon?'

Birdie'd had last period off, so she'd left school and visited the bank. She'd thought long and hard about the blackmail threat. She thought about the message from Stu: 'Dr Lee did not pay blackmail'.

She'd thought about a lot of things.

'I need to talk to you about something before we head off.'

Brad grinned. 'Sounds serious.'

'It might be.'

In the end, she'd taken a cancelled blank cheque and written the words: 'Go your hardest' on it. She'd put it in the deposit envelope and deposited it in the blackmailer's account. Whoever came in to withdraw their crooked $5000 would be getting one hell of a shock.

'I need to know exactly who your friend is,' Birdie said. 'The one with the "dirty little secret".'

His grin fell. 'Why?'

'You know your snide jokes about skeletons in my closet?'

Brad nodded, concern apparent.

'Well, you were right. I do have a rather large one in there and'—even though she'd decided she was ready to face the music and whatever came of it—'I'm scared it's about to jump out.'

She told Brad about her relationship with Jonathon – all of it.

He listened without judgement. Then hugged her fiercely. 'My friend is Dean Banks.'

The principal of Eastern Adventist College. The most conservative school in the area, it was a large school with students from kindergarten to Sixth Form. Birdie had done some casual work at Adventist in her first year. Dean was a lovely guy. He'd made her feel welcome and checked in with her at day's end. She'd even applied for a job there, which she didn't get, but just getting an interview – she was sure – had been down to Dean. He had called personally to tell her they had been impressed with her responses, although someone with more experience had got the job, and encouraged her to apply again.

As far as she knew, this was the only connection she had to Dean.

Why had Dean, a principal with a secret, been spared exposure? He was the prime target for *Shame Game, No Names*. Why had Jonathon, a man who was about to become the area consultant, a leader of leaders, not been unmasked? And why had Sy, Dom, Todd-the-Tool and Griff – Dr Lee, now, too, if he was to be counted – seen their stories told?

Brad slapped the steering wheel. 'Come on. Let's forget our troubles for the night and party like it's—'

'1999?' said Birdie.

Brad laughed. 'Yes!' He put his seatbelt on, then strummed the black strap like an air guitar. He thrust an arm with an outstretched finger into the air. He threw Birdie an innocent face. 'Prince *only* wants us to have some fun.'

Fidele's was awash with excited people when they got there. She and Brad were handed a glass of champagne and directed to squeeze down behind the chairs at the back of the room, joining the mass of bodies who were doing the same – including, Birdie noticed, Emer Garland. The lights were low; the atmosphere charged.

Despite her week, Birdie couldn't help smiling. 'Do you think she'll get a surprise?'

'Her birthday isn't until the end of May. Weeks away yet,' said Roseanne, the assistant principal. 'So hopefully, she's got no idea.'

'That's a clever way of doing it,' said Brad. 'Weeks before.'

'It will be sad to see her go from Joanie's. She's been a great French teacher. The students love her,' Roseanne added.

Birdie had forgotten Sabine was only on a temporary contract. The permanent French teacher would be returning for the new term. *I wonder whether holidaying in France is a tax write-off?*

'And to think, she's primary school trained, not trained in French at all, just fluent,' Roseanne continued. 'You know, Dom from next door's already booked her to cover a leave position for term two?'

'I heard,' said Brad. He turned to Birdie. 'Which means we can still all get together for lunch.'

Birdie waved a few fingers at her Fidele staff mates who sat in the window seats with the pretence of having an early dinner. The tables at the front near the door were the only ones lit up; a soft glow from overhead pendants teamed with the table candles.

'How does that work?' Brad whispered. 'How come she can teach in high school without the training?'

'We all graduate with a Diploma of Teaching,' Birdie whispered back. 'Technically, I suppose, we could teach anywhere.'

A few stragglers shuffled in. 'She's coming,' they hissed as they took their places up the back. Word spread like the wolf chasing the duck in Prokofiev's 'Peter and the Wolf'. A hush descended, and everyone crouched down as best they could.

Sabine and another small raven-haired woman, who looked just like her – a cousin from Queensland, apparently – chatted excitedly in French as they approached the doors. Fidele, ever the showman, opened them with a flourish of napkins and invited the pair inside.

The lights went up.

Sabine's tiny body froze on the spot, eyes wide with panic.

'SURPRISE!' A smile spread across Sabine's beautiful face as the arms of about fifty guests and their excited voices were thrown to the ceiling.

'Far out!' she screamed. A glass of champagne was placed in the birthday girl's hand. 'I'm shaking.' She brought the glass carefully to her mouth to drink.

Everyone was still facing her way.

'Alright.' She lifted her glass and motioned to the room. 'Everyone can drink now.' She shuffled through the crowd towards her parents, tears streaming down her slightly embarrassed yet gorgeous face. She turned to the crowd, who were mesmerised and quietly watching, held up her glass once more and cried, 'Let's party.'

There was no actual sit-down meal, just lots of hors d'oeuvres and Australian finger food, but Fidele's food was always amazing. Real champagne flowed among the beer, and he'd also created a dance floor where the young and young at heart were encouraged to live it up.

'How are you faring, Miss Mealing?' Brad pulled Birdie into a hug against his strong chest.

'I'm actually not too bad.' She held up the champagne. 'This is helpful.'

Without warning, Sabine was suddenly up in Emer's face, mouth moving a mile a minute. Although they were too far away to hear the exchange, Birdie watched as the birthday girl pointed at Emer's notebook, indicated Birdie, moved her arm in an arc to indicate the whole party, grabbed Emer's notebook and shoved it at the journalist's chest.

'Can you see this, Brad?'

'I'm seeing it,' he whispered. Although, with the party loudly pumping, it seemed – luckily – they were the only ones. How could the beautiful Sabine and the frosty, hard-shelled Emer be friends? Emer caught Birdie's eye before she made a retort to Sabine, bagged her book, turned on her heel and slinked away.

'Do me a favour, Brad. Go comfort Sabine and see what that was all about.'

Brad had his arm around Sabine, whispering in her ear before Birdie could blink. He directed Sabine onto the dance floor and moved in time with her. Arms aloft and body swaying to the music.

'Fidele, do you know Emer Garland from the paper very well?'

He made the symbol for small with his thumb and fore-finger. '*Une petit.*'

'Do you know why Sabine and Emer might be conversing in French?'

'Urm. Sabine is French.' He tilted his head and lifted a shoulder to say: This is self-explanatory. 'Emer is from Ireland. She would be taught *le Français* as schooling.' Fidele tapped his chin. 'Practice perhaps?'

'Maybe.'

Although the discussion at the back door of the paper yesterday looked more heated than mere practice.

Fidele gave her shoulder a squeeze. 'How does *l'investigation* go, *chéri*?'

'Slowly, Fidele. How's business?'

'*Tranquille*.' He shrugged his shoulders. 'The man is ...' He mimed the action of stabbing. 'Still free, non?'

No one believing Sister T was guilty and everyone believing the assailant was still at large, wasn't helping business.

'I'll find them, Fidele.'

'*Je sais*.'

His 'I know' made her smile.

Brad came towards them. A grin on his lips and a glint in his eye. 'Do I have some gossip for you.'

⇔ ⇔ ⇔

'Guess who was at Sabine's surprise twenty-first?' Birdie had rung Pia as soon as she got home from the party.

'Ralph Macchio?'

'Emer Garland,' Birdie said.

'So close.'

'She very clearly eavesdropped on conversations and even wrote in her notepad as she listened.'

'Subtle,' said Pia. 'What if Emer had been fishing for information from Sabine yesterday morning when you saw them in that heated argument?'

Don't touch Birdie Mealing.

'*Oui, c'est possible*,' answered Birdie.

'Sabine could have been angry that Emer was collecting information on one of her good workmates. Hence the argument after the article about Larry. Perhaps she'd badgered Sabine for story material.' Pia whistled as she thought. 'If Emer was even making observations at her own friend's birthday party, maybe Sabine's been down this road with Emer before.'

'Sabine was clearly angry tonight. She and Emer had another heated tête-à-tête. When Emer stalked away, Brad comforted Sabine – at my suggestion – and she told Brad she thought Emer was in the car park the night of Warwick's stabbing. She said as much to Emer at the party and told her to write *that* little piece of information in her *stupide* book.'

'Sabine saw Emer in the car park the night Warwick was stabbed?' Pia's voice held disbelief.

'Well. No. She couldn't have. Emer was up the coast following a story, remember? She wasn't even in town.'

'Then why did she say that?'

'Just to piss her off.'

'Have you told Herb what Sabine thought she saw?'

'It's superfluous. She couldn't have seen her.'

'Oh, I love it when you use big words.'

'Drop dead.'

'Very articulate. Emer might be planning another article about you or Larry. She's clearly trying to discredit him.'

'Well. I did kindly mention to Emer the other night that I'd find out who stabbed Warwick like I found out who killed Robert Crown,' said Birdie.

'You've got up her nose, Birds. She's out for blood.'

They were silent for a moment. Each in their thoughts.

'Tequila Sunrises!' Birdie burst the words through the phone.

'Not sure cocktails are appropriate at this hour.'

'Very funny. They were mentioned in the article.' Had she told Sabine what had happened last year? She couldn't remember exactly. It's not like she went around proclaiming her involvement. 'That's a detail only we would have known … *Brad* knew! He could have told Sabine we were drinking Tequila Sunrises the night we found Uncle Larry.'

'So, whether Sabine meant to give it to her or not, Emer's probably used the information Sabine provided. No wonder Sabine's pissed off.'

'It's Thursday tomorrow and I'm packing it.' Birdie said, changing the subject. It wasn't difficult when this worry rented a corner of her brain.

'You know how I feel about that.'

'All the people who paid were safe. All those that didn't were not.'

'Exactly!'

'Except we don't know about Sy, so that theory is twenty-five percent unsupported.'

'Are you channelling Stu?'

'Maybe.' Birdie laughed.

'Regardless, tomorrow's paper will not feature you, Birdie. I'm almost sure of it.'

'Whether it does or not, I've decided to tell Herb about the skeletons in my closet.' Take control of your destiny. She was sure she'd read that in *Cleo*. She filled Pia in on her bank deposit. 'I'm not sure how much detail I'm going to go into, but you are right, we have some issues with trust. He's keeping something from me, and I can't blame him. I'm keeping things from him, too.'

'Silly old duck. It happened ages ago. Way before Herb. Do you really have to disclose every questionable thing in the past you've done?'

'I can't go on knowing that he might find out about Jonathon. I think I'd rather just blab it out and take his reaction. I can't keep walking on eggshells.'

'You're fearless, Birdie Mealing. And that's why I love you.'

Fearless? Birdie didn't feel fearless.

THIRTY

WHEN SHE PICKED UP the *Gallie Wallen Gazette* at the Little Shops on the way to school, just as Pia had predicted, the *Shame Game, No Names* rumour was not about her. Birdie have kissed her amazing, loyal, talented, clever, spectacular friend.

The entry wasn't even about a teacher. It seemed the gazette had moved on to its next category of victims. Thank God it was finished with the education sector.

She drove the Gypsy out of the car park and pulled up at the beach. The waves glided into the shore slowly. The few people walking along the sand let the water flow gently over their feet.

She'd find Herb today and tell him they needed to talk.

Birdie took a cleansing breath of air, cool freshness filling her lungs. She drove on to Joanie's, knowing that whoever the blackmailer was, it no longer mattered. They could not touch her.

THIRTY-ONE

THE STAFFROOM HOUSED THE entire staff for the last morning meeting of the term, and Sister T was asking for a bit of shush. She spied Birdie and gave her a wink. She was about to announce Birdie's appointment as the acting form mistress. It had been difficult keeping it secret, especially from Sabine and Brad. Birdie was sure the response of 'I'm not allowed to discuss it' she had given the pair when they asked if she knew whether she'd been successful, had them seeing straight through her. Currently, Brad was grinning like the Cheshire cat.

'Good morning, lovely people.' There was a murmur of good mornings in response. 'Let's get straight into business. This morning I have the pleasure of announcing that the acting first form mistress will be—'

'Birdie Mealing?' All heads turned towards the commanding voice, not that of Sister T, but a different voice, loud and strong and coming from the entry to the staffroom. 'I would like to see Birdie Mealing.' The voice made its demand again.

Birdie stood up at the sound of her name.

'May I help you?' said Sister T, a frown on her face as she focused on who had interrupted. She peered impatiently over the heads of her people. 'We're just in the middle of a staff meeting here.' Sister T said something quietly to the assistant principal who walked towards the owner of the voice.

Stylish, in a black pencil skirt and fitted blazer, the owner of the voice was a woman. She wore over-sized, black-rimmed sunglasses and a black-and-white, wide-brimmed hat pulled low over her bobbed auburn hair. Birdie focused on the cherry red lips that were smiling in her direction. By reflex, Birdie smiled in reply. The woman moved further into the room. She conversed quietly with the AP who had caught up to her, halting her advance, and motioned in Birdie's direction. The AP could be heard asking the woman if she'd signed in at the office downstairs or had an appointment.

'It's a good thing you're standing, Birdie,' her principal said. Heads slowly drifted back to Sister T. 'Because, as I was saying, I would like to make an announcement that concerns you.'

The strange woman laughed. The sound cutting through Sister T's words. Birdie was mesmerised as the woman broke away from the AP and glided like an eagle towards her. She raised an arm and pointed a red manicured finger at Birdie. 'Birdie Mealing is having an affair with my husband.'

Brad's fingers spread out across Birdie's arm and squeezed tight. Sister T gasped, a hand flying to her chest.

Birdie's breath left her body. The world slowed down. Faces in various degrees of contortion swung – 'like the movements of astronauts walking on the moon,' thought Birdie – to look her way. She was aware of a sliding door scraping and Herb stepping in from the outside verandah, legs making big floating steps and a hammer swinging through zero gravity in his tool belt.

'I'm not sure that's following the Catholic ethos,' the woman continued.

Birdie's stomach dropped, rooting her in place. Sweat broke out across her skin. The intakes of breath from those around her battered her skull like a seagull's wings hovering over a hot chip.

Birdie's eyes locked with Herb's. Realisation slapped her like a wet fish. *Holy shit.* The woman was Linda Naylor – Jonathon's wife.

'Not only is she screwing my husband, she's also screwing him.' Linda swung her arm one-eighty degrees and pointed at Herb.

All faces – sockets wide and mouths agape – followed the path of Linda's arm. Herb stiffened.

'He's not a handyman, he's an undercover policeman, and they are *not* married,' she said with a tilt of her head.

A sea swirled around Birdie, legs sinking into sand. The pounding of her blood crashed in her ears like the waves on a stormy shore. A look of horror grew from Herb's perfect mouth to his beautiful caramel eyes, which fastened like periwinkles, onto hers.

'Your little message,' said Linda, who had moved closer to Birdie, murmuring so only she could hear, 'has set this chain of events in motion. I hope you renmember that. You're about to see what really happens when I *go my hardest.*'

The words, 'go my hardest' echoed in Birdie's tiny ear caves. Her focus on the scene clouded. Brad's cologne staled in her nostrils.

The world became sluggish. She saw Linda's face creep into unrushed smile, auburn hair swish in a slow motion arc as she turned to leave. The echo kept washing forwards. Birdie blinked, trying to correct the lagging pace, to push the sound away. 'Perhaps I am on the moon?' she thought, as gravity failed.

Then she heard nothing and saw nothing.

⊜ ⊜ ⊜

When it came to fainting, Birdie had experience.

Not a lot of experience, but she had fainted before once or twice, so she realised this weird feeling she was having was her regaining an understanding of her surroundings. She felt like she'd missed part of the conversation, like she'd woken from a deep sleep, like the comprehension part of her brain was returning from a walk.

A kettle was whistling. Voices were murmuring. A sweetly smelling, steaming cup of tea passed her nostrils, and Brad's strong arms were lifting her to her feet. Sabine placed the tea on the table, then held the chair out for Brad. She pushed the teacup into Birdie's hands as he secured Birdie's bottom on the chair.

'Tttthat ... woman, sshe's ...' Birdie's teeth were chattering.

Brad was holding her firmly in place. He bent down. 'Best not to speak of that woman, my love. Best not to speak at all,' he whispered into her ear. 'Might be a good idea if you faint again, actually.'

The entire staff was looking Birdie's way.

'But, that woman—'

'She's gone,' Sabine said, bending down to help. 'She was in a hurry to leave too, *la pute*,' Sabine spat under her breath in French. 'She mumbled something about another stop to make, or she had more work to do, or something.'

No wonder Griff had no knowledge of blackmail. He hadn't *been* blackmailed.

With complete clarity, Birdie realised two actors were at play here.

The phone call Dom's wife intercepted and ended with 'Please don't call here again' had most probably been from a disgruntled fling – not a blackmailer.

Who did she know for certain *had* been black-mailed? Jonathon, Dean and Birdie. The blackmailer was Jonathon's wife. And she had nothing to do with *Shame Game, No Names*, except to use it to her advantage for the purpose of extracting money. Linda Naylor was not the supplier of gossip to *Shame Game, No Names*, which was why Jonathon, Dean and Birdie's secrets weren't published. She was only the blackmailer.

Birdie's brain had regained its precision and was firing on all four cylinders.

Pia was right about the mixed-up pattern. Jonathon's wife was merely riding on the exposé's coattails and using *Shame Game*. She'd only targeted her husband, Birdie – her husband's lover, and Dean – her son's principal. She was seeking her own revenge and, in the process, grabbing some cash.

Birdie clutched Brad's tie. 'You ... you need to stop her, Brad. That's, that's ...'

'Shh. I figured out who it is, honey,' he whispered. 'But she's gone. She can't hurt you anymore. Shh now.' He pulled at his tie to get it out of Birdie's hand, but she was using it to keep his attention and also to try and get to her feet.

'Holy Mary Mother of God, this is a terrible business.' Sister T bristled. Her face darted left and right as a hand worried her rosary beads. 'Miss Mealing, we may need to have a chat in my office. If you could bring her along, Mr Foster,' she said softly. 'Miss Mathieu, you can come too.'

'She's the blackmailer,' Birdie continued, grabbing at Brad.

'What?'

'Detective?' Birdie called out.

'Here.' His tone suggested he'd prefer to be anywhere but. She'd have to deal with that later.

'Off to classes now, everyone,' Sister T urged. 'The bell's rung. The students will be waiting. Come along *now*, please, Birdie.'

'Jonathon's wife is the blackmailer. You need to stop her, Brad. Sabine heard her say she's got another stop to make, more work to do. She could be off to ... *another* ... school. To expose *another* person. Another person she's blackmailed. Another person she's got a beef with.'

Realisation dawned on Brad's face. 'Crapola! He's got an awards assembly on there this morning. Parents and dignitaries. It could be happening right now.'

Although Herb may not have known exactly what was going on, Birdie knew the detective's mind would be reading the situation perfectly. And she hadn't been wrong. 'Miss Mathieu, you stay with Miss Mealing.' Herb moved seamlessly into play. 'Foster, you and I will go after the woman.'

Brad kissed Birdie's cheek and ran out of the room. Her eyes searched for Herb, tears welling.

'Mr Foster! Where are you going?' Sister T called. 'For goodness' sake. Teachers! Off to class. NOW!'

Sabine held her tight. 'It'll be alright, Birdie,' she said.

Would it? Herb had gone and hadn't looked back.

Unavailability. There is
nothing more desirable than
something you can't have.

'What turns women on? Men tell!'
Cleo, September 1984.

THIRTY-TWO

HER REPUTATION WAS SHOT.

Her relationship was in jeopardy.

Her grasp on the form mistress position was slipping, not to mention her continuing role at a Catholic school where marriage came before any engagement in sexual activity, let alone the proclamation that she'd slept with *two* men outside marriage.

Her principal, already under scrutiny, would probably now draw even more.

Sabine and Birdie huddled together as they shared the wing-backed chair, meant for only one bottom, in Sister T's office. The nun was pacing. Sabine had her arm along Birdie's back, stroking her shoulder.

'Are you okay, dear?' Sister T asked.

Birdie nodded. She hoped Brad and Herb had got to Dean's school in time.

Linda's ready to murder someone. That's what Jonathon had said when they'd talked that afternoon in the staffroom nooks.

'You know I think you're wonderful, Birdie.' *Here came the 'but'* ... 'But unfortunately, I can't give you the leadership role now. Not after that.'

Birdie opened her mouth to speak.

'I'm not saying I can't give it to you at all.' Sister T slid her veil off with a shaking hand. 'Although, that might be something I'll need to discuss with the bishop. I'm saying, if you are to have it, I can't give it to you … now.'

Birdie admired Sister T's positive thinking, but Birdie would be lucky if she even kept her job.

'I feel terrible about this, Birdie.'

'It's okay, Sister.' Birdie exhaled a breath not really expelling all the air. 'I'm not having an affair with that woman's husband, if you're interested.'

'Oh. Well. I suppose that's good to know.'

'I did have an affair with her husband, over five years ago, when I was on my very first prac.'

The older woman stopped pacing and peered at her intently. 'You did?'

'Yes.'

'Did he take advantage of you?'

No. Not like Sy had taken advantage of the girl at the Christmas party.

'I wish I could say yes, Sister. But I was old enough to know what I was doing. As soon as we crossed the line, I stopped it. Not soon enough, though, as it happens.'

'We've all had relationships when we were young that could be seen in retrospect as … not of our best judgement.' She sat on the edge of her desk and absentmindedly swept a hand across its surface. 'Heaven knows I'm not innocent of indulging in a relationship with someone I shouldn't have,' she said, almost to herself.

It had always struck Birdie as odd that a beautiful woman such as Sister T, and the many other nuns she'd known over the years, would make a conscious decision to deny the sexual side of themselves. It didn't surprise Birdie that Sister

T might have had relationships. Perhaps one, as she referred to now, that she shouldn't have. At present, the nun's tunic pulled against her strong legs, outlining the curve of her hip, the roundness of her backside. She was all woman. She was beautiful. Strong and vibrant. Attractive.

Was she referring to the relationship Dom hinted at? The breaking of her vows. The one that led to the secret Warwick knew.

Sister T slid off the desk and stepped towards her. 'Take the rest of the day off, Birdie. I'll be in touch.'

Birdie glanced up at Sabine, who smiled down at her. Strong and steady.

The door flew open—'Terri'—and Dom Walker charged in. He grabbed Sister T's hand. 'Are you okay?'

She motioned with a barely-there nod to where Sabine and Birdie still sat in the lounge as she pulled her hand back. 'Fine, thanks, Mr Walker.' Her voice was clear and professional.

Dom turned his head. 'Sorry, I didn't realise you were still in the middle of it.'

Sabine squeezed Birdie's shoulder. Birdie hoped Sabine's loyalty didn't put her in a bad light in Sister T's or Dom's eyes.

Birdie exhaled. 'Word travels fast, Dom.'

'I was already at reception. One could say perfect timing. Everyone loves a good gossip, Miss Mealing. As I, of all people, should know.' He turned to Sabine. 'Good of you to show your support, Miss Mathieu.' *Thank goodness Sabine would not be scarred.* Dom's mouth flattening into a sympathetic line. 'Bad business, Birdie.'

'Yes. It is that.'

'You were young, my child,' Sister T said. 'It might be bad business, but it doesn't make you a bad person.'

THIRTY-THREE

BIRDIE WAS STILL PICTURING Sister T's sympathetic smile as she sat in stunned silence in the passenger seat of Sabine's VW. The *ticker-ticker* of the engine massaged her aching mind.

'How's your uncle going with trying to make a case in Sister T's favour?' Her beautiful colleague glanced over briefly and smiled, dark eyes catching the sun as she refocused on the road. 'Come on, Birdie, talk to me.'

About what? How her heart was breaking because Herb thought she'd been sleeping around?

'Why did you think it was Emer you saw the night of Warwick's stabbing?' Birdie asked.

'Well, I didn't at first. I was in the Little Shops' car park where the gazette office is. I heard a man's voice, but because it was coming from the gazette, I assumed it was Emer. She's got that deep Carlotta, *Les Girls* voice going on, you know.'

'Yep, I know.'

'I just put two and two together and came up with zero.'

'What were *you* doing there?' Birdie continued.

'I was meeting Fidele. He was helping me with some text I needed translated for one of the fourth form students; she's a genius at French. I wanted to confer with him, make perfectly sure I'd marked it correctly. HSC and all that.'

'Did Fidele see the person you thought was Emer?'

'No. I didn't really see them either when I think about it. The person was mumbling to themselves in Polish, which was why my mind also flew to the conclusion it was Emer.'

'Polish? You mean French?'

'Emer also speaks Polish. She speaks a few languages actually.'

Birdie pictured the articles in the editor's office that Emer had written. Framed and on display. All from various world papers. 'How do you know it was Polish?'

'I won't do it justice, but it's a phrase she's used before. The person said "*Zrobili mnie w konia*" and then in English "*I* don't *think*".'

'Do you know what it means?'

'It's got something to do with a horse.'

'A horse?'

She turned into Birdie's street. 'It couldn't have been Emer, though. Brad said she had an ironclad alibi.'

'She was up the coast,' said Birdie.

'So it must have been some man,' said Sabine.

Birdie nodded absently.

'And besides,' Sabine went on. 'I'm pretty sure Emer isn't the only person who can speak Polish in Gallie Wallen.'

⇔ ⇔ ⇔

Mrs N pondered Birdie with calculating eyes. Growing up, the older woman had often been attuned to Birdie's moods. Perhaps the dark circles were a giveaway. Sleep had eluded her last night, and the night before it had been spasmodic.

Thoughts of her plan for later today were also making her anxious, however strong she felt in her conviction to carry them out.

Birdie pasted on a smile and went through the motions of practising with the choir. After a while, it was easy. They were a joy. But she was relieved when she could finally be in her old friend's little room. Just the two of them.

She placed a cool drop of Oil of Ulan on the back of her hands and rubbed it in. The familiar smell of almonds, wisteria and cinnamon bringing her comfort. She picked up a tiny ceramic whale and let it sit solidly in her palm. She'd always loved the feel of it. She hefted it for a moment, the action calming her, before placing it back down. Then she slid a piece of P.K Chewing Gum from its packet and popped it into her mouth. Minty freshness burst across her tongue and rose up her nose.

She turned to find Mrs N sitting in her chair watching her silently.

'There's something I need to tell you,' Birdie said.

'I see this is true.'

Birdie took a deep breath. She hated to disappoint Mrs N. 'When I was eighteen, I slept with a married man.'

Silence stretched.

'Did you know of his marriage?' Mrs N finally said.

'Yes.'

Birdie told Mrs N the story about her and Jonathon. An edited version but still factual. The older woman listened. When Birdie had finished, they sat quietly for a few moments. Sparrows twittered outside Mrs N's window. The older woman opened the door to her little garden and collected a couple of flower bulbs a generous neighbour must have left on her doorstep.

Birdie concentrated on the little squeaks and chirps; the sound of the birds louder with the door open. The crinkle of the outer shell, like dried onion skin, that the flower bulbs made in Mrs N's soft hands. Mrs N stood next to Birdie. 'You are sorry for this, yes?'

'Yes. Very sorry. I was caught up in the moment, but in hindsight, I am sorry it happened. It's not something I will ever repeat.'

'He was married one.'

'I know.' Birdie turned and picked up the whale again. 'He was the one who broke his vows. Technically, I just slept with a guy. But I'm not sure that really makes my actions any better.' She placed the whale back down. 'I feel bad for his wife. She knows, and it's upsetting for her.' Birdie hadn't told Mrs N all the details about the scene in the staffroom. Her lips couldn't get themselves around that story.

'Actions have consequences. This is life. You understand this now.'

She certainly did understand this. More so now than before. Nothing like a bit of public humiliation to drive that point home.

'I don't know how to tell Mum.'

Mrs N put a hand on Birdie's. 'Always, truth is best.'

'I'm ashamed.'

'You forget, at this same age, she was growing baby. She was unmarried mother. She will understand.'

Falling pregnant young was shameful, but did it hurt others? Most of the harm seemed to land on her mother.

The side of Birdie's brain that was always hypothesising came up with a new one. Could Birdie have been the product of an affair with a married man? Perhaps that was the reason her mum was tight-lipped about her father.

'What does *Zrobili mnie w konia*, mean?'

Mrs N laughed. 'Where did you hear this?'

'Sabine, the French teacher at school, thought she heard someone say it in the car park behind the *Gallie Wallen Gazette* the night Warwick was stabbed.'

'I was made into a horse,' Mrs N answered.

Birdie frowned.

'It means *I was taken for the ride. Made to look like fool.*'

Was that what Jonathon's wife felt like? Herb, when he found out what she'd done?

She had yet to speak with Herb. Was she keeping her distance, or was he?

'This is reason someone stabbed Warwick?' Mrs N asked.

Was it? Had he made someone look like a fool? It was true; *Shame Game* had made a fool of many.

But exactly which fool had taken their revenge?

⇔ ⇔ ⇔

Birdie waited patiently as Vinny savoured whatever liqueur was in his tiny glass. 'I'm sorry I didn't stop that woman from her mission.'

'It's not your fault, Vinny. Sometimes the bad decisions you've made in your life catch up with you. Mine just happened to be on display for everyone to see.'

'Was it a bad decision?'

'To sleep with someone else's husband?' She held his scrutiny and tilted her head. 'Yes.'

Vinny poured himself another and pushed a tiny glass across the table for her. A slightly different atmosphere from the last time they'd met at this little café. This time, Birdie had dropped in on a whim after Evesong, without the comfort of Uncle Larry's company, without permission from Lenore.

Vinny looked her over as she lifted the glass to her lips; she was used to being scrutinised by him.

It was becoming easier to be in his presence. He was mixed up with Herb. He was protecting her home, her family. She studied him studying her as she sipped the alcohol.

'Shit!' She coughed madly at the harshness that clutched her throat. 'You're supposed to be keeping me alive,' she managed to push out, 'not killing me.' Birdie's normal experience of spirits was mixed in pretty cocktails.

Vinny laughed. He called out something in Czech to the owner who fired up the machine in front of him. He pulled the offending glass back to his side of the table. 'We all make mistakes, especially when we're young.' A reference to the sleeping with a married man and not to spurning his liqueur.

'I was eighteen, Vinny. I knew what I was doing.'

'Of course, you did. But when you are my age, you'll realise just how young eighteen is. You need to forgive yourself. Move on.'

'Is that how you do it? Just forgive yourself all the death and destruction, the maiming, the drugs, the eye for an ey—'

'Why does what I do disgust you so, but when it goes in your favour, you're fine with it?'

That was a good question.

A pot of tea appeared on their table. Birdie smiled a thank you at the tiny, wrinkled man who had placed it there and proceeded to make herself a cup.

'Where is he, Vinny?' She sipped her soothing brew.

'Where is who?' He sipped his tiny spirit.

She peered into Vinny's eyes. Is this how Lenore felt? Is this why she and Uncle Larry were drawn to Vinny, yet at the same time pulled away? 'He knows about the affair. We have to talk. There's no point avoiding it.'

'Most people would do exactly that.'

'I'm not most people.'

'One of the things I admire about you.'

'What happened to Herb while he was gone?'

'That is not my story to tell.' He sipped his drink again and moved on to the leftovers of hers. 'Be careful, Birdie. It might not be a story you want to hear.'

Was it a story she wanted to hear? What could be worse than finding out your girlfriend was having an affair? That's the story Herb heard. He didn't know it wasn't ongoing; she hadn't had a chance to tell him that. Perhaps it was time they both levelled with each other.

'Do you know where he is, *starý muz*?'

A hint of a smile brushed Vinny's mouth at her use of the Czech word for 'old man'. She smiled in return.

'Tell me where he needs to be, *holčička*. Give me a time and a place.'

THIRTY-FOUR

BIRDIE WATCHED THE EXODUS from church to the hall where a supper was prepared for Sister Verona's farewell. The same liturgy at which Jonathon would have been blessed as the new superintendent.

She hadn't attended the mass. But she could imagine he would have stood up in front of the congregation and made his pledge to serve God and the Catholic school teachers of Gallie Wallen and Gibber Shires. Totally juxtaposed to his personal promises.

Birdie was on a mission to make him sweat on that. She wasn't exactly sure what she hoped to gain, personally, from her next move – apart from the satisfaction of making him squirm.

She'd timed her arrival to coincide with the Friday afternoon liturgy's conclusion and slipped in the back door of the hall, keeping to the walls. As soon as Brad was aware of her presence, he hurried over. His enormous frame shielded her from prying eyes. Birdie was sure once they spied her, tongues would be wagging.

'There's the man of the hour,' Brad said, dripping with anger. 'Gets away scot-free, star on the rise, while the people around him are burnt to a crisp.'

'Speaking of, how's Dean?' Birdie said from behind Brad's back.

'Far out, Birdie. He's better than he would have been if Herb and I hadn't got there on time.'

'But you did. And he's okay. And you're okay.' She patted his shoulder blade.

'Dean paid the blackmail.' Brad popped an olive into his mouth. 'Why did she still want to expose him?'

Go your hardest. Had Birdie inadvertently poked the bear? 'I don't think she's in her right mind. Jonathon said she was ready to kill someone. Perhaps she just snapped or was high on adrenaline. Perhaps she was always intent on exposure as well as money. Anyway. I'm glad Dean was saved.'

'But you weren't, my darling.'

No.

'Herb is such a dish,' Brad said, turning his head to speak to Birdie over his shoulder.

Laughing with a colleague, Jonathon lifted his head in their direction. His twinkling-eyes faltered and did a double take. He'd spotted her.

Brad, oblivious, continued, 'Was he okay about the whole Jonathon thing?'

How would I know? He's disappeared again.

Birdie stepped out from behind Brad and headed towards Jonathon. The surprise on the new superintendent's lips quickly tamed into a polite smile. She could ruin this man, just like his wife had ruined her. Her reputation was already a towering inferno. It would mean nothing to her to watch *his* go up in flames. Perspiration gathered behind her knees. The heart's ability to keep going under the amount of blood her adrenaline was pumping through her veins, was a mystery. 'Your wife thinks we are having another affair.'

Jonathon's focus darted back and forth. He stepped closer to Birdie, frowning at her before plastering a smile on his face. 'Now is not the time or the place.' He nodded hello to a face in the crowd before looking at her again. 'Someone might hear you.'

'Don't worry. No one saw Linda's face. No one saw her eyes. She didn't mention your name. She just referred to *you* as "my husband".'

Jonathon exhaled a haggard breath. His shoulders relaxed. He gave his arms a shake and picked up a cup of lemonade from a server who walked by – his quivering hand visible to only Birdie's eye.

'She announced I was having an affair to my entire staff,' Birdie continued.

People walked past. They smiled and waved at Jonathon who smiled and waved back.

'Why would she think that?' Birdie asked.

Jonathon exhaled and moved her away from curious eyes and ears. 'I'm surprised you attended today.'

'I'm not your only extramarital affair, am I, Jonathon?'

'It's not becoming of a lady to engage in gossip and innuendo.'

'But it's fine for a gentleman to be rooting around behind his wife's back?'

'Your language is vulgar.' He surveyed the room again.

'Your behaviour is vulgar. Perhaps the people here should know that.'

He speared her with a look. *Yes, Jonathon. I can make your life as difficult as mine currently is. Your job is hanging by a thread, as mine is.*

'This discussion would be better had at a different time, in private.'

'No. Now. In public.' She waited.

He pushed out a breath. 'Linda must have been following me. She must have seen me at your school that afternoon and concluded we were together, saw me hug you the morning the paper came out, thankful we weren't in it. Not, in hindsight, that we ever would have been.' He sipped his lemonade. 'I don't know. I'm just guessing.'

Guessing? Linda's response was extreme. How many other women had she witnessed being hugged by Jonathon over the years?

'Were the other girls young? Were they under your supervision? I wonder whether *Shame Game, No Names* might actually like this little tidbit?'

His expression turned dark. 'What do you want, Birdie?'

'I would love for you to treat young women with respect. And even older women. Your wife, for example.' What would drive his wife to behave the way she had? Her son being in trouble could possibly be the reason, but was it the only reason? 'She's blackmailed people. She blackmailed you. Her *own* husband.'

'It was a cry for help.'

'Is she getting help?'

'That is no business of yours.' He smiled and waved at several more people. 'Rumours are already circulating about you, Miss Mealing. It would be good if you could remember where we are.'

'Everyone will believe that my purpose here is to plead a case for clemency, Mr Naylor.'

He wiped sweat from his brow.

Now that Birdie had made it clear what she could and was probably very capable of revealing, she tried her hand. 'And so that's what I'm doing. What can you do to make certain I keep my job?'

'Well, I'm not sure yet.' His attention was taken by a couple of principals who came over to give their congratulations. Jonathon ignored her while he engaged in chitchat.

Birdie turned away from their discussion until they'd moved on.

'I must mingle. This new position is all about communication.' He went to move away.

She placed a hand on his forearm. 'Everyone knows I had an affair with *someone*.' She dragged a finger along the material of his suit. 'All I have to do is mention who that someone was.'

'Bell.' He went to reach for her but thought better of it. 'Don't be like that.'

'People are already speculating. A couple of people already know.'

'Are you threatening me?'

'I trust you will do all you can to help my situation, Jonathon. As my superintendent, I'm relying on you.' She held out her hand.

Jonathon gawked at it.

She took his hand, placed it in hers and shook it. 'Congratulations, Jonathon. Thanks for this opportunity to talk.' She projected her voice so that those around them could hear, before leaning in and whispering, 'Enjoy your time in the light, big wig. Hopefully, it won't be short-lived.' She walked away.

She had a Seasons gig to get to.

So we bold, audacious young Lotharias might take a step back and notice that the objects of our pursuit are, oddly enough, just people. It's a rather shocking idea, but I think useful.

'Man-chasing:
Win and keep his attention'
Cleo, April 1985.

THIRTY-FIVE

There he was. Underneath the lamp. One leg held his weight. The other leg was bent at the knee; the sole of his shoe rested effortlessly on the brick wall he leaned against. He looked relaxed for someone who thought they were about to meet with Velvet Vinny Varva at one o'clock on a Friday night, or should she say, Saturday morning.

His head lifted as she approached. Eyes scanned the dark sky on an exhale. 'Shoulda bloody known,' he grumbled.

'Hi Herb.'

'Don't bloody "Hi Herb" me.' He pushed off the wall and pulled her into the light. 'It's the middle of the night.' He surveyed the length of the street. 'Shouldn't be moving in the shadows.'

'You're moving in the shadows.'

He released contact and shook his head, ran a hand over his face. 'Being in your world, Birdie, is something I'm not sure I'll ever get used to.'

'Interesting statement from someone who seems to have dropped out of it … again.'

They held each other's gaze. She'd gone from wanting to console him, explain her actions, plead forgiveness to once again playing with her friend, Anger, in the space of two seconds. Herb's fingers curled under and rubbed against each palm. Fire danced behind his eyes.

'What's wrong, Detective, can't handle the heat?'

The beautiful muscles of his jaw clenched, fury like lava bubbling beneath the rock.

'Least I know what made you retreat, this time,' Birdie continued. Molten heat spread along her *own* limbs. He hadn't even given her a chance to defend herself. 'Why is your first instinct to run?'

'Don't start, Birdie.'

'Start what? I'm just trying to understand you.'

'Or purposely piss me off.'

'Because that's how I spend my time. Steepling my fingers together'—she made that exact action and tapped her fingertips for a few beats—'plotting ways to piss off Herb Lawson.'

'Mature.'

'Oh. Maturity is what you're after? Who's the one buggering off every time the going gets tough? Is this how you do things? Because if it is, I need to know.'

'You don't think finding out my girl is sleeping with someone else is enough of a reason to step back for a moment?'

'I would have thought asking *your girl* if she had actually slept with someone else might have been your first response.'

His eyes glistened. They searched hers. A moment of relief followed swiftly by hurt. 'Your face said it all in that staffroom, Bird.'

Trust. It shimmered between them like the intro to a dream sequence in the movies. Never standing solid.

'My face,' she spat. The fire in her limbs licked and crackled, arms lifted like she had wings. 'Didn't.' Her fists slammed against his chest. 'Say it ALL.'

Did he think some lunatic was more believable than his girlfriend? *Arsehole!* She slammed her fists again and then stormed away.

Herb followed her, cuffing her wrist. 'Say it now, then.'

'Now. After I tracked *you* down? Why didn't you come and ask me yourself if you really wanted to know?' She ripped out of his hold. 'No, you just believed some deranged stranger.'

She continued down the street, tears streaming down her face. She didn't want him, not if that's what he was all about.

'Birdie.'

'Go to hell.'

'You're just going to walk away.'

Why not? Hadn't he already done the same? 'I'm not the one walking. You are.' She whirled to face him. 'Am I that easy to forget, Herb?' That cutting remark had come out of nowhere. If she wasn't so furious, she'd be amazed at what her anger was capable of.

'I said those words from my heart, Birdie. And now you're just throwing them back in my face.'

Yes! She wanted to hurt him.

'You truly are unbelievable,' he said.

'So *very* unbelievable that you haven't even bothered to ask for my version of events. Willing to believe someone else's.'

'Are you telling me you didn't sleep with Jonathon Naylor?'

Actually, no. She couldn't tell him that. 'Get fucked, Herb.' She pounded off again.

As if *he* was Mr Perfect. As if he had any right to make her feel any more of a bitch than she already did. He was supposed to be the one who was solidly on her side.

Sister T had been understanding. Vinny, Uncle Larry, Brad, Sabine, Mrs N, even bloody Dom had been sympathetic. She didn't need anyone to tell her how reprehensible her actions had been; she knew that already. *How dare he.*

She tried to push the anger down, but as usual, it simmered along her bones, making her twitch. She spun around, intending to give Herb a piece of her mind, and bounced straight into his chest. She poked a finger into the broad breastbone that met her nose. 'You know what?' He stepped back. She kept going. 'I did the wrong thing. I'm sorry I hurt Jonathon's wife.'

He lifted her finger gently, removing it from his chest.

She registered the pain in its tip, pulled it out of his hand. 'That she must feel betrayed and confused.' She held her finger and thumb a centimetre apart. 'A little bit less, because of me. But she is the *only* person who gets an apology from me, Detective. I'm not apologising to *you*.' Her finger pushed again into his chest. 'Or anyone else.' Tears swelled. How many times had she felt the shame of what she'd done? 'I slept with him once. When I was eighteen.' A soft waterfall of tears trickled down her cheeks. She pushed the next words through an aching throat. 'If you look at me now with any less respect or love, then that's your problem.'

'Birdie.' He tried to reach for her, but she was already storming away.

Rage rose from her centre and crept up her neck. She spun to face him again. 'You don't think for the last five years I haven't thought about what I've done over and over and over.' Tears streamed down her face. Pain throbbed in her jaw. 'I can't take it back, Herb.'

'I know how you feel,' he said softly.

'You've slept with a married man too, have you?' Her nose stung. Pressure rushed against her eardrums like a plane ready for take-off.

'I shot someone.'

The whoosh in her ears was deafening. 'I don't need your judgement, Herb Lawson,' she yelled over the roaring noise.

He pulled her towards him. 'He's dead, Birdie.' His expression a mixture of fear and sorrow. 'And I can't take it back.'

She frowned and shook away the thunderous turbulence. 'What?'

'I shot a man. Dead.'

THIRTY-SIX

Herb was in the shower. She'd brought him back to her place where she knew Lenore would be dozing in her gun-free bedroom after putting some very alive, definitely not-shot-dead boys to bed, waiting for her not-murderous husband to return from drinks with the innocent-of-homicide lads.

'He's struggling, Mum. I haven't made things any easier these last couple of days.'

Lenore poured a glass of Baileys and took a sip. She and Birdie stood in the kitchen. Her mother lifted her chin, closed her eyes and let the smooth, creamy liquid slide down her throat. She poured another, and one for Birdie. 'Do you think the police know?'

'They would have to know something. Someone connected to the police is the one who sent the man to silence Herb.'

'Sugar,' said Lenore. 'What about Larry?'

'He knows something went on. I'm not sure he knows all the facts.'

Lenore shook her head and drank back another swig of Baileys. 'Vinny?'

'Vinny knows, Mum.' She was sure of it.

Vinny knew many things. Herb said he was the one who organised a gun – one that wasn't NSW Police Force issue. Vinny had got wind of the fact that someone was sniffing around Herb. Knew that Herb had met with internal affairs.

'Where's Herb now?'

'He's in the shower. He's a bit wiped out. I think we might need to get him home. Properly. To Terrigal.'

'What happened, Birdie?'

'Herb witnessed Warren Lanfranchi's shooting.'

'Sugar,' whispered Lenore. 'No wonder he disappeared.'

'He decided to go to Country earlier than planned. Hoping he'd be safe. We'd all be safe with him gone, but ...'

'He wasn't.'

'On his way to Country, he was followed. A hitman attacked and tried to kill him. Herb killed the hitman instead.'

He'd gathered himself up and continued onto Country. *Thank God.* Being on Country had probably saved him. She'd need to call his brother if she were to get him home to Terrigal.

'That's why he wasn't honest with me. He was trying to keep me ... us ... safe. To get his shit as far away from us as possible.'

And she'd been angry with him for not letting her in. Angry at him for running. Now she felt like crap because her anger had been so fierce it had drawn a confession.

She understood Herb would always choose the path that protected her, but sometimes she wished he'd choose to involve her, rather than just protect her. She wished that they were in it together.

'Sugar, Birdie.'

'Mum, there's more.'

Lenore took another sip of her Baileys. Her eyes darted to the clock. 'Hurry, love. It's late. Glen might be home any minute.'

'Vinny has people watching the house.'

'What?'

'Herb and I were shot at, last week. In the car park of the Sailo.'

'Shot at! Are you alright?' She came around and raised shaking arms. Checking Birdie out like she did when Birdie was little; trying to locate the sore. 'Were you hurt?' Her eyes were glassy. 'I didn't hear anything about a shooting. Why didn't you tell me?'

'Sorry I didn't tell you.' Lenore enveloped her in a hug. Birdie spoke through the smothering. 'We weren't hit. Herb's bike and a wooden paling took a small beating, but not us.' Her mother released her. Birdie went on, quickly. 'They used a silencer. Still noisy but not as much. It was late. No one else was in the car park. Since then, Vinny has had people tailing all of us. Including Glen and the boys.'

'That bloody man.' Lenore sank onto a kitchen stool. 'This is what I hoped to avoid.' She ran a hand down her neck. 'I can still remember the day I told him to stay away from me. He told me he'd always be there if I needed him. He'd always keep me safe.' She launched off the stool and paced the kitchen, eye on the clock again. 'All these bloody years I distanced myself, made sure I was independent, on top of things. He'd be loving the fact that he's needed to keep me safe.'

'Sorry, Mum.'

'It's not your fault, love.' She lifted the remaining liquor, the quiver in her fingers noticeable, and swallowed it down.

She dropped the glass on the bench. 'Although, I'm going to kill Larry.'

The front door opened, and Glen wandered in. Birdie took the opportunity to call Cec as Lenore helped her very merry husband into his pyjamas and then bed.

A while later, Lenore came into Birdie's room and checked on a sleeping Herb. 'He's exhausted, love,' her mother said softly.

'It's partly my fault.' Birdie kept her voice low. 'I've put him through the wringer the last couple of days. Flew off the handle again tonight.'

'I'm sure he gave as good as he got. With you two, it seems to be the way.' She stared off, perhaps remembering another time, her own past sparring partners. *Vinny perhaps.* Birdie sat on her lounge, reluctant to leave him. Lenore sat at the opposite end.

'I didn't get the form mistress role.' She said in softly spoken words.

'Oh no.' Lenore put a hand on Birdie's leg. 'How do you feel about that?'

Birdie felt many things. Anger – because it was about to be announced as hers. Mortification – at the way everyone was party to the airing of her dirty laundry. Shame – at how they would know why, consequently, it hadn't been given to her. Her eyes welled with tears, sadness at having to tell her mum the truth of it. She didn't want to let her down, have her think less of the daughter she'd raised on her own.

'Oh, Birdie.' Lenore shuffled forwards and grabbed her in a hug. A week's worth of tension pouring out through tears over her mother's shoulder. 'There'll be other chances. What did Sister Therese Margaret say?'

'Sister T originally told me I got the job. She was about to announce it to the staff at a morning meeting.'

Lenore pulled back and studied Birdie 'But then ...' Her mother shook her head. 'She didn't?'

'Do you remember when Jonathon Naylor called and left a message?'

'Yes.' Her face took on an expression of irritation, her voice did too. 'Did he give you a bad reference?'

'Not a bad reference, more a bad reputation.' Birdie regarded her frowning mother. She would just have to say it, just blurt it out. 'I slept with him, Mum. When I was on prac, all those years ago. I slept with Jonathon.'

Her mother was silent. 'Right,' she finally said. She stood, holding one hand in the other, squeezing them. 'Did he tell her?'

'Sort of.'

'I can see how the Catholic Church may find that troubling. Sex outside of marriage and all. But there's nothing wrong with having sex. Seems unusual that he would make his love life common knowledge, though.'

'He didn't. There's more, Mum. At the time I slept with him, he was married.'

Lenore inhaled. 'Okay.'

'His wife made it known.'

'Did she?' Lenore paced the carpet in front of the lounge. 'Bloody cow,' she mumbled softly. 'You were only eighteen when you did your first prac. You were a child. Granted, not one of your most sensible moves, love, but he's the married one. He was the one who should have kept it in his pants. Not only that, but he was your supervisor. A position of power. Some might say he took advantage of that.'

'I know all that. It doesn't help the guilt.'

Lenore sat on the lounge again. 'I bet he hasn't missed out on a job because of it.'

'Well, no. In fact, he's just been promoted.'

'What? Well, if she can expose you, perhaps I'll expose him. Maybe I'll give the Catholic Schools Board a ring.'

'Thanks, Mum.' Birdie huffed a laugh. 'But don't.'

'No, of course I wouldn't,' she said, pushing her hair aggressively behind her ears. 'It's still not fair.'

'It was the wrong thing to do. I just have to deal with the consequences. Like, Herb finding out.'

Her mother raised an eyebrow. 'Herb knows?'

'Yes. It's okay. We'll deal with it later. I wanted to say sorry to you, Mum.'

'Oh, sweetheart. You're twenty-three years old. You don't need to apologise to me. You just said yourself you did the wrong thing. You're sorry. You've learned from it. And you've missed an opportunity because of it.' She pointed at Herb sleeping on the bed. 'Had a barney with your boyfriend. Plus, the scorned woman has taken her revenge. That seems enough, don't you think?'

'I didn't want to disappoint you.'

'You haven't.' She held Birdie's hands in hers. 'We've all done things we should have done differently. Look at me, fell pregnant out of wedlock at eighteen. Not that I think that there's necessarily anything wrong with falling pregnant, and I'm not apologising for it, but questionable behaviour was involved before and afterwards.'

Would Lenore ever level with Birdie? Perhaps now that she could see Birdie as someone who is old enough to have her own regrets, she might let her daughter in on that time of her life.

'You know, it might be a good idea for us to discuss some of this stuff,' Birdie said. 'The stuff about you and Vinny and Larry.'

A soft knock on Birdie's outside door took their focus.

'Cec,' said Birdie. She stood to answer it.

Lenore grabbed her hand as she stood. 'You need to forgive yourself and move on. Stronger and with more compassion. Take it from me.'

Birdie hugged her mum, tears welling again.

'I love you, my brave, beautiful girl.'

'I love you too, Mum.'

Birdie let Cec in. The next while was spent helping him organise Herb. By the time Herb and Cec had departed, and the adrenaline had drained away, Birdie was bone tired. It had been one hell of a night.

'Time for bed, Mum. Might have a sleep in.'

The phone started ringing. Lenore jumped. 'Who's calling this late?'

'Early, you mean. It's a quarter to four.' Birdie lunged for the receiver in her room. 'Hello?'

'The police left a message on my machine overnight. I only just listened to it.'

'Is everything alright?' She lifted her mouth from the mouthpiece and whispered, 'Uncle Larry,' to her mother.

'They've asked me to bring Therese in this morning.'

'Bit early to be letting us know,' she said to her uncle before speaking to her worried mother, 'Larry's fine.'

'I woke up early. Not sleeping well,' Larry answered.

She didn't mention they hadn't slept at all.

'They need to speak to her again. I think they are going to officially charge her.'

⋙ ⋘

Birdie wandered through the aisles of the Little Shops General Store on Saturday morning, looking left and right. 'If he doesn't tell us now, he's never going to,' she said to Pia. They were searching for Dom. They needed to know Sister T's secret. And they needed to know it now! If she was having 'sex', was that what she was doing the afternoon of Warwick's attack, and could the person she was doing it with be able to give her an alibi?

The shops were one of the stops on Dom's list of things to do this morning, according to the mate he'd been bunking-in with.

'Grab some chippies,' said Pia. 'I'm hungry.'

Birdie's mind ran to Herb – it often did – as she began to pull the last packet of salt and vinegar chips from one side of the display. She hoped he and Cec had got home safely; that Herb would be alright. Pulling the last Polly Waffle from the other side was Dom Walker.

'Hello, Miss Mealing,' he said, peering at her through the steel mesh that separated the now-empty shelves.

'Mr Walker. There you are.' She wandered along until the end of the aisle, until they were face to face, no barrier between them. 'I've been looking for you.'

'I don't know whether to be flattered or concerned?'

'Have you heard from Sister T today?'

'Should I have?'

'She's at the station, helping police with their investigations … again.'

'What?' he whispered.

'It looks like she'll be charged, Dom. Uncle Larry's with her now.'

'But she didn't do it!' He sounded very sure of that. His voice was loud even in the ample space.

'She visited Warwick just before he was attacked. Plus, she was discovered with the knife, and body, in hand. She has motive.' Birdie took a punt. Dom was clearly emotional. Could she shake him up a little more, see if he'd crack? 'Maybe I've been wrong about the secret. I thought it might help prove her innocence, but what if the secret is the reason she attacked Warwick? I have to wonder whether she was attempting to keep her secret, *a secret*, when she stabbed him.'

Dom's face paled. 'I can't believe they think she did it,' he said to himself. 'It's all my fault. If I wasn't so selfish.' He raked his hands through his hair. 'If I hadn't pushed.' He started to shuffle around the entrance to the aisle. 'If I'd just kept it in my ... all those years ago. If I could just control my carnal needs.'

His carnal needs?

Birdie's mind flashed to Sister T's office ... on Thursday morning ... the look Dom and Sister T had exchanged after the Linda Naylor ordeal; the way he rushed to her, held her hands when he entered the room.

'Is he alright?' Pia said.

Birdie gaped at Pia who was hovering at her shoulder.

Dom had started to pace the entry to the aisle, mumbling to himself.

'Pia,' Birdie whispered, pulling her back into the aisle, 'the entry about Dom didn't say "young". It said "tight". We *presumed* the backside belonging to the co-teacher was young, therefore, a young person on staff – Margie, even, for a moment. But … Sister T's bum is "tight".'

Pia frowned. 'I'll take your word for it,' she whispered back.

'She swims most mornings, plays basketball and rides her bicycle everywhere. She sat on the edge of her desk the other day. Her bum is tight.'

'Weird thing to notice, Birds.' Pia's face looked like she'd smelled something bad.

'I couldn't avoid it. It was right at eye level. I also noticed her running a hand across her desk. A faraway look in her eye. Like she'd been swept across it – or one like it.'

Pia's eyebrows rose. 'Okay. Officially grossed out now.'

'I just told Dom that Sister T had been taken to the station for more questioning, and he said, if he'd just controlled his *carnal needs*. That's what Sister T said to Dom in the chapel that day. *Our focus should be on serving the Lord, not carnal needs.* I thought she was speaking in general, like collectively, everyone's carnal needs, but I think she was talking about hers and—'

'Dom's,' said Pia.

Dom wandered, unfocused, around the stacks of lollies and chips, oblivious to the looks from the girls and the ones he was beginning to attract from other shoppers.

'Are you saying, the person Dom is having an affair with is Sister T?' Pia hissed softly.

Was it possible that Dom and Sister T were sleeping together? Was it possible they had been sleeping together years and years ago?

'He practically told us himself. He told us Sister T had taken vows. Without meaning to, his sloshed brain alerted us to the possibility that she'd broken one.'

'With him?'

'Why not him? Sister T is beautiful and would have been even more so as a young woman. They worked together at St Perceval's as new teachers.'

They were close – always had been, as long as she'd known them.

Dom had clocked up two failed marriages. Maybe because he loved Sister T and always had. He touched her all the time, like incidentally, like he had a right to. Birdie had watched him grab her hands just the other day out of concern. He gave Margie a job at his school. Margie, Sister T's niece. Percy's and Joanie's were next door to each other, like 'co-teachers' and, in fact, they were co-teachers years ago. There was a *history* between them.

'Do you think it's got anything to do with Warwick's stabbing?' Pia said behind her hand.

Dom was pulling at his shirt, loosening the button at the top. His breaths were coming fast.

'Like, retaliation for printing the rumour?' Birdie said. Had Dom stabbed Warwick because of his love for Sister T?

It's all my fault. Isn't that what Dom just said?

CRASH!

The girls gasped. Clutching each other more closely. Birdie focused on a fountain of milk that fanned out in a white rainbow on the ground where Dom had let go of his groceries.

The cashier looked up from serving her customer and craned her neck.

Dom shucked off his jacket and pulled his shirt from its place inside the waistband of his trousers.

The girls took a step back.

'The entry said, history never repeats,' Birdie whispered. 'I reckon they slept together all those years ago, and I reckon Warwick saw them. Dom's marriage has just ended. Perhaps they started up again, all these years later. That's the history. We thought it was because Dom's a history teacher, but it was a clue from Warwick. He knew about their *history*, their *past*.'

The Polly Waffle chocolate bar rolled, stopping against Birdie's foot. Had they ever found out if Dom had slipped into his car and driven away that Thursday afternoon before basketball?

'It was me.' Dom's vision was unfocused. His voice loud and hoarse. He was in a world of pain.

The girls took another step back. Birdie ogled Pia. 'Did he just say—?'

'It's okay, sir. We know they're yours.' The cashier lifted the microphone from next to the register. 'Happens all the time. We're getting someone to clean it up now.' She pushed the button and leaned into the receiver. 'Code ten, mop and bucket to the registers, please. Code ten,' she called in a singsong voice.

'It was me,' he panted.

'But I thought we decided Warwick didn't write the rumours. They came in the mail,' said Pia.

'Remember the blue paper the messages were typed on? The texture of the paper was whisper thin, except one. One was thicker and had a watermark.'

'Shit, you're right! It was the one about the desk-polishing new principal.' Pia stared at Dom. 'The one about Dom. We *were* right. Warwick must have seen the popularity of the column and thought he'd put one of his own rumours in. He must have sent it in on blue paper to look like the others.'

'And just after Dom's entry, Warwick was stabbed.'

'I'm the guilty one,' Dom yelled.

'Because Dom stabbed him,' whispered Pia, eyes wide.

The girls moved another step away from the now-crazed Dom.

People had stopped what they were doing, and all heads turned towards the front of the store. Dom was a wild man: hair askew, shirt undone and untucked, surrounded by cascading milk, pasta sauce, glass and oozing eggs.

He lunged suddenly and grabbed Birdie's arms. Pia let out a squeak. Pressure from his fingers dug into the slack muscle at the back of Birdie's biceps.

'I stabbed Warwick Woods,' said Dom.

Birdie heard the intake of breath from Pia like a blowfly at her ear, felt Pia's fingers clamp her shoulder, felt Stumpy pound into her sternum as Pia clutched Birdie tight and tried to pry her away.

People started to back away from the scene.

Birdie could see the cashier in her peripheral vision, distress unwavering as she picked up the phone from under her bench like she was in slow motion, turned the dial in a wide arc around the phone once, twice, three times – *000 emergency* – and gradually slid with the unit and handset to the floor behind her station.

'Crikey, Birds. He's lost the plot,' Pia mumbled as she valiantly tried to extricate her friend from Dom's vice-like grasp.

He did look murderous. Where were Vinny's men? Why weren't they rushing to help? She was being accosted by a would-be murderer.

'It's my fault,' Dom screamed into her face.

Birdie squeezed her eyes shut. She'd just pushed the lunatic, who had stabbed a man, into a confession in the middle of the Little Shops, and was now stuck in his psycho death grip. If she wasn't already done for, she'd definitely be dead meat when Herb found out.

THIRTY-SEVEN

T HE PHONE IN THE kitchen rang. Uncle Larry was already on the office phone line. A muffled one-sided conversation came from the nook behind the fireplace in the lounge room. Pia had dropped Birdie at her uncle's for a bit of a debrief after the events of the morning.

The kitchen phone shrilled again. Birdie strained to see that her uncle was not going to answer it and lifted the receiver.

'Hello.'

'Birdie?!'

Shit!

Herb.

During the incident at the Little Shops with the deranged Dom Walker, one of Vinny's men had swooped through the front door of the supermarket and tackled Dom to the ground. 'Ask for Constable Celeste Ford,' Pia had called to the cashier who was on the phone with the police. Vinny's man had held Dom still until Celeste was in sight and then swooped out again like a hawk but without a mouse.

'Birdie, is that you?'

How much about what went on at the Little Shops would Herb know?

'Bird!'

Far out! Why did I have to go and answer my uncle's kitchen phone?

Birdie put on a formal-sounding phone voice, *'Hello. You've reached the residence of Larry Kean.'*

'You little shit.'

'He can't come to the phone at the moment.'

'Eventually we will be in the same room again, teach.'

'Your call is important, so please don't hang up.'

'This is how we're playing this, is it? Confident with this decision, Bird?'

'Please leave a message after the beep, and he will be happy to return your call. BEE—'

'Jesus Christ.' Herb took a breath. 'Larry. Herb Lawson. Can you pass a message on to that girlfriend of mine, who is going to be very sorry when I get my hands on her, that if she doesn't cease and desist, I'm going to wring her beautiful bloody neck.' His tone turned dark; it brokered no discussion. 'Listen to me, Birdie Mealing. Stay away from any dangerous situation.'

'Dom's in custody. There is no more danger.'

'Birdie!'

Bugger! She swallowed. 'Hi, Herb.'

'If I believed for a minute that Dom's arrest meant you wouldn't find some other situation to get yourself mixed up in, I'd be a happy man.'

'All I was doing was getting some snacks at the shops, officer.'

'And in no way did you ask Dom leading questions or push him for answers or offer up information that coerced him into impulsive action.'

'It was a friendly chat. It wasn't my fault.'

'Please, baby, I'm too far away to protect you.'

The softness of that 'baby', something he'd never called her before, made her heart melt.

'Can you be safe for me, Bird?'

Birdie was mush all the way to her toes. The man felt the need to be the protector of everyone. He needed to worry less about her and more about himself.

'I'll try.'

'Miss you.'

She missed him too. 'Why don't I come up on Monday. Stay for a few days.' Dom had been arrested now. Uncle Larry's case was closed. They could all relax a little. 'I'm on school holidays.'

'I'd like that.'

There would be a little bit of beach weather left in the season. And then she was sure they'd find *something* else to do.

'You off to the Sailo tonight?' Herb asked.

'Yep, with Pia and Stu. Sabine and Brad will be there too.'

'Griff Wheatley?'

'Don't do that, Herb. My heart belongs to you, grumble-bum. You know that.' *Surely he knew that now.*

Larry entered the kitchen area. 'Warwick Woods is awake.' His loud proclamation flew off excited lips.

'That Larry?' said Herb from her earpiece.

'Yeah. He just ended his call on the office line,' Birdie said.

'Celeste is going to pop into the hospital and ask him some questions after Emer Garland leaves,' Larry continued. 'He can only have one visitor at a time.'

'Emer visited?' Birdie said to her uncle.

'Took over some flowers and a gift basket from the staff, apparently.' He made big eyes and shrugged a shoulder.

'Did Larry just say Warwick Woods has woken up?' Herb said in her ear again.

'I'm going to tag along,' Uncle Larry continued.

'Yes,' Birdie said to Herb, 'and Uncle Larry is going with Celeste to visit him.'

'Celeste said I can chat to him when she's finished,' he called loud enough for Herb to hear. He collected his keys from the coffee table in the lounge room. 'You will be right to see yourself out, Birdie?' He left before waiting for her answer.

'Birdie.'

She focused again on Herb's voice in her ear. 'Yep.'

'You're not off the hook just because we're friends again. As soon as that perfect arse is within reach, I'm gonna—'

'What are you going to do, officer? Take me in hand?' She heard him suck in a breath.

'Jesus, you're wicked.'

'Well established.'

'Love you, teach.'

'I love you too.'

Birdie hung up the phone. A smile spread across her face. Herb sounded good, cheeky, his usual bossy self. His family must have been giving him the care he needed. It would be good to spend some proper time with him, now that this was all wrapped up.

Just the two of them. Away from everything.

Birdie picked up her own keys from the coffee table. The yearbooks she and Herb had analysed days ago sat open, Warwick and Sy smiling from the left-hand page. On the opposite page, the staff stood proudly, Dom among them. Sister T absent. So that was that, then. Warwick was awake. He'd be able to point the finger squarely at Dom.

It felt like she could expel the breath she'd been holding over the last couple of weeks. Focus on Herb and the beach.

Her mind wandered to Sister T. How would she be feeling? Relieved? Concerned?

Birdie checked the clock. She had time before heading out tonight to visit an old friend.

⇔ ⇔ ⇔

Birdie had spent plenty of time over the last few days pondering what she would have done if Herb had never returned. If he had died at the hands of that hitman. Or if someone even found out what he'd done and arrested him for murder. They'd been shot at. He could have been taken from her.

So as she sat at the convent's tiny kitchen table and focused on the cup of tea and plate of biscuits Sister T placed in front of her, she couldn't help feeling sorry for her beautiful principal.

Sister T slumped into the seat opposite and picked up a biscuit herself. 'I'm sorry, Birdie. Shocked into silence, into stillness. I should have quelled that woman. I should have stood up for you. Mary Mac would be turning in her grave.'

Never see a need without doing something about it. That had been Mary MacKillop's motto. These words were written on the walls of the school, murmured in prayers, a catchcry when the girls were apathetic.

Sister T looked tired. The news that Dom had made a spectacle of himself, roughhoused Birdie and been detained by the police, had troubled her.

Birdie placed a hand on her friend's wrist. 'I'm okay, you know.'

And she *was* okay. She was okay about Linda's accusation. She was okay about Dom's bruising grip. She was even okay about Herb shooting someone. She was surprisingly okay.

'We're survivors, Birdie – you, me, Mary Mac.' She placed a hand over Birdie's. 'But Dom. I'm not sure he'll survive this. I honestly can't believe he would *stab* Warwick. Dom is many things. But he's never been violent.'

'Even to protect those he loves? To stop their secrets from being revealed?'

There she went again. Asking questions. Pushing for information. Far out, Herb was right. *I just can't help myself.*

Sister T stood, agitated. 'His father was a hard man. He was violent. Dom made sure he was the complete opposite. He's turned from the light many a time – he'd be the first to admit – but violence?'

'Perhaps it finally caught up with him. The whole nature versus nurture thing.' Though, Dom was a gentle man, even on the basketball court. 'You're good friends, aren't you – you and Dom?'

Birdie knew people were capable of anything, but Sister T knew Dom well. She'd known him for twenty years. Maybe more. They were family friends. He touched her like it was natural. Spoke to her in soft tones. Called her Terri. 'Feels like we've been friends forever.' *And they say history never repeats.*

'The secret Dom was worried about.' *Carnal needs.* 'It was you. You were the woman on his desk.'

Definitely dead meat. Herb is going to kill me.

'You always were the clever one, Birdie Mealing.' Sister T stood and busied herself at the sink. 'Sometimes I wonder whether I'm the only woman he has loved. Properly loved. He obviously admires women. Many women over the years.'

At least two other women. Especially, enough to marry them.

'But maybe he was trying to fill the void, perhaps, I left him with,' Sister T added. 'I must take some responsibility there.'

'So that's why he stabbed Warwick.'

'I was in the chapel that afternoon. In the confessional.'

Which was why no one saw her. The confessional. Birdie considered Sister T who had stopped her cleaning. *The confessional* – meaning ... she had something to confess.

'Yet you didn't tell my uncle that, even when the priest could have easily verified your whereabouts. He could have given you an alibi.'

'How would it have looked that the day the rumour was published, the day a man was stabbed, I was in dire need of confession?'

'The confessional is sacred. Not even the priest can recount what's been said in there.'

'And you suppose that was going to make me look any less guilty?'

No. In fact, it probably would have made her look more guilty.

'So if you weren't confessing to Warwick's stabbing, what were you confessing?' Her affair with Dom?

'The police asked me the same thing.'

'And what did you tell them?'

'The truth.' She paced the kitchen. 'Warwick was not going to stop printing the column. He'd told me as much himself. Said he could make life even harder for Dom. He had more dirt to print. "Payback" he called it. I was concerned for Dom, concerned for Margie. I knew she'd already been the brunt of whispers around the staffroom.'

Payback. More dirt. From before. What had happened years before? 'You're very protective of Margie.'

'She's my blood. My niece.'

And they say history never repeats. 'So you'd had an affair with Dom earlier. Years before.'

'Warwick knew about our affair. He was very perceptive. Noticed details others didn't. He was the child who watched quietly while the others acted boisterously.'

'Where was Rebecca's husband when the baby was born?'

Sister T began wiping down the bench top.

Birdie spoke again. 'Margie said you delivered her.'

'He was in America. Doing some professional development on new ideas in dentistry. X-rays, protective gear, expansion into nursing homes, that sort of thing.'

'Lucky you were with her then?'

'Yes, very lucky.'

'Was he in America when she lost the baby too?'

'It all happened at around the same time.' She moved on to drying the cups in the dish rack.

'I'm just wondering whether Warwick knowing you'd been with Dom was enough. If he'd revealed that, you could have denied it; his word against yours. But it might have been more difficult to deny if he'd had hard evidence.'

Sister T's hands stilled. She returned to the table and gingerly sat. 'I'm hardly surprised you can teach, play music and be a detective, Birdie.' She offered a tight-lipped smile and started fondling a doily. 'He found out I was pregnant when I had some phantom contractions. He and I were finishing up a prefects' meeting when I thought I was in labour. He never said anything, and neither did I, but he must have known. He was the oldest boy of ten kids with a very traditional but useless father. I'd say he'd seen it all before.'

'Margie.'

'Yes.' She briefly covered her mouth with her hands. 'She's mine. Mine ... and Dom's.' She grabbed Birdie's hand. 'Dom doesn't know, Birdie. I would appreciate your discretion.'

'He won't hear it from me.'

Sister T removed her hand.

Birdie sipped her tea. 'You could have told the police anything. Could have confessed to forgetting to pray, having impure thoughts, missing church. You could have just stood behind the sanctity of the confessional. All you needed to do was prove you couldn't have been at the gazette at the time of the stabbing.'

'Just more deception. More lies. I took a vow of obedience.'

'You took one of chastity too, Therese.'

'And look what happened when I broke that one. There are reasons these vows exist. Rebecca's husband doesn't know Margie is not his by blood. He had no idea I was pregnant. He had no idea his wife had miscarried. He would have felt guilty that he was overseas. But he was a good man. He was providing for his family. Making dentistry advancements.' She absently pushed her finger into some biscuit crumbs. 'He was so happy to be a father at last after having so much trouble falling pregnant, holding a pregnancy. Us sisters cooked up the whole scheme. The perfect solution.'

'But you must have been showing. If you were sleeping with Dom, how didn't he know?'

'I disguised the pregnancy under layers of habit and coats. Dom and I took our pleasure where we could. The luxury of a bed never presented itself.' She absentmindedly placed a hand over her stomach. 'I pretended I was distraught over our actions, that I couldn't live with what we'd done, that I couldn't face myself or him. That worked for a while. Then I said I needed to get away. Lies, deception. One after the other.'

Birdie thought about the absence of Sister T in the staff photo sitting open on Uncle Larry's coffee table. 'How did Dom react when you left?'

'He was devastated. He probably still blames Warwick for our relationship ending all those years ago. And I simply let him think it was Warwick discovering our liaison that drove me away. I often wonder what would have happened if I'd just come clean and told him I was pregnant. If I'd chosen him over my vows. If I'd brought up Margie as my own. How different our lives would have been.'

'Have you ever called Dom at his house? Perhaps his wife answered the phone?'

Birdie's questioning eyes met Sister T's. Recognition flared behind the older woman's clear blue irises. 'Maybe I wanted to hear his voice. Maybe I wanted to hear hers. Maybe I wanted to confess. I don't really know what possessed me to make that call.'

You called Jonathon's house once yourself, Birdie.

'When she answered, I just froze,' Sister T said. '"Don't call here again." That's what she said. Like she knew.'

Just when Dom had finally reconciled with the woman he loved, the only woman he truly loved, Warwick told the world. And hinted that he could reveal more with the little tag about history repeating.

'Will you ever tell Margie?'

'She has a mother.'

And I've got a father. Somewhere. Was Uncle Larry enough for Birdie? Was not knowing her *real* father's identity ruining her life?

'The truth is, I love Dom. I have for a long time. But my lies have made a gentle man – a lover, not a fighter – commit a violent crime. I might be able to seek forgiveness from a higher power, but how will I ever forgive myself?'

Chemistry. Something
happens between a man and a
woman, which may have
nothing to do with their
images of physical
perfection in the opposite
sex.

'What turns women on? Women tell!'
Cleo, September 1984.

THIRTY-EIGHT

T HE SAILO WAS IN full swing when Birdie, Pia and Stu finally arrived. Griff, Sabine and Brad had secured tables and were well into at least their first, if not their second, drink.

'Did you hear that Warwick has woken up?' Birdie said after she'd bought drinks and joined the others at the table.

They knew about the incident with Dom at the Little Shops. Pia had told Stu, who had told Brad, who had told Sabine, who in turn had told Griff.

'Uncle Larry was on his way to visit the hospital.'

Brad wiggled his fingers. 'The truth will be revealed.'

One of the truths.

She spotted Margie hovering at the entrance and waved her over. Birdie had asked her to join them. If the truth was ever revealed, Margie would need her friends. Probably even one as imperfect as herself.

'Another mystery solved,' said Stu.

Birdie scoffed. 'After Dom confessed.'

'After you worked out the clues and pushed for a confession,' said Stu.

'Speaking of working out clues, you told me Dr Lee had not paid the blackmail.' Birdie frowned at Stu.

Stu shrugged. 'He *didn't* pay blackmail.'

Birdie flicked his shoulder with the back of her hand. 'That's because he wasn't bloody blackmailed, Stuart!'

Stu grimaced. 'I was hoping you wouldn't notice.'

'Stu!'

'Perhaps my message was lost in translation. I had been plying him with brandy, and we were speaking in dialect.'

Pia leaned over. 'Did you get something wrong, boy wonder?' A grin splitting her face.

Stu crossed his arms. 'I'm not sure *wrong* is the correct word. Misinterpreted would be more accurate terminology.'

'Misinterpreted,' repeated Pia. 'Righteo,' she said nodding. Birdie got the feeling Pia would be storing this moment away to bring out at another time. 'More importantly,' Pia went on. 'I wonder how our friend Emer will feel about the eventual return of her boss.'

'Well, she visited him with a basket of goodies this afternoon,' Birdie said.

'Dressed as Little Red or the Wolf?' said Pia.

Sabine popped her chin forward. 'Emer will be spewin'.' She giggled. 'I think she was hoping he'd never wake up. She told me she'd missed out on a job in the city. Said being the editor of the *Gallie Wallen Gazette* was her redemption.'

'That woman is full-on,' said Pia, shaking her head.

Birdie placed a hand on both Pia's and Stu's. 'I'm going to head up to Terrigal on Monday.' With Pia concocting adventurous scientific breakthroughs with food and Stu working his fingers to the bone at the hospital, she was often left to her own devices during school holidays.

'How is Herb?' Pia asked.

'He's good, I think. He was threatening to smack my arse if I didn't pull my head in last time we spoke.'

'Sounds normal.' Pia patted her friend's leg.

Birdie still hadn't explained the real reason Herb had needed to take a break. Would she ever?

'Obviously forgiven your little indiscretion with Jonathon then, if he's threatening to get kinky on your arse.'

'Pia!' said Birdie.

'No judgement here.' Pia grinned. 'Wish someone would get kinky with my arse.'

Birdie laughed, her gaze catching on Stu – eyes trained wistfully on Pia. A look she'd often caught him giving her over the years.

'Tell me you're going to stay at Larry's unit, just the two of you, while you're in Terrigal?' Pia continued, oblivious. 'I'm living my love life vicariously through yours, you know?'

Keeping the truth to herself that Herb had shot someone – killed someone – felt like a betrayal. She, Pia and Stu had been through a lot together. They shared most things. But was offloading on her friends a wise choice or was keeping them safely in the dark a wiser one?

'Being away from it all might give us a chance to work on that trust issue.'

'I think he understands that you're not conventional, Birdie, said Stu. 'He knows you're not going to be apologising for it.'

'And how do you know that, Einstein?' said Pia.

'We chat,' said Stu.

Pia rolled her eyes.

Birdie grinned. 'His mum was part of the Black movement, a rebel, a revolutionary. She's a gutsy chick. He'll realise he doesn't need to save me or protect me or be the knight in shining armour all the time. I'm a strong, independent, capable woman.'

'Amen to that, sister!' The girls clinked their glasses together.

'Give me strength,' Stu mumbled as he stood up. 'I'm getting a drink.'

Their little party, joined by a string of friends, had blossomed out from the tables to a nearby lounge area. Birdie watched Pia pat Stu's head patronisingly as he sat back down. She was giggling away to herself when she felt Griff sit next to her on the double seater.

'Birdie Mealing.'

'Griff Wheatley.'

'For the record, I would like it noted that it was not me who stabbed Warwick Woods.'

'When did I ever accuse you?'

'I know I was in your little casebook as a suspect, Girl Detective.'

'Don't flatter yourself, Griff. Everyone was.'

Griff laughed loud and long. 'I once asked you if you'd like me to level with you?'

'I wasn't asking if you'd stabbed Warwick during that discussion, though; I was asking if you'd slept with that girl?'

'I'm not sure this will make you feel any better about me'—he dropped eye contact, focused on his hands, turned an ivory ring around his pinky—'but no, I didn't.'

Why was she not surprised? She'd always had the feeling he'd been wrongly accused. 'Why wouldn't that make me feel better about you?'

'Because it was my student's mother whom I slept with.'

Birdie stared at the man in disbelief. 'Oh, Griff.'

'We just fell into it, Birdie. Rhonda had a hard life. I offered some relief. Accidentally offered a little bit too much. *Crossed the line.*'

Crossed the line. She'd said those exact words to Sister T? She knew what 'falling into it without meaning to' felt like.

'I suppose you've heard about my little indiscretion?' Birdie said. *Who am I to judge?*

'Someone might have confirmed a rumour that was floating around. I heard the actual incident happened a long time ago. Water under the bridge.'

'Sweet of you to say.'

'I'm a sweet guy.' He gave her a cheeky grin.

Why would he let everyone think it was one of his students, which was way worse than an adult woman making adult choices? Why would the mother, Rhonda, allow her daughter's reputation to be damaged like that?

'Something tells me there's more to this story,' Birdie said.

'Are you ever not searching for clues?'

'Often. Tell me anyway.'

'Rhonda's husband, the girl's father, was a big man, had a reputation. He was capable of, and had already, done Rhonda harm. That's what I was helping her with. I was trying to convince Rhonda to get out, get away.'

'Shit, Griff.' She put her hand on his knee and gave it a squeeze.

'He found me at the house. Came home drunk from the pub. Rhonda's daughter, my student, cleverly stepped in and said it was her I was sleeping with.'

'To protect her mum.'

Griff nodded.

'Brave girl.'

'The bravest. She finally told Rhonda's brother, her uncle, what had been going on. When she'd convinced him, he took his niece to the police station to make a statement.' *Brave indeed.* 'Then Rhonda found out she was pregnant to her prick of a husband, yet again. It's been a slow, careful process.'

'You let me, let everyone, the whole town, for God's sake, believe you were a complete deadshit.'

'Yeah, but I knew I wasn't a *complete* deadshit. Just a little bit of one.'

'You're a little bit of a hero.'

'Heroes don't run "wee, wee, wee, wee all the way home".'

'They do to protect those who need it.' *Never see a need without doing something about it.* 'You gave them the courage to act.'

'Does it make you want to fall in love with me?' He lifted her hand from his knee and kissed the palm, his cheeky grin turning warm.

It did actually make her want to fall in love with him, a little bit. 'Why are you telling me this now?'

'Apart from the fact that I had to keep up the pretence until they were safe, which they now are, I have an ulterior motive. I noticed your off-duty policeman has skipped town.'

'Well, now. How do you know that wasn't because he, *too*, is a little bit of a hero?'

Griff laughed. 'Is he?' He held her hand between both of his. With his elbows on his knees, he leaned forward and stared deep into her eyes. He was so captivatingly attractive it was hard to look away. She'd read this man wrong, all this time. He was studying her in earnest now, all cheekiness gone. What might have happened between them in another time and place? His expression became serious. More serious than she'd ever seen on this particular beautiful face.

'You know my heart belongs to another, Mr Wheatley.'

He dragged his hand away. 'Can't blame a boy for trying, Miss Mealing.'

⟦ ⟦ ⟦

Birdie searched the night sky as they made their way to the taxi rank. Did Herb see the same stars all the way up the coast? His plea earlier, to make sure she stayed safe, had stopped her from drinking too much. *Damn his eyes.* She watched as Pia and Stu fell into step with Griff and Brad, who in turn had an arm slung over Margie's shoulders.

Would Stu ever tell Pia how he felt?

Would Griff's name be cleared? Did he want it to be?

Would Brad, one day, be able to be his true self. Love the person he wanted to?

Would Margie find out she was born out of a secret love that still ran deep?

'Umm,' Birdie called, 'where's Sabine?'

Birdie was sure the little Frenchie had left the club with them. She turned back towards its entrance. Was that Sabine just outside the front doors? Birdie watched for a moment. It was definitely her. What was she doing? Birdie started back to the entrance. It appeared Sabine was in conversation with someone. The person, wearing black, blended into the darkness surrounding the pair.

'Stop, you lot,' Birdie called over her shoulder. 'We need to wait for her.'

The others came to a standstill. Brad said something that made Margie giggle and Griff bark out a laugh. Birdie refocused on Sabine to dtermine of she was comingwas coming, only to witness the tiny woman in a scuffle with the much taller person she'd been talking to.

'Sabine!' Birdie's feet moved swiftly without thought.

Mere metres away, Sabine's head jerked back, and her little body hit the car park floor.

'Hey!' Birdie called.

'Birdie?' said Brad.

Birdie heard the discussion between the others in their little group drift away as she increased her speed. Sabine's lifeless body was being dragged across the pebbled asphalt and away from the club.

'HEY!' Birdie yelled again. She'd nearly reached her, her long legs flying. The head of the person in black turned to see Birdie approach. Angry eyes, the only facial feature Birdie could discern through what she realised was a balaclava, locked on hers. Birdie's heart pumped like an enthusiastic organist on their pedal as she hurtled herself at the stranger.

What she imagined would happen was that she'd be able to tackle Balaclava and release her limp friend from their clutches. What actually happened was that Birdie was struck by Balaclava's raised forearm – like they were palming off said tackle – momentum sending her backwards through the air, before her backside hit the ground with a thud. When she looked up, Sabine and Balaclava had disappeared into the darkness.

THIRTY-NINE

'THOUGHT I TOLD YOU to stay safe, Birdie.'

'Herb?'

She felt the vibrations of her friends' feet briefly under the muscle of her bum and the bones of her elbows, before Herb yanked her to her feet.

'Brad, you and Griff head around that way. Stu and I will go from this side. Girls, you wait here.'

Pia put her hands on her hips.

'You know that's not going to happen, Herb,' said Birdie, dusting the tiny gravel stones from her elbows and discretely from her bottom underneath her skirt.

The boys were on their toes, ready for action.

'For shit's sake,' Herb muttered into his stubbly beard.

'We'll find another direction to approach from.' She started to pull Pia and Margie in a third direction.

Herb's outstretched hand clamped down on her elbow, whirling her around. 'Don't even think about it.' He pulled her to him until his eyes were centimetres from hers, twirling their fiery dance. 'You. Are not going. Anywhere.'

She lifted her chin and met his force. 'It's either that. Or we go. With you.'

'Birdie, for the love of—'

'Time's ticking, Herb.'

He growled. 'Could one of you girls, please, head back inside and call the police, at least?'

'I will,' said Margie, probably happy to remove herself from the volcano that was Herb.

'Call triple zero. Then call the station direct and speak to Constable Celeste Ford.' Herb gave Margie the station's card. 'Tell her, I think we've found Dom Walker.'

The young woman's eyes grew wide. She stood stock-still.

Herb pushed the card into her hand. 'Go, Margie!'

She jumped at his bark, turned and ran.

'You two are with me,' Herb told Birdie and Pia.

Birdie gave Pia a secret wink.

'Stu, you go with the boys. Be careful. Dom was given bail but didn't appear at the station this afternoon as per the conditions. Let's hope Sabine's not his next victim.'

Herb leaned into her space. 'Now do you see why I get the shits with you, Birdie? The man had you in his clutches at the Little Shops. That Raggedy Ann doll he's dragging around could have been you.' Herb turned, pulling her with him as they started off, before clarifying over his shoulder to the guys. 'Circle around. If you see anything, call out.'

'What are you even doing here, Herb?' She tried to pull her arm away from his grip as all parties – including their own – set off at pace.

He held on tight. 'Saving you, at present.'

'I was fine.'

'You were on your arse.'

They trod softly and slowly around the perimeter of the building. Birdie registered the swish of the water against the shore, Pia's escalated breathing against her cheek, singing coming from the club's kitchen, three sets of feet crunching softly on gravel.

'Why Sabine?' Birdie asked.

'Work that devilish brain for good instead of evil,' said Herb.

Birdie narrowed her eyes at Pia.

'She must know the secret too?' Pia whispered in response.

'The secret Dom and Sister T were talking about in the chapel?' said Herb.

Birdie exchanged another look with Pia.

'Do you two know what it is?' Herb asked.

Birdie swallowed.

'Bird?'

Crap. She hadn't yet told Herb about her visit and questioning of Sister T (almost straight after he told her to stop asking questions). 'I might know it.'

'Jesus, Birdie. What the fuck?'

She hoped that her little visit, and Sister T's confession, didn't have anything to do with Dom's desperate behaviour tonight. He reefed her along. Apart from the gentle sounds of lapping water, and Herb's deafening disappointment, the expanse of land was dark and still, the only light coming in splotches. Eventually, they were back where they started, Margie coming out of the front doors of the club to meet them.

'The police are on their way,' said Margie. 'I still can't believe Dom stabbed Warwick,' she mumbled.

'Well, believe it,' said Herb, his tone blunt. 'He confessed.' he turned to Birdie. 'Now, what's Sister T's secret?'

The boys appeared from the opposite side, shaking their heads.

'Herb, I don't think now is the best time to—'

'Answer me, Birdie.' Herb's tone brutal as the night.

Birdie squeezed Margie's hand. 'Sister T and Dom were having an affair.'

Herb dropped his head. 'Jesus!' He gave Birdie a look that said *good one*.

She answered back with a *that's on you, mate* before turning to her friend. 'Sorry, Margie.'

'I'm okay,' Margie said. 'Probably not surprised when I think about it. Aunty Terri's always been close to Dom.' She scratched her head. 'Answers quite a few questions actually,' she mumbled. 'So he stabbed Warwick to save Terri's reputation.'

'*Uuugh*!' A muted groan echoed out over the still night.

The guys turned their heads and, with a nod from Herb, started back the way they came, to investigate.

The Sailo backed onto the bay but was surrounded by filtered parkland on both sides. Herb set off in the opposite direction. The girls in tow. There was a toilet block, heaps of large trees, a jetty, boats moored, a car park, a boat shed, a ramp, a barbeque area. All of which would provide a perfect place to hide. Where had the sound come from?

As if in answer, a group of young boys on bikes exploded onto the jetty. Stu, Brad and Griff paused as one, and then changed direction to approach the boys on the bikes.

Herb watched for a moment, obviously happy that the guys would be asking questions of the young boys, before steering the girls towards the toilet block. 'Celeste said Warwick hadn't been able to identify his assailant as Dom.'

The ladies' toilets were empty.

'Lucky, he confessed then,' said Pia.

The gents were also empty. They wove in and out of the trees – nothing.

'Might be thinking he's confessed too soon and be regretting it,' Herb continued. 'Evidence has yet to be collected.'

'What if,' Birdie said, 'someone could identify him as being at the scene of the crime?'

'That someone being Sabine?' said Herb.

They were jogging back the way they'd come.

'She heard someone in the car park that night,' Pia said.

'*Zrobili mnie w konia*,' said Birdie.

'What does that mean?' said Herb, taking them through the barbeque stations. They came up empty-handed.

'It's Polish. Mrs N said it's a saying, like an idiom. It translates to *I was made into a horse*. Which sort of translates to I was taken for a ride, which means I was made to look like a fool,' said Birdie.

'Mrs N said?' Herb raised an eyebrow at the girls. 'Jesus Christ.'

Pia ignored his angry eyes. 'But the speaker had added "I *don't* think" after it, which means I won't be taken for a ride. I *won't* be made to look like a fool. Sabine said she thought it was Emer's voice because it was *deep*, Birds.'

'But it must have been a man's voice,' said Birdie. 'Dom's.'

'Dom's first wife was originally from Poland,' said Margie quietly, interjecting. 'Dom picked up a phrase or two.'

Herb glared at Birdie like he had a couple of times tonight: intense, passionate, like he wanted to rip her head off. He took a deep breath and then spoke evenly. 'And you passed all this knowledge onto your uncle or Celeste or maybe even, I don't know, *your boyfriend who is investigating the crime?*'

Birdie exchanged a look with Pia, who grimaced.

'Birdie,' Herb said low and menacing, expression thundering.

Herb,' she began, 'I ...' It's not like she meant to keep any of this from Herb. It's just that things got away from her, and then Linda accused her in the staffroom, and her job was in jeopardy, and Herb told her he'd shot someone. She took a breath. 'In my defence, Herb—'

'Detective,' Griff called.

Above Herb's head, Birdie's attention was taken by the boys on bikes. A straggler had just caught up and was pointing to the small bay that had been fashioned into the shoreline. The foreshore was a popular place where families could picnic on the grass while children paddled in the water.

'That last kid said he saw someone go that way,' Griff said.

As everyone started to run in that direction, including Birdie, she felt Herb's strong arm pull her back. His hot breath threatened her ear. 'We are having serious words after this.'

'Over here!' Brad called.

Herb ran past Birdie along the shore towards Brad's cry.

Sabine was slumped forward over the edge of a rock. The water lapped at her hands and hair as they hung down. Brad was holding Sabine's floppy head out of the gentle waves.

'Careful with her neck,' Stu said. He squatted on the grass and checked for a pulse. 'She's alive.' he looked up at Herb.

Herb peered around, searching. He placed two fingers in his mouth and whistled, like an angry kettle, into the night.

Birdie covered her ears. 'What are you doing, Herb?'

He speared her with a look. 'Wouldn't you like to know.'

Yes, which was why I asked. But she stayed quiet. Herb was clearly in a mood, and Birdie's stomach churned knowing the little bits of information she'd kept from him were the reason.

She backed up a few steps to avoid his glare and was met by warm breath, slowly exhaling against the top of her spine, right where her ponytailed hair met her neck.

She froze.

The world turned in slow motion. The tiny fuzz on her arms reacted, standing on end while her heart hit *molto allegro* in her chest. She held her breath, back teeth clenched.

'You are right, *sědý*. She is never still.' The words accompanied the sigh that came from behind her. Cigarettes, expensive cologne and danger wafted over her shoulder.

She let out a harsh exhale. She knew exactly who had uttered those words, whose warm breath had splayed on her neck.

'Tell me about it,' answered Herb.

'Thanks for the heart attack, Vinny,' Birdie said, turning around. She forced her lungs to inhale and exhale.

'I didn't mean to scare you, *holčička*.'

'Well then, don't bloody sneak up behind me in the middle of the night when a madman who's dragging women around like ragdolls is on the loose.' She took another deep breath. 'And I'd appreciate you not siding with Herb at the moment.'

A faint smile lifted Vinny's lips. 'I am always on your side,' he said with a tiny bow. 'Ah, little Pia and Stuart. Good to see you again.'

Birdie's best friends stood gaping at the mob boss until they regained enough composure to greet him in return. They'd only met him once before, and on that occasion, he'd been safely behind bars.

'I think I might have spooked your madman. After depositing the ragdoll, he went that way.' Vinny motioned north. 'No cars took off. No one on the street. He's still out here somewhere.'

'Didn't expect you to be doing the hard yards, Vinny,' Herb said.

'Like to get my hands dirty every now and then. We going after him?'

Herb and Vinny took in the eager grins and ready feet of Birdie and her friends.

'I hope I don't live to regret this, *migaloo*.' Herb thumped Vinny on the back. 'But ... let's go after him.'

FORTY

Birdie couldn't ignore the incessant ache in her bum and elbows, a slight jarring in her neck, too. The adrenaline was starting to wear off; the aftereffects of the almighty shove from Dom were catching up with her. Their little gang had split up. Brad was currently supplying body heat to the groggy, 'hypothermic' and 'must be kept immobilised' – according to Stu – Sabine.

Griff had headed back to the club to ring for an ambulance and get some blankets, and Margie stood in the light of the club's entrance waiting for the police. Stu and Pia had gone with Vinny – Pia giving Birdie an excited eye lift as he clamped a bear claw on each of their shoulders, dragging them closer to deliver directions.

And then there was Birdie and silent Herb.

Often, she and Herb would sit together without words. Reading, watching TV, bodies close but mouths quiet. Just knowing he was there was enough. This was not one of those times.

'You called Vinny *migaloo*. What does that mean?'

His gaze sliced towards her, jaw muscles clenching, and then away. He was not going to answer her. She walked along behind him in silence. A silence that was killing her.

Eventually, he let out a deep sigh. '"White fella". A word from up north. It's … you know … an endearment.' He placed her hand in his as they moved along, her small palm swallowed by his larger one.

After a while, Birdie spoke again. 'And *sědý*?'

'Vinny's version of one. It's "grey" in Czech.'

Birdie wasn't sure how she felt about Herb and Vinny exchanging endearments. And what exactly was 'grey' referring to?

Her tired legs stumbled, on what must have been just a tuft of grass, and she lurched forward.

Herb steadied her. 'You okay?' he said gruffly.

'Do you care?' she mumbled.

He stilled for a beat before pulling her along again. She wondered if his heart felt as heavy, as raw as hers.

'Are you okay?' he tried again.

'I'm fine. Just a bit sore.'

He huffed a laugh. 'Your arse?'

She lowered her voice and whispered against his neck, 'You mean my perfect arse?'

Herb shuddered. 'I refuse to think about your arse and how perfect it is when I'm so angry with you, Birdie.' He rushed her against his side, an arm circling her waist, and kissed the top of her head. 'Why do you never listen to me? I feel like we have the same conversation over and over again.' He released her and they continued their crawling steps, Herb supporting her efforts.

'Herb, I—'

'You promised me you'd share information with me that was vital to my investigation.'

'I didn't intentionally mean to keep it from—'

'More importantly, Birdie, you promised me you'd stay safe, and I find you arse over tit, in the middle of a car park, after blindly confronting an assailant, in the dead of bloody night.'

'It's hardly the dead of night, Herb, and I was not, as you so eloquently put it, ars—'

'Why do you think I hit the highway back to Vantage as soon as I hung up the phone from you earlier? I almost knew this would be the case.'

'I couldn't have just left Sabi—'

'You're going to give me a heart attack, Bird.' *So maybe that was a yes on the raw heart thing?*

She tugged him to a stop. 'Herb, I'm sorry. I don't mean t—'

'You're not, though.' He turned to look at her. 'That's the thing. You're not sorry.'

She scooped into him until her chest was against his. She kissed him quickly. 'You're right. I'm not sorry.' She'd been wanting to touch him ever since he'd growled his first words at her; his beautiful hazel eyes burning fire below a frowning forehead, soft pink lips surrounding a chastising mouth. Since his long fingers had enveloped hers – sending a buzz straight to her heart – and lifted her like a feather, like she was floating through air, back onto her feet. She deepened the kiss.

He pulled away, holding her at arm's length. 'Distracting me, Birdie, is not going to help me find a madman.'

'Help *us* find a madman.'

'Jesus!' He ran a hand through his hair. 'No, not us. Me. Do you really think I'm going to let you—'

'Let me? You're not in charge of me, Herb Lawson, I'm—'

'A strong, independent woman. You make your own decisions, go where you want. You don't need me telling you what to do. But what if something happens to you?'

'Herb.'

He pulled her roughly against him. His mouth exploding onto hers. There was nothing soft in it; he was passion and burn. But she was floating again, the buzz returning. Filling her up. Making her giddy. She felt the heat warming along cool limbs. Pushed her body into his. Matched his intensity, his release of pent-up anger.

Herb broke apart from her on a breath. 'I wish kisses could silence my fear, Birdie Mealing.' His words wafted against her tingling lips. A shuffling noise from behind them made Herb still. 'Shh,' he breathed.

There were any number of reasons there might be a noise coming from behind them in the boatshed. Possums, rats, birds ... lovers like themselves. But not right now. Right now, the shuffle was probably Dom Walker.

'Okay, teach,' Herb whispered. 'What I want to say is "Stay here, Birdie. Stay put. Stay safe."' He pressed his soft lips to her forehead. 'But instead, I'm saying, are you up for this with your backside being sore?'

It was strange that in a time and place such as this, where Birdie's pulse was already galloping, that she'd be able to feel it quicken with love. 'I'm up for it, Herb.'

They made their way silently towards the shed. The door, which looked like it was shut, was a tiny bit ajar; not noticeable unless you were as close as Birdie and Herb were now.

As soon as they opened it, light would stream in. Dom would know they'd found him. Unless there was a back way out or a window.

'He'll know he's cornered.' Herb voiced Birdie's thoughts.

Herb did not have a gun or a torch, and the only other weapon he had, apart from himself, was Birdie.

'If he runs, which he probably will, he's gonna come right for us, Bird,' he murmured against her ear. 'You ready?' She nodded in reply.

Herb pulled the door open. A musty smell, laced with disinfectant, sailed outwards. In the dim light, Birdie could see canoes lined up vertically like books on a shelf and paddles hanging on the walls, life jackets and nets and fishing rods.

They moved further inside, the concrete slab sandy under Birdie's shoes. They must have spotted the top of the black balaclava skimming the rim of the dinghy at the same time because when she looked Herb's way, his eyes were already seeking hers. They locked, wide with recognition.

Herb beckoned Birdie forward. She took a few steps and refocused on him. He beckoned her forward again while he moved backwards towards the door. He was using his body to block Dom's escape. Herb pointed at her and made a lunging motion. Then, with his hands and mouth, made the universal sign for 'Rah'. He obviously wanted her to lunge at Dom, hoping to startle the man into flight.

Herb held up his palm in the signal for 'wait'. Birdie held still. He held up three fingers. She nodded.

Herb moved from foot to foot, preparing himself for battle. He held up his thumb. Birdie took a breath. He held up his index finger. She took another one. His eyes went wide as he held up the middle finger.

'RAH!' Birdie roared into life, exploding like a bunger on firecracker night.

As with many hastily made plans, this one didn't go as anticipated. Instead of running around the boat and into Herb's waiting body, Dom spun around and charged in the opposite direction ... right at Birdie.

Once more, she felt her body fly through the air. This time, she reached out and tried to break her fall. Her hand landed on the point of the nearest canoe. The action set it toppling down, which sent the next one toppling and the next, like dominoes. The noise was deafening in the tiny tin shed, the obstacles making it difficult for Dom to escape. He lumbered over one and then another. Birdie saw Herb's lean length lift above the debris.

'Omph,' Dom groaned, the air leaving his lungs as his body slapped the ground with a thud under Herb's weight.

They struggled. Dom's movements surprisingly swift and agile.

But Herb, a trained policeman, overpowered the teacher without much trouble. He placed a knee against Dom's back and pulled his arms up behind him, hands pointed towards his shoulder blades. 'You okay, Bird?' Herb said, a little breathless.

If Birdie's backside hadn't already been in bad shape, it would be now. 'Just my perfect arse being ruined once again.'

'Birdie,'—Herb looked up at her, flicking his head to clear ome wayward curls—'what did I say about drawing attention to your arse?'

'Actually, I'm pretty sure you said when you get your hands on it you're going to—'

'Jesus, teach.' He closed his eyes, Birdie guessed to wipe away the unsavoury – or perhaps in this case, savoury – image, before they fixed on her. Blue flames sparkling among the hazel in the moonlight. 'Maybe remind me of that later on, hey?' He smiled.

Sirens wailed in the background. Dom struggled and bucked.

Herb placed an arm against the back of Dom's neck to keep him still. He flicked his chin at Birdie. 'Hand me some of that rope.'

One by one, her friends appeared in the entry, rimmed in the glow from outside.

'Beat me to it, I see,' said Vinny, gun at the ready.

'And I didn't even accidentally get him shot on this occasion,' said Birdie.

Herb tilted his head at Vinny's gun. 'There's still time,' he said dryly.

Vinny holstered the gun with a grin as Herb pulled the balaclava from Dom's head.

Stu gasped. 'That's not D—'

'Pia,' said Birdie. 'It's—'

'I knew it!' said Pia.

Several pairs of eyes stared in disbelief. The sirens became louder. From the corner of her eye, Birdie saw Vinny nod at Herb and back stealthily out of the shed.

'The voice in the car park speaking Polish,' said Birdie to the assailant. 'It *was* you.'

The face was not that of Dom Walker as expected, but a red-cheeked, mussy-haired, scowling Emer Garland.

'Sabine *did* hear you,' said Pia. 'You were coming out of the back door after stabbing Warwick.'

'Impossible,' said Emer. 'I was up the coast.'

'An alibi we will be going over with a fine tooth comb,' said Constable Celeste as she and some uniforms charged into the shed. She lifted Emer from under Herb's hold.

Birdie stepped forward. 'And when Sabine told you, she'd heard you—'

'You had to get rid of her,' finished Pia, stepping up next to Birdie.

Birdie turned to Pia. 'Emer told Sabine that being the editor of the *Gallie Wallen Gazette* was her redemption.'

'For that job she missed out on,' said Pia.

'And who supplies references for a job?' said Birdie.

'He told me he'd give me a bad reference. He said he'd make sure they knew I was a fickle female, the type who would skip out on a contract.'

'"Fickle" and Emer do not belong in the same sentence,' whispered Pia. 'What a complete arsehole.'

'It was a job in Sydney at Fairfax, but I had to let it go.' Anger laced Emer's tone. 'I would have been set.'

'You might want to stop talking, Emer,' said Birdie. 'Anything you say can and will be used against you.'

Constable Celeste threw Birdie a 'whose side are you on?' look and began to move Emer away.

'Let me just say this then, Birdie Mealing.' Emer glanced over her shoulder. 'If you ever want to find out what I uncovered, but didn't print, about Larry, Vinny and a certain Lenore Mealing, I might be persuaded to tell you.'

**Women should be visible.
They should take front seats
at conferences and meetings
and speak with authority.**

'Have you got what it takes to be a
$50,000 a year women?'
Cleo, April 1985.

FORTY-ONE

A WAD OF SOFT fabric butted up gently against the dip of Birdie's waist.

'Stomach up.'

She moved her hands from where they were tucked under her chin, brought in her wings that had been pointing upwards, leant on her elbows and – as per Herb's request – lifted her stomach. From where he knelt behind her, in between the V of her legs, he bent forward and slipped one of the cushions that decorated Birdie's bed between her lower belly and the mattress.

'Drop back down.'

She placed her arms into their original position, and tried to relocate her comfy spot. Herb tapped her lamp onto its softest glow setting and took the little brown glass jar of soothing cream from the bedside table. She listened for the tell-tale twisting of the jar's lid, imagined him scooping out some cream and tensed in anticipation.

'Relax.' The word was accompanied by a feathery kiss to the base of her spine. Easy for him to say; he wasn't the one who was splayed across the bed, spread out in all his glory, like a beached starfish.

'You're a treat for the eyes on a good day, teach, but this view is something else.'

She sighed into the pillow beneath her chin. 'Glad you're enjoying it.'

'Enjoying it is an understatement.' She felt his body shift as his hand neared her bottom. 'And to think, if you'd listened to my advice and stayed out of trouble, I wouldn't have got the chance to do this.' He dabbed the cool cream on the abrasions that peppered her backside.

She flinched.

'*Relax*, Bird.' He dragged his right hand up the back of her right thigh, from the crease behind her knee to the underside of her bum cheek. 'I'll be gentle.' With delicate pats – light as mist – he began to rub it in.

Birdie's mind was still snagged on the previous sensation of his hand gliding along the underside of her thigh, getting closer and closer to her centre. 'Do that again, Herb,' she said dreamily.

'Do what again?'

She reached back and moved his hand up along her hamstring.

'Birdie.' Herb's voice was a mix of wanting and warning. 'You're too sore.'

'You just said you'd be gentle.'

'I was referring to the healing cream.'

'But you *can* be gentle?'

'You know I can.'

She placed her hand over his once more and directed him along her leg. 'Then be gentle, Herb.'

'Jesus, Bird.' He slid his hand along her skin once more.

'Higher.' She could no longer feel any pain, just growing arousal and his warm, strong fingers on her skin. 'Higher.'

'As much as I'd love to take advantage of one of my favourite parts of you propped up on a velvet cushion, on show like the Crown bloody Jewels, I'm conscious of the fact that your backside is littered with scrapes and bruises.' He stopped just short of where she needed him.

She shimmied backwards. 'Almost there.'

His growl vibrated along his limbs to hers as he dusted a finger against her.

Her satisfied sigh followed. 'Again.'

Herb stroked her again. His fingers lingering on the spot that throbbed for them. She was noisy. Appreciative moans falling loosely from her throat. He worked her into a quick rhythm, bliss building swiftly, evidence of her pleasure tumbling without care from her lips.

'Herb.' She pressed back into him.

'We have to be gentle, Bird.'

'But I need more.' She rocked against his hand. 'Have you still got your pants on?'

'Christ.' The bed jiggled as he shrugged out of his boxers then continued to stroke and circle, the head of his shaft hot and heavy and bouncing achingly against her entrance. 'More, Herb.'

The front of his body was suddenly against her spine, carefully avoiding any contact with her bottom, as his left hand slid upwards along her ribs. 'Roll to the right.' She did as he asked. His hand cupped her breast and she rolled back into the much needed pressure.

Like those silly sketches where a man twists a woman's nipple as if fine tuning a radio, Herb's tweaking and flicking and squeezing of her own nipple made every other sensation fine-tuned, volume dial turned way up.

'I need *you*, Herb.' She shimmied back towards him until his head slipped gently inside her; a deep sigh from Herb regestered in her foggy brain.

With his fingers around her nipple, hand massaging pliable flesh; his other hand stroking and circling, building the delirium; and his head poking softly at her entrance, she was consumed with sensation. Euphoria burst from her core, rushing across her stretched out limbs as she screamed her delight into the pillow.

Herb's sprinkled kisses, above the damaged flesh along the base of her bum cheeks, brought her slowly back.

'Where have you gone?' she said.

'I'm right here.' He gently squeezed her hip.

'I meant from inside me.' She reached over to the beside table and fished out a condom.

'Birdie? Your backside.'

She passed him the foil package.

His mumbles morphed into a different commentry as he settled himself inside her and began to move. 'Christ, teach.' His slid slowly in and out. Birdie focused on the length of him tracking her roof. 'The sight of me disappearing inside you.' His pace quickened. 'It's such a buzz.'

His fingers skimmed along the surface of the bedclothes, searching; his lips tickled her ear. 'Did you know you tighten around me when you orgasm?' She sucked in a breath; she vaguely remembered reading something about that in *Cleo* magazine. Finding what he was looking for among the bedclothes, he began working her.

Despite getting lost in his own pleasure, his fingers were steady and sure; her body chased heaven.

'Yes, Birdie.'

Chased, as it climbed the hill. 'Herb. Don't stop.'

'No chance of that, teach.'

His thrusts became erratic.

'Herb.'

The pressure from his hand increasing.

'Herb, I'm—'

His groans blended with hers—'Fuck, Birdie. Your body is bloody amazing'—as they reached the peak.

⸜⸝ ⸜⸝ ⸜⸝

Birdie stretched awake, aware of a tingling sensation between her legs – the aftershock of the earth-shattering previous night with Herb. Who knew sex could be that good. She turned her face back over her shoulder.

He sat, propped up on the pillow, leaning against the headboard, beautiful arms resting on top of the covers, curly hair wayward and dishevelled, gaze scanning her. She twinged as she rolled from one side to the other so she could face him, her bruised backside making itself known.

A tiny grin on puffy lips. 'Want me to kiss it better, Bird?'

'I've often dreamed about telling you to kiss my arse, Herb.'

'Christ, woman.' He huffed a laugh. 'Already with that cheeky mouth. You've just woken up.'

She kissed the closest part of him, his hip. 'I thought'—she continued her kisses down over the hill of bone towards the valley of his rather impressive thigh—'you loved this mouth.'

Herb gave a sigh as she continued inwards from his outer thigh, leaving no question as to where she was heading. She owed him one after last night. *Probably several, in fact.*

'God, help me,' he breathed out as he ran his fingers through her hair.

'Not even he can help you now, Detective,' Birdie whispered onto warm, delicate skin, hard and hot, as she lowered her cheeky mouth.

⬯ ⬯ ⬯

Machines blipped, the fluorescent lights buzzed, and Birdie's senses were pinging when she and Herb went to visit Sabine in the hospital after breakfast – and she'd thought schools were a plethora of interesting noises.

Birdie sat on the chair next to her little French friend's bed. 'You provided the gossip to the paper about these abominable men, didn't you, Miss Matthieu, or at least some of it?'

Sabine studied Birdie as she fiddled with her cordial. 'What makes you say that, Miss Mealing?' She sipped the liquid slowly through the straw.

'Constable Celeste found something intriguing when she looked into Sy Templeton,' said Birdie. Her attention swung to Herb who stood by the door.

'He was asked to consider a leave of absence from his position,' Herb added. 'After a young female teacher entered a verbal complaint about his conduct. Teacher had done some casual work at his school at the end of last year.'

'That is intriguing.' Sabine twirled the straw around her plastic hospital-grade cup.

'Lucky for the arsehole that coaching job became available,' said Birdie.

'Super lucky,' said Sabine, sarcasm dripping. 'But then, having only the control of men within his grasp means hopefully no women will get hurt.' She sipped her drink again.

'The teacher must have been terribly upset to have made a complaint,' Birdie added.

'Did you read the entry in *Shame Game, No Names*? He was very inappropriate at the staff Christmas party,' Sabine said. 'Apparently.'

'It wasn't hard for Herb to find out who had been a casual there during the last term of last year,' said Birdie. 'Or who lived next door to the people who lived next door to Todd the Tool.'

'Or whose cousin was an ex-student of the school where Griff Wheatly's dad was the principal and knew of the family of the girl Griff had the supposed affair with?' Sabine offered. 'Handy, you having a detective for a boyfriend, Birdie.'

She caught Herb's eye. It could be. Although he was currently working as a private investigator. Apparently, it was very important to make the distinction, and who knew what the future held for Herb and policing. Thinking about Herb made her blood warm and heat pool low in her belly.

Bloody Herb.

'It took guts for that teacher to have made such a complaint,' Birdie continued.

'Guts, you think? I'd probably go with outrage, desperation, misguided quest for justice, maybe even ... stupidity.'

'I'm sticking with guts.'

'Genius,' said Herb with an eyebrow lift. 'Balls?'

'I'd like to add creativity,' said Stu, as he entered the room. He lifted Sabine's chart from the end of her bed and examined it. Though she was no longer in emergency, Stu was hovering around to make sure she was cared for.

Sabine took the meds Stu held out and washed them down with her cordial.

'I'll check on you later,' Stu said, walking towards the door. He glared at Birdie. 'You two have three minutes. She needs her sleep.'

Sabine lifted her eyes. 'Other people got messed up in all of this. I'm sure whoever wanted to expose these men didn't consider that the women around them, like Margie, might end up as collateral. They may have even tried to stop the steamroller once it got started by meeting with the new editor, but to no avail.'

The angry encounter between Sabine and Emer in French.

Sabine frowned at Birdie and placed a hand on her leg. 'It appears the quest to make these men uncomfortable made the people close to them also look guilty.' She squeezed Birdie's knee. 'And inadvertently spurred Jonathon Naylor's wife to ride on their coattails for her own means.'

'It was only small minds that thought it was Margie,' said Birdie. Could she feel heat from Herb's eyes on the back of her head, or was that just her imagination? 'And Jonathon Naylor can't hurt me anymore.' *I hope.* Her teaching fate had yet to be decided.

'Whoever the whistleblower was,' Herb said softly, 'had every right to retaliate after the way she was treated.'

Birdie wondered if current events had changed Herb's point of view on justice. He'd always been a bit of a stickler, but she'd noticed a shift since his return.

'As did Linda Naylor in the staffroom that day,' Birdie whispered. 'They were both wronged.' Birdie placed her hand over Sabine's and squeezed it.

'And Griff?' Sabine said.

'That little gem worked in the woman he was protecting's favour, Sabine. You can't feel guilty for that.'

'I only gave Emer that one story. The one about what happened at the Christmas party, but she wanted more.'

'And more you had.'

She huffed a laugh. 'Yes, unfortunately. Teachers.' She shrugged a: *What more is there to say?* 'Do you really think Emer stabbed Warwick? What about her alibi?'

Birdie looked over at Herb with questioning eyebrows.

'She *was* up the coast. She *was* seen by the hotel staff. I got a clearer timeline. She was seen just before two. Warwick was attacked at around five o'clock. She was seen again after dinner, at approximately eight by the bartender.'

Sabine nodded, glassy-eyed. 'So she drove home and back up the coast again?'

'It's tight ... but possible,' said Herb. 'Warwick remembers he told her over the phone that she had to honour her contract with the gazette. Told her he wouldn't let her go.'

'She drove down to stab him,' whispered Sabine.

Birdie shook her head. 'No, to plead her case, and her begging fell on deaf ears, so she actually left the office. That's when you saw her, or rather, heard her.'

'I won't be made a fool,' Sabine said as she yawned.

'She went back in,' Herb continued. 'Picked up the knife and bam.'

'After Warwick woke up and couldn't remember his attacker, she was in the clear.'

'Except I told her I thought she was in the car park that night,' added Sabine.

'Needed to silence the only person who could possibly point the finger at her,' added Herb.

'We were correct in thinking Warwick was the one who provided the rumour targeting Dom. It wasn't you, was it, Sabine?'

'No. Dom is friendly, a flirt, but he's never been inappropriate. Plus, I was totally unaware he'd been with Sister T, or anyone else, on his desk. I mean, even for us scandalous teachers, that's bold.'

Birdie sat back. 'Warwick saw the huge response to the rumours so provided one of his own. He used similar paper and the same method of sending it in through the mail. Emer just thought it was more of the same and printed it. Warwick knew he would be making Sister T and Dom susceptible,' Birdie continued, 'and he didn't care.' She shook her head. 'He'd sat on the secret for a little over twenty years. He didn't like Dom because he'd sided with Sy all those years ago when Sy had bullied Warwick. He saw Dom as being complacent, the teacher who should have done something to assist him but did nothing. In adulthood, he finally had the power to hurt them both.'

'Oh.' Sabine covered a yawn. 'That's not nice.'

Stu wandered in again. 'But how did he know Sister T and Dom were back on?'

'I don't think he did until Emer did her own investigation into the subjects. She knew more about each incident than Sabine's little titbits gave her. She found out Griff's dad was the school's principal, Todd had already moved down south. She must have done some digging, looked more closely at Dom and put two and two together.'

'She turned my little morsels of gossip darker.' Sabine yawned again. 'When I stopped sending the rumours in, she wouldn't let up. She even tried to get dirt at my party. It was like she was obsessed.'

Obsessed or just doing a very thorough job. It seemed Emer could do nothing but. A tiny part of Birdie admired her attention to detail.

'Why did Dom confess? Let himself be arrested?' asked Sabine.

'He thought Sister T was going to go to jail. He was doing what he thought would save her.'

'Oh, that's sweet,' Sabine said on the verge of falling asleep.

'The patient is fatigued. Visiting hours are over for Miss Mathieu,' said Stu. 'You two, out.'

'What will happen to Emer now?' Sabine said, grabbing Birdie before she could lift from the chair.

'If she's proven guilty, she will be given a sentence,' Herb said.

'But Warwick was an arsehole. That hardly seems fair.'

'She did attack you, honey,' said Birdie. She brushed a wayward dark hair from Sabine's forehead as her bruised eyes fluttered shut.

Sabine was right. Aside from assaulting her friend – which could not be excused – she'd lashed out at the man who had taken everything away from her. The actions of dickhead, misogynistic, arrogant men would continue. Had justice really been served?

FORTY-TWO

HERB HAD BEEN TWISTING her hair around his finger. The motion had been slowly sending her to sleep.

'We need to talk, Birdie.'

It was late, and after the last couple of days, she was exhausted. 'Do we?' Talk or sleep. It wasn't really a choice for her.

'I need to apologise to you.'

Well. In that case, she could stay awake for a natter. 'Go on.'

'I can't help but protect you. I tried to strong-arm you into not getting involved the other night. Got aggro. I'm sorry.'

'I love that you want to protect me, Herb.' She ran a hand across his ribs.

'It frustrates the hell out of you.'

You're not wrong. 'It's not always frustrating.'

'You're all ... explosive strength and incredible intelligence and fierce attitude. I'm floundering, Birdie. Don't know my place.'

She rolled off him and onto her back. 'Why can't it just be beside me?' she said, taking his hand.

'I *want* us to be in this together. I want it to be the two of us against the world.' He kissed her hand. 'I so want that.'

She felt a 'but' coming.

'But I'm scared you'll get hurt. My world is not always safe. It's messy and complicated. Poison leaches out. I'm not as clean and shiny as you.'

'It might appear that way on the outside, but I'm not clean and shiny, Herb.'

'Not all the time.' He shifted on the bed, turned onto his side and propped his head up on his hand. 'But when being with me means you show your dark side, or you're okay with mine ...'

Like shooting someone dead.

'I'm not sure that's okay, Bird.'

'My dark side?' The side of her that sleeps with married men; that can turn on the charm, the flirtation, like a tap; that withholds the truth; that excites in her relationship with Vinny, a mob boss; that doesn't shy away from keeping some of her mother's secrets while trying to find others out; that is slightly competitive, especially with Herb. The side that goes down on a man first thing in the morning, after said man, who she's *not* married to – extremely against the Catholic religion – has slept over ... and is not at all ashamed about any of it. That side? 'Have you been watching *Return of the Jedi* again?'

'Your dark side, Birdie. The side that flashed through your mind just now'—he wiped a finger across her bottom lip—'while you tried to suppress that little grin.'

'Herb!'

'And you say I have no poker face.' He brushed her lips with his and held her gaze. 'Never know what you're going to do, Bird.' He kissed her again. 'Can't control it. You march to the beat of your own drum, and I feel like I'm a couple of rat-a-tat-tats behind.'

'I'm sorry, Herb.'

'Don't apologise. I actually wouldn't change it. *Wanted to*,' he said, pulling her against him, wrapping her in his long arms. 'But it's what makes you, you.'

She'd spent so long trying to make Herb accept that she was capable, trying to show him she was an asset instead of a liability. It didn't feel like he was saying she'd succeeded. It felt like he was about to end with 'Unfortunately, that's not the girl for me.'

'So, we're all okay?' A tiny bit of her cringed at her need to hear yes.

'It punches my heart, Birdie.'

Was he about to let her down gently? She needed to know, even if the answer hurt.

'You want something easier?'

'Easier would be good.'

'I'm not sure I can do easier.'

'I know.' He rolled onto his back, taking her with him. 'I'm not going back to the force. I'm out.'

Herb had to think about more than her – like shooting a man dead. He had to contemplate his culture, his future.

'Do they know?'

How would Inspector Draper react to Herb's decision? Herb's boss had mixed him up in underworld crime. He'd been caught up in some things that were difficult to escape from. What did that mean for him?

'They will soon, and it scares me, Birdie.'

Vinny was helping with that. Also a player in the underworld, he'd made things better for Herb. Birdie wondered, though, if that wasn't jumping from the frying pan into the fire.

'The danger has passed for you there, Herb.' *Hadn't it?* 'Hasn't it?' Wasn't Vinny on top of all that?

'Might never pass, Bird.' He was silent as Birdie rested her head on his chest. His heartbeat quickened suddenly.

'What is it, Herb? What are you thinking about?'

'Remember last year when we ran into each other up the coast?'

Interesting way of putting it. But she couldn't dwell on the specifics of the events of last summer, except to focus on why they were important now. 'Are you talking about when you said you needed to get out of town in a hurry?'

'Mick Drury's trial had ended a couple of weeks earlier, and although Roger Rogerson was *not* found guilty of attempted murder, he was convicted of bribery. Was given a suspension from the force. Was out for blood.'

'Yours?' she whispered.

'When I was face to face with that guy before I headed onto Country, he didn't just call you leggy, like I said before. He went on to say how your long legs were an advantage on the basketball court. What a great singer you were: "voice of an angel" was the term he used. He said you were a looker. That he had a thing for "carrot-tops". And I'm phrasing that politely, Bird.'

Birdie held her breath. They knew who she was, what she did, where she lived. Her mouth was dry. She tried to swallow.

'What if I can't protect you?' He traced a finger down her spine and back up again. 'You're like a trouble magnet, either gravitating towards it or it towards you.'

'What about Vinny?'

'Comes with a price. You'd be happy for me to get further into bed with him?' His finger continued its rhythm along her backbone. 'I know how you feel about that.'

He was right about her being a trouble magnet.

And about Vinny. Being *holčička* to Vinny's *starý muz* was the price she paid for keeping her family safe. Did Vinny know what the thug had said? Had Herb told Vinny he'd mentioned her legs, her voice, her hair? She shivered. Herb rubbed across her shoulders and pulled the covers up.

If she thought about who was lurking out there too often, fear would engulf her. Her thoughts spiralling, catastrophising. Would she be safer not being Herb's girlfriend?

She ran her fingers through the tiny hairs on his chest. A sinking feeling in her gut.

'It would kill me to be without you, Birdie.' He lifted her fingers from his chest and kissed her palm. 'I'm not sure I'd survive it if I had to go again.'

She dropped her head to his chest. 'Then don't.' Tears spilled down her cheeks. He'd feel the warmth of them on his skin, but she didn't care. How would she ever feel safe if Herb wasn't right beside her?

'But it also kills me being with you.'

FORTY-THREE

SHE HADN'T SEEN HERB for a few days. Hadn't phoned him or returned his unanswered calls. She wasn't sure whether he'd gone home to his folks; her plans to join him up the coast were trashed. She had purposely not asked Uncle Larry if they'd been in touch.

A little hurt, a lot confused, she would give him space to get himself sorted – and take some for herself. She hovered between anger and understanding and fear.

She conceded he had a lot to weigh up. He might love her, love being with her, but was it good for him right now? He'd been so angry at her during the events at the Sailo. She'd seen it in his eyes, heard it in his words, felt it shimmer from him. He already had enough to worry about. He had to consider his family's safety, hers, his job, changing loyalties. He had more important places to aim that shimmer.

Plus, was *he* a danger to her?

She'd survived Uncle Larry's abduction and now Emer's attack. Plus, she'd survived being shot at.

She'd engaged in sessions with a psych.

Life was uncomfortable. Why did you have to see the light at the end before you went through the tunnel? She would not live in fear.

She'd even visited Vinny. Emer's offer to tell her what she'd uncovered about him ringing in her ears; it would keep for another day.

'It is too soon to relax the detail,' he'd said through a swirl of cigarette smoke.

'So, you'll still be watching me?'

He considered her as he often did, like a puzzle – a child he'd like to scold, a woman he'd like to befriend, like her mother's daughter. 'You call it watching, I call it keeping you safe.'

She'd walked away, not before turning back and saying,

'You know, smoking will kill you, Vinny.' His laughter saw her out the door.

So Vinny would be abreast of her every move; that wouldn't stop her from being bold and free. She would see it as an edge. A challenge. Give him a show if he was watching. Her ears pinged onto the engine of a motorbike. Without thinking, she scanned the road to see where it was. What was she hoping? That Herb would come flying down the street in some romantic knight-in-shining-armour gesture and sweep her off her feet?

Herb was considerate, responsible, procedural. She was more of a fly-by-the-seat-of-your-pants-kind-a-gal. Creative, impulsive, fiery. She didn't need to know everything would turn out okay before she dived in. *It's more my style to come barging into town on a horse.*

She should have known from the very beginning. The way he'd checked her out at Fidele's when he was there with his mates, and then turned up at the restaurant, a respectable number of times, afterwards. She'd been the one to launch herself at him. She had always looked back fondly on that fateful night, the wildness of it, the thrill.

But maybe it had been she who was the wild and crazy one. Maybe she'd just swept him along in her wake; he'd followed the zany girl's lead. He'd reacted with surprise when she'd snuck out in the early hours of the morning. Her motto was girls just wanna have fun. No promises, no demands. He'd expected more.

She'd been planning to go overseas. Live it up. Then, even that had been turned on its head without much thought. She wanted to be with Herb. Wanted to stay around. All plans for the trip were unconsciously thrown out the window.

Maybe he was right. Her track record showed she'd jumped into bed with a married man, flirted shamelessly, eyeballed a mob boss at regular intervals. She faced off with danger; she'd even got Herb shot. No wonder he was second-guessing.

Maybe it *was* hard being with her.

She contemplated this as she sat pushing the special around her plate between the early and late sets at Fidele's on Thursday night.

'It is not good?' asked Fidele. '*La poisson de jour?*'

'Sorry, Fidele,' said Birdie. 'I'm a bit out of sorts.' She pointed at the fish with her fork. 'It's amazing, really.'

Fidele placed a hand gently on her shoulder. 'True love, *allouette*. It will conquer.'

Mrs N and a bunch of the residents at Evesong had been at the early sitting. Mrs N had made Birdie relay the older woman's part in working out who had stabbed Warwick Woods, much to the oldies' delight.

Stu and Pia, Griff and Brad, Margie and a much-improved Sabine had just arrived for the later sitting. Uncle

Larry and Shelly, who had no booking but wandered in, on the off chance a table might be open, were there too.

She'd be okay on her own, in a life without Herb. She had the support of friends and family.

'I'm thinking of expanding the business into the field of private investigating, my darling,' her uncle informed her as she dropped by his table on her way to her corner stage.

Birdie stopped dead and exchanged a 'He's what now?' look with Shelly.

'I told him he's already too busy,' Shelly said. 'But Herbert will be heading that part of the operation.'

Birdie's heart clenched at his name.

'There might be some part-time work in it for you too,' her uncle said, 'if you're interested.'

'I barely solved this one. I was convinced it was Dom. I only worked out the truth when the balaclava came off.'

'But you were incredibly close. All the more reason to hone your skills.'

Was she interested? She had a meeting on Monday with Jonathon, in his role as superintendent, to discuss her future at St Joan of Arc and in the Catholic system at large. Maybe she'd end up being Birdie Mealing – Girl Detective after all. How would Herb feel about the danger of that?

'Might be something to think about.' she leaned down and kissed the top of his head. 'Thanks, Uncle Larry.'

'Of course, sweetheart.'

My darling. Sweetheart. Her uncle was free with his endearments.

She had asked her Czech friend what *malý drobecek* meant. The phrase she'd heard her uncle whisper into the phone the night she and Herb were shot at. She took in her uncle now. He placed a forkful of food seductively into his fiancée's mouth. Birdie had presumed, correctly, that Uncle Larry had been talking to Vinny on the phone that night. She'd thought *malý drobecek* had meant something like 'much appreciated' or 'I owe you one' or 'I feel safer now', but apparently *malý drobecek* was also a term of endearment. Shelly and her uncle smiled at each other as she slid the food off the fork and licked her lips.

Why would her uncle be calling Vinny his 'little crumb'?

She settled herself on her chair, picked up the next piece of sheet music and placed it on the stand.

'So, a real *Charlie's Angel*?' said Pia, breaking into her thoughts. Birdie tilted her head and raised an eyebrow at her beautiful friend who stood blocking them off from the diners. Pia grinned. 'I couldn't help overhearing.'

'Eavesdropping more like it.' Birdie picked up her guitar.

'Potayto, potarto,' Pia said, wandering off.

'The next song is dedicated to my friends,' she said. 'Please feel free to sing along with the chorus because I'm pretty sure *they* will.'

There was a whoop from the table at which her friends ate and drank and laughed and relaxed. Birdie launched into Ringo Starr's, Sgt. Pepper's hit, 'With a Little Help from My Friends'.

👄 👄 👄

Lenore stood on tippy-toes and waved a hand towards the wine glasses that were behind the sliding, glass-fronted cabinet. Birdie stepped up behind her, clean and fresh from the shower she'd taken after getting home from Fidele's, and lifted them easily from the high shelf.

'Herb rang again,' her mother said.

'Did he?'

'Are you ever going to return his call?' Lenore pulled the cask of wine from the fridge and proceeded to remove the silver bladder.

'Do you think I'm hard work, Mum?'

'Hard work? All good things are.'

'Thanks, Yoda. Let's focus, specifically, on me.'

She stopped what she was doing and gave Birdie her attention. 'Is this about Herb? Is that what he said?'

'He said it was hard being with me.'

'Does the hard outweigh the happy?'

Birdie placed her fingertip on a speck of dust and removed it from the glass. 'He did also say it would kill him to be without me.'

'Ah ... A conundrum.'

'A paradox,' Birdie agreed.

'A puzzle,' her mother said again.

'An enigma,' added Glen, wandering over from the boys' room, having just put them to bed. They laughed.

'Well, you are all those things, love,' Lenore said. She squeezed the bladder, securing the last remnants of wine, and poured them all a glass. 'You are not one of those people who follow the straight path.' They settled into the lounge room.

Birdie snuggled into the cushy lounge and tucked her legs up. 'He said he'd like things to be easier.'

'But was that a condition? Do they *have* to be easier ... or would he just like it that way?'

Birdie didn't really know.

'There's nothing wrong with the way you lead your life, Birdie. It's game on, no holds barred.' Her mother drank her wine. 'But it's also important to understand the needs of others.'

Birdie was coming into some of her own challenges. Like, whether she'd keep her job. Whether she wanted to finally find out who her father was. She'd always thought Herb would be there to go through them with her. That they'd be in it together. Why couldn't they lean on each other through the uncertainty, the possibilities, the danger? Maybe she'd just have to rely on Pia and Stu – like she always had.

'And I'm not saying only *you* need to be understanding,' said her mother. 'You both do.'

Rusty wandered into the room and burrowed into her side. The smell of soap clung to his soft skin, lemon scented detergent wafted from clean pyjamas, apple from his shampooed hair. His hair had grown out a bit; no doubt Glen would take the twins for a haircut before school went back after the holidays. For now, the dark blond curls tickled her chin as she kissed his boofy head. It reminded her of Herb's.

'Is Herb here, Big Bird?' Rusty grabbed her hand and squeezed the pad of each of the fingers of her left hand in turn and then her right.

She did the same to his, knowing he only really did it to have it done in response. He loved the sensory contact. 'No, little man. He's up the coast with his family, I think.'

'Oh.' He smiled up at her. His two front adult teeth making a tiny appearance in his gappy gum. 'Who's in your room, then?'

Birdie jumped up. *Herb.* 'Someone's in my room?' She gaped at Lenore. Her mother raised an eyebrow as if to say 'perhaps there is your answer'.

'Come and look,' he said with a big grin.

Birdie hurried along to her room. Rusty in tow. The door was closed – a rare occurrence.

'Are you gonna open it, Big Bird?' His grin grew wider, taking up his whole face. The boys loved Herb.

'Did you want to come in and say hi?'

Rusty nodded. Birdie opened the door. The light had been turned off. She couldn't remember doing that, even though Glen was constantly reminding the lot of them to turn the lights off when they left a room.

She placed a finger on the light switch. When she turned it on, she would see him. Why was she looking ahead? She would just live for now. Perhaps by being here, in her room, that's what Herb had decided, too. After all, he did say it would kill him to live without her, and she couldn't ignore the dance that was happening in her tummy. A mixture of delight and anxiety.

She flicked the switch. Light flooded the space.

A large piece of paper was on her pillow. In Rusty's unmistakable six-year-old handwriting were the words: *Made you look!*

'Gotcha!' he yelled.

Herb isn't here.

Rusty smacked her bum and ran. 'Sucked in, Birdie.'

'You little bugger.' She took off after him. The child was a *Dick Dastardly* of genius proportions.

'I told you to expect it when you least expected it,' he called as he went.

Well, that was definitely unexpected!

She'd stupidly forgotten all about his threat weeks ago to get her back. How can a six-year-old hold on and wait for exactly the right time to exact revenge like Rusty just did? If it was Kick, he wouldn't have lasted five minutes before he got her back. Disappointment was quickly replaced with glee as she chased him around the house.

When she went to put her head on her pillow that night, she picked up Rusty's little joke message and dropped it into the bin.

Regardless of what would happen between them, when she'd switched on that light ... she had wanted it to be Herb.

"I have a great respect for
women. To me, they are
emotionally strong, and
they're not as prone to
aggression or thoughtless
behaviour. I think they have
a greater understanding of
the importance of the
preservation of life."

'Peter Garrett:
Folk hero of rock and politics'
Cleo, April 1985.

FORTY-FOUR

She'd had this dream many times when Herb had disappeared. She'd dreamt about him here in her bed. His warmth cradling her back, hot breath on her neck, behind her ear, long limbs dangling across her.

'Herb,' she breathed.

'How did I think I could ever stay away from you?'

Lean legs slid along the underside of hers, toes tickling toes. She shuffled back into his embrace. It wasn't until one of those limbs, an arm to be precise, slid up her side and a cool hand cupped a sleeping breast, that she jerked awake. Her eyes flew open as it squeezed the soft flesh, zeroing in on her nipple.

She twisted her head to see Herb's beautiful lips centimetres from hers.

'Morning, Birdie.'

'How did you get in?'

He kissed her in response. *Stupid question.* There were many tricks Herb Lawson had up his sleeve.

'Can you teach me how to break in, Herb?'

His hand left her breast and slid down her side and around the curve of her bottom. She sighed, heat spreading like wildfire and leaned back into him. His mouth peppered soft kisses on her ear, his moustache tickling her shoulder.

'No.' His palm moved along the underside of her thigh, then back up to her bum cheek; fingers walked along the most sensitive of skin, searching between her legs.

She clapped her hand on top of his, stilling it, holding it in place. She sighed. She wanted to let him do whatever he had in his mind to do, whatever he'd broken into her room to do. Her skin was already on fire, but she had to stop him. They needed to talk. If this conversation didn't go the way she hoped it would, perhaps she'd never melt under Herb's touch again.

She wove her fingers through his and held his hand. 'Can we make a decision, here and now, to lean on each other, Herb? You know, you'll never be in any messy situation alone if we meet it head-on, together. And it's not just about me being there for you, Herb. I could use you on my side, too.'

With fighting for her job and thinking about finally voicing her desire to find her real father, she would need him. If she were to continue helping Uncle Larry with his investigations, which might be a real possibility if she lost her job, he'd have to trust her skills. He'd have to let her in on clues and divulge important information and rely on her physically, like he had with Emer in the boatshed.

'I meant it when I said it kills me to be without you,' he said.

'It needs to be more than that. I need to know we're in this together. I need to have no doubt.'

'I can't promise I won't try to be protective, though.' He squeezed her hand. 'You don't want me to be.'

'I don't want you to stop me from participating in life.' She twirled around so she was facing him, the blue flecks in his caramel eyes reflecting the morning light. 'I don't want you to prevent me from being a part of what happens with the whirlwind that is us. I don't want you to not teach me how to protect myself … and maybe … use a handgun.'

'What?' His eyebrows rose. 'That's not gonna hap—'

'Open a safe?'

'Are you seriou—?'

'Break into a house?'

'Birdie!'

She kissed him quickly. 'I want your protection just as much as I'd give you mine.'

'Christ, I missed you,' he whispered. His fingers pulled from hers and started to work their magic, circling and stroking, gently but steadily.

She stopped his hand once again.

'Are you using sex as a bargaining tool, teach?' he breathed into the skin across her chest.

She would if she knew it might work, but it defeated the purpose if denying him also meant denying herself. No, this was more than that.

'I want to finish this.' She felt him stiffen, his eyes lifted to hers. 'This *discussion*, Herb. I want you to stop with your magic fingers so I will be able to think clearly until this discussion is done.'

He huffed a soft laugh. 'So, I'm allowed to offer my protection?'

'Yes.'

'Tell you to pull your head in?'

'No.'

'But you'll listen to my instructions.'

'If you listen to my objections as to why I should.'

He huffed another laugh. 'You're a ratbag.'

'You're only just working that out?'

'No, but I *am* beginning to realise I wouldn't have it any other way.'

'And the gun, the safe, the breaking in? I can already shoot a rifle, Herb. A handgun is just a littler version.'

He pinched her arse. 'Don't test me.' He turned her around, so he was spooning her again. 'I'm scared,' he whispered into her ear. 'This feels real, Bird. I don't want anything bad to happen.'

'With the way we live life, it might, Herb.' She tucked in her chin and kissed his shoulder. The scar he'd gained last year a little rough under her soft lips. 'But you'll be by my side in good and bad. And I'll be by yours.'

He nuzzled into her neck. 'Okay.'

'Okay?'

'Okay, teach.'

She released his hand. 'You may continue your ministrations.'

'Birdie Mealing, what am I gonna do with you?'

'Well,' she said, turning her head to kiss his lips, 'you can start with whatever it was you were doing before I stopped you.'

ACKNOWLEDGEMENTS

THANKS TO ALL THE readers who enjoyed my first Birdie mystery: 'Girl Detectives Just Wanna Have Fun'. My dream was to write a book that readers loved, and you did. Therefore, you must be thanked – and also blamed for the eventuality of this: the second Birdie mystery. I hope you love it just as much! (Or maybe more?)

To Jodi and my Write Squad girls, I love yous all. Champions and keepers of my sanity. We are very lucky to have each other, and I think we all know it. Let's keep making books and having fun (because that's just what girls wanna do! Lol!)

Being a romance *and* mystery writer means I get to move within two worlds, and I've made great friends in both. Too many amazing people to name, but you all know who you are and how much I love and appreciate you.

To the many associations and organisations that I belong to – and others – that give writers advice, a platform, opportunities, a community. We love you for having our backs. Everyone needs art.

My story contains diverse characters. Those who know me well would have heard me say 'Diversity is "normal". Therefore, the actual word "diversity" is a misnomer.' Wouldn't the world be a wonderful place if difference was normalised? If representation of all communities was 'normal'?

As an Inclusive Education Teacher and Lecturer, I thought I knew lots about diverse communities. I was a little naïve, however, and didn't realise what a complex world I'd stepped into when I modelled a character on my Aboriginal students and old school friends. There is a love story within this story – Birdie, a 23 year old white girl, falls in love with Herb, a 28 year old black boy. She's thrown into an unknown world and – just like we all have – realises the history she learned about Aboriginal people was not entirely correct. I'd like to acknowledge the First Nations People of Australia – the first story tellers of this land. Thank you to sensitivity readers, members of the Gadigal and Darkinung Communities – especially Aunty Donna and Aunty Bronwyn – the Metro Local Aboriginal Land Council, Radio Redfern, and the Aboriginal Legal Service (ALS). As requested, the own voices of the individuals who worked at the ALS in the 1980s – who documented their experiences on *The Story Project: 40 Years of the ALS* – was the source for historically correct and respectful representation of First Nations People and History.

Love and respect is all we need.

To Penny Carroll, editor extraordinaire. Gentle but firm would be Penny's motto and who can resist a juxtaposition. *Not this little ADHD duck!* Thanks for making my stories better and for your general wonderfulness. Sending you much love and a messy MS soon. You's think being a teacher, I'd know how to word, do speling good, Punctuation rite, grammar proper, sentence correctly a structure, and that all stuff.. Hehehe! To Jo at 'Nurturing Words' for the copyedit, much appreciation.

To Kah, the amazing woman who did my covers. A talented artist and a sweet soul. You were a dream to work with. (Anyone looking for an illustrator, she's your girl.)

To Are Media, thanks for permission to use snippets of *Cleo*. In 40 years, you'd have thought we would have advanced when it came to allowing men the power, but this snippet ... Women have as much right as men do to declare their intentions, to reach for what appeals to us, to court, woo or conquer as we please. Why should we wait to be asked, allowing men the power of asking? ... made me wonder. *I hope you're listening young women.* (Copyright Permission is included overpage.)

Finally, thanks to my family and friends, especially Cher and Issy, who think I can do anything and Cam, my eater of bone broth beta reader.

To my children, who add me to their manifestations and cross their fingers and toes when I ask them to. And to Steve – Twenty-five years of the best adventures; here's to fifty.

In the words of Sophie Green, 'You're allowed to have fun when you write,' and read too, I reckon. So go on, have some!

Love Pip xo

P.S. that research Stu quoted in chapter five about male brains being more analytical, which Birdie suggested might one day be proven the opposite – well ... it was.

⬿ ⬾ ⬿

To the extent that Are Media Pty Limited (previously, ACP Magazines and Bauer Media) owns copyright or any other *relevant right to the content the subject of the request in your July 10th 2025 email, we have no objection to that content being used by you, on a non-exclusive basis, in the manner set out in your email, provided that there is no derogatory treatment of the magazine masthead or of Are Media. However, we do not make any representation or warranty that the use of the content does not infringe rights held by any third parties.*

Are Media Pty Limited /*Cleo*

AUTHOR'S NOTE

Sallie-Anne Huckstepp, Warren Lanfranchi, Michael Drury and Roger Rogerson are all mentioned in this book.

Sallie-Anne Huckstepp, interviewed by Ray Martin on 60 minutes, was fascinating – beautiful and wild and romantically tragic – to a girl growing up in the 80s.

Her lover Lanfranchi was shot and killed by Rogerson witnessed by a man up a ladder painting a balcony. This man never gave evidence at the inquest into Lanfranchi's death; author John Dale, who wrote an article titled 'Death in Dangar Place', suggests he was too frightened to.

The fictional character of Herb Lawson is placed in the middle of this real-life event.

ALSO BY PHILIPPA KAYE
BIrdie Mealing Mystery #1

It's 1984. Hair is big, skirts are short and Birdie Mealing is just a girl who wants to have fun ... until her uncle goes missing that is.

With a little help from her friends, Birdie, a talented musician turned amateur sleuth, is determined to find her uncle. After all, he's the only father figure this daughter of a single mother has ever known.

Detective Herb Lawson, however, has other ideas. Battling with colleagues, family and his conscience he doesn't need any further complications. Birdie – a magnet for trouble – needs to back off and leave the investigating to him.

Fat chance, detective!

The closer Birdie gets to solving her uncle's disappearance, the more she uncovers about his connection to a fatal explosion on the harbour and the underworld kingpin who was jailed for it. And the closer she gets to the guarded but gorgeous Herb, the more she questions his motives and her own identity.

Having fun yet, Birdie?